The Moth Man

Also by Jennie Finch and
available from Impress Books:

Death of the Elver Man
The Drowners

The Moth Man

Jennie Finch

First Published 2014
by Impress Books Ltd

Innovation Centre, Rennes Drive, University of Exeter Campus,
Exeter EX4 4RN

© Jennie Finch 2014

Typeset in Sabon by Swales & Willis Ltd, Exeter, Devon

Printed and bound in England by imprintdigital.net

British Library Cataloguing in Publication Data
A catalogue record for this book is available from the British Library

ISBN 978–1–907605–67–3 (pbk)
ISBN 978–1–907605–68–0 (ebk)

Acknowledgements

Thank you to everyone who has read and commented on the previous two books in the 'Alex Hastings' series. Knowing there are readers out there who enjoyed and shared the stories makes it all worth while.

Once more I have drawn on Jackie's recollections and expertise for much of the detail, especially in relation to probation work in the 1980s. I have made some changes to this excellent information in places and any errors are mine alone.

Thank you to Sandie for the 'buried treasure' story. I hope you like what I have done with it. Also, Derek's expertise with goats has been invaluable. An especial thanks to Arnold who first told me the story of a real offender, very similar to the Moth Man. Once I had that it all fell into place.

I am fortunate to have such friendship and support from Alex Lewczuk and all at Southside Broadcasting/Siren FM. I'm proud to be part of the team. Many thanks also to photographer Shaun Cook for the cover image.

This book is dedicated to Janet Wright, one of the finest probation officers I have ever met and to Nigel Leech, an inspirational teacher and good friend. Both gone too soon.

Prologue

The spring sunlight warmed the gardens around the Somerset Levels and many residents opened their windows and doors, welcoming the fresh air into their homes. Despite the evening chill, the temptation to linger in the slowly-cooling conservatories proved too great for some and as the light faded from the sky lamps were lit, books opened and gardening journals resumed. Birds called for mates, rustling the new leaves and settling into hollows and eaves as they prepared the sites of their new nests. It was a soft and gentle evening, a time for supper and a chat with a loved one before closing up the house and settling down for the night.

Out in the dusk he waited, eyes fixed on the gap in the garden hedge and the view into the conservatory. When the lights came on inside he could see her as she sat, feet crossed neatly at the ankles and legs tucked under, relaxing in the big armchair by the window. As the last of the sun dribbled away beyond the horizon he began his preparations, glancing up occasionally to check she was still there. Finally he was ready. The wind was cold on his skin and he shivered, both from the cool evening and with anticipation. Inside the glass room the woman glanced up and he froze, afraid she had heard him or seen something but she turned back to her magazine and he breathed again.

His mouth was dry now, though the palms of the hands sweated as adrenaline began to run through his body. This was the moment. The moment he had dreamed of since first seeing the house three weeks ago. Inside, the woman reached up and tucked a strand of hair behind her ear and it was the most exciting, provocative gesture he had ever seen. He was shaking though he no longer felt the cold on his bare body. Pulling the stocking over his head to mask his features, he slid through the bushes surrounding the garden and ran towards the house, a human moth drawn to the light and heat of the woman inside.

They heard her screams the whole length of the street but by the time help arrived, he was gone.

Chapter One

Deep in the wing at Dartmoor prison, far from events out on the Levels, William 'Newt' Johns lay awake, staring up at the ceiling as the first light of dawn crept over the stone window-sill and into his cell. His cell-mate, a skinny and slightly pungent little weasel called Ron, snored softly in the bunk below giving occasional whistles through his chipped teeth. Newt ignored him, used now to an ever-changing roster of short-term inmates. He wondered if this was a deliberate ploy on the part of the prison staff. Newt's father, Derek Johns, had been a powerful and influential figure with a reach far beyond his immediate patch of the Levels in Somerset. In the first months of his sentence, Newt had benefited from the support and protection offered by the Johns' family connections and his reputation as the heir to Derek's little fiefdom had earned him a high level of respect and standing, especially considering he had only just had his twenty-third birthday.

Life inside, he reflected, had been tedious, uncomfortable and occasionally undignified but overall his sentence was passing without any great trauma. After an early escapade, an escape engineered to help his late father, Newt had been a model prisoner. Gradually the impact of his 'prison break' – in reality a short sprint into the village to make a phone call – had faded away and life rolled on in relative peace. He read a lot of books, worked wherever he was placed and stayed away from fights. Only his mother's most recent visit, this week past, had made any impact on him.

She had looked different, he thought, watching her cross the room to sit at the table in front of him. At first he thought it was her hair. Iris had always taken great pride in her appearance and her hair had remained resolutely (and improbably) peach blonde for as long as he could remember, but recently she had allowed the colour to fade and the first streaks of grey began to show through. Then, just last month, she had appeared with a different haircut. This was new in itself, for Iris had always grown her hair in a long, thick mane that flowed down her back, teased and twined into a French plait. She watched his face as she settled into the hard wooden seat, her expression guarded and just a little defiant.

'I figured it was getting too much, all that time spent colouring and brushing and carrying on,' she said. 'Reckon there's no need for it now.'

Newt wanted to reach out and hug her, to comfort her, as the loneliness within her poked its head out past the protecting shell, but he could not. Even if the rules hadn't forbidden physical contact, even if he hadn't been hemmed in by sharp-eyed, feral men watching for a moment of weakness, there was an air of reserve about his mother. Her innate dignity and the strength of will she projected had made the gesture unthinkable.

That last visit, though, something fundamental and deep had changed and his mind worried at it through the long nights and tedious days. It had been an unexpected visit, arranged by Alex Hastings, his probation officer in Highpoint, and he had sat frozen with horror as his mother described her ordeal at the hands of his father – his late father, whom he'd thought had died the previous year. Derek had disappeared down the main canal on the Levels, swept away at the end of a murderous vendetta against all the people he had held responsible for Newt's imprisonment and the death of Biff, Newt's younger brother.

'So where'd he bin then?' he demanded, trying to make sense of Iris's narrative.

'Don't know,' she said. 'Don't know and to be honest, lad, don't care much now. Just glad it's all over at last. Funny.' She squinted up at the strip lights, blinking in the flat, bright glare. 'Seems I never felt he was gone before. I kept finding myself lookin' over my shoulder, double locking the door. Didn't feel safe, not without them finding a body.'

'So is that why you never had no memorial service or nothing?' asked Newt.

Iris shrugged. 'Mebbe. Just didn't seem – right, somehow. Still, at least we get to lay him to rest now, proper, like his family wants. Your probation officer, she's talkin' to the prison, see if we can get you out for the service.'

Newt doubted very much he would be allowed to attend the funeral. His escape attempt, laughable as it had been, was still on his record and in addition to losing him half his parole it meant he was unlikely to be considered for compassionate leave. When word came down he was to be escorted to the church and allowed to go back to the house to support Iris on the day, his admiration for Alex knew no bounds but, still, he mused on the difference he perceived in his mother. She was sad – or maybe not so much sad as thoughtful. Catching her eye across the table, she had glanced away and when he pressed her, she simply shook her head.

'Just thinking about things,' she said and smiled vaguely. 'Lot has happened and it seems all the world's changed this past year or so.' She rummaged in her bag for a tissue and blew her nose before finally meeting his gaze. 'One thing, mind. He loved you and Biff, even if he'd not the words to tell you. Don't you ever forget that now.' She reached over and squeezed her son's hand, in defiance of the rules, and the officer seated off to one side glanced away, ignoring this breach of protocol.

The light grew stronger outside and Newt slid off his bunk, landing without a sound on the cold stone floor. Moving softly to avoid waking his cell mate, he shaved and washed his face and hands before sitting in his prison uniform for the warders to collect him. They would bring his court suit, the only smart clothes he possessed, and he wondered fleetingly whether he would get any breakfast this morning but the prospect of a day away from the prison, even such a terrible, grief-filled day, had him churning with excitement. Too roiled up to feel hungry, he forced himself to sit quietly and wait.

At the probation office at Highpoint, Lauren was surprised to hear Alex and Sue intended to go to Derek Johns' funeral.

'Don't reckon I'd fancy it,' she said as she sat in the staff room and demolished a bacon sandwich.

Sue watched her, amusement mixed with disapproval. Lauren's appetite still astonished her, even after knowing her for the last eighteen months. Lauren was only four feet tall but could out-eat (and probably out-drink) any member of the probation staff and most of the clients too.

'Only good reason for going,' Lauren continued stuffing the last of the roll in her mouth and lobbing the greasy paper towards a bin, '*Only* reason is to make sure he's really dead this time. I don't want to think what he'd look like, coming back alive again. Was bad enough last time.'

Alex smiled ruefully, shaking her head at Lauren's callousness. They had both suffered at the hands of the late, unlamented Mr Johns. Derek had stalked Alex for months, tormenting and hounding, before finally trying to lure her into a deadly trap. Lauren had been the bait, stuffed into a car boot and then almost killed in a mad, whirling escape down the flooded canal. Neither had any reason to mourn his passing, though Alex was a little more diplomatic about her feelings in public

'Anyway,' continued Lauren, 'I know Alex has to go on account of Newt bein' there on her say-so but I don't see why you is.'

'I'm going for Iris,' said Sue. 'She'll have all those other members of his gang hanging around her, all his family and I bet not one of hers will turn up. I think she'll need a friend. And I'm picking up Ada on the way.'

This was news to Alex who allowed the surprise to show on her face.

'What?' Sue demanded staring at her.

Alex shrugged. 'Nothing. Just – well, does Ada want to go?'

Ada had suffered at the hands of Derek Johns even more than the rest of them. He had murdered her husband and tried to frame her son, Kevin. Ada had defended herself robustly when he tried to break into the house out on the Levels and Alex had helped to prove Kevin was innocent, but even so, Ada more than anyone must have been relieved to have Derek's death confirmed.

'Reckon she really *does* want to make sure he's dead,' said Lauren as she slid off her chair and headed for the door. Alex and Sue watched her disappear round the curve of the staircase before Alex spoke again.

'There's something you're not telling me about all this. The police said you were with Ada and Iris when Derek arrived at the house and he was raving about something, even after he collapsed and they hauled him off to hospital. What happened out there that night?'

Sue stood up and carried her beaker over to the sink, making a show of washing up and putting it back in the cupboard before answering.

'I wasn't there when Derek arrived,' she said finally. 'So I didn't hear what was said to make him so angry. You'll have to ask Iris about that.'

Alex glared at her retreating back. Sue had been reluctant to talk about the night of Derek's death and Alex recognised the little tricks she was using to avoid revealing something without actually lying. She puzzled over this as she sat at her desk in the day centre, wondering what it was Sue was hiding and, more importantly, why she felt it necessary to keep a secret from her friends. Finally she abandoned all pretence of work and wandered out into the reception area looking for some company. There was no-one at the front desk but several young men fell silent and sat up straight in the chairs as she walked in. Nodding in recognition Alex carried on through to the main office where the clerical staff was hard at work.

Her own administrator, Alison, was off on a day's leave and Alex drifted over to her desk, looking for a file she had sent down for updating a few days previously. Rummaging through the piles of papers, forms and assorted memos lying on the cluttered surface, she spotted a familiar document tucked in a new, green folder. Pulling the file towards her, she read her own name on the front. The word 'Confidential', was stamped in big, red letters across the top and from the feel of it, there were a number of documents inside.

Alex resisted the desire to glance over her shoulder at the women busily tapping away around her. Instead she leaned over the desk to shield the folder from view before opening it and flicking through the contents. The personnel files had all been checked and reconstructed following the departure of Garry, the previous senior probation officer who had suffered a spectacular nervous breakdown. Increasingly obsessed by what he imagined to be the moral failings of his team, he had spent a number of nights supplementing the records, adding little touches of his own to the official files. When his actions were finally discovered, Alex's personnel record included a facsimile pamphlet of the Great London Plague, a number of deeply unpleasant photographs from a book illustrating 'moral degenerates', the title page torn from Aleister Crowley's *777 and other Qabalistic Writings* and some seemingly random caricatures by the eighteenth-century artist James Gillray. Alex had quietly removed the offending items and spent some time trying to work out their significance. Entering a mind as disturbed as Garry's was not a pleasant experience and she finally put the puzzle to one side. They had never exactly got on and she was already too familiar with his personal opinion of her character, her work and her ideals.

She didn't need all that extra paper to tell her Garry disapproved of just about everything she held dear.

Now restored to a more traditional format, her file held details of her job interview, her contract of employment, Garry's supervision notes (she glossed over these, knowing they contained nothing good) and, at the back, copies of her formal qualifications and certificates. She glanced at her degree certificate and was just closing the folder when she noticed the corner of another document sticking out at the back. Sliding it to the top of the pile, Alex was startled to read the full academic transcript from her university. She hadn't realised the service had a copy. Not that there was anything to hide, but still, it made interesting reading and raised more than a few questions. Before she could do more than glance over it, a shadow fell across the desk.

'Can we help you with anything?' asked Pauline, the senior administrator.

'No, no thanks.' Alex stuffed the page back into the folder hurriedly. 'Just checking all the unofficial additions have gone.' She managed a rather sickly smile as she tucked the folder back under a pile of client files.

Pauline was utterly unconvinced but, after all, the officers were entitled to access their own files whenever they wanted. They just needed to ask.

'There's a client in reception for you,' she said.

Alex raised her eyebrows. 'Did they give a name?' she asked.

Pauline shook her head. 'No, and I don't recognise them either. Are you expecting anyone new?'

Alex pondered for a moment. 'I think there was a referral from the court last week,' she said. 'I was off that day but Alison left a note.'

A few weeks previously, Alex had survived a bruising encounter with Max, a gang leader from Bristol, and the incident had triggered a series of short-lived but debilitating migraine headaches. Still weakened from a bout of meningitis over the previous winter, she had spent several days curled up in a darkened room, emerging only to forage for food that was not cooked by Sue. Although Sue was a good housemate and loyal friend, she was possibly the world's worst cook and Alex had vowed never to eat anything produced by her ever again, if it could possibly be managed. As a consequence of her illness she had missed the weekly allocation meeting, and with Alison on leave she was at a loss to identify her visitor.

Pauline hesitated and then took pity on her, reaching over the cluttered desk and pulling out a slim file. 'There you are. I think that's all we've got on him at the moment but there's a contact number in there somewhere for his old probation office.'

Alex took the folder and turned towards reception with a heavy heart. Great, she thought. An unknown recidivist client who just turns up out of the blue. Thanks team – I owe you one. She took a moment to glance at the name on the file before opening the office door.

'Mr Burton,' she said, extending her hand and forcing her face into what she hoped was a welcoming smile. To her surprise the new client was dressed smartly in a jacket, clean shirt and tie. His shoes gleamed so brightly they could have been lacquered and his hair was short but not so short he looked like a skinhead. A marked contrast to many of the scruffy, often grimy youths she encountered on a daily basis.

After an almost imperceptible hesitation Samuel Burton rose and gave a perfunctory handshake before stepping back again. As their hands touched Alex experienced a strange sensation, almost a sense of revulsion and she struggled to keep her face smiling and her voice welcoming. Studying him as he waited for her to speak, there was no apparent reason for her reaction. He was clean, tidy and seemed quite calm – almost composed. Then his eyes met hers and in an instant she read a spark of fury before he looked away once more. It was as if another person peeked through his eyes – someone utterly cold. Someone you really didn't want to meet.

Every instinct in her was shouting to get away from this man but her job was to work with him, to help him if she could. Alex had never allowed a probationer to frighten her off in her life and she was damned if she was going to do so now.

'Please wait for a moment,' she said keeping her voice steady. 'I think the upstairs room is available.'

Pauline gave her a puzzled look as she handed over the key to the 'secure' room on the first floor. Alex generally made a point of interviewing her clients in the less formal atmosphere of the day centre but Pauline trusted her judgement enough not to ask questions. The secure room had furniture bolted to the floor, a panic button under the desk and shatterproof glass in the door and windows. It also lacked a lock on the inside, a sensible precaution with the rise in higher-tariff offenders passing through the system. There had been a few cases of clients trying to hold their probation officers hostage in the last year or so. It was a rare occurrence but not one the Highpoint office wanted to experience any time soon.

'Please come with me,' said Alex and led the way up the stairs and along the corridor to the interview room. She was aware of him behind her, a few steps back and moving silently in her wake. Their footsteps were absorbed by the carpet and she realised she would probably have no warning if he did make a hostile move.

Calm down, she told herself angrily. He's given no indication of any real danger. Just that one, tiny glimpse, seen and gone in an instant. But Alex was experienced enough to know that was a warning. She needed to be very wary of this one.

Unlocking the door, she stepped back and gestured to a chair set behind the desk. Samuel glanced at her and a flicker of amusement crossed his face as he took in the layout of the room. Seating himself in the chair he settled his weight, testing for movement before brushing an imaginary fleck of dust from the lapel of his jacket. Then he folded his hands on the desk in front of him and sat perfectly still, waiting for her to make the next move.

Alex took her place in the chair nearest to the door and opened the file Pauline had given her. It was decidedly thin, just a few flimsy copies of his Part B records from a London probation office, a transfer form and, tucked away at the back, a rather smudged list of charges from his recent conviction. Make that last conviction, Alex thought as she scanned the page. Although there were no details given, a list of previous offences was included, along with a quick note of the sentence passed. Skimming through these she realised Samuel Burton had wriggled his way out of several additional sentences by cooperating with the police. Each court appearance included a number of other offences 'taken into consideration' but even at first glance some of these did not seem to tie in with his proven history. There was something wrong here, she thought as she closed the file and placed it on the desk.

He was still sitting perfectly still, watching her. With a start Alex realised his eyes seemed to have changed colour. When he had first looked at her they were pale, almost watery grey. Now they were blue, a startling and striking deep blue. Once again there was a flicker of amusement from the man across the table, almost as if he knew what she was thinking.

'I do not seem to have any contact details,' Alex said, trying to seize the initiative once more.

'I'm at the hostel,' said Samuel waving one hand dismissively.

Alex blinked at him, wrong-footed once more. It was the practice for hostel clients to be allocated a bit further up the food chain, the more experienced officers dealing with these potentially more difficult and dangerous offenders. She thought Eddie, the stalwart of mid-range probationers, or Margaret who specialised in sex offenders and those with mental health problems or psychological difficulties, would have picked up Samuel Burton. She had only been in the job a year or so – with a start she realised she had taken up the post almost two years ago. In the eyes of the service, she was an experienced officer. It was a sobering thought.

Forcing her attention back to the interview, she elicited a few personal details, his room number at the hostel and how long he had been there. The probation hostel was run by a team of middle-aged men and operated rather like a scout camp but with the added excitement that the residents could be sent back to court, perhaps even to prison, if they stepped too far out of line.

Part of the regime involved the gradual increase in privileges for residents. Everyone started off sharing a four-bed room. After several months they might have earned a place in a two-bed room. Only after six months of impeccable behaviour could a resident be considered for one of the coveted private rooms. Samuel's room number indicated he was still on the first floor, in one of the four-bed dormitories. She couldn't help wondering how he, not to mention his roomies, was coping with that.

There was little she could do without more information and his full court report with details of his day centre order seemed to be missing from her notes. Reluctant to ask the client for information that should already be in the file, she decided to set an induction day and kick him loose. It was obvious from the barely hidden sneer that he knew exactly what had happened and Alex locked the door and returned the key to Pauline, feeling more demoralised than ever.

Lauren watched her over the top of her typewriter, bright eyes studying her face and posture. As Alex turned to leave, Lauren beckoned her over.

'Don't know about that one,' she said softly, eyes following Pauline who was drifting around the office keeping everyone busy and occupied. 'Reckon he'd look right smart in a black and silver uniform.'

Alex thought of Samuel with his straight, bright blond hair neatly cut and his strange blue eyes and silently agreed.

The funeral of Derek Johns was a subdued affair. Newt arrived a few minutes before the coffin was carried into the church by a choice selection of cousins and the deceased's closest adherents. Sue and Ada sat at the back, ignored by most of the mourners. Only Iris, as she followed the plain wooden box into the church acknowledged their presence, giving a nod to Sue and favouring Ada with a fleeting smile. Alex, who had made a point of waiting outside the church, managed to prevail on the wardens to remove Newt's handcuffs, though the cost to her was being forced to sit on one side of him, surrounded by the remnants of the Johns clan. The two men from Dartmoor took up positions behind him, one of them nearer the door and sitting in a position the block the aisle if necessary. A third man waited outside, beside the car that had driven him the seventy or so miles from the prison.

'Would think I was one of they Kray twins,' Newt muttered to Alex as he took his place next to her. Despite Alex's request and Iris's pleading he had not been allowed to walk behind the coffin. All eyes were on his mother as she slid into the front pew beside her remaining son and the brief service began. Iris bore herself with a quiet dignity, head held high despite the brevity of the eulogy – what could anyone possibly say without either incriminating or perjuring themselves, thought Alex – and the obvious discomfort of the minister. When it was all over, Iris took Newt's arm and led him out of the church behind the coffin, one look at her face causing the prison officer stationed beside the aisle to step back and let them past. Alex followed the pair out at a discrete distance, uncomfortable under the stares and whispers of the small congregation.

As she emerged into the bright sunlight, Iris took her hand, staring at her with clear, green eyes.

'I want to thank you,' said Iris softly. 'Don't reckon Billy would be here now without you.' She nodded to her son who was standing beside her, his pale face made more sickly than usual by his mop of red hair. Alex smiled and shook her head slightly. Deep down she was not sure her efforts had made that much difference. After almost eighteen months inside, the authorities at Dartmoor had finally come to the realisation that Newt – Billy Johns – was not much of a flight risk after all. His moment of madness, early in his sentence, had only been staged to enable him to get to a telephone away from listening ears and even this had been at the instigation of the man they were now burying.

Unlike the prison authorities, Alex knew the truth behind Newt's 'escape' but, as his actions had unwittingly led to the murder of Ada Mallory's husband, she had never spoken to anyone else about the incident. In her mind, Newt was innocent of any blame and she wasn't going to be the one who brought any further charges down on him. It wasn't as if she had lied to the investigators or the prison service. They had never bothered to ask her if she knew anything about the incident. If they had, she would have been bound by her duty as an officer of the court to tell them about Derek and how he had used the information from Newt to murderous effect, but they hadn't bothered – and she hadn't volunteered.

The mourners trickled out of the church, most of them stopping to shake Newt's hand and exchange a few words with Iris. A number of them gave Alex a look, some surprised and one or two downright hostile. Clients, she thought, as she stepped back into the shade of the church porch.

'Well, that went off quite well, don't you think?' said Sue softly.

Alex glanced over her shoulder and saw Ada standing behind her, face hidden in the shadow of the doorway.

'Will you be coming back to Iris's after the burial?' she asked.

Sue and Ada exchanged glances.

'Don't rightly know as I'd be that welcome,' Ada murmured but at that moment Iris finished with the last of the line of mourners and stepped back into the porch.

'I want to thank you all,' Iris said, indifferent to the curious looks her behaviour attracted from the Johns clan. 'Means a lot to me, you comin' here. And especially having Billy here with me, even for the one day.' She turned to face Alex. 'I know is asking a lot but would you come back, to the house? Reckon they'll let him stay a bit longer,' she nodded towards the prison officers who were hovering by the car away from the crowd. 'Of course, you's welcome in your own right too,' Iris added hastily. 'Didn't mean it just on Billy's account. All of you – been good friends to me and – well, I don't reckon many of them have a good word to say about me now.' She glanced at the rest of the Newt's relatives, her face hardening as she watched them greet her son and shake his hand. 'Sooner I can get him away from that lot, the better,' she muttered.

Despite her misgivings, Alex found the rest of the afternoon rather interesting. Nursing a glass of orange squash ('You're a cheap round,' Ada commented) and a barely visible presence in the crowded downstairs of Iris's village council house, she watched the flow of people as they moved in and out of different groups, initiating or retreating from conversations. A lot of the Johns gang wanted to talk to Newt and there were several attempts to lure the prison officers away, presumably so that family members could exchange a few words in private. Newt, she was pleased to note, was having none of it. Like a dutiful son, he stood beside his mother, smiling and nodding at all who came to offer their condolences but never allowing Iris to be edged out of the way. He was the perfect gentleman and, from the sour expressions on some faces, a bitter disappointment to a few of those gathered around.

Halfway down her second glass of squash she began to muse idly on Newt and the family. He looked like Iris's boy today, she decided. There was something in the quiet dignity with which she moved and held herself that was mirrored in the young man. Same smile too, a sudden, wide, welcoming look that seemed to light up those around him. He was a charmer, all right. His brother Biff had been very different by all accounts. Alex had not met Biff, only encountering the Johns family after Newt's arrest some eighteen months ago but her colleagues described him as a brawler, like his father. He resembled him physically too. Alex had met Derek Johns just once, whilst out on the Levels visiting Ada's husband, Frank Mallory. Derek had killed Frank out of revenge, posing as him and going through the initial interview questions

16

whilst all the time Frank's body was mouldering in an ancient freezer in the kitchen.

It was not an encounter Alex liked to dwell on, but she remembered Derek's face quite clearly. Heavy, florid features, dark hair that hung in greasy ringlets across his forehead, eyes so dark they were almost black and, a strange detail, one gold earring in his right ear. Nothing like Newt, who obviously took after his mother. As she finished her drink and wondered how long the afternoon was going to last, she tried to recall whether the gene for red hair was a recessive or not.

Chapter Two

Acting Detective Constable Dave Brown chewed the end of his pen and stared out of the window across the main square in Taunton. Around him several of his new colleagues were filling in forms and completing reports to the steady swish of paper being shuffled around. In keeping with the times, the teams took every opportunity to catch up on the ever-rising tide of official housekeeping. Reluctantly, Dave turned his attention back to the statement form in front of him. He'd been on secondment to the detective squad for two weeks and in that time had barely been out of the building. He'd seen more action as an ordinary PC back at Highpoint, he thought ruefully as he began filling in the details of his actions and the events leading to the arrest of a Bristol-based drug dealer on the Levels.

On the evening concerned, Dave had gone out on his own initiative, looking for Alex after her flatmate Sue contacted him to say she had driven off alone to look for a probation client and his prompt action had possibly saved Alex from a watery death in the canals. That, and his previous success in locating Derek Johns and uncovering his hand in several murders, had led to the chance at a detective post – but the downside was none of his previous success counted to his assessors. He was starting all over again, desperate to impress, to show what he could do. Only there was nothing – absolutely nothing – happening in the area.

What he needed, he mused, was a nice, juicy murder. Or a couple of armed robberies, maybe. I'm a bad person, he thought as he bent over the statement form. I should be glad life is settling back down again now the Johns gang are out of business, not wishing harm on persons unknown just to further my own career. Still, he needed *something* to come up before his three months were over. The thought of returning to Highpoint, tail between his legs, was too horrible to contemplate. Whilst there he had often been the butt of his colleagues' jokes and his life was unlikely to get any better if he failed to make the grade in Taunton and was posted back to Highpoint.

Out on the Levels, in her little cottage between Kings Sedgemoor and Westonzoyland, Ada Mallory opened the back door to let in the cool evening air and call the dogs for their supper. Humming softly to herself, she rinsed their bowls in the sink, wiping down the porcelain basin and drying her hands on a towel before reaching under the sink for the bag of dog meal she kept out of sight. Mouse was no problem, she reflected. A gentle soul was Mouse – maybe a bit too quiet, and not the boldest of dogs, unlike his father, Mickey.

Now *there* was a character. She'd rescued him when he was just a skinny scrap of fur floating helplessly down the narrow stream that ran behind her garden. Alerted to his plight by shrill, desperate barks, Ada had waded in and scooped up the puppy a few seconds before the lump of bark he was clinging to rolled over and was sucked under the water as the stream met the junction of the main canal. Mickey had repaid her kindness with fierce loyalty, comfort and companionship through the long, solitary evenings. She had never been afraid as long as she had Mickey at her side, even if he was a terrible thief. She paused for a moment, hands reaching for the clean bowls, as she considered what she was going to do when Mickey went. His muzzle was grey now, he wasn't so quick on his feet and he was starting to lose his sight.

'Damn those dogs,' she said crossly. 'Where've they got to now? Mickey! Mouse! Come on, 'tis time for supper!'

She almost dropped the heavy sack of meal as a man stepped through the back door into her kitchen.

'What you doin' here!' she said, stepping back until she was hard up against the sink.

'Now then Ada, don't you be like that,' said the man, lifting the bag and placing it on the draining board. 'Can't an old friend pop by to say hello?' He stood in the doorway, smiling at her, his bright blue eyes twinkling with mischief.

Apart from a few streaks of grey in his hair and the network of fine lines around his eyes he had barely changed, Ada thought. Still the gypsy boy who had charmed her out of her shell – and, on more than one occasion, her bus money.

'Thought you was locked up,' she said crossly. 'So, I'm askin' again. What you doing here, Tom Monarch?'

'Well, what them *polis* got on me to lock us up then, eh?' Tom grinned at her, a devilish expression on his face. 'Was me as was stuck in the bog, right? Was that Derek Johns cut the ropes to the bridges an' almost killed us, so I reckon I'm innocent here.'

Ada snorted in disgust, turning away to pour food into the bowls for the dogs who crept round Tom, looking suitably shamefaced.

'Fine bloody guards you two is,' said Ada fiercely. 'First sign of some stranger and you both sit down and let 'um scratch your ears and walk right past!'

'Ah, don't take on so Ada, they can tell I'm not a threat,' said Tom, leaning on the doorframe. 'Don't know as I'm that much of a stranger neither. Known each other for years, we have.'

'Well, not when they's been around,' Ada pointed out. 'First time you've been here in their livin' memory. Don't know you from Adam, they don't. Should've had the arse out of your trousers, they should, not listen to your gypsy whispering and such like.'

She set the bowls down in front of the dogs and straightened up, flapping her hands at her visitor. 'Go on now, get out my light. Standing there in the way.'

Tom straightened up and strolled through the kitchen into the tiny front room, settling himself on Ada's worn sofa.

'Cup of tea wouldn't go amiss,' he called hopefully.

'Who invited you in there,' said Ada crossly, but she filled the kettle, set it to boil on the range and, after the briefest of hesitations, reached up to a top cupboard and pulled out her best cups and saucers. After all, she thought, it was a long time since she'd had much in the way of company.

The day after Derek Johns' funeral was a Friday and Alex was looking forward to a quiet morning at her desk. There was just one session planned for the centre, a couple of hours in the afternoon where she expected to spend a lot of her time helping her younger clients fill in forms for job applications. Gone were the days when they could turn up at a factory gate and try their luck, she thought. In fact, apart from the chicken factory there wasn't anywhere left and even those jobs – cold, tedious and rather repellent as they were – were in great demand. When even the chicken factory could afford to be choosy, things were very bad indeed. The giant plastics complex to the north was firing a good proportion of its workers and everything else needed some kind of qualification.

Lost in her own thoughts, she almost skipped up the steps, swung through the double doors and cannoned into Gordon, the acting senior. Unlike his predecessor, Gordon was a thoughtful, considerate and immensely likeable man and in the few short weeks since Garry, the previous senior officer, had been gone, he had done wonders for team morale. Despite his undoubted air of authority, Gordon worked by negotiation and persuasion, teasing the very best from the band of exhausted probation officers. Everyone agreed it was a great shame he was not going to stay in the post much longer. Well, almost everyone. The latest addition to the office, Ricky Peddlar, was already acquainted with the senior appointed by Headquarters and took every opportunity to compare Gordon's actions with how she would do things. In common with most of the staff, Alex disliked Ricky intensely.

'Ah, Alex,' said Gordon, recoiling from the collision. 'I wondered if I could have a word.'

A sinking feeling in her stomach, Alex led the way through the deserted day centre and down a narrow stone corridor to the converted storage cupboard that served as her office. Switching on the lights, she shuffled a pile of paper off the spare chair and gestured him to be seated.

'I'm sorry about this,' said Gordon. 'Really, this is most unfortunate but you are the only other officer involved with this particular client.' He paused, tugging at his neat, greying beard for a moment before continuing.

'I'm afraid I have to ask you to take the breach.'

Alex blinked at her senior for a moment before she recalled the last staff meeting. In an effort to save money (and probably to wring the last drop of enthusiasm out of the probation service) the government had decided the Crown Prosecution Service would no longer handle the return to court of probationers in breach of their orders. Instead they would be handled in court by the breaching officer, using the notes from the arrest and original trial supplied by the police. The move was deeply unpopular amongst officers and there had been a growing sense of dread as several weeks passed and offenders began to slip off the 'straight and narrow'. No-one wanted to be the first to go through the ordeal of what was, basically, presenting a prosecution in open court.

'But I've not breached anyone,' Alex protested. 'Mine are all behaving themselves for once, especially now we've got rid of the drugs coming into town.'

'He's a client at the day centre,' said Gordon. 'He's actually one of Ricky's but . . .'

22

'And Ricky's not turned up today, has he?' said Alex angrily. 'He's chickened out.' She sighed loudly. 'Who is it then?'

Gordon shook his head slightly and said, 'Martin – Martin Ford.'

'Flasher Ford? You're joking, right? I'm supposed to stand up in court and read out the police notes on *Flasher Ford*?' Alex felt a surge of fury run through her body and her already limited tact and diplomacy failed her utterly.

'The shiftless, spineless little shit!' She wasn't referring to Martin Ford, either. 'Look, I'll have to go home and change. Have I got time?'

Gordon glanced at his watch and nodded. 'Just about. You're due in at ten. Alex – I will have a word with Ricky about this if he's not genuinely sick. He's the court duty officer today and I do feel he needs to ensure he's playing his part in the team.'

Not in the least mollified, Alex set off down the old towpath beside the river, heading to her little terraced house in search of her court suit. Just one more thing to make the whole business more uncomfortable, she thought. Skirt, tights and stupid shoes – when would the damn magistrates drag themselves into the twentieth century? She recalled one of her tutors telling her there used to be a 'court hat' at most probation offices as some magistrates demanded women appeared in hats and gloves. The idea was so ludicrous she gave a snort of laughter as she hurried through the front door and upstairs to her room.

When she arrived at the magistrates' court there was a flurry of consternation amongst the clerks.

'We were expecting Mr Peddlar,' said the chief clerk, his eyes darting around anxiously as if hoping to spot Ricky lurking in a corner.

'Well, he's not in today so you've got me,' said Alex grimly. 'May I see the notes please?' She put out her hand and, very reluctantly, the clerk passed over the folder. He hovered next to her, anxiety oozing from every pore.

'Um, if you look at the front pages – er, here to here, are the relevant sections. I'm afraid there's rather a lot of it . . .' His voice trailed away and he looked round again, hoping someone would intervene and call him away.

Alex skimmed over the first of the pages and felt her heart sink. It was written in Police English, a strange and rather stilted form of language that presumably aimed at clarity but frequently provoked hilarity amongst the initiated of the court. Even the short, formal statements could not do much about the content, however, and she wondered how she was going to get through the prosecution's evidence without either collapsing with embarrassment or succumbing to hysterical giggles. She was hard pushed to say which would be worse.

'That's fine, thank you,' she said, heading towards the bench outside the court. The previous hearing was still going on inside and she had a few minutes to read through the prosecution evidence from Martin Ford's trial. She had just reached the statements from the two main witnesses when a shadow fell across the page and, looking up, she recognised one of the local solicitors. One of the original team in the prosecution of Martin Ford, in fact.

'May I?' he asked and sat down next to her before she could answer. 'This is not right,' he said, tapping the case file.

Alex shrugged and tried to convey professional resignation without showing too much impatience. It was very nice, this display of solidarity from the court, but at the moment she needed every second to study the file. Although Martin was ostensibly a client at the day centre, she had hardly seen him and had sent several notes to Ricky Peddlar highlighting the non-attendance. As the officer holding Martin's order, it was Ricky's job to issue a breach and send him back to court for sentencing. Alex could only point out his client's non-conformity, but here she was, stuck with the very first order to be presented by a probation officer for Highpoint. She realised the solicitor – what was his name, she wondered – was still talking.

'We're not happy with the whole issue, you know, but to expect you to present this particular case, well . . .' He shook his head and twisted his long, thin face into what he presumably thought was an expression of profound sympathy. Alex thought it looked more like a bad attack of wind. The arrival of the clerk saved her from further platitudes and she rose, gathering up the file to follow him into the court.

There were more sympathetic looks as she made her way to the front amid a murmur from the small public gallery. Glancing up, she saw Martin Ford's family – father, mother and three brothers – sitting in unaccustomed splendour, the men in slightly shiny suits and a job-lot of carnival club ties. His mother sat in the centre of the row, squeezed into a polyester dress of quite shocking peacock blue and clutching a green handbag that looked large enough to hold several sawn-off shotguns. Given the family's reputation for solving disagreements with violence, Alex wouldn't have been surprised if it did.

She tried to sneak another glance at the statements but the clerk called the court to its feet and the magistrates entered and seated themselves at the bench. One of them, a woman called Veronica House, nodded to Alex and raised one eyebrow, either in sympathy or perhaps querying the absence of Ricky. As the ushers escorted Martin Ford to the seat behind the defence table there was a rustle from where his family were seated and the Chair of the Bench turned to glare at them.

'I want to say that we will tolerate no interruptions or remarks from the gallery. This is a serious issue and we expect it to be treated as such.' He nodded to the clerk who rose and began reading out the charges.

Alex had appeared in court many times before but always in a supporting role. Often she merely had to acknowledge a report submitted days or occasionally weeks earlier and at most had to respond to questions from the bench. She'd never had to get up and actually prosecute someone and the shaking in her hands and legs made her feel sick. As her name was called, she rose to her feet, convinced everyone could see how nervous she was.

'Are you ready to proceed?' asked the Chair of the Bench.

Alex nodded, then swallowed and managed, 'Yes, thank you Sir.' Her voice sounded squeaky in her ears and she took a deep breath before turning her attention to the pages from the prosecution's original case.

It started reasonably well, with an outline of the times, days and places of the offences and some dry and factual notes on Martin Ford's arrest and initial interview. It was when Alex got to the crucial statements from two witnesses that things began to go wrong.

This was the part of the file she had not been able to read properly beforehand and as she embarked on her recitation, she realised with sinking heart that had been a terrible mistake. As she skimmed ahead, her voice faltered and the bench leaned forwards, straining to hear. She cleared her throat again and started at the beginning of the first statement. There was only one way to do this, she thought fiercely. Absolutely deadpan, just straight out with it. And be sustained by the knowledge she would have Ricky-bloody-Peddlar's heart on a stick for putting her in this position.

'Witness statement from Mrs Vera Bond,' she read. 'On the morning of February 12th, 1987, I was walking with my daughter, Mabel Smith, on the beach at Hinkley Point. We had been walking towards the power station for about fifteen minutes and there was no-one else around. Just as we decided to turn round and go back to our car Mabel grabbed my arm and pointed to something near the fence. We were quite close by now and I could see a figure standing there and sort of waving . . .' Alex hesitated, wondering how anyone could 'sort of' wave but there was silence in the room and she hurried on.

'Mabel tugged at my sleeve and pointed again. "I think he's flashing at us," she said. I stopped walking and tried to see what the man was doing but I couldn't make out any details so I put my glasses on to check. Mabel put her glasses on too but we wasn't sure.'

A ripple of laughter ran floated round the room but Alex kept her eyes fixed firmly on the notes in her hand, not looking up as the chairman gave a warning sign to the court. As order was restored she sneaked a glance at the defendant. Martin was scowling, hunched over in his chair and chewing angrily at a large wad of gum – one of his numerous delightful habits, she recalled.

Alex resumed her reading, desperate to get to the end without laughing.

'I took my glasses off and cleaned them as they were a bit smudged and we went a few steps closer, to be sure, and it looked like he *was* flashing at us. I think he was a bit upset about something because he made a gesture in our direction and pulled up his trousers. I heard him call out a rude word before he ran off.'

The room was rocking with laughter as Martin Ford sprang to his feet, his face scarlet with fury.

'Was cold!' he yelled. 'Was February, all right?' He thrust his hands back in his pockets and glared round him, jaws clacking loudly on the gum in his mouth.

The magistrates all leaned forwards and Veronica House whispered something to the clerk of the court who held up one hand, calling for order and gesturing to the usher as he did so. The court usher on this occasion was a tiny woman who probably weighed less than seven stone wringing wet. She was also in her sixties but when she bustled over to Martin and rapped him on the shoulder, he glanced down at her and fell silent. Alex hid a grin. She had seen this before. It must be a bit like being scolded by your granny in public, she thought.

'I will not have this sort of behaviour in my court,' said the chairman when some semblance of order was re-established.

'And you.' He pointed at Martin. 'Yes, you, stop masticating!'

Martin shot a horrified look at the bench and jerked his hands out of his pockets.

Back in the probation office, Alex related the story to a fascinated audience that had gathered in the day room within minutes of her return. When she got to the part about the gum Lauren shrieked and covered her mouth in horror. Sue, on the other hand, was almost helpless with laughter, rocking on her chair as she revelled in the young man's discomfort.

'Serve him right,' she managed, gasping and giggling. 'Sleazy little oik.'

'So what was the outcome?' asked Pauline, ever practical. If Martin Ford was on his way to prison then Ricky had room for another probationer and after his oh-too-convenient sick day, she had several interesting candidates in mind. Pauline was the consummate professional and she was very slow to anger but she made a bad enemy when finally roused. From the glint in her eyes, Ricky was going to regret his actions on his return to work.

'Back on probation,' said Alex. 'There was a long speech from his solicitor arguing he hadn't re-offended so the probation order was doing some good. Don't know how, seeing as he hardly ever attends the day centre,' she added with a twist of bitterness.

'I think you should have a word with Gordon,' said Pauline. 'He needs to make sure Ricky reads the riot act to Martin this time. One more slip and he's back in court with a strong recommendation he doesn't get a third chance.'

'They just seem to keep sending them back, like unwanted parcels,' said Sue. 'I know we are often a better alternative than prison but when they don't bother even turning up, there's not much we can do to help them. It just means we waste a load of time that could be spent on someone who wants to do something positive.'

'Speaking of which, I've got a group coming in at two,' said Alex. 'See you later.'

'She works too hard,' said Pauline eyeing Alex's retreating back.

Sue nodded in agreement. 'Still, do you want to tell her?' she asked sweetly.

Pauline shook her head. 'Maybe another time,' she said.

Highpoint Probation Hostel was only half-full, partly owing to a recent swoop by the local constabulary who, acting on information gathered by then-Constable Dave Brown, rolled up a network of minor drug dealers and couriers. Out on the Levels, a gang of local opportunists led by Tom Monarch had been forced into an uneasy alliance with Max Long, a young but enthusiastic criminal from Bristol. Max used the traditional smugglers' routes across the emptiness of the Levels to bring in a lethal cocktail of 'recreational' drugs, with tragic consequences for at least one of his inexperienced customers. Max's capture and the removal of his fledgling dealers was a cause of great relief to the local men, who used the confusion surrounding his arrest to disappear into the background. The successful operation had left the hostel with a lot of space, however, and Samuel was finding it hard to understand why, with so many empty rooms, he was crammed into a four-bed dormitory with three strangers.

'That's the system,' said Peter Marks, the warden. 'You start in a four bed room, just like everyone else. You get to move up if you can prove you're trustworthy. This 'ent just a place to sleep you know. Is part of your rehabilitation and the 'Ladder of Achievement' is an important aspect of that.'

He gestured to the wall behind his desk where a diagram of the 'Ladder of Achievement' was pinned up, slightly crooked.

Samuel studied it for a moment before turning his unblinking gaze back to the warden. He had a strong – almost overwhelming – urge to rip the stupid thing from the wall and force it down the throat of this smug, petty little man. For a second he allowed himself the image of that podgy face, the eyes bulging in terror between his hands, before taking a long slow breath and without a word turning on his heel.

'I suppose we get a certificate if we get to the top, do we?' he called over his shoulder as he left the room.

Oblivious to the sarcasm in Samuel's voice, Peter beamed in what he mistakenly thought was a fatherly way.

'Well, no. But you do get a reference and a recommendation to take with you when you leave. Much more use, don't you agree?'

Samuel was already gone, heading upstairs to the airless, cramped room he was forced to share for at least the next three months. As the door opened, the smell hit him, a mixture of sweat, cheap aftershave and feet. He stood in the doorway for a moment, glaring at the dozing form of Charlie Dodds, a resident who had managed to slip back after breakfast to catch some illicit extra sleep.

The place was a pigsty, Samuel thought. Clothes and shoes were scattered across the floor and strewn on the furniture. Two of the beds had been made by pulling the covers roughly up and cramming the surplus between mattress and wall. One, Samuel's, was made with close to military precision, its covers smooth, pillows squared off and not a wrinkle on the surface. Even the sheets, hidden beneath the neat blankets, had mitred corners.

The floor around *his* bed was clear, two pairs of shoes lined up at the foot of the locker and the few clothes he possessed folded neatly in the small cupboard. On arrival he had taken one look at the communal wardrobe and turned away in disgust, going straight into town to invest in a zipped hanging bag for his suit, an outfit so vital for court appearances and job interviews. It now hung from a hook fixed to the wall behind Samuel's bed, away from the polluting squalor of the rest of the room.

Stepping swiftly across the room, Samuel jerked the curtains open and flung the window wide, ignoring the protests of the now-roused sleeper. He leaned out into the fresh air, relishing the cool tang from the river that ran below the building. As Charlie continued to protest, he turned and looked down at the recumbent form.

'Shut up,' he said softly. 'It's disgusting in here and I don't see why I should be expected to live in this filth. This window will stay open until the smell in here is gone and if you don't like the draught you can get up and leave.'

He crossed the room, settled himself on his own bed and pulled a book out from a cardboard box under his locker. Settling himself comfortably against the wall, he resumed his reading of Aldous Huxley's *Brave New World*. As always, he found himself torn between admiration at the author's perfectly rational caste system and bewilderment at the fact he spent a good half of the book attacking such a perfectly thought-out idea.

A wisp of smoke floated into his consciousness and he raised his eyes from the page to glare at the young man sitting on the bed by the window, sucking at a clumsily rolled cigarette.

'Put it out,' said Samuel.

'Bugger off. 'Tis my room too an' I've been here longer'n you. So if you don't like it, *you* can get up 'n' leave.'

Samuel was on his feet and across the small space before Charlie could take another drag. With no apparent effort, Samuel hoisted him up off the bed and bundled him head-first out of the window, where he dangled him over the river two stories below.

'You can drop that filthy thing or I'll drop you,' said Samuel ignoring the struggles of his victim. He waited a few seconds after the skinny little roll-up landed in the dark mud of the river before hauling his room-mate back inside and tossing him on to the bed.

'Reckon I should be by the window,' he said as he wiped his hand on the curtain. Charlie opened his mouth to protest and then shut it again without speaking.

'No, I'm not sleeping on your grubby mattress,' Samuel added as the young man reached out to pick up his pillows. 'Swap the beds. And don't touch anything of mine, neither.' Turning back to the cool of the open window, he ignored the scraping of furniture and the ragged breath of his room-mate struggling with the bed frames. 'And don't forget to pick up your mess before you go,' he added, eyes fixed on the town that was laid out before him, fascinating and tantalising, like an ants' nest before it was overturned by a thoughtless boot. Leaning on the narrow sill, he watched the townsfolk moving through their daily routine. The door to the room opened and then closed as Charlie left, his task complete.

Silently, Samuel lifted down his suit and hung it up behind his new space. He frowned at the floor by the window, the dirt in the carpet a source of great irritation. He considered going after Charlie and making him clean up but decided it wasn't worth it. Might disturb the warden and anyway, none of the others could clean worth spit. He'd get the vacuum cleaner up in a minute and do it himself. Samuel's eyes swung back to the window, his attention once more fixed on the little ant-like people swarming below, oblivious to his bright, hard gaze.

Chapter Three

Friday nights were always a bit special at Alex's house. The most anti-social of people most of the week, she was happy to welcome her friends, and their friends, to the small terraced house she shared with Sue. Often it was just her and Sue, sometimes joined by Lauren with or without Dave Brown. Occasionally, Jonny joined them, accompanied recently by Kirk, his new friend from Glastonbury, and Alex would watch Lauren and Jonny together, marvelling at the easy friendship between brother and sister that was so different from her relationship with her own siblings.

Alex cooked, of course. Sue was not comfortable in a kitchen and Alex hated to see good food ruined. Sue, on the other hand, was a good host and could get people talking, set the fire burning in winter and lay the table all at once, with seemingly consummate ease.

None of them had much money – no-one seemed to these days – and the food leaned towards 'hearty peasant'. Stews with a lot of vegetables, pasta and salad or rice with peppers, beans and a touch of salami or a few sausages were all staples on Friday nights. The visitors brought what they could – normally a bottle of wine, sometimes a cake or something for dessert. Alex was a good cook and somehow conjured something rich and exotic from the most unlikely ingredients and Friday evenings had become a fixture for the friends, a warm, happy end to even the hardest of weeks.

The evening following her court appearance to breach Martin Ford, Alex was standing by the cooker humming to herself as she chopped a rabbit into pieces so small as to be unrecognisable. Rabbit was one of the few meats they could afford and it was freely available in town but Sue had wrinkled her nose up at the thought of it the first time Alex had brought one home for dinner.

'I couldn't,' Sue said firmly. 'I had a rabbit as a pet when I was at school and I just couldn't eat one.'

For once she had stuck to her word – unusual where food was concerned – and subsisted on burnt toast and jam for several evenings while Alex munched her way determinedly through the rabbit casserole she had made for the weekend. For several weeks they had got by on vegetables and whatever cheap meat Alex could find but there was a limit to even her ingenuity where mince was concerned. With just a twinge of guilt, she sneaked a rabbit home, cut it into cubes and served it as stew with dumplings.

Sue enjoyed every bite but brought Alex up short when she asked what the unfamiliar treat was. Such curiosity was unusual coming from Sue who normally ate what she was offered, happy just to escape having to cook. There was a heart-stopping moment when Alex felt her habitual honesty begin to form the word 'rabbit' before, from nowhere, she conjured up 'Somerset beef'.

'Oh,' said Sue, blinking in surprise. 'Well, it was jolly good. Is it cheaper than other beef?'

'Oh yes,' said Alex. 'Much cheaper. It's local you see.' She felt a twinge of guilt but despite that, 'Somerset beef', became a popular staple, both on weekdays and for the Friday gatherings.

As she diced, seasoned and browned the meat she reflected on her on-going financial predicament. Despite having what many might consider a well-paid professional job, she brought home scarcely enough to cover the monthly bills. Without Sue's rent she would find herself in real trouble and even with that welcome addition, something as trivial as a car breakdown would find her scratching around for money. In the last two years the mortgage on her tiny house had gone up by almost £200 a month. In contrast her salary had risen by just £40. If it carried on much longer, she'd have to take a second job – if she could find one.

These gloomy thoughts were interrupted by the shrill ringing of the telephone in the front room and she hastily rinsed her hands and scuttled through to answer it.

'Hello? Hello – it that Alex?' came her mother's voice. The sound was slightly hollow, as if there was an echo on the line. In the background she could hear the murmur of voices and then a laugh, abruptly stifled but startling none the less.

'Mother – where are you?' she asked, but she already knew.

'Oh, still in East Sutton Park,' her mother replied casually. She said it as if she were referring to a rather nice spa out on the Downs. 'Actually, that's why I'm ringing, dear. They're letting me out on Monday and I do not want to go back to your father quite yet. I'm still cross with him, and your brothers, over the way they behaved and I want him to apologise. I don't suppose you could come and get me, could you?'

East Sutton Park, the women's prison in Kent, had been Dorothy Norman's 'home' for the last three weeks. Her mother, incensed by the high-handed actions of the police towards the demonstrators protesting the export of veal calves in crates through the tiny port of Brightlingsea, had defied the magistrate's court by refusing to pay a fine for 'obstruction'. The sentence of 30 days had seemed harsh but Dorothy had gone off gladly, a martyr to what she considered freedom of expression. Her family, especially her husband and Alex's two brothers, had been horrified. It had taken all Alex's efforts to prevent them paying her mother's fine.

'It's a disaster,' moaned Hector, the younger of the two boys. 'There's no-one to look after Father and he's furious. Spends his days sulking in his study until he gets hungry. Then he starts shouting and complaining about the dinner.'

Alex had been slightly less than sympathetic. 'So who's looking after him?' she asked.

Hector snorted down the phone. 'Nesta was here for a bit but she left after Father demanded something different to eat. I don't know where she's gone but Archie and I have been taking it in turns for the last week. I don't suppose . . .'

'Forget it,' Alex snapped back. Good for Nesta, she thought privately. Her younger sister was showing some spirit, defying the males of the household. Alex had the excuse of being on the other side of the country but Nesta had returned to the family home after completing her degree and still worked in the town. Alex wasn't surprised her mother didn't want to go back just yet, but it left her in an awkward position. She hated the thought of Dorothy being released, standing outside the prison gates with no-one to greet her and nowhere to go, but it was going to be difficult getting over to Kent on Monday.

'I'll do what I can,' she said to her mother. 'I'll be there or I'll arrange for a taxi – promise. What will you do for money?'

'Oh, I'll be fine dear. I'll have my card so I can stop at a hole in the wall.'

This was news to Alex who was under the impression it was her father who controlled the finances, the way he seemed to control most aspects of their family life.

'Don't ask,' said her mother briskly, interpreting the pause correctly. 'I don't suppose I could stay with you for a few days could I? Just until things settle down a bit . . .'

There was a shout from the back room.

'Just stir it so it doesn't burn,' she called through the door. 'I'll be back in a minute'

'You're busy dear so I'd better let you go.' There was a thread of disappointment in her mother's voice and Alex felt her stomach clench with anxiety. Her mother had always had the ability to reduce her to a desperate child.

'No, it's fine. I'll talk to Gordon and pick you up on Monday.'

'Thank you,' and the line went dead. Alex replaced the receiver and took a deep breath. She had no idea how she was doing to get over to Kent in time – in fact she wasn't sure she could afford the petrol, but she'd agreed to go now. The smell of burning onions greeted her as she stepped back into the main room.

'I said to stir it! For goodness sake . . .' Alex nudged Sue away from the simmering sauce and pulled it off the heat. It had only just caught and was probably salvable, especially if enough grated cheese was added to the pasta.

'I've got it,' she said gruffly. 'You set the table and see to everyone's drinks.'

Despite the slight taint from the onions, the pasta was received with enthusiasm and the evening passed quickly, several hours around the table, talking and drinking wine. When Jonny and Kirk finally left it was gone midnight and Alex shook her head and closed the kitchen door on the debris.

'Tomorrow,' she said and made her way upstairs, already wondering how she was going to manage the extra couple of days off.

Ada Mallory was humming to herself as she wandered around her vegetable garden, checking the progress of the early salad and securing nets over the new seedlings. Despite having lived on the Levels all her life, she was still captivated by the great flocks of birds that formed over the watery landscapes, their aerial displays darkening the sky and forming patterns in the air. She was not, however, willing to feed them and exercised considerable ingenuity where her kitchen garden was concerned. Old fishing nets were hung over wooden posts set in between the neat rows of baby plants and above them string and ropes coiled around, looping across the patch and supporting a selection of tin cans and a few old bells from cattle. Any bird brave (or stupid) enough to land on the posts immediately set off a cacophony of rattles and clangs, double insurance as Ada was out of the back door, clutching a slightly less than legal shotgun, and she was not averse to a taste of rook pie if she got a lucky shot in. A croaking call floated across the Levels and Ada squinted up at the trees behind her land.

'Don't you be getting any ideas!' she called.

There was another, almost mocking sound and a large, black bird flew out of the nearest tree, floating on wide, dark wings over her garden before circling lazily away towards Westonzoyland. Ada scowled after it, shaking her head in frustration. Her shotgun was lodged safely upstairs, in the back of a cupboard and she was unlikely to get such an easy shot again. Just as she turned her attention back to the seed beds there was a short bark and Mickey bounded around the corner of the house, his tail wagging.

'Afternoon Ada,' said Tom Monarch, striding down the path closely followed by Mouse.

'What you doin' back here, Tom?' Ada asked. She tried to glare at him but could not keep the pleasure out of her voice.

'Reckon I'd just pop in, seeing as I was passing,' said Tom.

Damn, he was still a handsome devil, Ada thought. Standing there in the spring sunshine, hands in his pockets and that cheeky grin on his face – hardly a grey hair on his head, though he was at least the same age as her.

'Been here all my life and you never had cause to be passing before now,' she grumbled. 'Suddenly you's here twice in a week.'

Tom grinned at her and raised his eyebrows. 'Maybe I weren't sure of my welcome,' he said. 'Anyway, that was afore I knew you was such a good cook. Don't suppose you've got none of that fruit cake left?'

38

Ada snorted, heading for the back door with Mickey trotting happily behind her.

'Just so's you know,' she said over her shoulder. 'I'm only lettin' you in 'cos the dogs seem to like you. Supposed to be good judges of character, they say, though I reckon maybe this is an exception.'

Tom stood for a moment, smiling after her. He glanced around the little garden, taking in the neat beds, the homemade cold frames and the shed that was cobbled together from scrap metal and gleanings from nearby trees. It was a testament to Ada's pride, her indomitable spirit and determination to live entirely on her own terms. Tom's eyes swept across the Levels, vast and echoingly empty on all sides. A lonely life, with her son was gone off with the travelling Fair to all corners of the land. Almost as lonely as his own was now.

He went inside, stooping to duck under the low frame of the kitchen door, and saw Ada had set beakers and plates out on the kitchen table.

'What, no best china?' he asked, trying to make a joke of it.

'You was a guest then,' said Ada shortly. 'Now you's just Tom – same as I've known you all these years. Besides, is getting warmer so I 'ent wasting wood putting the front fire on except in the evenings. Is warmer in here with the stove an' all.'

Tom settled himself at the table, next to the old wood-fired range and nodded as Ada offered sugar and milk for his tea.

'That's good,' he said, sipping the warm brew. 'So, how's you doing, out here on your own?'

Ada put down her tea and stared at the table for a moment before answering.

'If I'm honest,' she said, 'Is a bit hard sometimes. Kevin was ready for going away, I know, but was good to have a bit of company, 'specially in the evenings. And he was even a bit handy around the place sometimes. Right good shot with a catapult, he was. Saved me all kinds of bother with rabbits and such.' She took a sip from her beaker and looked at him. 'Still, I'm managing. Got to, 'ent you?'

Tom nodded and they sat in thoughtful silence for a few minutes.

'Was sorry to hear about your Bella,' said Ada finally.

Tom gave a tiny, involuntary gasp. The memory of his loss was still too recent, too raw to leave him for long but still, so few people ever touched on the subject, it was a shock to hear another person speak his dead wife's name.

'Thank you,' he mumbled, tears forming in his eyes.

'Oh, didn't mean to upset you,' said Ada. 'Must be hard for you an' all, what with both your families still bein' stubborn about you two.'

Tom gave a tiny smile. He wasn't sure 'stubborn' did justice to the fury he and Bella had faced when they announced their plans to wed. As son of a Roma Chief, Tom had been expected to marry the woman chosen by his father, not a half-Roma from a family that lived in a house. Bella's family were equally upset at the thought she might take up with a Gypsy, attracting unwanted attention from their more settled neighbours and tying them to the Roma once more, for future generations. With the determination of youth, Tom and Bella had pressed on, alienating both sides of the family in one simple act but despite that they had been happy together. Tom found his place amongst the smugglers of the Levels whilst maintaining a more acceptable public persona as a trader in the local markets.

All that was blown away in a few months by a short, brutal illness that seized Bella, burning her up until just the bones were left. After her death, Tom had thrown himself into a new project in an effort to forget his grief. His attempts to forge a wider network of contacts and routes for clandestine goods had come to nothing when one of his new partners decided to remove anyone who opposed them with extreme prejudice and it was only lack of evidence that had spared Tom a lengthy spell in Bristol prison. The late, unlamented Derek Johns had done most of the actual killing and the smugglers had disappeared into their respective hidey-holes waiting for the fuss to die down. Tom now found himself at a bit of a loose end, without a second income stream for the first time in many years and he was forced to look at his life, and his future, making some hard decisions.

Ada poured them both some more tea and they sat, sipping in silence for a few moments.

'Is right evil, cancer,' Ada observed, watching Tom over the top of her cup.

Tom nodded, not trusting himself to speak. After a moment to recover his self-control, he put down his drink.

'You heard about this bloke then?' he asked. Ada shook her head and he continued. 'Seems there's been a couple of incidents now. Folks sittin' around in the evenings, just quiet like, and some weirdo comes flying over and starts rubbin' hisself against the windows. No clothes on neither.'

Ada stared at him in astonishment.

'You mean . . .' She gestured towards her body and shook her head in disbelief. 'They know who it is then?'

'Seems the only thing he's wearing is a stocking and that's over his face,' said Tom. 'Mind, seems to be mainly posh houses, with them big conservatory things on the back.'

'Well, sitting in one of them at night, might as well be in a fish bowl,' said Ada scornfully. 'Asking for trouble, that is.'

Tom frowned. 'Don't seem right, folks can't sit up of an evening in their own place without nutters like that pickin' on 'em,' he said. 'Should be safe, inside your own home.'

Ada finished her tea and set the mug down on the table.

'Sensible women know that 'ent always so,' she said firmly. 'Maybe in an *ideal* world would be fine but there's more and more creeps out there and seems they don't ever get caught. Half the time the police think 'tis funny. So if they don't take it serious then is up to the woman to be a bit sensible. Curtains is good – and when you's all alone, curtains is essential.'

Tom glanced at her over the top of his beaker and took a final swig before answering. He respected Ada's point of view and it was typical of her fiercely independent (some

41

would say hard-nosed) approach to life, but the idea that it was somehow the fault of the women – and it was, invariably women who were targeted – did not sit easily with him.

'Still reckon it's not right, having to act like there's always someone nasty around. Person should be free to sit and look out of their own windows if they want to.' He changed the subject before Ada could respond. 'Anyways, now, I was lookin' at your garden. Seems you's using just about every inch you got. Real nice, the way is all set out.'

Ada smiled, nodding her agreement.

'Got to make the most of what you got,' she said. 'Mind, could do with a bit more, 'specially come summer. Seems a waste, all this decent land around and no-one using none of it.' She glanced towards the window and sighed. 'Is heavy work, though, what with clearing and fences and so on. Should have got some turned and cleared when I had Kev here but he weren't much of a one for garden work.'

Privately Tom thought Kevin hadn't been much of a one for any type of work but he wisely kept silent on the subject.

'Tell you what though,' he said. 'Friend of mine, he's got a goat he's looking to lend out. Big old male, but right gentle, he is. Nothing like a goat for clearing scrub and such. Even eat that hawthorn you got growing out on the sides of the garden.'

'Goats eat everything,' said Ada. 'My Nan, she had one and it ate her washing one time. And chewed up my boots too. Don't know about no goat . . .'

'I'll help with decent fences,' said Tom. 'Have to keep it away from the garden but I reckon it could clear a couple of extra beds each side, we adjust yer boundary a bit and no-one's any the wiser. What do you say – give it a go?'

Ada was not entirely convinced but the thought of some extra growing space was very attractive. By the time hard winter came she was often running out of home-grown produce and forced to rely on shop-bought vegetables. Apart from the cost and the difficulties inherent in the long journey into Highpoint, they just didn't taste as good. Even food from the weekly market was, in her opinion, inferior to her own and you never knew what had been put on it or who had been handling it. Those extra few square feet could make all the difference to her life and she was sorely tempted by the offer.

'Just a few weeks you reckon?' she asked.

Tom nodded. 'I'll bring over some posts and wires,' he said. 'Make it all secure afore he gets here.'

Ada had a thought. 'How's I goin' to transport a goat?' she asked. 'Don't fancy walking it however far it might be and I don't reckon the bus'll be happy taking him.'

Tom laughed at the notion of Ada trying to persuade a bus driver to accept her goat as a passenger.

'Reckon if anyone could then is you,' he said. 'No, don't you worry. When we's ready, I'll bring'm over. So, what you say – ready to expand a bit?'

Ada grinned at him. In her head she was already planning how she would use the extra space.

Tom got to his feet, clearing the beakers into the sink. 'Right then. I'll go have a word and pick up some stuff. Bit later this week be okay for you if I'm back to set a few fences?'

Ada assured him that would be just fine. She watched from the kitchen window as he ambled down the path, closing the gate carefully so the dogs wouldn't get out. Tom Monarch, she mused. Who'd have thought he'd be back, after all these years. He was good company too – always had been, even as a boy. She gave herself a little shake, annoyed at getting all sentimental. Calling to the dogs, she went back into the garden to see where her new seed beds could go.

One advantage of being on the detective team, Dave discovered, was that most of the work was done during the working week, provided there was nothing much going on. Of course, if something big and nasty happened then it was back to weekends and cancelled leave, but the detectives didn't maintain a regular weekend rota. Consequently he was both alarmed and excited when the phone went early on Sunday morning and he was called in, part of a new team to investigate a second incident involving a naked man in some poor woman's garden.

Lauren had quite understood when he rang to cancel their planned cycle trip out to Cannington. She knew how important these three months were for his career, much more important than getting used to the specially adapted tandem he had designed as a 'making up' present a few weeks ago. For the first time in her life, Lauren felt as if she were someone's first choice, someone who mattered in another's life. It might not last but then again, maybe it would – and she was determined to enjoy every day they had.

'I reckon it comes with the territory,' she said to Sue, sitting at the table in Alex's back room. 'And 'ent so bad as when he was stuck in Highpoint. They was runnin' him ragged, calling him out every weekend and half the nights too. Reckon they was tryin' to make him quit, him being an in-comer and all.' She reached out and lifted another biscuit from the plate between them. 'Where's Alex?' she asked, screwing up her face as she munched on a Garibaldi. 'She's not took bad again?'

Sue reassured her. 'No, she's just having a bit of a lie-in. Remember the phone call on Friday?'

Lauren nodded, her mouth full of crumbs.

'Well, it was her mother who is getting out . . .' Sue stopped abruptly. Lauren, dear as she was to them both, was the worse gossip in the office. Congenitally incapable of keeping a secret, she happily and unwittingly shared the most intimate details of life – both her own or anyone else's.

'Out where?' Lauren asked, her words slightly muffled.

'Oh, just – out of the family home for a bit. Like last Christmas when she came to stay for a few days.' Sue waved her hand vaguely before hurrying on. 'Anyway, Alex is going to drive over and get her tomorrow and you know she doesn't really like driving, especially if she's not really familiar with the roads.'

Lauren was not fooled by Sue's evasiveness but she just nodded and reached for another biscuit. Time enough to ferret out the truth when Alex's mother arrived, she thought.

Over in Taunton, Dave was being briefed by the Inspector in charge of the new team.

'This is the second incident of this type,' he said pointing to a map of the area around Highpoint. 'The first took place here, near Goathurst. Not much around there really but a few big houses with large gardens. The woman was sitting in her conservatory, reading a book so she didn't notice anything until the man just – well, plastered himself up against the glass. Stark naked he was, except for something over his face.'

There was a stirring amongst the officers and a soft snigger, hastily silenced. The Inspector glared at the men.

'This is not amusing,' he said angrily. 'The second woman was extremely frightened. She came to no physical harm but she didn't know if he was trying to get in or what he was going to do. Now she's too afraid to sit in her own home at night without someone with her all the time.'

The group subsided, heads bent like naughty schoolboys and the Inspector resumed the briefing. 'Friday night it happened again but this time over here.' He pointed to a small village further to the south. 'West Monkton. Again, not many properties around, a few large houses and some posh gardens. Same thing – woman on her own, sitting out the back of her house in a conservatory and he runs up and starts rubbing himself against the window.'

Dave hesitated before raising his hand.

'Yes?'

'Are we sure it's the same man?'

'I bloody well hope so,' said the Inspector. 'The thought of a gang of them running around the countryside doing this is a nightmare. We're operating on the assumption it's just one man, though it's hard to be sure without any clear description. We have to go with the MO – which is pretty distinctive. Now, you, Detective Brown.' He pointed to Dave. 'I'm pairing you with Sergeant Lynas for this one. You go out to interview the victim, a Mrs . . .' He consulted his notes. 'A Mrs Singleton. She is expecting you. When you've seen her,

45

I want you to go back to the first victim, Miss Taylor. See if you can get anything useful in the way of a description and talk to the crime scene boys. They're looking for any indication of how he got there, any signs that could help us find him. The first scene's probably useless by now but you never know your luck. Off you go.'

Dave got to his feet and hurried after Sergeant Lynas, a stocky middle-aged man known for his forthright manner and solid common sense. Of all the sergeants, Dave reflected as they set off along the A38, Lynas was probably the best option. Several of the older men, those closest to retirement, were resentful of his rapid advancement. It was very unusual for an ordinary constable to get a chance at detective as soon as he had. Barely two years out of Hendon and here he was, on the brink of his big career breakthrough. Lynas, in contrast, was only interested in how well his partner performed. If Dave could do the job then that was fine by him. If he didn't – well, Dave knew he deserved to be tossed back into the ranks at Highpoint.

'So,' said Sergeant Lynas, breaking the silence in the car. 'Fast-track, eh? What's that mean exactly?'

'It means I've got a hell of a lot to learn,' said Dave, keeping his eyes firmly on the road.

Lynas chuckled softly. 'Reckon it does,' he said. 'Least you knows it though.'

They drove in silence for several miles until the sergeant directed Dave off the main road and towards the little village at West Monkton. A typical settlement on the fringes of the Quantock Hills, it was little more than a couple of streets with an imposing church, parts of which dated from the thirteenth century. The most exciting thing to happen there recently (before the arrival of the mystery flasher, of course) had been a spectacular display of bell-ringing the previous Easter. As Dave drove slowly down the main street he saw a post office, a couple of small shops, all of them closed, and a pub off to the left. A few families, dressed in their Sunday best were walking back from the church, heading home for a Sunday roast and a quiet afternoon with the newspapers. It was difficult to imagine anything untoward happening in such a peaceful place.

'Down here,' indicated Sergeant Lynas and Dave turned into a narrow, unmade road. They jolted a few yards down the track before drawing to a halt outside a solid but not ostentatious Georgian house.

'Right,' said Lynas opening the door on his side. 'I'll do the interview and you take notes this time. We'll do it the other way round at the next call if you're confident, right?'

Dave nodded, suddenly and inexplicably nervous. He'd interviewed witnesses and victims at numerous crime scenes in the past but this felt different. More serious, perhaps. Certainly more important for him personally. However much the sergeant acted as if they were a proper team, Dave knew he was being watched and judged on everything he did.

The front door opened to reveal a large man with a heavy beard and angry eyes. He inspected their badges before stepping aside and gesturing towards the back of the house, closing the door and replacing the safety chain behind them.

'Through there,' said the man gruffly.

Down the hallway the back of the house opened up into one large room. A small, slight woman in her mid-thirties sat, her legs curled under her, arms wrapped around her body, in a large red armchair. Despite the fact the day was warm and bright, a fire burned in the grate and the sunshine was hidden behind closed drapes. Her husband hovered in the doorway, his anxiety and anger boiling away below the surface.

'Melanie?' he said gently. 'Melanie, love. These gentlemen are here from the police.'

The woman turned her head away from him and seemed to slip further into the cushions of the chair.

'Mrs Singleton,' said Sergeant Lynas softly. 'I'm sorry to bother you and I know this must have been a terrible experience but if we could just have a quick word, I hope we can catch this man.'

Melanie Singleton made a soft, squeaking sound, muffled by the chair, but she did lift her head a little.

'I'll get some tea, shall I?' said her husband.

Sergeant Lynas shook his head. 'We're fine,' he said firmly. 'Perhaps your wife would like something but if she'd rather you were here with her then you should stay.'

Dave opened his mouth, then closed it again without speaking and pulled out his notebook, trying to be as unobtrusive as possible.

'We've not had that conservatory long,' said Mr Singleton, gesturing towards the closed drapes. 'Melanie's been wanting one for ages. Thought it would be nice, sitting out and looking at the stars of a night.'

Melanie gave a sound like a sob and turned her head to look at them.

'Might as well pull it down,' she said bitterly. 'Don't reckon I'll ever want to sit there again.'

Dave kept quiet until the two detectives were back in the car and he was heading back towards the road into the village.

'Didn't get much there,' he said turning left and heading for the A38.

'Oh, I don't know,' said Sergeant Lynas. 'Reckon there's some useful stuff to start us off. They never heard nothing, right?'

Dave nodded, trying to listen and concentrate on the road at the same time.

'So what does that tell you?' Lynas said.

'No car?' ventured Dave.

'No car – no motor vehicle at all. Not unless he parked a bit away from the house and walked, in which case he must have stopped and got ready somewhere right close by. Don't reckon he was walking there stark naked, do you?'

'Ah,' said Dave and thought for a moment. 'Locard's Exchange Principle. Every encounter involves an exchange of materials. Somewhere out there he left a trace.'

'Well, I wouldn't have put quite like that,' said Sergeant Lynas, hiding a grin. 'Still, you'm right. And if we ever get the bugger, there'll be something on his clothes he took back from here too. All we need to do is find where he was waiting. That's what we need the crime scene lads to tell us. Hopefully they's still at Goathurst and we can check with them.'

'Can I ask you something?' said Dave after a pause. 'How come you turned down the offer of tea? I thought we always said yes, even if we don't want it. To help make it seem a bit more – well, normal.'

'Good question,' said the sergeant. 'Generally we would sit down, have a cuppa, bit of a chat, but Mrs Singleton, she was close to being traumatised by it all. I reckoned she wanted us to be as official as possible. In, ask our questions and out again. Last thing she fancied was more strange men tramping around her home. Next time, when she's feelin' a bit more herself, that's the time for tea. You get to judge these situations after a bit.'

The occupant of the Goathurst house was a very different character from Melanie Singleton. Miss Taylor opened the door herself, tilting her head back to look at the two men.

'More of you,' she said, waving their badges aside and leading the way through her house. The walls of the hall were lined with bookshelves, Dave noted. He wished they had a chance to examine the contents – he always found other people's books fascinating – but they hurried past and out into the back where the conservatory looked out over the garden. In the far corner several figures in boiler suits were poking around under the trees and Dave recognised the police photographer from Taunton hovering in the background. Despite the sunshine, he looked decidedly chilly and Dave felt a moment's pleasure at the thought of his own new duties, inside in the warmth.

This time tea was accepted and they sat in around a rattan table, nibbling at their biscuits and exchanging the necessary initial information. After confirming the basic details with Miss Taylor, Sergeant Lynas nodded to Dave to take over.

'Ah, well, can you describe what happened for us please?' he began hoping his nervousness didn't show too much. There was something about her that made him uneasy. She reminded him of one of his teachers from secondary school – one of the old-fashioned, no-nonsense women who had taken no prisoners, demanded his best efforts and, ultimately, helped put him where he was. Miss Taylor was watching him, a tiny gleam of sardonic amusement in her eyes. Dave returned her look, keeping his face as neutral as possible. He had a horrible feeling she knew exactly what he was thinking.

Miss Taylor's record of events was clear, crisp and impersonal, as if she were describing events that had happened to someone else. She confirmed there had been no obvious sounds of a vehicle stopping nearby and her description of her assailant was similar in enough ways for Dave to conclude this was the same man. Of course, she could not give much in the way of detail, to help identification.

'He had something over his head, squashing his face. Probably a stocking or something similar,' she said when he pressed for some identifying features. 'I could not see his face at all. I did not notice any scars or anything like a tattoo either, though it was all over rather quickly. I was a bit ashamed of the fuss I made after it was over but the surprise rather shook me up and I was reading a horror story at the time.'

She gestured to a small bookcase under the long window crammed with paperbacks by James Herbert and Stephen King.

'My guilty secret,' she murmured with a wry smile.

Dave smiled back, nodding in understanding. 'Well, he got here somehow. We must hope the scene of crime team can help us with the details. It's a lot easier with some idea of the suspect's appearance, obviously.'

Miss Taylor gave a little frown. 'Perhaps I can help with something,' she said. 'I couldn't tell you the colour of his eyes but he was blond.'

Dave glanced up sharply. 'I thought you said his head was covered? How can you be sure . . .'

A sharp tap on his ankle from Sergeant Lynas stopped him mid-sentence.

Miss Taylor blinked at him and gave her wry smile again. 'Oh yes, he was definitely a *natural* blond.'

Dave bent over his notebook, scribbling an unnecessary and elaborate series of notes as he felt himself begin to turn red.

'Ah, of course – well, thank you. That is very helpful,' he mumbled and stood up so abruptly he almost overturned the rattan table.

Miss Taylor reached out and steadied the tea tray before rising to her feet and holding out her hand.

'I believe your crime scene colleagues are still at the back of the garden,' she said. 'If it is any help, I have not cleaned the windows since it happened, though it has rained several times and so anything . . . useful, shall we say, may have gone by now. Perhaps you could let me know when I may scrub everything down?'

'Certainly,' said Dave, shaking her hand. 'Thank you for the tea. You have been very helpful. Oh.' He turned back from the door. 'We may need to check a few things later. Would it be alright to contact you?'

'Please, any time,' said the indomitable woman as she guided the two men towards the conservatory door. 'This is much quicker, out to the back garden. Last time I looked your colleagues were over there, under the willows.' With a nod and a smile she was gone and Dave heard the faint click of a key in the lock. Despite her calm exterior, this incident had rattled her, he thought.

Sergeant Lynas was grinning as he picked his way across the lawn, sticking to the paving stones to avoid any lingering trace evidence that might be left on the lawn.

'You're going to share that all round the station, aren't you?' said Dave gloomily.

'Nah,' said Lynas. 'Just the Detectives' room. Actually, you did pretty well for a first interview. Don't you look so down-cast – least we know he's blond.'

'A *natural* blond,' said Dave and then his sense of humour reasserted itself. 'Let's hope he doesn't dye his hair green or something. I don't fancy the identity parade if we have to rely on this sighting.'

Lynas grinned at him. 'I'll make you organise it, if it do,' he said.

Chapter Four

Gordon, Alex mused as she embarked on the long, solitary drive to Kent, had been very decent about her request for a day's leave, especially considering the lack of notice.

'I think you deserve at least a day off after your sterling efforts last week,' he had said when she phoned him on the Saturday. 'I hear nothing but praise for your professionalism. Don't worry about covering your duties. I've got Ricky pencilled in for most of them, including an extended shift in the family court.'

Alex grinned at the thought of Ricky Peddlar, the scruffiest and most egregious of officers, forced into the pit of conventional misery that was the family court. It required tremendous tact, patience and sympathy – all qualities Ricky, in Alex's opinion, lacked completely. She was glad she had no groups scheduled for the day, however. She didn't see why they should have to put up with him. It was bad enough being on probation and having to attend the day centre every week without having three hours of Ricky Peddlar thrust on you.

She started out very early in the morning, before dawn, her route written out on a large piece of paper beside her on the passenger seat. Deciding she wanted to give the motorways a miss, she cut across the Levels on the Westonzoyland Road, skirting the old airfield and passing Iris Johns' house in Middlezoy. It was eerily still on the marsh at night and she was glad to see the end of the rynes and canals when the road reached the relative civilisation of Somerton. She stopped for a sip of coffee from her flask before turning on to the A303, a road that led past Stonehenge as it headed east. She had timed her journey perfectly and the sun was rising as she pulled into the car park opposite that most magnificent of monuments. There was no-one else around and she slipped through the gate, marvelling at the size and setting of the great stones.

She felt strangely privileged to have the circle all to herself. There were rumours the authorities were considering fencing it off more permanently, a typical knee-jerk reaction to the recent free festivals and the violent events nearly two years past when the New Age Convoy had clashed with local police, an encounter now glorified with the title 'The Battle of the Beanfield'. Whilst the truth of that incident was still hidden in layers of contradictory witness statements, the impact on the free movement of travellers was considerable and the possible loss of access to something as beautiful and important as Stonehenge saddened Alex deeply.

After a quick rest she drove on, concerned now about the likely traffic and possible delays around the capital. Already well acquainted with horror stories about the new M25 motorway, she had planned a route away from the ring road but as her journey began to slow to a crawl at junctions and through the towns of the south-east she began to question her decision. One town seemed to bleed into another as she tried to count them off in her head, one house-lined road indistinguishable from another. Dorking, Reigate, Godstone, Sevenoaks – would this journey never end, she wondered as the minutes ticked by, but the miles covered seemed stuck at the same place on her trip monitor. Finally she turned off towards Maidstone and cut across the rolling downs towards Sutton Valence and the entrance to the prison.

She pulled into the car park and collapsed, exhausted by the stress of the last seventy miles. The coffee was beginning to wear off and she felt gritty, sweaty and utterly drained. Just the idea of the return journey made her head pound and a familiar sense of panic swept through her body. Forcing herself to take slow, deep breaths, she leaned forwards and rested her head on the steering wheel, closing her eyes and trying to think calm, cool thoughts. A rap on the window made her jerk upright, her vision blurred and heart racing.

'I thought you had fallen asleep,' came a familiar voice and her mother opened the passenger door and smiled at her. 'I'll just put my bag on the back seat, shall I?'

Unfastening her seat belt, Alex opened her door and went round to greet her newly released mother. Dorothy Norman looked – well, just the same as ever really. Her brief sojourn as a guest of the Prison Service seemed to have had remarkably little impact on her.

'Well,' said her mother, meeting her daughter's gaze with a steady look of her own. 'Did you expect me to be shaven-headed? A few tattoos, perhaps?'

Despite herself, Alex laughed and reached out to hug the indomitable woman.

'You never know,' she said. 'Some people find it a real trauma. I sometimes think all sentences should be about a week long. After that people get to know the system and it stops being so frightening. Give them a week and most prisoners would never go back again.'

Her mother returned the embrace and then, glancing over Alex's shoulder, pulled away.

'Wait here will you?' she said and hurried over to a small group of women who, having emerged from behind the fence, were clustered in the car park, looking around at the empty space. Alex leaned on the car and watched as her mother spoke to each one, exchanging brief hugs and smiles. One woman stood a little apart from the rest, a thin and bedraggled figure dressed only in a light dress and knitted cardigan. She was clutching a handbag but seemed to have no personal possessions or spare clothes with her. Dorothy reached out and touched the woman's shoulder, leaning forward to speak to her. The woman shrugged and began to pull away, glancing up towards Alex before finally nodding her head. With a sinking heart, Alex watched her mother lead the woman across the car park towards her.

'Alex, dear,' said Dorothy. 'This is Muriel. She has no-one to collect her and I said we could give her a lift to the railway station in Tonbridge.' The tone was bright and friendly, but underneath Alex could hear the unspoken words so familiar from her childhood. 'So do as you are told and don't make a fuss', was the rest of the sentence. She managed a smile and slid into the driver's seat, trying to avoid her mother's approving eyes.

She was a grown woman, she thought angrily as they began the long journey back to Highpoint. A grown woman with a life of her own, opinions of her own and free will, dammit! Except, of course, there often is precious little free will where mothers are involved.

Back in Highpoint, Ricky Peddlar was receiving a regular dressing-down from Gordon. Although he was generally a quiet man, the epitome of politeness, softly spoken and seemingly unflappable, Gordon was not a soft touch and he was extremely angry with the young probation officer.

Ricky shifted in the chair set in front of Gordon's desk, his eyes sliding over the bookcase, the notice board covered with official bulletins and timetables and coming to rest finally on the acting senior's desk. It was a mess, a jumble of paper, files and stationery interspersed with pens and a couple of small picture frames.

'Well?' said Gordon, cutting through Ricky's self-absorbed inner dialogue. 'I would welcome your explanation for last Friday's absence.'

Ricky blinked and turned his attention back to the older man.

'I just didn't feel very well,' he said, waving one hand vaguely. 'Perhaps I picked up a bit of a bug during the week.' He smiled in what he thought was an engaging manner, an effort that fell horribly flat.

Gordon looked at him, wondering just how this idle, smug and incompetent specimen had managed to qualify as a probation officer. More puzzling was why he had chosen the job in the first place. He seemed to have no particular area of expertise, loathed the court duties and acted towards his clients with something akin to contempt. He had, Gordon thought, the empathy of a brick and the tact and tolerance of an enraged pit viper. Most days he was about as likable, too. Gordon tried very, very hard not to allow personal feelings influence his professional actions but Ricky pushed him close to breaking point.

'I know you have not had any consistent supervision since your arrival,' said Gordon smoothly. This was true, owing to the extraordinary breakdown of the previous senior probation officer, a man who had been found roaming the building stark naked in the middle of the night.

Ricky's eyes narrowed slightly as he tried to work out what Gordon was up to. He'd expected some come-back for his absence last week but not any sympathy – real or otherwise.

Gordon opened his desk drawer and pulled out the master diary for the whole team, flipping through the pages and making soft sounds as he scribbled notes on a blank piece of paper.

Ricky resisted the temptation to lean forward as he tried to read what Gordon was writing but the distance and the angle made it impossible. The silence stretched out between them, broken by the sound of Gordon scribbling and an occasional voice from the adjoining offices.

Finally Gordon seemed satisfied with his plan, checking between the diary and the paper. He placed the pen on his desk and looked straight at Ricky who suddenly felt unaccountably nervous. There was a glint in Gordon's grey eyes, a hint of anger that took him by surprise.

'It is difficult, working in a new environment and a strange place,' said Gordon softly, his calm voice at odds with the hardness in his eyes. 'I sense you may be finding the court work particularly challenging so I think we should ensure you get more practice. You have a light case load at present, right?'

Ricky nodded, reluctant to give any encouragement to what, he suspected, was going to be a deeply unpleasant outcome.

'Yes,' Gordon continued checking one of the diary pages. 'You had eighteen clients as of last week. That should leave you with at least half the week free so I'm putting you into the family court for the next two months as well as Monday's magistrates' court and alternate Fridays.'

Ricky stared at him in horror. Court duty was never popular and the proposed schedule would ensure he was working flat-out every day just to keep up with his work.

'I'll speak to Lauren about the admin work involved,' Gordon continued before Ricky could protest. 'Obviously there will be a few more social enquiry reports to do and you need more experience with these but you won't be expected to do them all. You will bring the list to me at the end of each court day and I'll allocate them. You will do some, of course, but I think you would benefit from a little more guidance. I'll speak to the team and an experienced officer will go with you for the first few.' He slapped the diary down on his desk, making Ricky jump. 'We'll see how it goes after the first month or so.'

Ricky opened his mouth, closed it again without speaking and rose to his feet. He felt sick at the thought of all that court duty and a slow, deep anger began to burn inside. All those provincial, small-town little know-it alls, watching him and reporting on his work – how dare they!

'Oh, Ricky?' said Gordon as he reached the door.

Ricky took a moment to compose his expression before turning back towards the desk.

'Use today to contact your clients and arrange their appointments for the next month. I'll check the lists before you leave this evening and you'll be ready for family court tomorrow. They start at nine so you will need to be here early, in time to pick up the files.'

Gordon managed to keep the smile off his face until the door had closed behind the young officer. He hadn't wanted the acting senior's job and was looking forward to handing over to whoever Headquarters appointed, but just occasionally it was worth all the problems it brought with it.

Lauren had left early, taking a little of the time owed her from the extra hours she had put in to Ricky Peddlar's notes. She was proud of her role as a specialist administrator for first year officers. It involved a lot of patience, the ability to persuade new members of staff to take things slowly and even occasional hand-holding, but overall it was very rewarding. She liked working with the new recruits, often wide-eyed and idealistic but still untouched by the layer of cynicism that came with years of work for relatively little return.

Lauren was a believer in the system and when it worked it was just wonderful – a life pulled from the ashes of prison, a second chance only a few managed to reach out and take – but she knew the successes were the exception and most of the clients slipped away into the twilight of routine offending, a life in and out of prison and a poisonous legacy for their families. She knew she could play a part in the forming of a new officer, helping them develop the skills and attitude that gave resilience, a sense of humour and enough optimism to carry on.

She had supported Alex through part of her first year and still filled that role for Sue. Both were turning into fine officers, but she was struggling with Ricky. Maybe it was his lack of professionalism, maybe it was partly personal but Lauren found him difficult, unsympathetic and lazy. He had a habit of dumping a few scribbled notes on her desk along with the clients' files and disappearing – who knew where. It would be nice, she reflected, to catch him hanging out in one of the many local pubs but that was unlikely. He never came back after lunch smelling of drink, though he trailed the sour smell of his hand-rolled cigarettes behind him wherever he went.

Lauren had spent most of the afternoon struggling to bring Ricky's files up to date and wishing she could ask him what some of the scribbles and abbreviations actually meant. He acted as if she were just a typist, someone to transcribe his words of wisdom. Actually, Lauren and the rest of the team knew as much about probation work as the officers and considerably more about the clients than some of them. They acted as a first line of defence for many probationers, solving minor problems, re-scheduling appointments and helping with letters, travel warrants and visiting schedules to prisons. They knew who was related to whom, which families were best kept apart in the waiting rooms and could spot the signs of glue-sniffing or illegal pill-taking with a single glance across the room. Most of the officers were both grateful and appreciative of their experience. Ricky was neither, though he needed the input more than anyone else in the office.

Sighing in frustration, Lauren put the whole mess of her working life behind her and slipped behind the wheel of her specially adapted car. A modified version of the new Nova, it was her pride and joy and she loved the sense of independence it gave her. As a child she had watched her school friends begin to explore the world around them. Starting with bicycles, the boys moved on to mopeds or motorbikes before they clambered into second-hand cars, cheap and battered castoffs from relatives or friends that helped to carry them away, out of her life. Lauren had tried and tried but was unable to ride a bicycle and could barely see out of the windows of most cars. She had watched, sick with envy, as her friends grew up and moved on, leaving her stranded at home.

The car was a major triumph, a victory won by determination, hard work and the stalwart support of her brother, Jonny. For years he had driven her around, out to parties and the houses of her friends, taking her shopping and on occasional trips to Bath or Bristol. Lauren had managed with the local bus whilst they lived in town but when her mother decided they were moving out to Nether Stowey, she rebelled.

'I 'ent going all that way out there,' she had said, so angry she stamped her foot in fury. 'Might be alright for you, maybe, but what about me? How'm I supposed to get into work then? 'Ent more'n one bus a day and that at the wrong time. Often times I got to work a bit late and then I'm stuck. So I reckon either I gets my own car or I'm lookin' for some place of my own.'

She had slammed out of the door and into her room, flinging herself on the bed where she was overwhelmed by tears of frustration. There was a knock at the door announcing the return of her brother and she wiped her face hastily, sitting up to face him.

'Suppose you heard then?' she'd said as he peered round the frame. Lauren loved Jonny dearly but she had a bit of a temper and had been known to throw things when upset.

'Reckon they heard you back in the office,' he'd said, grinning as he slipped in and settled in the armchair by the bed.

'I mean it,' said Lauren, setting her jaw stubbornly.

'I know you do,' her brother had said softly. 'And I agree with you. You need your own car and you need more independence. How long you been working now – about four years?'

Lauren nodded.

'Suppose you got a bit saved up then?' he'd suggested. 'After all, would need a deposit and such for your own place if you stayed round here.'

Lauren had nodded again, eyes narrowing as she wondered where this was going.

'Well then, we get in touch with the Mobility people and see about a car for you. Soon as we got that, I'll teach you to drive,' he said.

The car meant freedom for Lauren. A little bit of independence, a few choices and the chance to work, just like everyone else. She mused on her life as she travelled along the road unwinding from Highpoint towards Nether Stowey. She certainly had more choices than most people had thought possible when she was at school. This was partly down to her mother who had resisted all attempts to move her daughter to a 'special school', arguing the mainstream environment, though rough on occasions, would best equip her for later life.

There had been moments when Lauren had rather wished her mother had agreed to the easier and more sheltered atmosphere of the special school, times when the big boys (and some of the big girls) crowded round her, bouncing and jostling with scant regard for her small frame. There were occasional outbreaks of bullying when she found her school bag or books placed on top shelves or thrown back and forth above her head and once, just once, a particularly unpleasant boy had picked her up and held her off the ground until his mocking laughter attracted a crowd. For some reason this was considered going too far and a score of hands seized her, placed her safely on the ground and hustled the offender off behind the bike shed.

Lauren did not know exactly what transpired after that but the culprit never so much as looked at her again. In fact, her refusal to give his name to the teachers who rushed to the scene too late to be of any real help, earned her the respect of most of her peers and from that day onwards she was never lonely at school. A number of the friends she made after that final outbreak of bullying were still close and those experiences, along with twice weekly karate classes, helped to give her the confidence she needed to do her job at the probation office.

All in all, she had a pretty decent life, especially now Dave Brown – *Detective* Dave Brown, she thought smugly – was her boyfriend. Resisting the urge to laugh, she nevertheless could not resist a happy grin spreading over her face. Dave was marvellous – thoughtful, clever, funny and, when he wasn't at work, attentive. He treated her as if she were special but not as if she were fragile. Dave knew how physically tough Lauren could be and had no qualms about suggesting outings into the hills or increasingly long rides on the modified tandem he had designed when he learned she had never been able to ride a standard bicycle. No, Dave was one of the best things that had ever happened to her. As she bowled along towards Nether Stowey, the Quantock Hills rising up before her, she wondered if she would get a chance to see him any time soon.

Detective Dave Brown returned from the canteen with a tray of tea and coffee and nearly dropped the lot when he saw his desk. Slap in the middle was a shop mannequin's head, obscured by a black stocking. What was so startling, however, was the long, brassy blonde wig flowing down from the head and trailing over the desk. Putting the tray down on a spare desk, he was aware of several pairs of eyes watching him and there was a smattering of laughter, hastily stilled. Dave took a deep breath, strode over to the desk and picked up the head.

'Well,' he said waving it at the other men. 'Who arrested this little beauty?'

The laughter was unrestrained this time.

Dave lifted the wig and pretended to examine it before shaking his head. 'Don't think it's him though,' he said.

'Why not?' called someone from the back of the room.

Dave waved the wig at the voice. 'Our victim was most insistent,' he said. 'Our man is a *natural* blond.'

'Told you,' said Sergeant Lynas as he stepped out of the Inspector's office, a grin on his face. 'No fooling this lad.' He nodded approvingly in Dave's direction before stepping up to the whiteboard at the front of the room.

'Right, settle down. I've got some results back from forensics.'

Dave sank into his chair, his hands toying idly with the hair of the wig. He felt inordinately pleased with himself. No-one had teased him at Highpoint. They had played tricks and made jokes at his expense but he had never had the sense he was invited to join in. He recalled his mentor from Hendon Training College, a man who had given Dave the skills and knowledge he relied on every day. 'Remember,' he had said just before Dave left for Somerset. 'No-one teases someone they don't like. It's too much trouble.'

Dave turned his attention back to the briefing. Sergeant Lynas was recapping the collection of evidence from the two crime scenes. Most of it had come from the most recent incident, in West Monkton. Here the officers had gathered a rich haul footprints, a number of them of bare feet, as well as signs of someone watching the house from amongst the surrounding trees. The glass of the conservatory had yielded some smudged handprints but nothing clear enough to be of any use for identification. The technicians had taken swabs from the surface and found sweat and what seemed to be spit on the glass.

'Now, that's the good news,' said Lynas as he noted the evidence on the board. 'The bad news is he's not a secretor.'

There was a soft groan of disappointment from the assembled detectives. The majority of men – around 80 per cent – secreted a type of marker that could be found in most bodily fluids. This indicated their blood group and associated enzymes – the PGM. As the two markers were inherited independently, there were many different combinations and this information could narrow the field of suspects considerably, especially with the rarer blood types. Whilst the information from a secretor couldn't identify an individual, it was very valuable in eliminating a suspect.

Sergeant Lynas held up his hand for silence. 'Now then, at least we can rule out anyone who *is* a secretor,' he said. 'And the redoubtable Miss Taylor was right.' He held up a small plastic envelope and waved it in Dave's direction. 'These hairs were found on the glass of her conservatory. And they come from a natural blond. When we find him, we've got something to match him against. Now all we have to do is find him. And hopefully before he decides to do this again.'

Chapter Five

Ada was weeding her vegetable garden in the warm midday sunshine when she was interrupted by the unusual sound of the post van stopping on the road outside. Alerted by the frantic barking of the dogs, she slipped around the side of the house and peered at the postman suspiciously. In her experience nothing good ever came through the letterbox, especially if it was in a brown envelope. Since her son Kevin had left home to travel with the Fair there had been a lack of any sort of mail. Ada took heart from this, seeing the absence of court summons and official correspondence as a sign that he was behaving himself and keeping to the conditions of his probation. Alex Hastings was still nominally his probation officer and she had arranged for him to report into a number of offices around the country. She was, Ada reflected, a thoroughly decent person but she took her job seriously and if Kevin failed to stick to the agreement, she knew Alex would haul him back to Highpoint and breach him.

The postman was a new one, a young man she'd not seen before. Despite this he still approached the front door with some caution and stepped to one side before reaching for the letterbox. Ada suppressed a grin at this. She had a reputation for slamming the fingers of unwary delivery men in the letterbox and had, on a couple of occasions, menaced unwanted visitors with an old carving knife she kept in the drawer of an ancient hall stand.

'I'll take that,' she said popping her head around the wall. The young man jumped and stared at her, eyes wide with fear.

'Oh, don't be soft. Give 'um here.' Ada put out her hand for the envelope – a white one, she noted with surprise – and waited as the postman sidled towards her, the letter held arm's length. She had an almost overwhelming urge to shout 'Boo!' at him, just see how he would react but at that moment a battered green van drew up and Tom Monarch stepped out and waved at her. The young postman took advantage of her momentary distraction and, thrusting the envelope into her outstretched hand, beat a hasty retreat down the path and into the safety of his own vehicle.

Tom glanced at Ada quizzically. 'What's that all about then?' he asked as the postman roared off down the narrow road.

Ada shrugged, her attention focussed on the letter. Her name and address were printed in block capitals and the postmark was from Nottingham. She turned the envelope over in her hands, puzzled. As far as she could remember she knew no-one from Nottingham and although the handwriting was vaguely familiar she couldn't place it. Still, it was certainly addressed to her.

'Reckon you could just open it,' Tom suggested.

She scowled at him without speaking, still turning the letter over and over.

Tom sighed. 'Why is it you has to fight with everyone?' he asked wearily. 'Just open it will you, then we can get on with this here fence.'

He turned and walked back to his van, opening the back doors wide and hauling out a home-made ramp.

Ada slipped into the house through the back door and took a seat at the kitchen table, setting the letter on the worn wooden surface in front of her. Letters were a rare commodity in her world and demanded the correct ritual. They were not to be ripped open and gobbled down, to be dropped into a pocket and forgotten in an instant. Letters were for sipping and savouring – except those in brown envelopes of course. They were for stuffing behind the clock and ignoring.

After another minute staring at the letter, Ada took a small knife from the dresser behind her and slit the top open carefully. Inside was a single sheet of paper, folded in half. Setting the envelope to one side, Ada unfolded the letter and read it slowly. When she reached the end she took a deep breath and read it again before placing it gently on the table. Her hands were shaking and there were tears in her eyes as she stood and reached for the kettle.

'Tom,' she called through the open door. 'Come in and have some tea afore you get started.'

There was a shout in reply and she heard the doors to the van slam shut, followed by Tom's footsteps up the path. A few moments later he peered around the door, the dogs at his heels.

'You alright, Ada?' he asked as he stepped into the kitchen, concern on his face.

Ada waved him towards a chair by the table and lifted the teapot, placing it between them. Tom's eyes slid over the letter but he was too well-mannered to ask until she nodded.

'Have a look,' she said, pouring the tea into two mugs and adding milk to both.

Tom picked up the letter and read it silently, then glanced at Ada over the top of the single sheet of paper.

'Well, is nice to get some news,' he said. 'Seems he's going on alright.'

Ada reached out and plucked the letter from his hands.

'Don't get it, do you,' she said gazing at it once more. 'Kevin can't read – couldn't read, anyroad. Times we sat here and I tried to teach him his letters – could just manage to write his name by the time he left school. Could scarcely struggle through a book for infants. Soon as he learned a word it was gone again. But here, look.' She smoothed the paper out and beamed proudly. 'Is all in block printing but is Kev's writing. He done this his self. My boy, he sent me a letter!'

Tom took a sip of his tea and nodded his understanding.

'Bit of a special moment then,' he said. 'Don't suppose you fancy popping out for a drink, to celebrate?'

Ada glared at him and folded Kevin's letter again, placing it in the envelope.

'You'll not get round me so easy,' she said. 'You and your opportunism!'

'Big words,' said Tom with a grin. 'Sounds like you swallowed a dictionary sometimes, hearing you talk. Well, can't blame us fer asking. I'll unload this stuff I've got for that fence and I was hopin' to maybe have a quick dig around, see what we got under all them brambles afore I settle on the sort of posts we need. That okay with you?'

'Help yerself,' said Ada, but her eyes followed him as he rose from the table and strode back to the van. Strong he was, she reflected. Always had been a decent sort, if truth be told. Carried himself well too, despite him being – she reckoned up in her head – must be early sixties by now. Couple of years older than her. She shook her head, annoyed at the turn her thoughts were taking. Better be up and see what he was doing, she decided. He was charming, helpful, attentive – reckon he needed watching. Never knew what he was after. She tucked Kevin's letter under the clock on the mantelpiece and hurried out into the sunshine.

Alex was exhausted when she dragged herself into work on the day after collecting her mother. Never a confident driver, she had found the distance hard. Compounded by the unexpected detour to Tonbridge and the stress of having her mother in the car, she was a wreck by the time she reached home late on Monday night. Sue had been waiting up for them and offered tea, sandwiches and a glass of wine. Alex declined the latter and, after a couple of bites, rather wished she had passed on the sandwich too. Whilst Sue was out in the back kitchen looking for biscuits, Alex's mother leaned over and whispered.

'What's in these – do you know?'

Alex peeled the bread back and squinted at the filling but was unable to identify the bright pink substance inside. Poking at it cautiously, she dislodged several large chunks of onion and, with a bit more digging, what was probably sweet corn.

'Ah, perhaps some sort of savoury?' she hazarded.

Her mother sighed and took another bite.

'Well, it was a nice thought,' she said. 'Eat up, dear. I raised you to have better manners than that.'

Alex opened her mouth to protest but at that moment Sue bustled back through the door clutching a packet of chocolate digestives and the tea pot.

'Everything all right?' she said brightly.

Alex managed a sickly smile and took another, decidedly reluctant, bite. 'I'm not very hungry actually,' she said, trying to swallow without chewing. 'It was a long drive and I started out before dawn.' She set her sandwich aside and tried not to look too longingly at the biscuits.

'This really is most kind of you,' said Alex's mother. 'It's quite an unusual filling. You must have made it yourself?'

Alex had always envied her mother's gift for somehow saying just the right thing. Such a polite way of asking, 'What the hell is this?' Instead there was a hint of praise for going to the trouble of providing something home-made whilst satisfying their mutual curiosity.

Sue dropped into a chair on the opposite side of the table and beamed at them both.

'I was going to try it with tuna,' she said taking one of the digestives and nibbling at it. 'Tuna Savoury – they make it up at the Royal Arms in Woolavington. Then I thought, some people don't like fish or can't eat it so I decided I'd try making it with corned beef instead. Well, it was such a busy day I didn't get out to the shops at lunchtime but it was okay because I found a tin of Spam in the back of the cupboard.'

'How very ingenious,' Alex's mother murmured taking another small, delicate bite.

Alex repressed a shudder. She remembered her encounter with the Tuna Savoury at the Royal Arms. A large, rambling building set on the road just outside the village, the pub had been the place where Tom Monarch and his gang had planned to set up a new criminal franchise, hoping to control the Levels and the lucrative smuggling operations following the demise of Derek Johns and his followers. The fact that rumours of Derek's death had been somewhat premature had led to a series of nasty killings and brought Alex into contact with Max Long, a particularly unpleasant drug dealer from Bristol.

After the police arrived in the shape of Dave Brown and arrested Max and his local dealers, Alex and Sue had visited the pub, talking to Phil and Marie Watson in an effort to untangle their young probationers' involvement in the scheme. Phil, the landlord, had been desperately apologetic about events, genuinely upset that his establishment had been hosting a criminal gathering on a regular basis. Times were hard, he said, and they had been in dire need of the income. They were trying out a new, cheaper menu and looking at different events in an attempt to bring in more customers. He and Marie insisted they try the latest addition to the menu and Alex found herself facing a plate piled high with tuna and sweet corn sandwiches.

'There's just something wrong about them,' she said to Sue as they drove back to the office in Alex's car. 'Fish with onion is bad enough but adding *sweet corn* – and they were almost liquid, there was so much mayonnaise mixed in.' She shuddered at the memory. 'Gull vomit.'

Sue looked up sharply. 'What?'

''It was like eating gull vomit,' Alex repeated.

'Well, thank you for that. Now that image is stuck in my head,' said Sue who folded her arms and stared out of the windscreen for the rest of the journey.

The conversation came back to Alex as she contemplated the plate in front of her. It was very possible this was Sue's revenge.

With smarting eyes and heavy steps, Alex hauled herself up the steps and into the reception area of Highpoint probation office. Despite the early hour, there were already several young men sitting on the slightly battered chairs in the lobby, waiting to see their probation officers. She cast her eyes over them and with a sinking heart, recognised Brian. A tall, skinny young man with a striking Mohican-style haircut, Brian Morris had been a constant in her life since her arrival two years ago.

Originally classed as a juvenile, Brian had been transferred to her list when he reached the age of seventeen and in spite of support from his previous officer, Paul Malcolm, and Pauline from the office, he had succeeded in sabotaging just about every chance he had been given. He had even broken Alex's wrist the previous winter whilst fencing with a pool cue in the day centre. Alex had refused to report his actions, arguing he had been under the influence of an unknown intoxicant at the time and certainly his behaviour had improved for a few months after the incident. He had, Alex reflected, been almost polite the last few times they had met.

'Hello Brian,' she said, managing a not-too-unwelcoming smile.

The young man looked up and jumped to his feet, beaming with excitement. He was in a good mood, Alex noted.

'I done it!' said Brian, his grin revealing the chipped front teeth he had damaged in a fight several years ago.

'Oh, right – well done,' said Alex, scrabbling around in her memory. Should she be congratulating him, she wondered. Perhaps he was talking about something criminal – or maybe his girlfriend was pregnant. The thought of more little Brians running around made her want to shudder.

'Come on, I'll show yer,' he said and scurried out of the front door.

Hopefully not the pregnant girlfriend then, Alex thought as she turned and followed him.

The yard looked almost empty when she got to the top of the stairs and she looked around, puzzled by Brian's abrupt disappearance. Suddenly Lauren turned into the car park, her little Vauxhall heading straight for the reserved space by the foot of the stairs. At that moment, Brian shot out of the old bike shed at the rear of the workshop, feet turning the peddles of his bike at a frantic pace as he wobbled towards her. His shout of triumph was cut short as he ploughed towards Lauren who braked as she tried to turn out of his path. At the last moment, Brian hauled the bike to one side, tipping over and sliding into the office wall.

Alex ran down the steps towards him, her heart thumping, but Brian was on his feet, a broad grin stretched across his face as he brushed himself off.

'Reckon I should work on them brakes a bit,' he said, picking up his bike and examining the front forks.

'You dozy bugger!' yelled Lauren, slamming the car door and stamping across towards them. 'I almost hit the wall! Think I can afford to get my car fixed? Why don't you look where you're going?'

Alex knew there was little love lost between Lauren and Brian. Whilst at school, Brian and his mates had spent a considerable amount of time and ingenuity tormenting her and when she took the job at the probation office, they were there, waiting to greet her. Alex's first encounter with Brian had been to admonish him – rather severely – for taunting Lauren and their relationship had veered from mutual dislike to grudging respect ever since. Despite Lauren and Brian's history, Alex did think her attitude was a bit callous, even for Lauren. After all, he had come close to disappearing under the wheels of the car.

'Don't,' said Lauren holding up a hand to Alex. 'I know what you's going to say and I don't care. Sick of this stupid behaviour, I am. And you,' she rounded on Brian who was still grinning foolishly. 'You watch what you's doing and grow up a bit. Gonna get yerself killed one day and it'll be some other poor driver as has to live with that.' She turned on her heel and marched smartly up the steps and into the office.

'Harsh words – but with an element of truth,' said Gordon emerging from the inside of his car, which was parked off to one side by the dustbins. 'Perhaps you should take your bike back into the workshop and get the brakes looked at now,' he said to Brian. 'Certainly before you try it out on the road.'

Brian nodded and began to wheel the rather battered machine across the yard. Turning back he called to Alex. 'What you reckon then? Girt fun, this. Never knew I could ride no bike afore!'

Alex shook her head but still couldn't prevent a smile creeping through her mock sternness.

'I think he means this is a positive in his life,' she said. 'Though sometimes I still get lost in all the double negatives.'

'I would say it gets easier,' said Gordon as he started hauling out the mats from the back of his car. 'It would be a lie however. I grew up with the dialect but still encounter something that confuses me on a regular basis.'

Alex watched him for a moment. Gordon always seemed to be cleaning out his car. Every week he had the mats out or was scrubbing at the upholstery. When she had first arrived she thought he must be obsessively clean or ridiculously proud of his motor but now she knew he had been helping someone out. A lot of the clients or their families had no car of their own and little access to public transport either. Gordon, despite having the newest and smartest vehicle of all the staff, was ever-willing to provide a lift to the lost, the drunk and the extended family, no matter how ill or dirty they might be. Sadly his rewards included car-sick children, incontinent dogs and pints of spilt cider.

Alex stopped at the reception desk on her way back to her office and had a word with an unrepentant Lauren.

'It was your boyfriend who taught him to ride in the first place,' she pointed out. 'He should have instilled a little more discipline.'

Lauren snorted in disgust. 'Dave only taught him 'cos you insisted,' she said. 'Anyway, don't reckon 'tis possible to use the words discipline and Brian Morris in the same sentence. Seems he's always swingin' from one mood to the next. Never did know where you was with 'un, not even at school.'

Alex pondered this, sitting at her desk in the cool dimness of her office, a converted store cupboard behind the main day centre. During the winter there had been an influx of 'recreational' drugs, a potent mixture of LSD, amphetamines and barbiturates, brought into the area by Max Long, the young dealer from Bristol. Brian had been one of his most enthusiastic customers and his mood swings had become even more extreme whilst under the influence of some of Max's offerings. Even so, there remained a core of erratic behaviour evidenced by his continuing inability to stick to anything for more than a few days. Brian, she thought, was recidivism incarnate.

There was a tap at the door and the subject of her musings stuck his head into the room.

'Reckon I wanted to thank you,' he said as he flopped into the chair in front of her desk. 'Never had no chance to ride a bike afore and could never have afforded one, neither.'

His hair was sticking up, the Mohican slightly askew, but apart from that he seemed none the worse for his close encounter with Lauren and the office wall.

'Was wondering,' said Brian, leaning over the desk. 'My Dad's comin' home soon and I don't want to be around when he does. Is any way I could be staying at the hostel or mebbe getting a place in town?'

Alex's heart sank. It was a good sign, Brian wanting to be away from the toxic influence of his drunken, petty criminal of a father but the odds on finding anywhere he could afford to live, let alone a landlord willing to take a chance on someone with his history, were vanishingly small. Even the tiny stock of rooms held by the semi-official 'probation landladies' was under severe strain, both from financial pressures and the sheer numbers of newly released or unemployed clients desperate for somewhere to live.

'I can't just place you in the hostel, Brian. You know that. I'll check around for you, but I'm not promising anything. There's a real shortage of bedsits at the moment. Look, is there anywhere else you could go? Maybe a friend?'

Brian's face fell and he stared down at the table for a moment.

'Reckon I've used up most of my friends,' he said. 'Don't see much of a welcome, most places.' He lifted his head and she saw he had tears in his eyes. 'My Dad – I don't like leavin' my kid brother there but 'ent nothing I can do. If'n I is there, he'll just turn on us, soon as he's pissed. Figured is maybe time I looked for a job or summat, got a place of my own and our Josh, he could come stay with me when Dad's around.'

Perhaps Brian really had finally begun to grow up, she thought as she worked her way unsuccessfully through the list of possible lodgings later that afternoon. The last year had not been kind to him, with the impact of the drug use, several return trips to court and the death of his friend, Darren, who had drowned himself at New Year, his blood stream awash with LSD. Sometimes it took that sort of shock to get through to someone like Brian. Still, he'd had a lot of chances in the past, and thrown every last one away. She had a horrible feeling that, however sincere he might be now, he was too late.

Walking through town, he enjoyed the sense of anonymity, the disregard for his presence that a new environment offered. No-one knew who he was. No-one knew anything about him and so no-one cared enough to give him a second glance. He settled on the seat in front of the Cornhill Market and spent an amusing half hour watching the people, all the little people with little lives and tiny, tiny concerns. His relaxed pose gave no indication of the contempt he felt for each and every one of them and the bright blue of his eyes was hidden behind dark glasses.

What was the best part, he wondered. The excitement of the actual event was almost overwhelming, of course. That sweet, perfect glimpse of fear in their eyes was surely one of the best moments in life. There was ultimately very little difference in their reactions. Some took a few seconds longer to slip into hysteria but they all succumbed in the end. It was the shock, he thought. The sudden realisation someone had been watching them, studying them – stalking them. And none of them had the slightest idea it was happening until it was too late.

He felt a brief shiver run up his spine, causing him to bite his lower lip in an effort to retain a calm, controlled façade. It had been a while, he thought. Time to move on to the next one. He already had someone in mind and the security at the hostel would prove no obstacle to his nocturnal visits. The whole place was a joke – but he needed the cover it offered for a little while. He focussed on behaving himself, making himself follow all the stupid, petty rules. He made sure he reported in to the probation officer he was stuck with for the next few months too. Discipline was important, and he was quite capable of giving the impression of compliance when it suited him.

The pleasure of the day slipped away abruptly as he remembered he had an appointment to discuss his day centre attendance after lunch. Glancing at his watch, he decided to forego the nauseating spectacle of his fellow residents wolfing down their food at the hostel. Rising from the bench, he strolled across to the market, selecting several pieces of fresh fruit and washed them carefully under the tap in the gents. Walking through the town he ate, using the time to memorise the layout of the unfamiliar streets. You never knew when such planning might be needed and Samuel was always very, very careful.

Chapter Six

It was all a bit serious, Alex thought, contemplating her plans for day centre groups. Of course, it needed to have some demonstrable value to the clients and so classes in literacy and the new sessions on budgeting, cookery and basic hygiene, cunningly dressed up as 'life skills', were easy to sell to the magistrates. It was a lot harder to get the clients on board however. There was a good take-up for the workshop days especially with a new influx of unclaimed bikes recovered by the police and donated to the service. Some lads also enjoyed the basic woodwork on a Thursday morning and Alex was grateful for the help offered by her colleague, Eddie Stroud, in running it. Her expertise was limited to simple repairs and changing a front door lock – not something she thought they should emphasise, given the clientele.

There were some issues she was desperate to tackle, principally alcohol education, and she had a lot of ideas on how to make this effective and fun but there were a couple of obstacles to overcome. Gordon had read through the outline earlier in the week and sighed.

'I can see why you want to do this and I think you have some really good approaches,' he said. 'However, there are a few issues. Here,' he pointed to the plan. 'We cannot serve alcohol on the premises. I know,' he held up a hand to forestall Alex's objections. 'Tiny, taster glasses, we are not charging anything, it is for a very laudable cause but . . .' He hesitated before continuing, 'How do you think the magistrates will react if they find out they are sending someone with a drinking problem to a group where they are offered more alcohol? And what do you think the press will make of it – because they *will* hear of it and they most certainly will write something sensational and damaging.'

Alex returned to her office, depressed and despondent. The two strongest sessions both depended on using real beer. Not a lot, but enough to have an effect on the clients. The two most common arguments she heard from her drinkers were 'It don't affect me none anyway, I can hold it' (manifestly untrue, otherwise how did they end up on probation for being drunk and disorderly) and 'I just likes the taste – that fake beer 'ent the same.'

Alex had just treated herself to a small computer, a 64k machine that plugged into the back of her television. As well as trying to write simple programs to draw pictures and learning to use a database, she had experimented with the free games that came with it. Despite the fact they took an age to load and the tapes did not remember any high scores, she soon found herself hooked. Running a tiny ant around a maze or piloting a seemingly mentally defective builder across scaffolding full of holes was enormous fun and she and Sue had once sat up until two in the morning, reluctant to stop playing when they were still winning.

Amongst the cassettes she had found a motorcycle racing game and several weeks ago had challenged her friends to a tournament. She was amazed to find how rapidly her ability to manipulate the bike on the screen deteriorated. One glass of wine was all it took for her to start crashing out on previously easy corners. If only she could get the Alcohol

Education group to try it, she thought. Let them play a round, then take a small drink and then try again. The results could be striking – but how on earth could she manage it?

Setting the plans aside with a sigh of her own, she pondered the idea of setting up some more creative groups. Perhaps photography, she thought. It would get them looking properly at their surroundings and offered the chance of some trips out of the town. The office had a minibus that was chronically underused, though Alex was not keen on trying her hand at driving it. There was also the cost of the equipment but she had started drifting round the auction rooms on a Saturday morning and only last week had spotted a box of cameras, old fashioned but quite serviceable. Some of those, a cheap enlarger and a bit of money for supplies and she could get a small darkroom set up in the room next to hers. It was just a dumping ground at the moment and was more poorly lit than her office. Of course, she would have to supervise it very closely. A lot of the day centre clients were young and almost exclusively male. They were not much more than a bunch of kids sometimes and there were some types of photography she definitely did not want to encourage.

The ringing of her telephone interrupted her train of thought.

'Yes?' she snapped into the receiver.

'Oh . . .' There was a pause before a vaguely familiar voice said 'Hello? I'm trying to get hold of Alex Hastings . . .'

It took her a few seconds to identify the caller but then an unfamiliar, broad smile spread over Alex's face.

'Hey,' she said. 'It's me. Wonderful to hear from you.'

Tom was as good as his word and the next week he was back at Ada's house, complete with a trailer-load of fence posts, a shovel and several rolls of heavy duty wire mesh.

'Don't know as this'll keep him in, mind,' he said as he and Ada unloaded the van and carried the material across the garden. 'Would be better if we had maybe an electric fence or summat.'

Ada snorted. 'Don't have no money for lights and such, never mind running no 'lectric fence.'

Tom was busy sorting out the posts and placing them on the ground at regular intervals.

'Well, we'll see what can be done fer that,' he said. 'Is only a small area so we only need a little 'un, and that just runs on a battery.'

'Where'm I supposed to get this batt'ry,' Ada objected. 'An' special wire, I suppose?'

Tom gestured towards the van. 'No worries,' he said grinning slyly. 'I thought of all that. Borrowed some, seein' as is only for a few weeks. Battery's fully charged an all, so should be good for a week or so.' He held up his hand to forestall further objections. 'Don't be worrying about chargin' and so on. You leave that to me. You is doin' my friend a favour, taking his old stud goat off'n his hands for a few weeks so is right you don't need to pay nothing.'

They worked in companionable silence for a while, Ada clearing the ground and Tom digging the holes for the posts. Together they set up the framework for the enclosure on the left of Ada's garden before stopping just after noon.

'Got a bit of rabbit pie,' said Ada. 'Bit of spring greens to go with it, if you fancy.'

Tom straightened up from filling around the last of the posts. 'Sounds just what we need,' he said following her into the kitchen.

Ada busied herself with the meal whilst Tom washed off under the kitchen tap and bumbled around looking for plates and cutlery. Finally, Ada pointed him towards the kettle. 'Get some tea on,' she said. 'Never mind about the other stuff. I'll do that in a moment.'

Tom sat at the table, content to watch as Ada rinsed and chopped the greens and added some sliced mushrooms to the pan.

'St George's,' she said, noticing his curiosity. 'Don't often get 'um round here but they was growing out by the edge of the church at Westonzoyland. Verger there, he got no taste for suchlike so I figured I might as well bring 'um home rather than leave 'um to be dug over. Left a few mind, so there'll be some next year too.'

Tom nodded his approval, and shortly turned his attention to the plate she put in front of him. There was a nudge from under the table and he looked down to see Mickey at his feet, nose turned towards him hopefully.

'Don't reckon,' he said. 'Is much too good. Anyway, is mushrooms bad for dogs?'

Ada laughed. 'Don't know,' she said. 'Them two'll eat anything put in front of 'um though, and doesn't seem to do no harm. Oh come on in, will yer,' she added as Mouse peered around the door.

'Didn't know you had company,' came a familiar voice and Kevin walked in, stopping in the doorway to stare at Tom.

'That were right rude,' said Ada when Tom had returned to his van and was busy putting his tools away, out of earshot.

Kevin shrugged, his face that of a sulky teenager.

'Didn't think to be comin' home to find some didicoy sitting in my kitchen,' he said.

Ada rounded on him. 'Firstly, 'ent your kitchen,' she snapped. 'Is my kitchen, my house an' I'll have what friends I want in here. Second off, don't see you bein' so sniffy about Tom. He's proper *Rom*, anyway. And what about all them Fair men you is spending all your workin' days with? Most of them's didicoys – or much worse. Bunch of Irish tinkers, half of 'em. You tellin' me you act like this 'round them?'

Kevin shrugged again, turning his head to stare out of the back door. 'Work with 'un,' he said. 'Drink with 'un too. Don't mean I want to find none of 'un hangin' around my mother.'

'He's a good man, is Tom,' said Ada. 'He do help I.'

'He do help himself and all,' said Kevin looking at the remains of the lunch on the table.

Acting Detective Dave Brown sat at his desk, face set into a frown as he went back and forth through the notes on the two incidents. With typical grim humour, the investigating team had given their unknown suspect the nickname 'Moth Man', a title that seemed to sum up his actions rather neatly, but there was something disturbing Dave. He was sure there was something missing in their analysis of events.

There were too many unanswered questions – how did the Moth Man get to the scenes, for example. What did he do with his clothes, for it was obvious he didn't travel naked. Had he been watching the women for a while, Dave wondered, or did he just stumble on them? In which case, there was the question of how he found them in the first place – and back to how he travelled to two scenes, a good distance apart, arriving at just the right time to find a woman sitting alone in a brightly lit glass room.

Dave sighed and pushed the notes to one side, running his fingers through his hair in frustration. There had to be something to indicate the mode of transport, he thought. Then at least the team could pin down a rough area to watch and start asking questions in the search for witnesses. Their best chance would be to find someone who saw him en route, unless they were going to wait for another attack. Dave grimaced at the thought and pulled the pile of notes back towards him, picked up a pen and began to sort through, searching for the one, tiny, elusive piece of information he needed.

'How's it going then,' said Sergeant Lynas as he dropped heavily into the chair beside him.

Dave shook his head. 'I don't see how someone so visible can be so totally *invisible*,' he said. 'Somehow he manages to get into the gardens, probably waits for the right moment, strips off, pulls a stocking over his head, does – what he does – and escapes without anyone except the victim seeing him. I reckon you've got to be pretty deranged to do something like this but the execution is so controlled, more the work of a planner. This isn't an impulsive crime, I'm sure of it.'

Lynas nodded thoughtfully. 'Reckon you're right,' he said. 'There's too many ways it could go wrong if he was just drifting round hopefully. He's chosen these women for some reason and he's almost certainly been there before. Maybe watched them for a few evenings.'

Dave felt a chill run down his back. Sergeant Lynas' analysis was compelling. It was the pattern of a sexual predator and from all his reading Dave knew most predators were on an escalating path. More 'incidents', more frequently and growing more extreme – that was the pattern. Somewhere out there was a very dangerous man and the police didn't even know how he was getting around the area. He turned his attention to the victims, trying to establish any common ground between them. Something attracted the Moth Man and if they could establish what it was, perhaps they could prevent another attack.

Alex finished work on time, for once, and left the office looking unusually cheerful. Lauren joined her at the front door and looked up at her quizzically.

'You's lookin' right happy,' she commented, unlocking her car door and throwing her bag onto the passenger seat.

'Mmm,' Alex said. 'I'm catching up with an old friend this weekend. Well, someone I hope will become a friend . . .' She stopped, looking a bit flushed, much to Lauren's surprise.

'Right,' said Lauren and waited, hoping for more details.

'Ah, remember when Kevin was in Bristol?'

Lauren nodded. Kevin Mallory had been arrested for murder soon after Alex's arrival at Highpoint and his time in Bristol Prison had been neither happy nor comfortable. In fact, it was generally agreed he would not have lasted much longer if Alex had not been able to prove his innocence and get him released on bail. It had been a personal triumph for Alex, though professionally a bit of a disaster as the probation service took rather a dim view of what they saw as her over-involvement in police matters.

'There was one prison officer, a woman called Margie,' Alex continued. 'She was really helpful. She got him into the sick bay for a week and tried to look out for him. I don't think it went down too well with some of the other officers, to be honest. Anyway, she's applied for a job at Shepton Mallet and we're meeting up before she goes back. She's got a couple of days over there, sort of trying things out and seeing if it suits.'

Lauren was puzzled by Alex's reaction but nodded along to her friend.

'Where you thinkin' of going?' she asked. 'Wouldn't mind meeting her myself – not often you hear good things about a screw.'

'Don't call her that!' snapped Alex. 'She's interested in all the training work they're doing at Shepton Mallet. It's getting some really good results and she's more suited to that sort of work. They're not much for rehabilitation at Bristol.'

'Sorry,' said Lauren. 'Still, I always wondered what makes someone want to earn a living, locking other people up. So, where's you going?'

Alex gritted her teeth. Lauren was always eager for a trip out and normally she enjoyed the company. Irreverent, clever and tough, Lauren could enliven any gathering. This time, however, Alex had other plans.

'We've not decided,' she said, waving one hand vaguely. 'Probably just get together to catch up a bit, you know.'

There was an uncomfortable silence before Lauren slid into her car and slammed the door shut. 'Suit yerself,' she snapped and reversed out of the space with alarming speed.

Alex felt a rush of remorse and raised one hand to call her back but Lauren was gone, having executed a screeching turn in the car park that drew several young men attending an evening session to the door of the workshop to see what was going on. Waving them back inside, she set off down the path by the river, still choking on the hard crumbs of guilt that seemed to lodge in her throat. The sun was shining and she stood for a moment, eyes closed as she savoured the first warm evening of the year. Taking a deep breath, she blinked away the red dots clouding her vision and turned under the road bridge, heading for the back gate to her house. On the river, a swan glided majestically past the banks of vivid daffodils. The flowers were fading as spring edged towards summer but the bright, nodding heads of the last, brave blooms still cheered her.

'It's my life and I can do what I want,' she muttered, a mantra against the intrusions of the world surrounding her.

'What was that, dear?' asked her mother who was standing at the sink in the kitchen.

'Nothing,' said Alex. 'Just talking to myself. What are you doing?'

Dorothy gave the cleared draining board a final wipe, wrung out the cloth and spread it out on the tap to dry. 'I thought I'd tidy up a bit,' she said as she filled the kettle and set it to boil. 'Would you like some tea?'

Alex actually felt like a large glass of wine but she nodded and smiled before making her way through to the dining room. She loved her mother dearly but somehow, having her around all the time, she felt herself drifting back into the old role of 'child'. She almost expected her mother to call up the stairs, reminding her to hang up her work clothes. She could not help wondering, rather uncharitably, how long Dorothy intended to stay.

Lauren was still upset when she got home, her bad mood signalled by the slamming of doors and heavy tread as she marched through the house to her downstairs room. Jonny was lying on the coach, one arm draped elegantly over his face as he basked in the sunshine from the open windows.

'What's up, Sis?' he asked, without moving.

'Nothin'. Don't stir yourself,' said Lauren.

Jonny sat up, uncoiling and stretching as Lauren disappeared into her room, banging the door behind her. He was used to Lauren's moods and waited patiently until the sound of the radio floated out from the back before ambling over to the door and knocking.

'So what's happened?' he asked, peering round the frame.

Lauren was sitting in front of her dressing-table, chin propped in one hand as she stared moodily at the reflection in the glass. She was struggling to understand why she felt so hurt by Alex's reaction and so her explanation sounded both lame and petty, even to her own ears. Jonny listened without interruption, his long frame draped over the bed. He loved his sister dearly but knew how short-tempered she could be. Too often in the past, she had spoken without stopping to consider and her harsh words had lost her opportunities, new friends and even, on one occasion, her job.

'Well,' he said, once Lauren had finished her rather mangled tale of woe. 'You shouldn't take this so personally. Everyone has secrets, everyone's a bit of a mystery really. So Alex wants to go off on her own this weekend – so what? Besides,' he added, 'you did call her new friend a "screw".' He hesitated, wondering whether to push his luck as Lauren's reflection glared at him from across the room. 'Is not exactly designed to endear you to her, is it? I don't think I'd want you along after that.'

There was a long pause before Lauren sighed and spun round to face her brother. 'I suppose,' she said somewhat reluctantly. 'Just – maybe I'm missin' Dave a bit, with him out all hours on this case of his. Don't seem to have much fun at the weekends at the moment.'

Jonny grinned at her. 'You make it up with Alex tomorrow,' he advised. 'With a bit of luck we'll get an invite to her house on Friday and I'll see about a trip out for us if it's fine.'

Lauren smiled as she slid off the chair. 'Deal,' she said. 'Still, can't help wondering why she's so secretive . . . I know, I know, 'tis none of my business.'

Jonny shook his head as he followed her through to the kitchen. Despite what she said, he knew his sister would use all her cunning to ferret out the truth about Alex and her new friend.

Most of the time he had it under control. That was what he kept telling himself, and it was true – in the main. Most days he just got up, showered and dressed, ate what was put in front of him (or not, if it was too horrible), tidied his personal space and went out to see what the day had in store. There were appointments to be kept, of course. That went with the whole set-up and he did his best to appear calm and responsive to all the busy-body people who seemed intent on interfering in his life. He gritted his teeth and nodded, keeping silent as some thick half-wit with the brains of a cabbage told him how to do something.

The workshop was particularly difficult, full of young men who had been there a few weeks and thought they knew everything. The stuff they produced was terrible too. Shoddy, ugly and unimaginative, all made to a template with no care or skill. It took time to make something properly but no-one was interested. The supervisors moved them from one project to another without any concern for their skill level, let alone personal preference. Worst of all, he was constantly shuffled from one workspace to another, paired with an endless succession of lazy, incompetent partners who regarded his attempts to maintain a clean environment and decent tools as risible. If this was the future of small workshops, he thought, they deserved to be torched, their ashes turned over and stamped down into oblivion.

Working with his head down, shaving the surplus wood away to make a smooth, neat joint, he closed his ears to the sea of vulgarity that swirled around him. Inside his head he was far away, watching and waiting in the cool silence of evening, just him and the woman sharing the moment. His tongue flicked out to touch his lips and he swallowed, taking a deep breath to calm his emotions. His body jerked forwards and he narrowly missed running the plane over his fingers as he was shoved from behind.

'Oh, sorry – didn't see yer there,' said a mocking voice and he swung round to face Andy, a hulking, clumsy lad who fancied himself as a bit of a hard man.

He wrinkled his nose in disgust at the miasma of stale tobacco smoke and sweat that wafted towards him. 'Reckon I should have been more careful,' he said and Andy and his cronies shuffled closer, moving in at this sign of weakness. 'Yes,' he continued. 'Should have smelt you coming and got out of the way – you stupid oaf.'

Andy stood for an instant, a look of bewilderment flitting across his face.

'He's sayin' you stink,' said one of his henchmen helpfully.

'I got that,' said Andy rounding on his followers angrily.

Taking advantage of their momentary distraction, he reached behind him and located a chisel, a long and exceptionally sharp tool he had selected in the first week and moved from one workbench to another. Holding it casually in his hand he waited, facing down the bullies who were suddenly rather less eager to continue the conversation.

'Is only one of him,' said someone from the edge of the group. For an instant the dynamics swayed back and forth and the lads at the back urged those at the front onwards – and those standing right in front of the chisel edged away.

'Stopping a bit early for lunch aren't you?' cut in the supervisor as he materialised in the doorway bringing a strong smell of cigarette smoke with him. The group melted away, relieved at the interruption. Andy gave a sneer before sloping off, hands in his pockets as he shouldered his way through the rest of the young workforce. The chisel was back on the table before the supervisor noticed anything was amiss and he turned his back on them all, sweeping up the wood shavings and putting the off-cuts in the bin before washing his hands in the tiny cold water sink and heading for the door. Another morning done, he thought. He tried not to count up how many there were left to complete before he could sign off and move on. It made him too angry.

Chapter Seven

Margie stopped her car outside Alex's terraced house by the river at Highpoint and sat for a moment before getting out. The sun was shining, it was Saturday and she had the whole weekend off for the first time in months and she was meeting up with someone she liked and admired. What, she thought, what could possibly be the reason for the sudden desire to turn around and flee to the security of her room at the hostel in Shepton Mallet. What indeed. There was always this moment, this certainty that she had made a mistake. Forcing herself to open the door, she stepped out into the empty road and, locking the car door behind her, strode across the street to knock on the front door.

Alex had been up for several hours, showering and spending an inordinate amount of time wondering what she should wear. Normally immune to such trivialities, her bed was strewn with outfits once considered and then cast aside as too casual, too smart or just plain wrong. She hadn't realised she had so many clothes and after finally settling on new black jeans, a silk shirt and her favourite jumper (thank goodness it was clean, for once) began clearing up and hanging garments in the cupboard before abandoning the mess in favour of coffee and a quiet sit at the dining table. The house was quiet as she shuffling around the kitchen, moving carefully to avoid waking the others as she prepared to enjoy having the downstairs to herself for a while.

She drank her coffee standing at the back door, watching the morning light wash across the jumble of plants, soil and rubble that comprised her tiny back garden. Sue had dug over one of the beds by the gate during the last summer and the display of colourful annuals had attracted bees and butterflies as well as lifting her mood every time she looked out of the window. As she watched, several small birds swooped down and began to peck at the head of Sue's now-fallen giant sunflower. Under her amused gaze, they flew off with a seed in their beak, only to return a few moments later. Or perhaps it was a couple of different birds, Alex thought idly. Either way, it was nice to see them.

Her peace was disturbed by the sound of a door slamming next door and her neighbour, a retired man who lived a quiet life with his wife and maintained his garden perfectly all year round, hurried down the path, waving his hands at the feeding sparrows.

'Get off now,' he called. 'Out of it yer greedy little . . .'

'Good morning Mr Pond,' said Alex stepping out of the door.

Her neighbour swung round, startled by her sudden appearance. 'Oh, yes – good morning. Didn't see you there.' He rubbed his hands together nervously. 'You's up early this morning.'

'It's a lovely day,' said Alex. 'I thought I'd go out and enjoy it' – for once, added a voice in her head. She changed the subject abruptly. 'You're not a fan of sparrows, I take it?'

Next door, her neighbour shifted from one foot to another, looking round the garden before answering.

'This time of year, they's a menace,' he said finally. 'Pull up seedlings and such and eating all the berries.'

Alex blinked at him, taken aback by his vehemence. 'I'm not sure sparrows eat seedlings,' she said after a moment's thought. 'And there aren't any berries in your garden. I think it's starlings that pull up seedlings.' She nodded towards Mr Pond's freshly planted vegetable beds, the earth turning a pale green with the first growth. They were all covered in fine meshed nets, bright strips of plastic and cloth rippling above them in the light breeze. 'I think it would need to be a sparrow Houdini that managed to get in there.'

The joke fell flat as a squashed rat, her attempt at humour greeted by a basilisk-like stare as the old man stood his ground, presumably waiting for her to go inside so he could continue his harassment of the sparrows.

'Well,' said Alex. 'I'm off out to find a bird table.' As she closed the door behind her, she almost bumped into her mother who was standing in the kitchen, pretending to rinse out an already clean beaker.

'That was just naughty, dear' said Dorothy. 'The poor man is obviously worried about his garden.'

'They weren't in his garden,' Alex retorted. 'They were in *my* garden, eating *my* sunflower seeds. Honestly, he's got so much netting and stuff out there on his precious seed beds, anything smaller than a Roc would fly away screaming in terror.'

'You do exaggerate sometimes,' murmured her mother. 'Still, I think he's mainly concerned about your raspberries.'

Alex put down the cup she had been clutching and looked at her mother. 'What raspberries? I don't have any raspberries,' she said. 'It's a wilderness out there. I'm surprised I don't come across Stig of the Dump.'

'*Which* raspberries, dear. And you do, actually, in the bed just outside the bathroom window, between the path and your neighbour's garden fence. They are in need of a prune, of course, but the flowers are out so you might get a decent crop this year.'

Alex opened the back door again, setting the sparrows whirring off into the trees behind her back wall where they rustled and agitated, uttering annoyed chirps at this second disturbance. Dorothy followed her out into the back garden and pulled aside a thick growth of weeds growing so tall they threatened to cover the bathroom window entirely.

'There,' she said, pointing, and Alex found herself confronted by a bed of raspberry canes. A tangle, certainly, and rather neglected, but still, there were almost two dozen plants, all with a scattering of creamy white blossom.

'Of course, they are planted much too close together,' Dorothy continued. 'Or perhaps they are spreading. They do that, you know. That's why it is so important to prune them every winter.'

As far as Alex was concerned, her mother might as well have lapsed into Cantonese, for all the sense she was making. She was still staring in astonishment at this unexpected bounty.

'So there will be fruit here?' she said finally.

'Oh yes,' said Dorothy absently picking some stray greenfly off the nearest plant. 'These horrid little things need to be controlled though. Pour some soapy water over the plants and that should get rid of them. Your washing-up water will do. And when they do fruit, make sure you harvest every couple of days. That helps bring more berries on.' She leaned over the raspberry canes and examined the plants, turning them carefully to peer at the blossom.

'That's interesting,' she added.

'What?' asked Alex. She looked at the plants her mother was examining but could find nothing at all different about them. They all looked the same to her untrained eyes.

'The plants here are much more productive,' Dorothy continued. 'Look, they've got more flowers and they look much healthier. Almost as if this part of the bed has been cared for by someone.'

Mother and daughter looked at one another for a moment and then Alex grinned broadly.

'About an arm's length in from next door,' she said. 'Well, that explains why old Mr Pond is so annoyed about the sparrows, the cunning old . . . .'

A loud knock on the front door cut across this rare moment of shared humour.

'That is probably your friend,' said Dorothy. 'Now, you go and have a nice day out and don't worry about me. I might go up into town later. Would you mind if I did a bit of gardening this afternoon?'

It was the first time Alex could recall her mother ever asking her permission for anything. 'Please, help yourself,' she said.

'Thank you,' said Dorothy and she turned her attention back to the jungle surrounding the raspberry bed.

Weekends were supposed to be restful, an opportunity to rest and recover from the stresses of daily life. This was not, however, the case for the staff at Highpoint probation hostel. Weekends were an endurance test. Shift patterns were different, with staff working up to twenty-eight hours without a break. The worst stint began on Saturday at 1pm and finished on Sunday at 5 in the afternoon. To make matters worse, it was a solo shift from 9 on Saturday evening. Every two weeks the residents received their benefit cheques on the Friday and most of them spent a good part of the following weekend ensuring the local publicans could continue to thrive in what was turning into an endless and brutal financial recession. The hostel, always a volatile environment, could be a dangerous place at weekends.

Despite this, it had become customary to allocate the long weekend session to a female member of staff. The reason for this had little to do with the skills and experience of the staff nominated for this deeply unpopular shift. It was based solely on the fact there were no kitchen staff over the weekend. This meant that after working for almost 24 hours with very little sleep, the weekend warden was expected to produce a decent Sunday dinner for up to twenty hungry residents at midday. Women, of course, could all cook and so were much better suited to the task. Well, that was the theory and none of the men were going to contradict it.

Samuel Burton rose early on Saturday mornings and signed out of the hostel as soon as the doors were unlocked. He did not wait for breakfast, a meal he scorned as fit only for weaklings. He also escaped before he could be roped in to any of the unofficial work parties the weekend staff set up. This was one reason he was not progressing as rapidly as some of the more indolent but easily manipulated residents. 'Being a team player', was seen as a sign of improving social skills and if there was one thing Samuel was not, it was a team player.

His sole concession to social norms was a curt nod in the direction of Bennie Sands, the deputy warden, on the way out of the front door. Bennie raised her hand in greeting but Samuel was gone before he could be engaged in conversation. Sighing with frustration, Bennie opened the day book, a log of all events and activity in the hostel, and noted the departure. Flipping back through the pages, she saw the pattern repeated every morning since Samuel's arrival. He had tried the breakfast just once, on his first day, and not given it a second chance.

Samuel remained rooted to the lowest rung of the warden's 'Ladder of Achievement', his silent refusal to engage with any of the hostel's activities and neglect of the housekeeping chores allocated to him condemning him to a continued existence in the four-bedded room designed for new arrivals. Samuel's only achievement, Bennie reflected as she closed the office door and hurried off to start preparing breakfast prior to the handover to the weekend staff, was he had not yet re-offended. Or at least, he had not yet been caught.

Samuel stood for a moment on the pavement outside the hostel, breathing in the fresh air and feeling the familiar thrill that came with anticipation. His moment of calm was broken by the first of what would be many cars rushing past, the roof-rack loaded with cases, sleepy children's faces peering at him from steamed-up windows. The half-term holiday was in full swing, bringing the first early influx of tourists.

Samuel glared at the vehicle as it swept along the road and passed from view around a bend. Unlike a lot of the locals, he had nothing personal against the many, many tourists flooding through the county from late spring to mid-autumn. He just found the noise, the dust and the sight of pale, grubby children crammed into the back of cars offensive. It wasn't as if he felt sorry for them either. He didn't like children. Or animals. If the truth were told, most people left Samuel cold – and they were the lucky ones.

Pushing the irritation from his thoughts, he cut around behind the hostel and scrambled down a steep grassy bank to the remains of the old tow-path. This particular route was a favourite of his, crossing the countryside that surrounded Highpoint and following the disused canal that ran straight and true towards the edge of the Somerset Levels. When it turned to head towards Taunton there were a number of different paths and tracks snaking off into the undergrowth or running parallel with the narrow strips of gritted tarmac that passed for roads around the empty, open water meadows.

Samuel had already spent many hours out on the Levels, ferreting out the shortest and safest routes from the town to a number of the surrounding villages and hamlets. He had discovered that shortest was not always safest early on in his exploration, a plunge up to crotch level into stagnant, icy water teaching him a valuable lesson. Now he checked the smaller, more obscure paths with a stick, testing the ground beneath the surface, for out on the Levels nothing seemed to stay the same for long. A good downpour and the safe route from one road to another could become muddy, slippery or even deadly if the surrounding marsh seeped too close to the surface. Today it was sunny and the paths seemed firm, but he proceeded with caution, eyes fixed to the ground, ever alert to darker patches or the glint of water that might suggest a new danger.

Around him the grasses whispered in a light breeze and in the distance a lark shot out of the undergrowth, flinging itself skyward with a burst of song. The high trills of its call floated around Samuel as he walked on through the long grasses, oblivious to the beauty that surrounded him. His only acknowledgement of his surroundings was an irritated wave of his left hand as he batted at a cloud of insects buzzing around his face. Samuel hated insects, especially midges – though they seemed to love him.

As a child he had suffered through the summer as midges, mosquitoes and wasps flocked to surround him, feasting on his sweet blood and rewarding his frantic flapping with bites and stings. One particularly humid year he had spent most of the school holiday curled up on his bed reading a book, his arms and face a mass of red blotches and dry, itchy patches of camomile lotion. Already vain about his appearance, he had refused to go outside until every pink spot had faded. His strength of will was already apparent as his parents discovered when all their blandishments, bribes and attempts to order him out into the fresh air were met with hard stares and silence.

Since that miserable summer, he had avoided anywhere that could be considered the insects' natural habitat, but that was difficult around Highpoint, surrounded as it was by open countryside that was crossed by rivers and streams and nestling up against the great marshy expanse of the Levels. Samuel had little choice but to venture out into the midges' home ground, but that didn't mean he had to enjoy it and the first mile or so was covered at a brisk pace, dodging the damp areas and ducking around fine clouds of insects as he cut across the edge of the marsh towards the firmer ground of Kings Sedgemoor and its small villages.

Emerging from the surrounding brush and reeds, he set off at a trot, following the narrow path that ran next to the great drainage ditch, his feet kicking up small clouds of white dust from the chalky gravel surface. It felt good to be running again, to feel the rush of air past his face and the prickle of sweat break out along his back and Samuel began to run faster, falling into the familiar and seductive trance induced by the exercise. Reaching the footbridge over the canal, he swung to the right and continued down the ancient track marking Sedgemoor Drove. New leaves rustled on the branches overhanging the path and there was a fine line of grass growing down the centre, a sure sign few, if any, motor vehicles used this route.

At the next sharp bend he skirted the boundaries to a disused farmhouse and hopped over a tiny feeder drain. Pushing through the hedge that barred his way, he stepped out onto a large, open strip of concrete, cracked in places with more grass pushing up between the crumbling slabs. Off to the right were several grassy humps, the overgrown remnants of bunkers left behind when the military withdrew from the airfield at the end of the Second World War, finally abandoning it completely in the 1960s. With no-one guarding the remains of the runways and surrounding land, it was the haunt of BMX riders and underage drivers during the school holidays but this early in the morning it was still deserted, just another noisy skylark disturbing his peace with its shrill, mindless warbling.

Glancing around to make sure he was completely alone, Samuel headed for the overgrown bunkers where the remains of a rotting door hung away from the frame. Sliding in through the narrow gap, he waited for a minute, allowing his eyes to adjust to the darkness. The smell told him he was not the first person to find the way in but an earlier examination of the floor had suggested the room had not been used for a long time. Stepping carefully around the edge of the low walls to minimise his footprints, Samuel moved further into the remains of the shelter.

Once beyond the outer walls, he could use the torch he carried in his pocket without risking unwanted attention. The pale yellow beam flickered over the dust covering most surfaces. The interior of the shelter had been stripped of anything useful a long time ago and only a scattering of broken furniture and rotting wood remained. Samuel repeated his crab-like sidle around the walls, trying to keep as close as possible without brushing against decades of grime and accumulated filth. Everything he was wearing was going in the wash tonight, he vowed as he reached the back of the room.

Hidden under a new groundsheet was a backpack containing a complete change of clothes, a trenching spade folded up and fastened to the back and, off to one side, a large round tin with a tight fitting lid.

Samuel was pleased with the tin. It had taken a lot of searching to find something air-tight, big enough but still easily carried. In the end he had spotted it on a pile of scrap metal waiting for the recycling lorry next to the old quay. The inside had been slightly sticky and smelt of fruit – pineapple, he thought. It had taken a lot of scrubbing but now it gleamed inside, though the fruit trace still lingered, especially when first opened. It couldn't be helped, he decided. He was unlikely to find anything as good in the time he had and anyway, the smell was so faint it would soon fade completely. He had been tempted to leave the tin open to speed up the airing process but the thought of mice or rats crawling around inside made him shudder. Better pineapple than rat piss, in his opinion.

After checking everything was still in place and undisturbed by human or animal, he pulled a second torch from his pocket, a smaller, rubber covered model in a plastic bag. He unwrapped it, checked it was working and then turned it off and placed the package in the rucksack with the clothes. Nearly there, he thought and his eyes glinted in the light from the torch he propped up against the wall, its dim light reflecting feebly from the ceiling, fading to grey as it was absorbed by the thick cobwebs strung around the roof. When he was satisfied all was secure, he edged back to the doorway, torch in hand. As he emerged into the open air he blinked, blinded for a second by the bright sunlight. That momentary loss of concentration meant he missed the lanky figure of Brian Morris slipping out of sight amongst the trees at the far side of the runway.

Brian watched from the shadows, startled by the abrupt appearance of someone way out on the Levels at such an early hour. Keeping very still, he squinted across the concrete trying to identify the figure silhouetted against the grassy mounds. For a moment he thought he'd been spotted, but then he realised the figure was rubbing at his eyes as if dazzled by the sun. Strange, he thought. Maybe he was sleeping rough or just been poking around in the shade. As the figure turned towards the gap in the hedges leading towards Westonzoyland, Brian got a good look at his face.

'That new bloke from the hostel,' he muttered. 'Now, what the hell's he doin' all the way out here?'

He waited until the new bloke disappeared behind the boundary hedge before stepping out into the sunlight, dragging his latest acquisition behind him. Brian had need of some sort of income, and quickly. He really did want to get away from the family home before his father returned in a few weeks and recent events had caused him to pause and reflect on some of his recent life choices. Laudable as this all was, however, he was still not exactly looking at his situation in a truly realistic manner. His delight at finding the abandoned metal detector he hauled behind him was evidence he still tended towards the quick-fix sort of solution.

The metal detector had been lying in a large patch of brambles, presumably flung there in disgust by its previous owner. It was old, battered and in need of a new battery pack but Brian was undeterred by the weight of his find or its awkward shape. He reasoned it would be easier to hide the machine on the airfield somewhere and take the battery into town to source a replacement. He was surprised to discover most of the weight *was* the battery but, still undeterred, he managed to prise it loose without damaging the connections and put the leaking, corroded pack to one side as he considered the possible hiding places for the rest of the machine.

The obvious place was in one of the overgrown ruins, but the appearance of Samuel Burton from the doorway of the largest building rather put paid to that idea. After some thought, Brian dragged the metal detector off to the side of the runway where the concrete was broken up and piled off to one side. A few minutes hard work, and his find was covered with lumps of hardcore and an artistic dusting of leaf debris and twigs. Brian stepped back to admire his handiwork from several angles. Not bad, he thought and, hefting the battery up in both hands, set off towards the main road. A trickle of fluid seeped through the broken casing and coated his fingers but he ignored the discomfort, intent on getting into town before he was spotted. Behind him, on the side of the runway, a trail of dusty footprints marked his path away from the metal detector.

Kevin had become used to rising earlier in the day whilst off on his travels with the Fair and Ada was surprised to see him sitting at the kitchen table, a fresh pot of tea in front of him, when she came in after collecting the eggs from her hens.

'Morning,' said her son, rising from his chair and pouring her a cup.

'Morning,' she replied, taking the beaker and folding herself into the chair opposite. Momentarily lost for words, she took a sip from her tea before placing the cup on the table. 'Sleep well?' she asked finally.

Kevin nodded, his mouth full of toast. He'd learnt to make his own breakfast too, she noted.

'Fancy a boiled egg to go with that?'

Kevin grinned and nodded again. 'Reckon,' he said. 'Don't find nothing to match they eggs from your hens. Right special, they is.'

Ada stood up and turned to the stove, hiding a smile of delight. There had been few enough compliments in her life and her son's new attitude seemed to light up the whole morning.

Pushing his chair back from the table after wolfing down his breakfast, Kevin said, 'I got to go into town today, see to a few things. Anything you wanting from Highpoint?'

Ada's mouth dropped open in astonishment. 'No, reckon I'm good,' she managed.

Kevin nodded and gathered up his dishes, carrying them to the sink to wash.

'Hold on,' Ada said. She leaned over and plucked the empty egg shell from the plate, dropping it into an old plastic box where it joined several others lying in a mess of tea leaves. 'Slugs,' she said in response to Kevin's unspoken question. 'They's a bit too fond of the leaves but when they go sliding over the shells, they comes all unzipped. And no need to use no poison or nothing on my veggies, neither. Oh, don't you give me that sad face,' she added. 'If they stays off my garden they don't come to no harm. Now, hang on a moment.'

Seizing a spoon, she pounded the eggshells into sharp edged fragments, mixing in the leaves before handing the box to Kevin.

'I've got some herbs growing out front. Patch of thyme, bit of rue – just put this round the roots will you – leave the box on the step and I'll get it later.'

Kevin picked up his denim jacket and slung it over his shoulder, tucking the plastic box under his arm as he headed out of the back door and around the corner of the cottage. The front of the house was a mixture of flowers and greenery with clumps of small bushes placed in the sunniest locations. Bees clustered around the rosemary and buzzed contentedly amidst sprigs of early lavender. Kevin shook the slug mixture round the bed, then stood for a moment, blinking in the bright sunlight and just enjoying the warmth as it soaked into him like warm honey.

His good mood was ruined when he opened his eyes and met the cynical gaze of Samuel, standing across the narrow road and staring in at him.

'What you looking at then?' Kevin shouted.

Samuel shrugged and turned away.

'Don't know,' came his reply. 'The label's fallen off.'

Kevin felt his temper rising, his fists clenching as this stranger sauntered off down the road.

'Bugger off! Don't you come round here again, you!' he yelled.

Samuel swung round and glared back at him.

'I believe this is a public road and I'll walk along here whenever I want. Understand *boy*?' He stretched out the last word in a mocking imitation of Kevin's accent, walking backwards with a mocking sneer on his face before turning away again.

Six months ago Kevin would have been over the fence and after this insolent stranger but that was before his recent travels. He had grown up over the winter, learning to curb his temper and starting to see some things from another person's perspective. He was physically bigger too – all the lifting and heaving around of the Fair's complex infrastructure had helped develop some decent muscles. It was ironic he was now more than capable of holding his own in a fight but far less inclined to throw the first punch. Instead he contented himself with a universally recognised rude hand sign.

There was a scuffling sound behind him and Ada appeared around the corner.

'Just some dickhead hanging around across the road,' he said, hastily lowering his hand. He glanced at his wrist and added, 'Better be off or I'll be missin' the bus.'

Ada nodded as her son slipped his jacket over his shoulders and held out the empty box. He was wearing a watch, she realised. Not a fancy one, just one of those cheap plastic ones you could pick up from a garage. The sort with numbers – what did they call them? She puzzled for a moment before it came to her. Digital – that was it. A digital watch. He'd never had a watch before, but then he'd never bothered with a job before neither. First he was writing letters, then making his own toast, now he was paying attention to the time. Seemed like the Fair was going to be the making of him, she thought with a nod of approval.

'You be wanting any dinner then?' she asked.

Kevin thought for a moment and then shook his head. 'Don't wait for us,' he said. 'I'll get somethin' in town if'n I is hungry. Bye now.' He gave a little wave and headed off down the narrow track towards the main road, leaving his mother smiling fondly as she watched him stride off into the distance. Definitely a turn for the better, she thought as she went back inside and began tidying the kitchen.

Chapter Eight

Lauren was up early that Saturday morning, flinging open the curtains and smiling as the sun shone through. Dave was working again but Jonny had promised her a trip out and she had already decided where she wanted to go. Along the coast there were a number of small coves, each with their own character. Over the years, Lauren had explored them all, but her favourite was Kilve, a rocky bay with one of the best fossil beaches in the country. A trip to Kilve was always a favourite day out, especially if it was combined with a pub lunch at the old inn nestling behind the sand dunes.

The phone rang as she was finishing her breakfast and the unexpected voice of Dave Brown made her smile.

'I'm really sorry I can't go with you today,' he said.

'Is all right,' Lauren replied, licking the last of the jam from her fingers. 'I know you got to work. Is more important you get this weirdo so just you crack on and show 'em all how good you really is.'

Before his move to the detective squad, Lauren had suffered a severe fit of jealousy, the strains of his long hours and weekend overtime making her feel neglected and unloved. They had come close to breaking up and only Dave's determination to hang on to her had kept them together. Since his transfer, however, Lauren had developed a bit more patience. She understood how important this chance was and although she tried not to show it too obviously she was proud of Dave and his achievements. If that came with a few weekends without him, well, it was worth it as far as she was concerned.

There was the sound of footsteps on the stairs and Jonny, wearing only his boxer shorts and a tee shirt, poked his head round the corner.

'Was for me,' she said replacing the phone on the hook. 'You getting up now?' She tilted her head to one side, scrutinising her brother's face. 'Look a bit rough, mind.'

Jonny glared at her, his eyes bloodshot as he stepped rather gingerly down the stairs. Alex had called off the usual Friday night dinner, unsure of how her mother might react to some of the more unorthodox opinions and relationships of her friends and so Jonny had spent the evening in Highpoint, returning long past midnight in a taxi, humming tunelessly as he stumbling upstairs.

'I'm fine,' he snapped. 'Any coffee on the go?'

Lauren gestured to the enamel pot on the stove and waited until he shuffled back to the table, mug in hand.

'So, where do you fancy going today?' said Jonny after taking a restorative gulp from his coffee.

'Reckon is going to be a lovely day,' said Lauren. 'Tide's out around lunchtime so I really fancy Kilve.'

Jonny groaned softly. Kilve beach was a walk best described as 'energetic', the approach little more than a farm track and the path around some of the more interesting outcrops of rock was uneven and rough underfoot. There was a distinct lack of shade out by the sea and in the summer sun, the light was blindingly bright, glittering off the sea and the white rocks. He had enjoyed a rather good night last night but he suspected he was going to pay for it today. Still, he thought, he'd promised Lauren the day out of her choice and he didn't intend to disappoint her.

'Give me a couple of minutes to finish this,' he said, holding up the mug. 'And I'd better be putting a few more clothes on. Don't want to end up frightening the public like dumb ol' Martin Ford.'

Dave Brown put the phone down with a sigh. He was relieved that Lauren was taking all this overtime so well. It certainly made his life a bit easier, knowing she was happy and was going out to enjoy the day but he could not help wishing he was going too. He had spent the last week going over and over the same information, reading and re-reading the interviews, notes and reports. When he closed his eyes at night, he could see the photographs from the two crime scenes in his mind, as clearly as if they were taped to his eyelids. He bent over his latest attempt to plot the links between the two incidents, a complex matrix that tried to make comparisons in every area he could think might be relevant but he kept coming to the same conclusion.

The most important bits of information were all missing. What the two incidents had in common was 'don't know'. Don't know what the motivation might be, don't know if the actions were premeditated, don't know whether they were complete or if he was interrupted – that was especially ominous and Dave didn't like to think what might happen were he to chance on a victim without neighbours or someone else within earshot. Didn't even know how the hell he was getting to the houses in the first place.

Dave flung his pen down in disgust, rose from the table and stood in front of the incident board, studying the map with its two pins. The door opened and Sergeant Lynas walked in.

'Anything you can add?' he asked.

Dave shook his head angrily.

'I don't know if he's clever or lucky,' he said. 'I only know we don't have anything like enough to catch him at the moment.'

The sergeant nodded, staring at the map. 'It's like that sometimes,' he said softly. 'We have to wait, hope he makes a mistake.'

Dave's shoulders slumped as he heard his own thoughts spoken out loud. 'You mean we need another one, don't you. You're hoping he's going to strike again.'

Sergeant Lynas gave him a hard look. 'I'm not *hoping* he'll strike again,' he said coldly. 'If anything I'm *hoping* the bastard falls into a deep ditch and lies there in agony until we pick him up the next morning. However, I have to admit, we need more than we've got right now. A lot more.'

Dave flushed, squirming uncomfortably before his superior's wrath, and started to stammer an apology.

Sergeant Lynas waved his hand, silencing him.

'I know exactly what you mean,' he said. 'But you need to watch how you say it. A member of the public hearing you talk like that – doesn't bear thinking about. So, exactly what *do* we have and where do we go from here?'

Dave walked back to his desk, anxious to make up for his hasty words.

'Similar time of day,' he said. 'Both early evening, just as it's getting dark. Could be because of the need for darkness, for hiding perhaps, or it could be – maybe he works during the day?'

Lynas nodded and made a note on the board.

'Good. Now you're thinking like a detective. Anything else?'

Dave felt the tension leave his chest a little.

'Some distance apart,' he said. 'The Monkton attack was around five kilometres south of the incident at Goathurst.'

Lynas shook his head.

'Don't give me all that metric rubbish,' he muttered. 'How far in real distances is that?'

Dave did a quick calculation in his head.

'Just over 3 miles,' he said. 'And almost exactly due south – only a few degrees off. But there's no direct route between them so maybe he's coming from the east. There's High-

106

point out there – Taunton to the south or Petherton perhaps. Maybe he's from one of them. Mind you,' he continued, lost in speculation, 'could be he's travelling from work. Both days were working days, nothing at weekends – so far anyway.'

He glanced up to see Sergeant Lynas nodding in approval.

'Right. Well, you write that all up and see what else you can tease out of this mess. I'm off to the lab to see if they've got anything else for us.'

Dave nodded, his attention already fixed on the notes in front of him. What did they have so far, he asked himself. A man – a tall man, blond – here he suppressed a grin – with a stocking over his head . . . Dave stopped and blinked his eyes, then started rummaging through the folders in front of him. No stocking found at either scene so he'd taken it away with him. Either he was knowledgeable and careful or he needed to keep hold of it for next time. Maybe both. So where did a man get hold of a pair of stockings? Easy enough nowadays – every supermarket and corner shop sold them. But a single man might be wary of buying them regularly and the type of behaviour this man displayed suggested he was probably not the sort to have a regular, loving girlfriend.

His hand stopped over on piece of paper, a transcription of the notes from Miss Taylor, the first victim. It didn't say specifically but he got the impression the stocking was dark – darker than most every-day stockings, anyway. Otherwise she would have been able to tell his hair was a light shade, he reasoned. Black stockings might be easier to trace, a bit more memorable if it came to checking shops and supermarkets. He realised he was clutching at straws but even so, he went in search of his sergeant. He had an idea and they needed to do another interview with the victims as soon as possible.

Alex sat in Margie's car, trying to enjoy the sensation of being driven by someone else but she was uncomfortably aware of the beating of her heart, fluttering and twitching in her chest as she sat, pulled tight by the safety belt against the seat.

'You comfortable there?' asked Margie, risking a quick glance away from the twisting road.

Alex nodded and managed a sickly smile.

'Fine,' she said, tugging at the seat belt where it was cutting into the side of her neck. 'Really, I'm just a bit tired.'

Margie glanced in her mirror and pulled the car over to the side of the road, stopping hard up against a hedge.

'Here,' she said, leaning over Alex. For a moment Alex felt Margie's body pressed against her as she reached for the bracket holding the belt. There was a popping sound and the pressure on her neck eased suddenly as Margie slid the anchor point down the door pillar.

'I don't hardly ever have passengers,' said Margie as she shifted back into her seat and put the car in gear again. 'Last time was my hulking girt brother and it was a bit low for him, even right up at the top. Don't reckon they designed these bloody things for women anyway.' She tugged impatiently at her own belt as it pulled across her chest. 'Is alright for men but we got a lot more stuff in the way to get hurt.'

Alex felt herself begin to relax as she grinned, nodding in agreement.

'Yeah. Across the waist and straight down both shoulders would be a lot more comfortable but I can't see that ever happening.'

They drove in silence for a few minutes, but a more comfortable silence as the car sped through the little tree-lined lanes towards the coast. Sunlight flickered through the leaves, a continuous rippling pattern of green and gold. It was a very beautiful day, with Somerset looking its best and Alex smiled as she leaned back in her seat.

'So, where we going?' asked Margie.

Alex looked out at the scenery and said, 'Just a few miles further along this road, then we turn left. Off the Levels and towards the coast. Have you ever been to Brean Sands before?'

Margie shook her head, eyes still fixed on the road.

'Nope. Heard about it, mind. Big holiday camp there, and some of my old colleagues used to go there when they was kids. Didn't fancy it myself – all that community spirit an' joining in and stuff.'

Alex couldn't agree more. Never one for 'joining in' herself, the idea of a week in a holiday camp filled her with horror.

'It's okay,' she said hastily. 'We're not going to the camp. There's an enormous beach – miles of sand dunes and so much space out there. You can see Wales across the estuary on a clear day and the sand is amazing. You wait 'til you see it – it's covered in a layer of tiny shells and in the sun it looks like a rainbow.'

Margie risked a quick smile in Alex's direction.

'Sounds just what I need,' she said. 'That our turning?'

'Down here,' said Alex. 'The road gets a bit rough a mile or so further on. We go down a bit of a track and then follow the dunes up to the beach.'

A bit rough was an understatement as far as Margie was concerned. After half a mile she found herself edging along a narrow strip of lumpy tarmac, driving in second gear and trying to avoid the worst of the potholes.

'Well, I can see why we is using my car,' she said.

'I've already driven mine up here too many times,' said Alex. 'We're using yours 'cos mine probably won't make it.'

Margie laughed and added, 'Mind you, I tend to make it a rule never to drive along no road as has grass growing down the middle. I reckon there's probably good reason cars don't use it and I don't want to find out what it is.'

They turned right at the end of the track and bounced along, sand dunes rising to block any view on the left and flat, dry scrub land to their right.

'I hope this beach is worth it,' grumbled Margie as sand flew up around them, sticking to the windows. At that moment they reached the end of the road, the dunes fell away and the bay stretched out before them, gleaming in the sunlight.

'I think it is,' said Alex, enjoying her companion's astonishment.

Margie turned off the engine and they sat for a moment, just enjoying the silence and the view. The car made soft ticking noises as it cooled and Alex wound down her window, letting the rich, salty air wash over them both. It was still early and they were the first car in the little car park at the end of the lane. Around them the birds resumed their calls and a soft breeze rustled the grass planted along the dunes to help them resist the pull of the winter tides.

Margie took a deep breath and smiled.

'This looks right lovely,' she said. 'Fancy a walk?'

The sand, with its covering of tiny shell fragments, crunched beneath their feet as they made their way along the beach. Margie had been reluctant to walk on the wide ribbon of colour at first, looking down at the fragile beauty and not wanting to damage it. Alex remembered how she had felt the same on her first visit with Lauren and Jonny and how Lauren had teased her.

'Is only shells,' she had said. 'They's all getting broken up by the sea anyway. Where do you think sand comes from then?'

'It's just part of a natural cycle,' she said to Margie. 'Anyway, you can't get far along the beach without walking on some of them.'

Together they strolled along, the soft crunching of their footsteps and calls of the gulls flying across the estuary almost drowning out the whisper of the waves, far out in the distance. Margie stopped and looked around at the magnificent solitude, taking a deep breath and letting it out with a great sigh.

'You'm right,' she said with a broad grin. 'Is certainly worth the drive. Come on, I fancy a paddle!' She set off towards the distant sea, running and skipping as she went.

'No!' Alex yelled. 'Wait – don't go any further!'

Margie stopped, swinging round to look in surprise. Then she glanced down at her feet and gave a lurch as the sand slipped away a little and her heels sank below the surface.

'Lean forwards and walk slowly towards me,' Alex called and, arms out for balance, Margie obeyed. Alex ran forwards and seized her hand as she reached a firmer stretch, the pair of them stumbling together up the beach.

'What the bloody hell . . .?' Margie looked down at her shoes, soaking wet and full of fine, gritty sand.

'It's like quicksand,' Alex explained. 'I thought you knew, you being local.'

Margie snorted in disgust. 'From Bristol,' she said. 'Not from round here and we don't have much of a beach down my way. Course, I heard about all them dumb tourists getting stuck at Weston but generally they was in cars. Serves anyone right, if they's daft enough to drive a car out on the beach but walking? Didn't know about that.'

Alex felt utterly wretched. The lovely day she had planned was ruined, the gently growing closeness she felt was gone. She wanted to cry and her feelings must have shown as Margie put out a hand and touched her lightly on the shoulder.

'Is no matter,' she said. 'I got a towel and some spare shoes in the car so we can just go back and get 'um. As my granddad always said, worse things happen at sea.'

Alex felt a surge of relief. 'You know,' she said as they set off back to the car park, 'my granddad used to say that too.'

Miss Taylor had greeted them warmly when Sergeant Lynas and Dave knocked at her door later that morning. The officers sat in the conservatory and waited whilst she made tea before Dave helped her carry the tray through and they settled in the bright, warm sunlight.

'It's getting a bit hot during the day now,' said their hostess when Sergeant Lynas ran a finger round his collar. 'I keep going to open the back door but – well, you can imagine I'm a little reluctant.'

Dave nodded, thinking how sad it was someone as nice as her could be robbed of such a simple pleasure. More than ever, he was determined to find this 'Moth Man', so this brave woman could enjoy sitting in her own garden again.

'We've got a few more questions, if you can spare the time,' said Lynas reaching for a biscuit.

111

Miss Taylor sighed softly but nodded her head.

'I don't know what I can add,' she said. 'To be honest, I'm trying to put it all behind me, not dwell on details. Still, if you think it might help . . .?'

'Thank you,' said Dave. They had decided he would do most of the talking and Lynas would take notes, stepping in if he were needed. That way, Dave could maintain eye contact and keep the illusion this was more of a conversation than an interview. Time was passing, memory would begin to fade and there was a limit to how often they could make the victims re-live their experiences before they met resistance. Dave needed to get this right the first time.

'I want to go over the description of this man,' he said gently. 'I know it is not pleasant but there are some details that might really help us.'

Miss Taylor gestured with her hand, the sort of 'carry on then,' gesture Dave remembered from his school days. He took a moment before beginning, trying to banish the idea he was questioning his form mistress from Year Five.

'I need you to concentrate on his appearance,' he said. Ignoring her raised eyebrows, he continued. 'Was he fat or thin? Did he seem to have good muscles or was he flabby – or a bit weedy.' He stopped, realising that was not really precise enough. And he had to ask just one question, not a series, if he wanted to get useful answers.

'So, fat or thin?' he repeated.

There was a pause as Miss Taylor considered the question. 'Thin, I suppose. Certainly not fat. And, yes, he was a bit weedy looking. Skinny legs – but his shoulders . . .'

Dave waited, resisting the impulse to jump in and perhaps break her chain of thought.

'He had quite broad shoulders,' she said after a moment. 'And his upper arms seemed in proportion to them so they must have been quite muscular. Certainly not scrawny little chicken arms,' she finished with a smile.

Dave smiled back at her. 'That's really good,' he said. 'Now, did you notice whether he was pale skinned or was he tanned?'

He knew it was early in the year for holidays. If their man had visible tan lines the chances were very good he worked outdoors.

Miss Taylor half-closed her eyes, tilting her head to one side as she strove to recall the events of that evening.

'I'd forgotten,' she said softly. 'His body was very pale but his arms were quite brown. Another thing – when he ran away I think his shoulders looked a bit red. Almost as if he'd caught the sun. I had a silly thought, just before the shock of it all hit me. He reminded me of a Neapolitan ice cream. We used to get them when I was young,' she continued seeing the look of puzzlement flicker over Dave's face. 'Three types of ice cream in one block – chocolate, vanilla and strawberry. The back of his neck was brown, then there was a mix of white and pink. Yes, I'm sure of it.'

Dave nodded and smiled encouragingly. 'That's really helpful,' he said. 'Just one more question, I think. Which parts of him touched the glass? Apart from . . .' he tried, unsuccessfully, not to blush. 'Apart from the obvious, of course.'

Miss Taylor sat very still for a few seconds, staring through glass of her conservatory. Dave could hear the bees buzzing outside in the garden and in the distance a dove cooed, its mellow call floating above the idyllic scene. It was difficult to imagine anything disturbing the peace of this little haven and he felt a pang of sadness, knowing that it would never feel entirely safe for Miss Taylor again.

'Well,' she said, breaking the stillness. 'Apart from the obvious,' here she grinned unexpectedly, causing Dave to flush slightly once more. 'You know, I'm sure he put his hands on the window. About level with his shoulders but stretched out a bit.' She stood and demonstrated, her arms slightly extended, palms facing the two officers.

'You could see his hands?' Dave asked excitedly. 'Not just the shape but actually see the hands themselves?'

'Oh yes,' she said, taking her seat once more. 'They were the same colour as his arms, anyway. Oh,' she looked at the two policemen sharply. 'That might mean he left some finger-prints, doesn't it?'

'There weren't any prints thought, were there,' said Dave as they settled back in the car and headed back to Taunton.

'Right,' said Lynas, reading through his notes again. 'They were very careful, the crime scene people. Would've spotted something like that right off. So, what's that tell us then?'

Dave concentrated on the road for a few seconds, negotiating one of the many treacherous blind corners round which an army of tractors and dairy herds seemed to lurk whenever he ventured out of town.

'Either he was wearing gloves – see-through ones that is – or he has no fingerprints.'

Sergeant Lynas grunted. 'Seems the former's a bit more likely, don't you think? Everyone's got fingerprints. Thank Christ. Be a right sorry show if we didn't!'

'There have been a few cases where people have sanded them off,' said Dave. 'And some types of workers lose the prints, at least for a while.'

'What is you blathering on about?' snapped Lynas. 'What sort of workers?'

Dave realised he had started down a path fraught with danger but he couldn't help himself.

'I knew a lighting technician, from our local theatre, and she burned her fingers really badly on one of the new halogen bulbs,' he said. 'All the skin just peeled off and it never did grow back properly.'

'Well, I think we can rule *her* out of our enquiries, for fairly obvious reasons,' snapped the sergeant.

'Well, yes – that's just an example,' said Dave. 'I read that some people who work in canning factories lose their finger-prints too. If they work with pineapples a lot.' In his head he was shouting, '*Shut up, shut up!*' but he couldn't seem to stop. 'There's something in the juice that eats the skin away and their fingerprints just disappear . . .'

Lynas turned his head slowly and blinked at him.

'Pineapple?' he said, disbelief dripping from that one word.

Dave kept his eyes fixed on the road.

'Don't work with chicken then, nor tomato?'

Dave swallowed and shook his head, staring firmly in front.

''Cos that's what they do in the cannery down Wembden. Making baby food, that's all. Wouldn't like to think of that baby food being strong enough to take off fingerprints. Don't sound healthy.'

They drove in silence for a few minutes before Dave ventured, 'Maybe he's not from round here.'

'Go on,' said Lynas.

Dave considered his words before continuing.

'There has to be a reason he's started this now,' he said. 'Something set him off – or he's just arrived here from some-where else. Maybe we should check, see if there've been any more like this in other areas.'

Sergeant Lynas nodded, making a note under his record of the interview. 'Anything else?'

'I think he might work outside,' he said. 'At least, he does now – he's tanned but not very much. It sounds as if he's sunburnt on his back so he's new to whatever he's doing, oth-erwise he'd probably have a bit of brown already. It's been a reasonable spring and most builders and farm hands will have much more exposure to the sun by now.'

'Good,' said Lynas. 'So, where do we start looking?'

Dave knew he was being tested but he was much surer of his idea now.

'I think we should put out a shout around the regions for anything similar and while we're waiting for any answers, look at new men taken on by builders, farmers – people like that.'

'The theory's good,' said Lynas. 'A terrible load of work though. Most builders is starting their busy time on the large sites round about now. Same with farmers. And there's all types of others we might need to check on – scaffolders, for example, road men – council gardeners even. He might easily work on his own account. Lots of blokes do now, what with all the cut-backs and the state of most industry around here.'

Dave's shoulders slumped. It had seemed so logical when he first proposed the theory but now Sergeant Lynas's reasoning was punching holes in the whole idea.

'Don't look so glum,' said Lynas. 'You've got a place to start from, which is more'n we had this time yesterday. And that point about why he's suddenly doing this now – that's a good one. That could be what cracks it wide open. I'll put the bulletin out when we get back and you get on with working out some sort of reason for all this. Like you said, why these women – and why now.'

Out at Kilve, Lauren wasn't enjoying herself quite as much as she had expected. It was hot – unseasonably hot, according to Jonny who seemed to have run through the boost from his morning coffee and was nursing a rather unpleasant hangover. Lauren left him in the relative cool of the car, making her way over the rocks to the beach where she began to comb the edge of the sand, turning stones and occasionally banging a couple together to see if there was anything inside.

There was talk of restricting the public's right to search for fossils on the beach following a recent raid by professional fossil collectors from out of the area. Arriving in the late evening, they had worked under cover of darkness, hammering at the rocks and low cliffs and stripping several sections of beach of anything of interest. Even worse was the damage caused by the almost industrial scale of their efforts. Broken rocks and the remains of numerous specimens littered the coast the next morning, many damaged or crushed and discarded as commercially worthless.

Lauren had some sympathy with the authorities' plans but did not see why it should apply to her, or other local people who walked the beach, turning the rocks, admiring the many different specimens and only occasionally removing one for themselves. As she strolled her way along the shoreline, she spotted something interesting, half-covered by a fall of white scree. Scrambling across the litter of rocks, she hauled herself up onto a flat platform shaped by the waves, a reminder the sea reached the cliffs each high tide. Kneeling in front of the pile, she carefully picked her way through the lighter stones until a big, flat rock was exposed.

Her heart leaped with delight as she gazed at a large, perfectly preserved ammonite embedded on a rock of deep green. It was beautiful and she knew she had to have it, but it was huge – the largest specimen she had ever found. Sliding it clear of the remaining stones, Lauren stood and lifted the ammonite, puffing as she took its full weight. Holding it in front of her she began the precarious journey back down to the sands. Feet sliding and ankles rocking with the effort, her progress was measured in inches but finally she felt firm ground beneath her and she placed the fossil on the ground, thankful for a brief rest.

As she leaned against the rocks, now warm from the morning sun, she looked around her. Where was Jonny when she needed him? When sending out fierce mental instructions to her brother failed to bring him down to her aid, she heaved herself up again, lifted the ammonite and resumed her tortuous path across the shore and up towards the road where the car waited. Her shoulders felt as if they were coming loose from the sockets, her arms were shaking and she was covered in sweat by the time she made it to the top but Lauren was determined not to let her prize go, whatever it cost her.

As she emerged over the top of the cliffs, staggering and swaying with effort, Jonny leapt from the car and hurried towards her.

'Sis, hey – give me that,' he said.

Exhausted but triumphant, Lauren let him take the fossil, shambling after him as he carried it to car. Placing it safely in the boot, Jonny turned to his sister.

'Why didn't you call?' he asked. 'You could have hurt yourself, lugging that great thing all that way.'

Lauren decided not to tell him about climbing the cliff, something frowned on by most sensible adults. Jonny was a wonderful brother but he did tend to be a bit over-protective on occasions.

'I reckon I've had all my luck here today,' she said opening the passenger door and sliding into the front seat. 'Fancy going on somewhere else?'

Jonny was feeling a bit better after a quick snooze in the car, but he was relieved they were not going back down to the beach.

'Where do you fancy?' he asked reaching for the keys.

Lauren considered for a moment.

'I know is a terrible long way,' she said, 'but I got a real hankering to see Brean.'

Chapter Nine

Kevin caught the bus into Highpoint, something that had been a rare luxury in his past life as an unemployed probationer but was now a routine occurrence for him. The driver had pulled up and frowned at him suspiciously until he handed over the fare and made his way towards the back, sitting alone as he watched the landscape of the Levels flit past the window. It was so familiar to him, yet the changes were apparent, signs that were in contrast to his memories. Small things crept up on those living out on the great marsh but to his eyes the area was beginning to undergo a transformation.

Most obvious was the shift from older houses with small-holdings to clumps of modern, brick-built houses, huddling together around a raw, new piece of tarmac as if seeking shelter from the empty space around them. The bus ambled through the narrow lanes and Kevin had plenty of time to look over the low walls and see the gardens. Thin, patchy lawns were laid out around and behind the houses, the grass struggling to gain a foothold on the ancient soil of the Levels.

Kevin wasn't a great one for gardening but he looked in scorn at the feeble planting. Waste of growing land, as far as he could see. Not one of the few occupied dwellings had so much as a vegetable garden, let alone a run for a few chickens or rabbits. All that concrete and tarmac and stuff all over the ground was stupid too. Nowhere for the water to drain away when the rains came, for one thing, and there'd be no game or wildlife in that sterile environment. He had been away a while, but Kevin was a child of the Levels and he knew what was right and what was not. The new patches of housing, springing up like dry, crusty sores along the road, were most definitely not.

Turning his attention to his fellow passengers, Kevin noticed the driver seemed to be giving him rather too much attention, glancing in the mirror and frowning as he manoeuvred the vehicle around the lanes. No-one else seemed to be watching him so he slid off the seat and walked along the swaying aisle until he was opposite the driver's cab.

'Problem, mate?' he asked, dropping on to the bench seat at the front.

The driver kept his eyes firmly on the road ahead but lifted one hand from the steering wheel to point at a notice affixed to the front of the bus interior.

Kevin squinted at the sign, his lips slowly forming the words as he deciphered it.

'Do not – speak to the – driver or dis ... distr .. act his att .. en .. tion when the bus is in m ... motion,' he managed, spelling out the sounds. 'Right. Okay then. Just wondered why you was givin' me the eye, is all.'

The driver slowed and pulled the bus over to the side of the road, opening the doors for a woman who hauled herself up the stairs, puffing with the effort. Kevin sprang to his feet and offered a hand, receiving a smile and a nod in thanks.

'Just into town, please,' said the woman. Taking her ticket, she motioned for Kevin to move up a bit and practically fell on to the bench seat as the driver closed the doors and swung the bus back out onto the road.

'Oof,' she said, clutching a battered black shopping bag to her. 'Thank you. No manners, some people.' Here she scowled at the driver who ignored them both as he made as much speed as he could along the narrow, rutted road. 'I wondered when you was goin' to visit, Kevin,' she added giving him a sly glance.

Now, don't you look so surprised,' she added. 'I know your Mam – she's been a good friend to me and to my Charlie too.'

Kevin looked more closely at his travelling companion and then smiled.

'Mrs Dodds – I didn't recognise you for a minute. How's you doin' then?'

Lily Dodds nodded, squinting out of the window opposite as the bus trundled on towards town.

'A sight better now my Charlie's got a place in the hostel,' she said. She made it sound as if he'd got a scholarship to a rather nice college. 'I was getting' a bit worried about him, runnin' around with the wrong sort. They's good about keeping an eye on the lads in there and to be honest, is rather nice having my house back for a bit.'

Charlie and Kevin were old friends and Kevin knew how hard Lily had struggled to raise her young grandson. With his new-found maturity, Kevin appreciated how difficult it must have been for her to take on a wild boy like Charlie, especially as he seemed incapable of learning from his mistakes. His choice of friends had always been suspect – Kevin could mentally consign his younger self to that group – and, lacking any educational qualifications or noticeable skills, he was virtually unemployable in the current climate.

'So he's doin' all right?' he said.

Lily nodded again and then twisted round, staring out of the window over Kevin's shoulder.

'What?' asked Kevin, turning his head in an effort to see what had attracted her attention.

'What's he doin' out here?' muttered Lily fiercely. 'Up to no good, I'll be bound!'

Kevin got a glimpse of a figure trotting with seemingly little effort along the road. He could have sworn it was the same man he'd seen outside his house earlier.

'Nasty piece of work, he is,' Lily said. 'Bullies my Charlie – took his space by the window and was right threatening to 'um too. I was going to go talk to that warden chap but Charlie said not too, seein' as he was moving to another room anyway. Don't seem right though, just letting him get away with it.'

Good for Charlie, thought Kevin privately. It was about time he started sorting stuff for himself rather than letting his Gran do it for him. With the righteous conviction of the newly reformed, Kevin was happy to feel superior towards those less fortunate, to those left behind. When they arrived at the final stop in Highpoint, he helped Lily off the bus, promised to convey her best regards to his mother and, ignoring the surly driver, set off through the town, hands in his pockets and a spring in his step.

He stopped on the steps of the Cornhill and waited for his eyes to adjust to the relative gloom of the interior. The calls of the stall holders and chatter from the crowd bounced around the stone market hall, making his head ring and the scents of flowers, leather goods and fresh bread swirled about him, a heady rush of sensations. Feeling suddenly and unaccountably nostalgic, Kevin stepped into the cool space. It wasn't large or fancy but in his mind it was one of the best markets he'd seen in all his travels.

He was jolted out of his calm mood by a thump on the back. Swinging round, he found himself staring into the grinning face of Brian Morris.

'Wotcha Kevin!' said Brian. 'You back then? What was it like eh? Travelling and that.'

Kevin looked at Brian, a young man who had seemed rather intimidating before he left Highpoint. Someone he'd looked up to but at the same time treated with caution. Now he saw a dishevelled boy with a defiant but slightly crooked Mohican hair cut, his shoulders bent under the weight of a bag slung over his back. He could not remember what it was he had found so impressive.

'Brian – yeah. Just back for a few days. Bit of a quiet time afore we start the summer season so I thought I'd do a visit.' There was a pause as the enormous difference between their lives sank in. Brian seemed to shrink a little, diminished in his own eyes as he looked at the new, confident Kevin.

'What you got there then?' Kevin asked, more to break the uncomfortable silence than out of any real curiosity.

Brian tugged at the bag, his eyes darting round as if expecting the crowd to lean in and eavesdrop on his answer.

'I'll show yer, but not here,' he whispered theatrically. ''Tis a secret.' He glanced around once more and sloped off into the bright light shining down onto the market steps. Kevin hesitated but finally set off after him, striding to catch up as Brian hurried down the street towards the park beside the river Parrett. Together they ducked under the bridge carrying the main road, the roar of early holiday traffic echoing around them before emerging into dappled sunlight. There were a few groups of picnickers scattered around the open spaces and in the distance they could hear the sound of children splashing in the paddling pool, but the seats under the ancient oak tree were empty and offered a measure of privacy.

Once settled on the wooden bench in the shade, Brian opened his bag to display the battery and casing from his metal detector. Kevin blinked at it for a moment, singularly unimpressed.

'So what the hell's that then?' he asked finally.

Brian started explaining about the metal detector, his hands waving around with excitement as he detailed all the promising sites he had identified around the Levels. The battery lay on the ground between them, oozing gently over the grass.

Most of the ideas were pure fantasy, Kevin thought, but he was struck by Brian's plight. He could identify with the need to escape from his abusive father, the desire to take control over his own life. Kevin had always been sheltered from his father by Ada and never known that type of fear but he too had reached the point where he needed to make his own choices, even if that meant making his own mistakes. He didn't think for a moment that Brian was going to find anything of value with his metal detector but he felt compelled to offer him a hand.

'Don't know about that,' he said interrupting Brian's excited monologue. 'Looks a bit past it. You could try gettin' a new battery but chances are this'n's done a lot of damage. Rotted away some important bits, maybe. Might be better spendin' yer money on a place for you an' yer brother to stay. Then you'll be able to sign on an' try for jobs around town.'

Brian's face fell, disappointment visible in the sag of his shoulders, the droop of his head.

''Ent much of anything round here at the moment,' he said. 'An' if there was, don't reckon no-one's gonna take a chance on me, is they?' He lifted his face and stared defiantly at Kevin. There was envy in his eyes as he took in the clean tee shirt, new jacket and smart black jeans his old friend was wearing. Next to Brian, Kevin, one of the lowest of the hierarchy in the Fair, looked pretty successful.

Kevin fished in his jacket pocket and came out with some money.

'Here,' he said. 'I still reckon you should try for a place in town but if you is set on repairing this,' he gestured towards the battery. 'Well, you give it a go.'

Brian stared at the money in his fist. Used to only small change in his pocket, if anything at all, he jiggled the unfamiliar feel of the new pound coins. His eyes widened as he saw the edge of a fiver peering out from the palm of his hand.

'Just – use it, will yer?' said Kevin getting up and brushing his new jeans down. 'Don't go off an' spend it on "natch". Promise me?'

Brian nodded his head vigorously, still too startled to speak.

'Yeah, right – promise,' he finally managed.

Kevin walked through the gardens and under the road, struggling with the temptation to look back over his shoulder.

He had little faith in Brian's ability to resist the lure of 'natch', the lethal natural cider sold at many farm gates around the area. For a moment he thought about going back and accompanying him to the large electrical superstore on the edge of town, for even Brian's plan for the metal detector was better than drinking away his little windfall, but Kevin resisted that impulse too.

He had done a lot of thinking and a lot of talking to his new friends in the travelling Fair and he had come to the realisation it wasn't possible to make people change. It was fine and good to give them a hand but in the end they needed to do it for themselves.

'Don't stick otherwise,' he muttered to himself as he headed back to the market in search of something nice for dinner. 'Don't mean as much so it don't stick.' He'd learned that the hard way, almost losing everything through a combination of bad judgement and bad luck. He hoped Brian would be more fortunate.

Out on Brean Sands, Margie had dried herself off, rinsed her muddy feet under the cold-water tap beside the road and surprised Alex by fishing in the back of the car and producing a picnic hamper.

'I'm impressed,' said Alex. 'Really – I thought only my family still had anything like this.' She ran her hands over the smooth, woven willow, admiring the finish on the handle. It had an over-the-shoulder strap as well as a suitcase style handle and Margie slipped it over her head and settled it on her back before locking the boot.

'So, where's a nice, quiet spot for some lunch?' she asked handing Alex a bright red tartan rug.

Alex stood for a moment, considering their options. As the sun rose in the sky, more cars began to appear, crawling along the track towards the lure of the beach. It was going to be hot, she thought, despite the beginning of a breeze coming in from up the estuary to the east. Somewhere sheltered from the wind with a bit of shade – and far enough away to have some privacy. Alex loved her mother, enjoyed Sue's company and was passionate about her work but she did miss the quiet of her own space sometimes. At the moment the world seemed rather full of other people. She glanced at Margie and smiled. Right now she was with the one other person she wanted to spend her time with.

'Back along the beach,' she said pointing to the dunes rising from the sand. 'We need to go a fair way because the holiday camp people often come out in the afternoon. The damn Bluecoats sometimes drag a load of kids out to play games on the sand.' She pulled a face. 'Don't get me wrong,' she added hastily. 'I like kids – I just can't eat a whole one.'

Margie blinked at her for a moment and then burst out laughing.

'So we go down a good way and let's hope you like the food I've got made up in here, shall we?'

Alex grinned at her. 'Believe me, just having someone else make lunch is a rare treat. Unless you can cook as badly as Sue – well, it'll be wonderful.'

'Sue?' asked Margie, a note of concern in her voice.

'She's my room-mate,' Alex explained over her shoulder, already heading off to the far end of the dunes. 'She's a terrific friend but her cooking – oh, I can't tell you how bad it is! I always cook at home, in self-defence.' She missed the flicker of disappointment as it ran over Margie's face, intent as she was on crossing the sands without tripping or getting too much in her shoes.

Alex loved the beach but hated sand in her shoes – or any of her clothes. As a child, on holiday in Wales, she had once changed her clothes six times before running out of sand-free options. She had spent the rest of the day sulking in a rock pool until carried back to the car by her father. In fairness, she had been only five years old but her family had never forgotten and still teased her about it on the rare occasions they got together for a day out.

It was a long trudge to Alex's selected spot but when they arrived and spread out the rug, the view was wonderful and they were sheltered on three sides from both the breeze and prying eyes. Margie flopped down onto the sand and stared out at the sea, smiling with delight.

'Now, this is just what I imagined,' she said happily. 'When I was thinkin' of moving down here, this is just like the picture I had in my head.'

'Why are you thinking of moving?' asked Alex.

'Don't enjoy my work in Bristol no more,' said Margie. 'Looked around and most prisons, they's moving in the same direction. Too many inmates, banged up most of the time. Is stupid and is dangerous. Not many places like Shepton Mallet around, where there's a focus on training. What's the point, lockin' 'em up for all that time and then kicking them loose with no chance of a job or nothing? No surprise they keep coming back. Is the only time some of 'em get a decent meal or a roof over their heads for more'n a couple of days on the trot.'

She snorted in disgust and turned her attention to the picnic basket, now lying beside them on the sand.

'I should have asked you afore – you're not veggie are you?'

Alex laughed and shook her head. 'Oh no,' she said. 'Big old carnivore, I am.'

Margie let out a sigh of relief as she set out plates, cutlery and two glasses before lifting a foil-wrapped chicken and a tub of mixed salad onto the rug. A small French stick of bread followed, with condiments in neat, individual pots. Alex was more than impressed.

'This must have taken you ages,' she said.

Margie shrugged her shoulders. 'Just a bit of organisation,' she said modestly, pouring some fizzy water into the glasses. 'And 'ent like there's much to do of an evening, with all the others bein' local so they all go home. Is a nice enough lodging I've got but not much goin' on.'

The chicken, Alex noted, was home-cooked, not a coloured and flavoured supermarket offering.

'They let you use the kitchen?' she asked.

127

Margie nodded. 'Got its own little kitchenette attached,' she said. 'Just as well, seeing some of offerings in the local pub.'

The women set to with a will, demolishing the salad and eating the meat with their fingers. As Alex sat back, sighing contentedly, Margie reached into the hamper and pulled out a bottle of wine.

'Ooh,' said Alex. She was very fond of wine, though often it did not seem so fond of her. As Sue had remarked on one notable occasion, she couldn't drink a hamster under the table.

'Tempting,' she said. 'Very tempting but I've got to drive and, to be honest, it goes straight to my head.'

Margie grinned and shook the bottle gently.

'I thought maybe we could drink it this evening, at yours?'

Alex closed her eyes for an instant and sighed.

'We'd have to share it with my mother,' she said finally.

There was a moment's silence before Margie said, 'I didn't have you down as someone who still lived with their parents.' She tried to make a joke of it but only managed to sound a bit critical.

'I don't,' said Alex. 'She's living with *me* – at least for the moment. She . . . okay, being totally honest – she's just got out of prison and won't go home until my father and brothers apologise.'

Margie's mouth fell open and she stared at Alex in astonishment. Whatever she had expected to find out about her new friend, it certainly wasn't this.

'You are a bit of dark horse, 'ent you,' Margie managed finally.

'Not half as much as my mother,' Alex retorted. Then their eyes met and the pair of them collapsed into giggles.

'Alright, alright – tell me,' Margie gasped, lying back in the sand.

Alex related the tale of her mother's protest at Brightlingsea, her fury at the males in the family who tried to pay her fines and her recent incarceration at HMP East Sutton Park.

Margie listened, fascinated by the family drama that was so different from anything her relatives might do, yet so familiar in its echoes of her working life. An awful lot of people ran foul of the law through bad luck, bad choices or a single, desperate act. If they used their time inside to reflect and maybe find better solutions to their problems, they need not ever return, but the opportunities to do so were limited. It was one reason she wanted to move to Shepton Mallet, with its regime of training and education.

'So, there you have it,' said Alex. 'My criminal mother. I don't know how long she intends to stay but for the moment she's firmly ensconced in my spare room and shows no inclination to head back home.'

'She sounds something special,' said Margie. 'I like to think I'd be brave enough to stand up for something I believe in like that but I don't reckon I'd cope on the other side of the bars. You should be right proud.'

Alex blinked in surprise. She hadn't been sure what to expect from her revelation but it wasn't such whole-hearted approval.

'Will it cause you any problems, at work – you know, consorting with a newly released prisoner?' she asked.

Margie shook her head firmly. 'Not like she's one of mine,' she said. 'And who's to know? Is your family business and is not like she's a desperate bank robber or nothing. Unless you're holding out on me?'

Alex laughed. 'No, just the public order stuff,' she said. 'I wish I could be as confident of my lot at the probation office. I'm not sure what they'd say if they knew about her – especially as we're due a new senior soon.' There was a pause before she finished rather wistfully, 'I've not had a lot of luck with my seniors so far.'

'Was it just this last one you found so difficult?' asked Margie. 'Only sometimes if you expect someone to behave badly they always seem to. Like with the lads in prison. You behave like you expect trouble and they'll act up for sure. Start kind of neutral and often they'll be quite different. Mind you,' she added, screwing her eyes up against the glare of the sun. 'Don't mean you shouldn't watch your back, just in case.'

Alex looked out over the beach, turning this over in her mind but suddenly her attention was captured by two figures walking towards the dunes.

'Bloody hell!' she shouted, jumping to her feet and kicking sand over the remains of the picnic. 'I don't believe this!'

Lauren sauntered along the beach, revelling in the warm spring sunshine. It was very bright and she regretted leaving her dark glasses in the car but despite that, it was turning into a perfect Saturday. Suddenly Jonny stopped just ahead of her.

'Hey, look Sis,' he said, pointing towards the sand dunes. 'Isn't that Alex over there?'

Lauren squinted through the sunlight at the two figures seated in the shade of the dunes. Then one of them leapt to their feet, gesturing towards her and Jonny.

'Oh heck,' said Lauren. 'Looks like it is. And I don't think we're going to get much of a welcome, neither. Come on Jonny – let's go back the other way.'

A furious yell from the figure in the dunes caused Jonny to hesitate and Lauren to start back to the car as fast as she could. Torn between the two, Jonny turned from side to side, as if watching a frantic but invisible tennis match. Lauren was not slowing down, he noticed. Alex, on the other hand, was heading his way. Mentally cursing his sister, he walked towards the dunes, with what he hoped was an innocent and welcoming smile on his face.

'We didn't expect to see you here,' he called when a furious Alex was still a few yards away.

She stopped, frowning at him. 'Just co-incidence then?' she said mockingly.

Jonny nodded. 'Honest Alex, we was out at Kilve but Lauren found a huge ammonite and was pretty knackered after hauling it up to the car so we decided to come down here. Bit more restful, we reckoned.'

Alex was not totally convinced and the sight of Lauren

130

fleeing the scene did nothing to reassure her but she was very fond of both of them and didn't want to make a fuss in front of Margie.

'We're off anyway, I reckon,' said Jonny, gesturing towards the figure of his sister. 'Where you goin' next? Wouldn't want to keep doing this, would we?'

Alex laughed and shook her head. 'I suppose not,' she said ruefully, glancing over her shoulder to see Margie making her way across the sand towards them.

'Better introduce me or your friend might think you're trying to keep her away from us,' said Jonny, a smile on his face to take any sting out of his words. 'Hello. I'm Jonny – nice to meet you,' he said smoothly as Margie arrived at Alex's side.

'Oh, hello – I'm Margie,' she said, a little flustered. 'Um, who was..?' she pointed in the direction of the rapidly receding Lauren.

'That was my sister,' said Jonny. 'She's a bit shy but I'm sure you'll get a chance to meet her soon. I'd better go after her – I've got the car key.' He grinned wickedly at Alex, threw another charming smile in Margie's direction and set off towards the car park leaving Alex confounded by the whole encounter.

'He seems very nice,' said Margie as they picked their way back to the remains of their abandoned picnic.

'You have no idea,' said Alex. 'I've rather spoilt the rest of this – I'm really sorry. It was just such a shock, seeing them. To be honest . . . ' she paused, wondered if it were too late to back out and decided it was. 'Well, Lauren wanted to come with me today, to meet you. But I wouldn't let her and I thought she might have been following us.'

Margie looked at her for a moment.

'Why didn't you want her to come along?' she asked softly.

Alex took a deep breath before plunging on.

'I wanted you to myself, at least today,' she said. 'I really like Lauren – I like all my friends – but I hoped this might be a special sort of day – just us.' To her horror she felt her voice wobble and for a moment feared she was going to cry. This time the pause seemed to stretch between them for ever until finally she felt Margie's hand on her shoulder.

'It is,' she said. 'I think maybe we both been trying too hard but, in spite of that, 'tis girt special.'

Alex grinned at the sudden, thick accent and the day was bright once more.

Kevin hadn't been gone long before there was a tap on the door and Tom poked his head into Ada's kitchen. She was sitting at the table, sipping tea from her favourite china mug and reading from the last week's local paper.

'Come on in then,' she said. 'You can smell tea bein' made, you can.'

'Reckon I will, if you's offering,' said Tom. He lifted a mug from the top shelf, poured some milk into it from the fridge and replaced the bottle before sitting opposite her.

'Didn't know you was that superstitious,' said Ada waspishly as he added tea from the pot.

Tom stopped pouring and stared at her before finishing and placing the pot carefully on a mat in the middle of the table.

'I heard,' he said adding three spoons of sugar and stirring thoughtfully. 'I heard if you put milk in first it stops you having ginger kids.' He took a slurp, sighed with pleasure and raised an eyebrow at her over the mug.

'Seems Iris should'a tried that then,' said Ada folding her paper and putting it down next to her elbow. 'Could have saved her a might of trouble.'

Tom stopped mid-slurp and lowered his mug carefully.

'Didn't know you was one for gossip, Ada,' he said.

Ada pushed her chair back and rose from the table, gathering her empty mug and turning to rinse it in the sink.

'Anyone with a pair of eyes could see there was something odd about young Newt,' she said scornfully. 'Decent enough lad mind, not like his brother. *That* one took after his Dad, no matter what Iris done to set him right.'

'What about Newt?' asked Tom. 'Does he take after his Dad?'

Ada turned and stared at him. 'Nice try, Tom. Like you said, I 'ent one for gossip, so as far as I'm concerned, was his hair I was talkin' about and I don't know no more'n that.'

Tom smiled and finished the last of his tea.

'If you say so,' he said mildly. 'You ready to give us a hand with this wire then? Ol' Bert, he's a bit eager to get his stud goat off the farm for a bit. Says he's got a young'n he's trying out and they fight something awful. Having trouble keeping 'em apart, with both of 'em pulling at the fences,' he added hastily seeing the look of alarm on Ada's face. 'Don't you worry now, is right placid when he's on his own, this old'n.'

Out in the garden, new fence posts stood awaiting the electric wire and reinforced metal netting that would, hopefully, keep the goat corralled safely and away from Ada's crops. Tom had set the new boundaries stretching from the edge of Ada's official patch several yards out in each direction, the stream bordering the far end of the new enclosures.

'Need to put some along there too,' said Tom, hefting the shiny rolls of chicken wire and dropping them on the rough scrubland. 'Goats is quite capable of wading downstream a bit and coming out on your seed bed.'

'You do that,' said Ada. 'I need this,' she waved her arm over the densely planted land. 'Don't look much but is what I live on most the time.'

Privately Tom thought it looked grand. It was one of the most efficient and productive cottage gardens he'd ever seem and he was full of admiration for Ada's efforts. Working in companionable silence, they rapidly strung the netting, two layers thick, between the new fence posts and Tom set to laying the electric wire around the inside whilst Ada examined the fixings on the posts, hammering home metal staples and adding a few extra, just to be sure all was as goat-proof as possible.

As the sun rose over the garden, they stopped for lunch, sitting in the cool kitchen and eating the fresh salad and a vegetable pie Ada had prepared the night before. After another cup of tea, they went back to work, constructing a portable but robust goat shelter from some old pallets Tom swore he'd found just lying around and some heavy-duty plastic from empty feed sacks. It wasn't elegant but it was certainly efficient and, with the addition of some straw liberated from the edge of the field on the other side of the stream it looked quite comfortable.

'You got an old bucket?' Tom asked. 'Metal if possible. Plastic don't last too long round goats. They don't generally eat it but once it gets stepped on, well, is not good for much.'

Ada rummaged through one of her sheds and produced a large galvanised bucket.

'For water,' said Tom. 'He'll need it changing couple of times a day. Otherwise he's more likely to try and get to the stream, if he gets thirsty. I'll bring a trough when I come next.'

'Trough?' asked Ada. 'I thought he was goin' to eat all this.' She gestured towards the newly enclosed rough land. 'Was the whole point, I thought.'

Tom shrugged, suggesting he was newly wise to the ways of goats.

'Mostly he'll eat all this,' he said. 'He just needs a bit of other stuff, for vitamins and such I think. Ol' Bob, he's sending some goat nuts over to keep him healthy. A couple of scoops a day is all he's needing.'

Ada nodded her head. This goat was turning out to be a bit more bother than she's expected but still – her eyes took in the newly fenced areas. Tom had been bolder than she would have been and together they added almost as much again to the size of her garden. She was already planning what to do with all that wonderful land. Fruit trees, she thought. She had a longing for fruit trees but they needed so much space and up to now she'd needed every inch for her vegetables. Maybe some soft fruit too – that was a real indulgence, taking up space for just a few weeks of produce – but what produce.

She snapped her attention back to the present, nodding more firmly this time.

'I can manage that,' she said.

Tom looked at her and smiled. It was a long time since he'd seen her look so relaxed, he thought. Life had been somewhat relentless for Ada and she had experienced some horrible things over the years. It pleased him to make her happy and, just for a few moments, he forgot his recent loss. He was happy too.

That afternoon Samuel retired to his room, closing the curtains and revelling in the solitude. One of his room mates had started to follow him but a fierce glare sent him scurrying back to the games room where a day-long tournament was underway around the battered pool table. It was the quiet weekend, mid-way between dole cheques, and few of the residents had any money left to squander on real cigarettes or a trip to the pub. In an attempt to keep them from drifting around the town causing trouble, the assistant warden had arranged a series of competitions to keep them amused.

About ten young men gathered in the recreation area, glad of the distraction as they vied for the small prizes on offer. The sound of pool balls being pocketed, bars on the table football machine spinning and rising shouts of laughter grated on him and he was happy to leave them to their inane pleasures. He lay on his bed, relaxing in the cool breeze from the river as it stirred the curtains, clearing the air of the smell of three fellow residents. There was a lot to think about.

Everything was in place for his next excursion, safely hidden out on the old airfield. Planning, he knew, was vital to success and despite the growing urge to act, the pull towards speedy gratification, he knew he had to wait a little longer. The travelling was proving difficult, for the distances were greater than he was used to and the terrain unfamiliar and potentially hazardous. He had not come close to being caught yet and he intended to keep it that way, with a few simple precautions.

Leave nothing behind, he thought. Take nothing with you when you leave. Be silent and invisible and always check, double check their routine. Patience was the key to it all. And night – the darkness of night was his friend. Closing his eyes he let his imagination wander as he drifted off into a world of his own making. First there was the watching, then the visualising where the whole event was set out and planned. Then came the imagining, the pleasure that came from anticipation of past acts revisited and new, stronger actions savoured. But soon, very soon, it would be time.

Chapter Ten

The office was buzzing when Alex arrived for work after the weekend. Relieved of the burden of court duty for the next few months, thanks to Gordon's intervention, she found she had time to set out some detailed ideas for workshops and groups. Photography was high on the list and she hoped to persuade Gordon to let her attend the local auction later in the month.

According to the list of lots, there was a box of darkroom equipment on offer and there were always old cameras for sale. Highpoint was blessed with a large number of independent shops, family businesses still holding their own against the relentless incursions of the chain stores, and one of these was an old fashioned photographic business. As well as offering a wide range of photography ('Wedding's, Christenings and Masonic Functions a Speciality', it boasted ungrammatically), it stocked the widest range of film sizes Alex had encountered, including several that would work in a Box Brownie. She was confident that, whatever the cameras' specifications, they would find a film to fit.

First thing on Monday, however, Gordon called a full staff meeting.

Alex tramped up the stairs from her tiny office in the old storeroom on the ground floor, joining her colleagues as they settled, somewhat apprehensively, in the day room. Sue arrived in the nick of time, sliding into a chair next to Lauren's special seat and puffing with the effort of running up two flights of stairs.

'Without the benefit of coffee, mind,' she whispered to Lauren in response to her assistant's raised eyebrows. 'I couldn't find anything in the kitchen this morning.' She shot Alex an accusing glance, as if suspecting her of hiding the coffee on purpose. '*Someone's* been tidying up!' Alex pretended she hadn't heard, though she had a good idea who the 'someone' might be. She resolved to leave a few minutes early and have a quiet word with her mother before Sue got home.

The murmuring amongst the staff died down as Gordon entered, a slim grey folder under his arm. Casting a quick smile around the gathering by way of welcome, he wasted little time on formalities.

'Thank you for all attending so promptly,' he said opening the folder. 'I am pleased to be able to inform you the new senior probation officer has been appointed and will begin work on the first of July. This is, of course, a Monday – eight weeks from today, in fact, and I expect everyone to be ready for their arrival.'

There was a hum of conversation before Eddie Stroud asked what they all wanted to know.

'Any idea who it is, Gordon?'

Gordon laid the folder on the table in front of him, pursing his lips before replying.

'She is from out of the area,' he said.

That was the first surprise. Although there were a number of female SPOs, Highpoint had always had a male senior.

'I believe she is from London,' he continued. 'Until recently she was working as a training consultant and has been instrumental in formulating some of the revised policy and protocols that are currently being instituted.'

Alex blinked at Gordon in surprise. Normally the most down-to-earth man she knew, he was suddenly talking fluent 'management-speak'. There was a message hidden in amongst all that jargon, and she was not sure she liked the sound of it one little bit. She raised her hand to attract his attention.

'Is she an experienced senior?' she asked. 'I mean – has she run an office before or is she mainly a training person?'

There were nods around the room as the staff considered the implications of a pure theorist trying to run the many and diverse operations of an office as complex as Highpoint.

'I am sure she has all the skills and experience we need,' said Gordon sternly. 'Headquarters seem particularly pleased with her appointment and she will expect – and receive – our full support and assistance during the early days when she is finding her feet.' He looked around the room, stopping to focus first on Alex and then Lauren. There was a moment's silence, broken by the door flying open.

'Sorry I'm a bit late,' said Ricky. 'Have I missed anything?'

'Saved our bacon, he did,' said Lauren at lunch time. She had a box of home-made sandwiches in front of her and was munching her way through them with an air of grim determination. 'Don't know why Gordon was giving me the eye, though. I 'ent said nothing. Not like you, going on about experience and so on.' She nodded towards Alex before taking another bite.

'That is because you are a noted troublemaker,' said Sue. 'No – *the* noted troublemaker in this office.' She cast an envious eye over Lauren's sandwiches. It seems she had been unable to find anything for lunch in the kitchen either.

Taking pity on her, Alex divided her own sandwiches in half and offered Sue the box. 'I was only wondering how much we might have to do if they're new to it all,' she said. 'It can be a bit tricky, especially if they're used to knowing everything and being the one to tell everyone else how it works.

After all, training's all right but you learn the job on placement – and then you find yourself in a real office with a real case load and you realise you know bugger all and have to learn it all over again properly.'

Lauren shrugged, glancing over at Ricky who was sitting with his back to them, pointedly going through his court files for the afternoon session.

'Seems some don't recognise that,' she said. 'I hear tell this new senior's an old friend of his.' She jerked her chin in Ricky's direction. 'If'n she's been mixed up in his training, don't look too promising, now does it?'

Alex waved her hand at Lauren to warn her Pauline was just behind them. The senior admin officer was a stickler for professional conduct and criticising the senior, especially before they'd even started, was not likely to go down too well with her.

'Let's just wait and see, shall we,' said Sue with uncharacteristic tact. 'After what's happened here recently, all they really need to do is keep their clothes on and cover the court sessions if we're short-handed. I mean, how hard can that be?'

Out on the boundary of the old airfield, Brian sat in the shade, resting from the effort of hauling a new battery all the way back from Highpoint. Resisting the siren call of a cider-drenched weekend, he had made the rounds of the hardware stores, Kevin's largesse clutched tightly in his hand, until an old-fashioned ironmonger unearthed a replacement for him from the back of a dim, dusty cupboard. He'd even given Brian a discount, 'On account of it being a bit out of date,' he said. Closer examination showed the battery was marked 'Best before Aug 1985', but Brian reasoned it was still sealed up so how was the electricity going to get out anyway? Science, along with a depressing number of other things, was not his strong point.

There had been a bit of change left over from this purchase and so he'd caught the morning bus out to Westonzoyland, sitting under the suspicious eyes of the driver who counted the stops to make sure he didn't try to ride past his ticket.

'What's with you lot?' the driver asked as Brian got and rang the bell. "Ent seen none of you for months and suddenly you's all flitting around all over the place. Seen that Kevin, Saturday just gone. He out again, then?'

'That's all you know,' said Brian scornfully. He's off working. Proper job he got, with the Fair. Just back to see his mum for a few days, he said.'

The driver raised his eyebrows in disbelief at this. In his opinion, Kevin, in common with Brian and most of the other young men he saw hanging around in town, was unemployable. He'd pack the lot of them off to join the army if he could. What the country needed, he thought as he watched Brian lurching over the stile and off towards the airfield, what it really needed was another war like the Falklands. Short, successful and far away – something to restore a bit of pride in the nation. He didn't continue this train of thought consciously but a part of him also considered it no bad thing if it thinned the ranks of the unemployed a bit too. He swung the heavy wheel to the right, pulled out into the middle of the narrow road and set off towards Middlezoy, dust rising behind him to hang in the warm, still air long after he was gone from sight.

Once he'd stopped panting, Brian scrambled to his feet and set off across the long patch of open concrete towards the place where he had hidden the metal detector. He was feeling relaxed, pleased and a little proud of himself so, in the midst of an introspective haze, did not take proper note of his surroundings. He barely registered the angry shouting off to his right before the growling of an engine made him leap up in fear. He looked around frantically. For a moment he froze in terror as a two-seater plane touched down behind him, rolling straight towards where he was standing. Mouth open and eyes popping, he was rooted to the spot as the aircraft hurtled down the runway, the propellers still spinning as the pilot tried to steer away from him. At the last moment something hit him, slamming his inert body out of the way of the aircraft as it roared by, close enough to feel the wind from its passing.

The man who had shoved him out of harm's way stood up and brushed himself off.

'Girt stupid fool!' he said. 'Now I missed the number.' He shook his fist in the direction of the little plane which was now once again airborne and heading away over the trees towards Bristol.

Brian lay in the dust, winded and still in shock from his brush with death. The man looked down at him, shaking his head in disgust.

'Get up will yer? There's more coming and I can't be charging nothing if you is in the way. Go on, bugger off. 'Tis private property, this.' He turned on his heel and marched off towards a chair set up beside the concrete runway, stopping to retrieve a notebook from the ground on the way.

Brian struggled to his feet, his head buzzing from the force of the impact, and limped slowly into the safety of the surrounding trees. He knew the airfield was supposed to be private property – he passed the signs every time he came out here – but he'd never heard anyone actually lay claim to it before. Resting in the shadows, he watched as the man sprang to his feet at the approaching drone of another light aircraft. He had a wooden paddle painted bright yellow with black stripes and he waved it at the pilot as the tiny plane circled round, touched its wheels down and then, with a roar, took off back over the Levels.

Dropping the paddle, the man scribbled something in his notebook, glanced at his watch and added the time to his records before sitting back down to wait for the next arrival. Despite his recent scare, Brian was intrigued. Surely this man had said something about charging the planes. Sitting in the sun and getting up occasionally to wave a stick didn't seem much like work to Brian. He thought maybe he could manage that, if he could find out how the money arrived and from where.

'Thought I told you to bugger off,' said the man as Brian approached his chair.

'I was just interested,' said Brian casually. Now he got a good look, the man wasn't much older than he was, a bit overweight with a red face and thin yellow hair. Not so intimidating close up. Still, he'd packed quite a wallop when landing on top of him, so Brian kept a bit of a distance between them.

'Always thought this belonged to them Ministry of Defence lot,' Brian continued. 'Signs say that, and was used in the war by the Yanks. Remember my Grandad saying about them all hanging around town with their cigs and sweets, chatting up anything in a skirt.'

'That's as may be,' said the man, squinting up at him from his chair. 'Was my family's land, out here on the open moor and when they give up the base we wanted it back. Is my Aunt's land by rights and all these planes, they come here, do a landing and take off for training. Costs 'em a lot more, doing that up Bristol or over Exeter so I reckon is a bargain, couple of quid a time. I takes the numbers and send a bill off to the flying schools every couple of weeks. Long as I got the paddle, they's had warning this is a proper airfield. Informed consent, see. If'n they land, they've agreed to pay.'

In the distance another plane droned into view and the man leaped to his feet, shoving Brian out of the way as he waved the landing paddle at the pilot, who responded with a rude gesture through the cockpit window.

'That's goin' to cost you a fiver,' muttered the man, scribbling frantically in his notebook. 'What you still here for?' He glared at Brian, who finally took the hint and turned away, sauntering off across the runway with his hands in his pockets. 'And get off my runway!'

Brian carried on walking across the cracked surface until he reached the tree line. There he spotted the remains of an overgrown path running parallel to the landing strip and he continued along this, dodging the occasional patches of nettles, until he reached the back of the mound where his precious metal detector was hidden. A quick glance around showed that the owner – if indeed he was the owner – was busy with his notebook and Brian slipped out of the shadows and dug around under the branches and leaves for a moment. His hands came away empty and he scrabbled in the dust, shoving the covering stones and twigs in all directions before finally slumping to the ground in despair. With a groan, he dropped his head in his hands as he accepted the metal detector was gone.

Another plane touched down and departed with a waggle of its wings before Brian found the energy to clamber to his feet. He hoisted the bag with the now-redundant battery onto his aching shoulder, resisting the urge to hurl the useless thing into the undergrowth. Slowly, each footstep dragging in the dust, he made his way back along the runway towards the road.

'Hey – you looking for the old metal thing that was hid over there?' called the plane man.

Brian stopped and turned slowly to face him.

'Maybe,' he said. 'You 'ent got it have you?'

The plane man laughed. 'Not I,' he said. 'Got better things to do with my time than mucking around with one of them stupid things. Still, I seen the lad as took it. Was shaking it about a bit and I don't reckon it worked but he took it anyway, maybe to sell for scrap. Was yours then?'

Brian nodded mutely. It really was gone, taken by some unknown passer-by out searching for scrap – or anything else they might be able to sell. Brian had subsisted on the deposit coins from returned bottles he'd salvaged from bins in the parks before now. He knew the detector would fetch a few quid even in its damaged state and with no battery. He dropped the bag on the ground, sick of lugging it around. For the first time he regretted the money he'd spent on it, counting it instead in pints of cider and cheap packets of crisps.

The plane man nodded to the bag lying in the dirt.

'What's in there?' he asked.

Brian shrugged. 'New battery,' he said miserably. 'Thought I might repair it. Give it a go, any road. Got no use for this stupid bloody thing now though. Don't see the sense in hauling it all the way back.' A feeling of utter misery engulfed him as he remembered he didn't even have enough money left for the bus. Kicking the bag in fury he turned and began to walk off.

'Why not go see the lad 'as took it,' suggested the plane man. 'Could do a deal, perhaps?'

'I didn't see him,' Brian pointed out. 'You saw him but I don't know who the hell he was or where he's gone to.'

'Well, I told him he were trespassing,' said the plane man. 'He laughed, said to go on an' report him 'cos weren't much more they could do seeing as he was already in the hostel at Highpoint anyway. Skinny lad, he was. Curly hair – bit younger'n you but not much. Had a red mark on one hand – looked like he'd had a burn or something there.'

A slow smile spread across Brian's face as he recognised the description. Charlie, he thought. Little Charlie Dodds from the probation hostel. He knew him, of course, and he was sure Charlie could be persuaded to hand over his find, if he could get to the hostel before he had time to dispose of the booty. His face fell again as he contemplated the long walk – and the damn battery.

The plane man watched Brian closely, reading the emotions as they flickered across his face.

'How'd you get out here anyway?' he asked. 'Long way out from anywhere – less you's from Westonzoyland and I don't recall seein' you around there much.'

'Come out from Highpoint,' said Brian miserably. 'Got the bus, far as I could but I don't have no fare back now. Is a bitch, carrying that thing, but that detector 'ent no good without 'un.'

The plane man nodded understandingly and thought for a moment. 'Tell you what, I'm starving. Was out here almost afore sunrise and is a long time since breakfast. Last few planes is coming over the next half hour, then is a break 'til about two this afternoon. You can read, can't you?'

Brian nodded.

'Well then, you take this here paddle an' get the numbers so as I can get summat to eat and I'll have time to drive you back home. Deal?'

Brian took the wooden paddle and stepped over to the chair where the notebook resided.

'Why you doing this for me?' he asked suspiciously.

The plane man shrugged. 'Like I said, I'm right hungry. 'Sides, you's at least willing to put some effort into something, even if 'tis probably a waste of time. 'Ent no fun, being unemployed – been there myself for a time. Some stranger gave me a hand so I is just passing it on.'

There was a moment's hesitation and then Brian grinned.

'Deal,' he said happily.

Gordon considered Alex's request for a couple of hours out of the office and came up with what he thought was the perfect solution.

'We'll call it part of the life skills programme,' he said. 'You go to the auction with the group so they can see how this sort of buying works. Get them to think about how to bid properly and you can start them considering how they spend their money and the importance of researching a purchase, not just acting on impulse. You could try the weekly market too – let them see food in the raw, so to speak. They might even realise it's a good thing to speak in turn rather than all at once.' He sat back looking mightily pleased with himself.

Alex suppressed a groan. She had some rather tricky clients enrolled on the life skills option. Those with less than usual social graces, some who had difficulties with anger and several who were just plain perverse. The thought of dragging them around the market with her – let alone the sale room – made her contemplate resignation.

'It would be a useful lesson for them,' Gordon continued. He was well aware of Alex's reluctance but he was not going to back down on the issue. If she wanted a chance to set

146

up the planned darkroom, she was going to have to earn it, and justify the time and money spent too. Gordon had been watching the changes in probation practice for some time and unlike the rest of the officers, he read the fortnightly bulletins from cover to cover. He had a bad feeling about what was coming, though his position as acting senior prevented him from sharing his concerns openly. Alex didn't realise it but he was trying to protect her and the day centre.

'There is no guarantee we will be able to continue with the centre,' he said. 'It is still experimental and the new management team may decide to change our provision – or even scrap it entirely.'

There was a ghastly silence as Alex stared at him, open mouthed.

'That would be the worst-case scenario,' Gordon continued smoothly. 'I would hope the value of your excellent work and the level of success with a high tariff and notoriously difficult group will be recognised. I think, however, we should ensure everything is done . . . by the book, shall we say.'

The equipment allocation he offered was not exactly lavish but times were hard for many people and Alex hoped there would be a lack of interest in the photographic equipment. Deciding to make the best of a bad job, she scribbled down some notes for a preliminary session when the group met that evening. She had started running some groups later in the day when a couple of clients took places on the community programme, a government-sponsored work scheme ostensibly offering experience at 'the going rate for the job'. The going rate for every job seemed to be around £15 a day, with many of the 'trainees' working only three days each week. They got a bit more than they had on the dole but not much, and they lost their entitlement to some of the fringe benefits that helped make life bearable. Still, Alex thought it was something that should be encouraged – any experience of work could only help her charges in the future and it offered some of them the chance to engage with the community in a more positive way than most had previously.

It did mean some of them were struggling to meet their commitments at the day centre, however, and rather than have them turn down what was often the closest thing to a job they had ever been offered, Alex undertook some rescheduling, opening both the main centre and the workshop for a couple of evenings each week. Trading heavily on her colleagues' good will, she had managed to cover all the groups without needing any additional staff but this was probably not really sustainable in the long term and she was especially concerned about what was likely to happen over the summer.

She could see it all – officers off on holiday, new priorities flooding forth from headquarters in Taunton, larger case-loads for everyone and precious little money to attract someone who could contribute more than basic baby-sitting skills to the day-centre experiment. She set her notes aside with a sigh. There was nothing she could do until the new senior arrived and worrying would only take valuable time and energy. Think positively, she told herself sternly. The telephone on her desk rang and she picked it up, answering absently.

'Alex? Hi, am I interrupting anything?' said the voice of Dave Brown. Without waiting for her reply he hurried on, 'I wonder if I might pick your brains a bit?'

Alex wasn't sure she had much in the way of brains to offer but gave him a non-committal grunt by way of encouragement. She was very fond of Dave and besides, he had come to her rescue out on the Levels earlier in the year, arriving in time to apprehend the nasty little drug dealer called Max who was threatening to drown her in the Avalon Marsh.

'It's about these incidents,' said Dave. 'The "Moth Man" – you know, the man who flings himself naked against some poor woman's conservatory at night. I'm really struggling to make any sense out of the information we've got and I wondered if you . . .' His voice trailed off as the silence from Alex's end of the line seemed to push back at his eagerness. 'Hello? Alex – are you there?'

'Yes,' she answered, reluctantly.

'Oh – good. So, could I come over and maybe go over a few things. It's a bit unorthodox but . . .'

Alex cut him off abruptly. 'I don't know why you think I could be any use. I'm a probation officer – that's all. I run a day centre and try to get jobs for petty criminals with brains the size of a flea. That's what I do, Dave. I don't know anything about detective work so, sorry, I can't help.'

She hung up the phone and tried to turn her attention to the notes for the evening session but her thoughts kept returning to Dave's request and all it entailed.

'Damn!' she muttered. 'Double damn!' She flung her pen across the room in disgust and stormed off to find a coffee from somewhere in the main building.

First came the selection, then the planning, he thought. A lot of planning that involved travelling and studying his chosen one from afar. Working out every detail of the arrival, the act and the escape, because only fools with no patience, no sense of the occasion, acted on impulse. You had to know your special woman. Understand and anticipate how they would react when finally, finally you came calling for them. Every step was walked through in the mind before the actual event. All the options considered and all the choices made so it was one seamless, perfect moment.

Only after all that came the watching – a time to anticipate the pleasure that was to come. Books and films were full of characters who knew they were being spied on. They stopped whatever they were doing, often giving a little shiver as if they could feel the observer's eyes on them, twin pinpricks of laser light crawling across their bodies. They would look around, in these stories, turning abruptly just in time to catch a glimpse of their stalker. This never happened to him. Perhaps he was more careful than all those characters from fiction. Or the objects of his affections were particularly insensitive. Or maybe that just didn't happen in real life, because he could watch, hidden in the shrubbery or behind a tree and the focus of his desire just carried on with whatever they were

149

doing. There was no twitching of shoulders, no sudden stares or uncomfortable glances out of windows. It was just him watching, sharing a secret moment with the woman in the glass case who was posing and performing just for him, even if she didn't know it yet.

Yes, the watching was most pleasurable.

In the detectives' room at Taunton, Dave replaced the handset and sighed. It had been a rather long shot but worth a try, he thought. Lauren had let slip about Alex's twin degrees a couple of weeks ago and Dave was most interested in her qualification in psychology. He'd done a bit of reading around the subject himself and knew enough to realise it wasn't a magic key, opening up the personality for examination. Still, he also thought there were some interesting aspects of this offender's behaviour that might bear closer scrutiny and Alex was the only person he knew who had the right background for the job.

Chewing on his biro, he went back to the notes, searching for the one link that might help him track down the Moth Man. There had been no reports of any suspicious activity for several weeks but Dave suspected this was because the perpetrator was getting ready, preparing and perhaps following his intended victim. The lack of evidence, the care taken to leave as few traces as possible and the complete blank surrounding any form of transport convinced Dave of one thing. These were not random attacks and they were not committed on impulse. He was hunting a cunning, careful predator who was going to strike again.

Chapter Eleven

On the train down to Dartmoor, Iris sat and stared out of the window, her stomach twisting and clenching with anxiety. She had put it off so often, she scarcely knew how to broach the subject of Newt's father now. When she had hinted at the fact that her husband, Derek, was not his biological father, Newt had listened but not pursued the topic. He had seemed more concerned about Biff, his younger brother. Despite being so different, Newt and Biff had been very close and Iris knew her son missed his little brother very much.

'You can't blame yerself,' she had insisted at their last meeting. 'Was not your fault the police was waiting for you at the post office. And was nothing you could do once they'd separated you both. Biff made his own choices, though God knows, they was right stupid ones.'

She stopped, unable to continue as she blinked back tears. Locked up alone in a custody cell, left to sweat it out in the hope he would give up the rest of the gang who were targeting local post offices, Biff had managed to hang himself with the blanket they'd given him for the night. In theory, someone should have checked on him every half-hour or so but somehow he was forgotten, left alone with his own thoughts and fears.

There was the suspicion it was all a horrible accident and Biff had been trying to gain sympathy and attention, a play for leniency when he was up in court, but if so he had misjudged the whole situation badly. Newt still felt responsible for his brother's death, she knew. He was the clever one, the leader who directed and moderated Biff's undoubted talent for violence and intimidation. Newt was the one who devised the post office raids.

He had the uncanny ability to shin up walls as if he had suckers on his hands and feet, a talent he put to good use when indulging his propensity for burglary. Together the brothers had wrought havoc across the Levels until they were betrayed, caught red-handed breaking into their fifth post office in a month. Sentenced to two years in Dartmoor, Newt had plenty of time to think about his future. With his father and brother gone, his view of the world changed dramatically. He watched his mother struggling with her grief, reflected on the events that had brought the remains of his family to their current sorry state and decided he needed to look for another line of work when he got out.

As an 'escapee', he found his options severely limited for the first part of his sentence. The authorities took a dim view of his escapade and for a number of months showed no signs of restoring any but the most basic of privileges. Their suspicions were further raised when news of his father's actions filtered through to the prison. In their eyes he was the son and sole heir to Derek Johns' criminal empire, a little gang-lord in the making, and they kept a strict look out for any signs of the organisation within the walls of Dartmoor. Prison life was hazardous enough without allowing imported gang rivalries to flourish unchallenged.

Newt resigned himself to a long, Spartan stretch inside, an hiatus in his young life made lonelier by his determination not to play leader to the men from the Levels who appeared and then vanished with depressing regularity. The Somerset inmates were hurt and angry at his rejection of their homage and many of the other prisoners were too scared by his family's reputation to respond to any overture of friendship he might make. It was only when Alex Hastings, on one of her regular visits, raised the subject of post-release employment that the authorities agreed to let Newt attend the classes available to his cohort.

Choices were limited, centring round basic educational skills and a very small range of manual jobs. Newt was never going to be allowed out into the gardens or farm again and he was already fully literate, so apart from maths there was little to attract him. Despite this, he greeted the chance with enthusiasm and proved to be a fast learner, attentive, eager and popular with his teacher. It was a sad day when he reached the end of the highest available curriculum, but as he was making his farewells at the end of the lesson the teacher put out a hand to stop him as leaving the room.

'Perhaps I might have a word?' he said, nodding to the guard.

'I'll need to lock you in,' said the warder as he rounded up the other prisoners. 'Be back when I've delivered this lot, right?'

The teacher nodded his agreement, signalling to Newt who sat down at a table and waited.

'You have done extremely well Johns,' he said once they were alone. 'I only wish we had time to enter you for the O level,' he said. 'Sadly, the last papers are in a couple of months and then a new exam is being introduced. Hopefully you will have left us by then.' He smiled, a crooked little smile and Newt, despite himself, responded in kind.

'Reckon,' said Newt. 'I figures I should be out round about September. Lost half my parole but still got three months left of 'un.' There was a pause and Newt shifted uncomfortably in his seat.

'Mr Norris . . .' he hesitated. 'If'n that's all, I should go. Is dinner time and they don't like latecomers.'

Norris nodded but made no move to summon an escort. Instead he walked over to the corner of the room where a large, square shape stood on a bench, covered by a dark cover.

'Come and have a look at this,' he said and somewhat reluctantly Newt rose and crossed the room to join him.

Norris slid the cover up and folded it carefully, placing it on a desk beside him.

'What do you think of that then?' he asked.

Newt stared at the machine in front of him. It was big – about a foot square and standing about four inches high with an equally large television screen standing on the top. There was a long, grey keyboard attached by a wire and a strange little box with two buttons next to it. Newt, who had lived on the Levels all his life and left school seven years previously, had never seen anything like it.

'Where's that to then?' he asked finally.

Mr Norris was from Bath and has a reasonable grasp of the Somerset dialect. 'It's called a PC,' he said. 'A personal computer. They teach them in a lot of schools now and I put in for a machine a little while ago. We only got the one, but this is a good one.' He laid his hand on the top of the television screen possessively. 'This is IBM standard, it's got a colour monitor and it runs a lot of the programs used in offices and businesses outside.'

He stopped and looked at Newt thoughtfully.

'It's been sitting here for a few weeks now. To be honest, I've been almost afraid to use it. We'll not get another one in a hurry. In fact, I'm astonished we got this one. Anyway,' he realised he was possibly sharing a little too much with a prisoner, 'I thought you might like to be my first student. You've a very good head for maths and a knowledge of simple programming would be most helpful to you when you leave. I think we can cover the basics – word processing, databases, spreadsheets and so on, in the time you have left. What do you think?'

Newt blinked at the machine, shaking his head slowly.

'Being honest I 'ent sure,' he said thoughtfully. 'I heard of computers, of course, but most of what you just said – I 'ent got a clue what it all means.'

There was the sound of the door being unlocked behind them and Norris slid the cover back over his PC.

'Think about it anyway and let me know what you decide,' he said.

Newt glanced at the warder who peered round the doorway, impatient to be off. 'Reckon I'll give it a go,' he said. ''Ent nothing else they's offering and is nice, getting off the landing and doing something new.'

It was not quite the whole-hearted enthusiasm Norris had hoped for but he smiled encouragingly as Newt was led away to his late, cold dinner.

There was some discussion between the prison officers on his wing as to whether he should be allowed through to the visiting room. Knowing any intervention on his part would only make things worse, Newt sat in his cell, listening to the voices outside the open door as he struggled to keep calm. He minded missing the visit for himself – of course he did. He still felt homesick, even after eighteen months in Dartmoor. In some ways, it was getting worse as he crept close to his release date. Most of all, however, he hated the thought of his mother travelling all this way, only to be turned away through no fault of her own – or of his.

He'd not asked to be kept back by the teacher and it wasn't his fault he was late for his meal but that didn't count for much with some of the screws. He tried to make out who was winning the argument but just when it sounded as if they had come to a decision an angry voice interrupted and they went back to the beginning again. Resisting the urge to slam the cell door in their faces, Newt made himself lie down on his bunk, opening the library book he kept under his pillow. He presented a picture of serenity when one of the warders finally looked round the door and yelled.

'Hey, Johns! On yer feet. Got a visitor and you'm been late already once today.'

Keeping his face neutral, Newt marked his place in the book, put it neatly under his pillow and jumped to the ground. He followed the warder along the gantry to the stairs and down onto the main floor. Their footsteps rang on the metal steps, a constant, harsh cacophony that had formed the background to Newt's days for the duration of his sentence. He thought sometimes he would never get the sound out of his ears, wondering in the long nights if he would be able to sleep without hearing the sound of steps advancing towards his door.

Through a maze of corridors and gates, he progressed fitfully, standing, waiting, lifting his arms to be searched, turning round before the warders' hard gazes, before finally donning a bright yellow tabard and being ushered through the door to the visitors' room. Iris sat at a table near the far corner, her head held up as if refusing to show weakness in the midst of the surrounding misery. Family groups, huddled around larger tables, juggled with small children who wriggled and fretted at being held and bounced around by men who were strangers to them. Toddlers stood, wide-eyed and suspicious, leaning against their mothers for reassurance whilst their older siblings feigned indifference, attention held by a book or toy they guarded fiercely in this den of thieves.

Newt picked his way around the tables, settling in to the chair opposite his mother.

'Starting to think you wasn't coming,' she said with a quick smile to take away the implied criticism.

'Starting to think the same thing,' said Newt.

Iris reached into her bag and took out a packet of cigarettes, handing one to her son and lighting it with a cheap disposable lighter. Newt nodded his thanks and took a single puff before putting it out carefully, hiding the scarcely-smoked tube in his hand. After a moment, he slid it behind his ear casually, teasing his hair down a bit. Cigarettes were precious, an alternate currency in a place where only the most valued and industrious could earn more than a couple of pounds a week. Newt didn't smoke but he knew a lot of men who did.

Iris watched her son go through the same rituals as her husband had before him but the resemblance ended there. Newt was growing up and he neither looked nor acted anything like Derek. Not surprising, she thought. Not in the least surprising.

'You's getting more like your Dad every day,' she said.

Newt sat very still, aware that the topic, now raised so directly, could not be easily ignored.

'Look at you and I can see 'um, all them years ago.' She scanned his face for any reaction but Newt sat mute before her.

'Is three things you got from him,' went on Iris doggedly. 'Yer hair, yer name and seems you's growing up real nice, thoughtful like he was.'

A frown flitted across her son's face.

'Thought I got my hair from you,' he said. 'You was sort of red, before . . .' He stopped, embarrassed by the direction the conversation was taking. 'I mean, I reckon it looks fine now – just, well . . .'

'Oh don't be so soft boy,' said Iris crossly. 'Think I went grey overnight with the shock of Derek turning up like that, and him half dead and mad too? Been turnin' for a while now but I never could let it grow in. Started to colour it a sort of red when I was carrying you and could never stop once you made yer appearance, you with that carrot-top.'

Newt was thoroughly confused. Name – well, he was a Johns, like his mother and Derek. Regarding his hair, he was surprised to learn Iris wasn't (and never had been) a redhead. He thought for a moment but could not recall anyone in his past with red hair and certainly no-one who might fit the role of absent father. As for growing up thoughtful, well there were a lot of ways he could describe the late Derek Johns but thoughtful was certainly not one of them.

Iris watched her son's face as he puzzled over what she told him.

'Seems we did a better job of keeping our secret'n we realised,' she said. 'Wouldn't 'a bin so worried if I'd know you had no clue. Don't get me wrong,' she added hastily as Newt leaned forward, anger on his face. 'I never wanted to lie to Derek. He was a decent father to you and Biff, and some nights I wanted to just cry over what'd happened but wasn't safe. You know what a temper he had. What do you think he'd a done if he'd found out you was someone else's? There was three of us I was having to protect – was me, and you and yer real dad.'

She dropped her head and stared at the hands, clenched together on her lap. There was genuine anguish in her voice and Newt felt his anger melt away.

'Must'a bin hard,' he ventured.

'Wasn't easy sometimes,' Iris conceded. 'Yer Gran, she said I'd made my choice an' was only right I stood by it. Set myself to being a good wife to Derek and the best mother I could to you an' Biff. I wonder sometimes . . .' Iris hesitated for an instant. 'Maybe if I'd not been all roiled up with feeling guilty, mebbe I would've been a bit firmer with him – and you boys too. Might 'a stood up to him more. Maybe this all wouldn'a happened.'

Newt had spent a lot of his time in Dartmoor reliving the events that had brought him to the door of his lonely grey cell and had wondered how much blame he had to take for events. Quite a lot, he'd decided. Biff followed his lead – always had. Newt himself had been proud of his skill at breaking and entering, sure he could continue to outwit the local police and becoming foolish in his over-confidence. The one person he never thought to blame was his mother. She stood apart from the rest of the family and although she had been utterly loyal to her husband and sons, she had not liked their chosen career path.

'Wasn't your fault,' he said. 'Would'a happened sometime anyway. Was always something wild about our Biff.'

There was a clanging from the doors at the far end of the room and around them families began their farewells, some with tears in their eyes, others with barely concealed relief.

'Won't be long now,' said Newt as he rose to his feet. 'I'm out in a few months and – Mum?' She looked at him, eyes searching for the little boy she had sacrificed herself to protect. 'Will be different. I'm doin' classes – learning to use a computer, even. Will be better – I promise.' With a last smile he was gone, swallowed up by the crowd of men that slouched its way through the barred door and back into the belly of the beast that had devoured the rest of her family.

News of the third attack sent the people of Highpoint into a fury. Despite all the efforts of the police, rumours had begun to circulate in the town, each more lurid than the previous, but the impact of this, a confirmed incident, was worse then anyone had anticipated.

'Seems we got a serious problem on our hands,' said the Inspector at an emergency briefing. 'People are scared and they're angry – not a good combination in my experience. Now, you've all got details of this latest incident. Take a moment to read through what we know and then I want any ideas you have. We need to catch this bastard – and fast.'

Dave sat with Sergeant Lynas in the front row. He kept his head down, re-reading the slim folder and studying the map of the three attacks but he could feel the Inspector's eyes on him. The man had high expectations of all his detectives and Dave knew he had so far failed to impress. His probationary period was trickling away and his big chance was heading home with it.

'Well?' There was silence in the detectives' room, broken by the soft sound of shuffling feet. 'Come on – anyone? There must be something, however stupid – or obvious.'

Dave lifted his hand tentatively.

'This is miles from the second attack,' he said. 'But not all that far . . . um, less than two miles from the first one.' The Inspector regarded him, nodding to show he should continue. 'Well, they've got a couple of things in common. All of the houses are off the main roads. Up footpaths or something similar, and I bet this was the last house in the row, or on its own.'

This time the Inspector nodded in approval. 'It was actually. How did you know that?'

'Maybe it's actually Detective Brown,' said one of the men behind him. A snort of laughter greeted this witticism, attracting a scowl from Sergeant Lynas.

'Don't have time for all of that,' said Dave easily. 'Too busy trying to catch myself in the act.' He glanced back at the Inspector and hurried on with his thoughts.

'I think they must all be the same person. Same type of behaviour, same disguise, same type of victim and we were very careful about details for the first two so I don't think this is a copy-cat.'

'Same hair colour too,' muttered a colleague, but this time the Inspector silenced the voices with a raised hand.

'Enough. This is a very serious business and if any one of you thinks it is funny then I suggest you go to see some of the victims. Try talking to them and see just how badly they've been affected.' There was a shamed silence in the room as he continued. 'These innocent women had been attacked *in their own homes*. They may never feel safe anywhere ever again. Now, I want the forensic teams out there now looking for any trace, any shred of evidence. You,' he pointed to Dave. 'You and Lynas did a good job interviewing the earlier victims so I want you to speak to this . . .' He consulted the note from the dispatcher. 'Miss Bradshaw. Eleanor Bradshaw – she owns a shop in Highpoint apparently. Uniform are there at the house and she should have a WPC with her by now. The rest of you, look for any signs of how he got there and how he got away again. For God's sake, he's human – he didn't fly to Enmore so there should be something.'

'Yeah, if Uniform haven't trampled all over the scene,' said one of the specialist team sourly.

Uniform, in fact, had done very well. The call had gone to Highpoint, Dave's old station, and the Inspector there had taken charge personally. Both the garden and the lane leading up to the house were marked off with uniformed officers guarding the entrance and trying to ensure only essential personnel used the road. All cars were parked on the main highway and police and forensic teams shuffled along a narrow strip of grass running next to the track, leaving the main access untouched.

'Don't know what good it'll do though,' said Sergeant Lynas as he peered through the evening gloom at the muddy surface. 'Look at the state of it!'

The lane was certainly badly churned up, an uneven mix of tyre marks and hoof prints. It had rained the previous evening, Dave remembered. The softened surface could have been the answer to all their problems, yielding just the sign they needed – but once again the one vital piece of information had eluded them.

'Is them bloody kids,' said the uniformed PC from his post at the end of the track. 'Riding them stupid little bikes everywhere. They been up on the Quantocks, tearing up the footpaths and frightening the deer last week. If'n I had my way I'd take them bikes off'a anyone caught doin' damage.'

'He lives out by North Petherton,' said Lynas softly as he and Dave turned away and picked a route up the road. 'Had a bunch of BMX lads racing down from Kings Cliff and messing up the paths last month. Seems to think they's second only to skateboarders in major public nuisances!'

Dave grinned but then composed himself, ready for another interview with another potentially traumatised woman. They had to get a breakthrough soon, he thought. The whole thing was getting very nasty and this man, whoever he was, was making the whole of the Avon and Somerset police force look like fools.

Alex started the day in a meeting with one of her least favourite clients. Jake Hollis was a petty thief, a recurring nuisance who had been in trouble in several countries and never seemed to learn from his mistakes. He had been blissfully absent from the area when she arrived but a couple of months ago he had landed on their doorstep following a spate of minor break-ins at local pubs. In his twenties but looking at least five years younger, he was tall and thin, a pale, washed-out looking individual. The fact he had an inflated opinion of himself and his abilities did little to endear him to his peers and Alex spent a lot of the time in interviews fighting an urge to reach across the desk and slap him.

'How are you getting on at the workshop?' she asked.

Jake managed a sneer as he flicked at a microscopic speck of dust on his sleeve. 'They are mainly morons,' he said. 'Apart from the two cretins and the bully.'

Alex waited but it seemed that was all he had to say on the subject.

'The foreman – uh.' She searched through her notes but could not find the man's name. 'He speaks very highly of you. He says you're one of his best workers and they might have a full-time job for you at the end of your placement.'

Jake looked suitably unimpressed by this news. A lot of her probationers would view this as a way out of their problems, a chance to start again and work towards a better life. Jake, by contrast, thought he was far too good for the Community Programme in the first place. By the time he finished his year he would certainly be above working next to unskilled, underpaid young men – young men just like himself.

'I shouldn't even be here,' said Jake angrily. 'There was a big misunderstanding in Rotterdam and the Dutch police were just looking for someone to blame. Picking on the foreign workers, as usual. I was completely innocent and they had no right to do what they did.'

'Deport you once you had completed your sentence,' murmured Alex glancing back at the file in front of her. 'Well, unfortunately as a convicted criminal, they had every right. And sadly for us, that means you are our problem now.' That was, she realised, rather less supportive than it should be but there was something odd about Jake, something unpleasant that set her on edge.

'It is a complete waste of my intelligence,' said Jake, folding his arms and leaning back in the chair.

His fingernails were bitten, Alex noted. The sight of those torn, red hands turned her stomach and she looked away.

'Perhaps you should look at one of the apprenticeships?' she suggested.

'Modern-day serfdom,' said Jake. 'Why should I work for years, for a pittance?'

Because you might learn something, thought Alex. Like a valuable skill, or perhaps some manners. She studied the file in front of her, avoiding the sight of Jake staring out of the window, for as long as possible. Finally she closed the folder and pushed it away in disgust.

'You have almost a year of your order to run,' she said. 'This includes another six months in the hostel.'

Jake shifted in his chair and turned his head to glare at his probation officer.

'I don't like it at the hostel,' he said.

There's a surprise, Alex thought. She waited, hoping to force something further from the young man before her. Despite all the meetings and the reports in the file, she still knew hardly anything about him and that worried her. The pause stretched into a silence, a wordless contest between them. Alex forced herself to sit absolutely still, a slight smile on her face as she waited. Finally Jake looked away, the fingers of his left hand drumming a rapid tattoo on the desk and Alex tried not to let out her satisfied smile.

'Unless the court decide to reduce your order – and that is such a rare occurrence I don't know why I even mentioned it – you have to stay there and work where directed until your time is up,' she said.

Jake glared at her. 'You can change it,' he said. 'I know you can. You did something for that loser Kevin Mallory so he could go off with the Fair.'

Alex blinked at him. 'Where did you hear that?' she asked.

'Everyone knows,' Jake sneered. 'It's all round the hostel. So what do *I* have to do before you help me like that?'

163

Alex felt an awful rush of apprehension as she looked at his smug face.

'Your favourite little criminal,' Jake sneered. 'Back last week, lording it around the place with money in his pocket – for doing nothing. Just hanging around the Fair. How did he get that then?'

Alex was not about to discuss another client with this man, but she did need to stop any further gossip about Kevin. An accusation of favouritism could be disastrous, especially now, with a new senior arriving in the next few weeks. And it wouldn't do Kevin much good either.

'Every client is entitled to confidentiality,' she said firmly. 'Mr Mallory is fulfilling his obligations and keeping to the conditions of his probation order. I would suggest you focus on your own situation as a good employment record and success under the hostel regime will stand you in good stead in the future.' God, I sound pompous, she thought.

For a moment it seemed Jake was going to answer her back – or worse – but he just shrugged his thin shoulders and looked away again.

Alex felt compelled to offer him something. She wasn't going to help him leave the hostel and she didn't trust him, but her job was still to assist his rehabilitation, despite the changes outlined in the new Criminal Justice Act that was going through parliament. Perhaps, she thought, he might find one of the new groups at the day centre more to his liking than the workshop evening.

'I'm starting a photography group in a couple of weeks,' she said. 'You might like to transfer on to that. The workshop is a bit basic for you I know and it must get boring, doing the same thing all day and then during the evening too.'

'You don't want me on the raft race team then?' asked Jake.

Alex had forgotten about the raft race. Or, to be more accurate, had deliberately pushed it from her mind. Press-ganged into the team last year to make up the numbers, she had experienced some of the most terrifying hours of her life as the home-made raft wallowed and ploughed its way around the coast from Watchet to Minehead, only to almost sink a few hundred yards from the safety of the quay. Alex had gone overboard and almost drowned when her life jacket, sabotaged by Newt's deranged father, had failed. It was not an experience she was eager to repeat.

'Of course you should stay with the workshop team if you want to do the raft race,' she said. 'It's quite an experience. Still, there are other groups you are welcome to try as well if you like.'

Jake shrugged again and she gave up the unequal fight.

'Well, let me know about the job next week,' she said gathering her notes together. 'I'll have a list of the new groups for you to look over then.'

When he was gone she riffled through the file but a glance at her watch reminded her the Monday auction was due to start in less than an hour and she needed to speak to the little band of clients who would be accompanying her before they set off for the sale. Notes on Jake Hollis would have to wait for a few hours she thought as she left her dictaphone in the desk drawer. Locking the office door behind her, she thought of all the other notes she needed to bring up to date. The paperwork was getting seriously out of hand again and she'd probably be back in the office over the next weekend, scrambling to catch up.

There was a babble of voices from Reception and Alex hurried through the day centre to meet her charges before they caused too much disruption.

Chapter Twelve

Despite her initial misgivings, Ada was looking forward to the arrival of her first goat. That morning she rose early and was hovering in the garden, ears tuned to the sounds of approaching vehicles long before Tom's battered van appeared round the bend from Middlezoy dragging a small horse box.

'What-ho, Ada,' Tom called cheerily as he swung the vehicle up next to the hedge and killed the engine. Ada hurried down the path, stopping just shy of the garden gate to sniff the air.

'What you been driving through, Tom?' she said. 'Smells awful.'

Tom kept his back to her as he fiddled with the trailer door. 'Well now,' he said over his shoulder as the ramp fell down with a loud thud. 'I don't rightly know.'

As he reached into the vehicle and hauled at his passenger the smell intensified and as the goat emerged the stench seemed to roll around her, acrid and all enveloping. Ada stepped back, flapping her hands in front of her face in a vain effort to dispel the horrible scent.

'What in all holy hell is that?' she demanded, eyes fixed on the animal standing next to Tom, its twisted horns splayed up and out from its head and its strange golden eyes regarding her with intense curiosity – or malevolence. It was hard to tell which, thought Ada, what with them slitted pupils. She had been expecting a neat, fawn coloured animal with a white beard and fox-like head not this huge, shaggy beast with a long nose and ears hanging down the sides of its face.

Tom stroked the animal's nose gently and the goat shook its head, chewing reflectively whilst never taking its eyes off Ada.

'He's an Anglo-Nubian,' said Tom. 'Looks a bit frightening at first but is a real softy underneath. Come and say hello.' He began to lead the goat through the gate but Ada back off as the aroma washed over her again.

'What about that smell?' she persisted.

Tom grinned, looking a bit sheepish.

'Well now, they is stud animals and so – well, they wee on their heads. Makes them more attractive to the lady goats, so I hear.' He rubbed the animal's nose again, taking care to avoid the top of its head.

Ada was astonished by this information.

'What, they wee on one another?' she asked after a moment.

'No,' said Tom. 'On their own heads. Very flexible and agile animals is goats.' He tugged at the halter gently and the goat clattered obediently down the narrow brick path behind him, stopping for an instant to nibble delicately at Ada's washing line.

'Come on Marmaduke,' said Tom firmly as he guided the goat between the neatly planted beds and into the fenced-off area beyond.

'What did you call it?' asked Ada.

'Well, Bob, he calls him Marmaduke. 'Cos he's a bit lanky and clumsy like that cartoon dog, I think.'

Ada folded her arms and gave both the goat and Tom her best hard stare.

'There 'ent no way I'm shouting for no goat called Marmaduke,' she said firmly. 'I'll be calling him Pongo on account of how he smells so awful.'

'If you says so Ada,' said Tom hiding a smile. He had wondered, after a journey in close proximity to Marmaduke, if Ada would agree to have the animal at all. She could christen the goat 'Lollipop' if she wanted, he thought. He was just relieved she was going to keep him.

Brian Morris dressed in his best clothes for the visit to the hostel. His leather jacket was brushed and polished as were his black Doc Marten boots. He had even put new laces in, carefully threading the fourteen eyelets and tying them with a neat bow at the top. His shirt was ironed and was a crisp white and his hair stood up proudly in its full Mohican. As he walked down the path to the front door he had an almost overwhelming desire to strut.

The reception he received left him startled and bewildered.

'What the bloody hell do you think you're doing, coming in here done up like that?' demanded the warden, rising from his desk and barrelling towards the office door.

Brian stepped back, away from the figure advancing towards him.

'I was just comin' to see someone, Pete,' he said.

'Not like that you're not. And it's Mr Marks to you.'

Brian found himself out in the hallway, moving backwards as Peter Marks barged through the office door, his face twisted into a furious scowl.

'There's no gang uniforms allowed in here. I expect all my lads to dress decently – and that goes for you as well, if you want to come in. Now clear off and come back when you've found something respectable to wear. And wash that stuff out of your hair!'

Brian retreated down the path, hurt and angry by the man's words. He had spent a long time getting ready for this visit, hoping to impress the hostel warden with his diligence. Instead he had somehow alienated him completely. To add to his misery, it began to rain and his wonderful Mohican was starting to droop. Brian made a dash for the bus shelter a hundred yards down the road and huddled under the safety of the sagging roof until the shower passed. He couldn't afford proper hair spray, especially now his dole was about to be stopped and he'd resorted to soap in an effort to make his hair stand tall and proud. A glance at his reflection in the glass panels confirmed his worst fears. His head was covered in bubbles, soapy water was dripping on his jacket and he looked a complete mess. Nothing, it seemed, was going his way at the moment.

Samuel Burton stood at an upstairs window in the hostel, watching as the skinhead in the ridiculous get-up scuttled out of the front door and ran for the dubious shelter of the bus stop. Amused by his predicament, Samuel hovered for a moment too long, hoping to witness the complete collapse of the lad's hair. There was a sound behind him and he swung around to see Bennie Sands, the deputy warden, glaring at him from the top of the stairs.

'What are you doing here?' she demanded. 'I thought you had an appointment at the Job Centre this morning.'

Samuel regarded her bleakly. He didn't particularly like women – not as people anyway – and it was particularly galling to find himself under the supposed supervision of two such inferior creatures as Bennie and bloody Alex Hastings. Interfering bitches, the pair of them. None of this was made obvious as he kept perfectly still, hands relaxed at his side and his face expressionless. Only the spark of blue in his flat eyes betrayed his fury.

Bennie climbed the last couple of steps to the landing and stood for a moment, hands on hips as she waited for an answer. When it became apparent there wasn't going to be one, she stood aside and gestured down towards the front door.

'Go on, out with you. You know the rules – unless you're in a class or on the rota you're not allowed inside during the day.'

Samuel stalked past her, close enough to just brush shoulders as he stepped on to the stairs. Bennie tried, unsuccessfully, not to flinch at his touch. Samuel was considerably more successful in hiding his satisfaction at her reaction.

Bennie watched as he strolled across the lobby and out of the front door, shaking her head in frustration. Samuel was becoming a real problem. He was bright enough, that was obvious. He was clean – perhaps almost *too* clean for he took two showers a day and sometimes three if the weather was hot or he had been at the day centre workshop. He dressed well and took care of his clothes yet there was something unpleasant about him.

He was still in a four-bed room and after almost a month had made absolutely no progress as far as the hostel programme was concerned. Bennie didn't think a great deal of her boss's 'Ladder of Achievement' but the idea of making the lads earn their little privileges was a sound one. Samuel, however – he didn't seem to care. Standing at the window looking down onto the road below, she found herself hoping his attitude wasn't catching. There were some difficult and potentially dangerous men in the hostel and Peter Marks' 'Ladder of Achievement' was a very flimsy shield indeed.

Responding to Lauren's call, Alex left her office and hurried through to the reception area, stopping only to warn a couple of lads hanging around the pool table about their language. For a moment she thought the lobby was empty but then she spotted a hunched, lonely figure slouched in the far corner. Brian Morris was a sorry sight, streaks of soapy water running down his face and spotting his leather jacket and a pool of grey water forming at his feet.

Lauren was at the counter, leaning on the edge as she craned forwards to see what was going to happen next. From the glint in her eyes, it was obvious she was on the verge of laughing aloud. Alex caught her eye and gave a tiny shake of her head in warning. There was a lot of bad feeling between Brian and Lauren, most of it Brian's fault, but as she looked at the wretched figure in front of her Alex felt nothing but concern for the boy. All the fight, all the spark had gone out of him. She'd seen people look like this before and rarely had there been a good outcome.

'Come on Brian,' she said gently, walking over and touching his shoulder. The boy flinched slightly but didn't answer or lift his head to look at her.

'Lauren, can you see if you can find a towel please?' said Alex over her shoulder. There was a scraping sound as Lauren clambered down from the high stool and headed, somewhat reluctantly, in the direction of the office.

'Come on,' said Alex more forcefully. She shook Brian's shoulder, trying to get his attention. 'Brian! You came here for a reason. You've come to see me – right? Now, we'll go into my office where it's quiet and private. I'll make you a cup of tea and you can tell me what's wrong.'

Slowly, as if every movement caused him pain, Brian rose to his feet and began to shuffle after her, his head still bowed. He looked like a statue by Giacometti come to life, thought Alex. Tall, horribly skinny with spindly legs and those great big boots . . .

The lads at the pool table glanced up as she led her charge through to the office and one of them opened his mouth to say something, only to shut it again at her fierce glare. All of them suddenly developed a fascination with the game in front of them and she hurried Brian through to the room down the corridor without mishap.

After mopping himself off with the towel produced, eventually, by Lauren, Brian muttered and rambled his way through a tale of woe.

'So – let me get this straight,' said Alex. 'You found this metal detector thing and bought a new battery. Then someone else – you think it's Charlie Dodds – found the metal detector. So you've got the battery and he's got the metal detector. Right?'

Brian nodded glumly.

'Well, the solution is obvious,' said Alex. 'Talk to Charlie and both of you share the metal detector. After all, neither part works on its own.'

Brian scowled at her. ''Tis *mine*,' he said. 'Don't see why I should share nothin' with no thief as took it.'

Alex sighed. Sometimes it was very hard to reach any common sense solution with her clients and Brian was one of the most stubborn people she had ever encountered. And she included her own family in that calculation.

'You found it in the first place,' she pointed out. 'What if the original owner came to you and demanded his metal detector back?'

'Was just thrown away,' Brian protested. 'Let under a pile of junk an' stuff. Fair game, that is – don't see as how I should be givin' it back.'

'Charlie found it buried in a hedge,' said Alex. 'There was no battery in it so it was obviously scrap as far as he could see. What's the difference?'

She watched as Brian struggled with the logic of this argument, a range of emotions flitting across his face. Finally he shrugged and said, 'Well, Charlie 'ent so bad. Leastways, is not some stranger.'

Taking this for acquiescence, she picked up the phone and dialled the workshop, summoning Charlie to her office. It was nice, she thought, when common sense prevailed. Unusual but rather nice.

On leaving the hostel Samuel turned left and headed out towards the canal path. The rain began to fall steadily and he had left his jacket behind in his room. The water seeped through his thin sweater and gathered in his hair, forming drops that ran down his face and neck. Ignoring the discomfort, Samuel fell into a fast trot, his arms swinging as his feet sped along the increasingly muddy path out beyond the town. Turning on to the Levels just beyond the canal bridge, he headed for the airfield and the shelter of his hiding place.

The path was slippery underfoot and after about a mile

the strain was beginning to make his ankles and calves ache. Despite the growing discomfort Samuel increased his pace, his clothes now damp from the inside as he started to sweat. By the time he reached the bunker on the airfield he was hot and breathless, his legs burning from the effort. I'm getting soft, he thought as he sat on the floor, his hands trembling slightly from fatigue. After a few minutes his breathing slowed to a more normal rate and he shivered a little as his clothes clung to his body, clammy and cold from the rain.

He rose to his feet and walked to the doorway, peering out into the grey morning. The rain fell steadily, a fine mist of water obscuring the surrounding countryside so he could scarcely see to the end of the runway. Wrapping his arms around his body in a futile search for warmth, he retreated into the interior and settled once more on the bare concrete floor. For a moment he thought of the pineapple drum with its stash of dry clothes, gloves and shoes. Then he put it out of his mind. Far too risky, he thought. It would be stupid, chancing everything just to avoid a few minutes' discomfort. That sort of thing was for fools and weaklings. He waited, leaning back against the wall, for the rain to stop, brooding all the while on the wrongs he was forced to endure from the hostel and the staff at Highpoint probation office.

Alex hummed to herself as she walked along the tow-path by the river on her way home. The weather had cleared up half an hour before she finished work and the bright evening sunlight caught the water droplets on the few remaining daffodils, sending rainbow sparkles glittering across the river bank. She had waved Brian and Charlie off to collect the various pieces of their metal detector and Bert, who had been an electrician before 'retiring' to the post of evening janitor at the probation office, had offered to help them repair it in the workshop. All in all, she thought, a very good outcome.

Her good mood lasted less than thirty seconds after stepping through the back door and into her kitchen. Dorothy was busy, slamming a huge lump of dough around on the main work surface, muttering to herself as she pummelled at the bread. This was a bad sign. From her earliest years, Alex could remember her mother retiring to the kitchen to cook up a storm on the rare occasions she and her husband had 'had words', as Dorothy had put it.

'Um, how was your day?' Alex asked rather tentatively.

Dorothy gave a decidedly unladylike snort, ripped the dough from the board and flung it down again, tearing and pulling at it before dropping it back into a large mixing bowl.

'Your father,' she said through gritted teeth. 'Your father has seen fit to deprive me of my right to have a say in who will rule this country.' She turned on the tap and washed her hands before flinging a towel over the bowl. 'And close that door. I'm trying to get this to rise and that won't happen in a draught.'

Alex opened her mouth, ready to respond angrily, then closed the door and followed Dorothy through to the dining room. Her mother removed an envelope from the apron pocket – an apron, Alex noticed. Where the hell did that come from? – and was smoothing it out on the table in front of her. Trying not to be too obvious, Alex sneaked a look at the back. It was addressed to her mother, at this address, and was undoubtedly written by her father. Alex recognised the handwriting – firm, controlled and almost excessively neatly formed. Rather like the man himself, in fact.

Dorothy hesitated and then pushed the letter over towards Alex who picked it up, suddenly reluctant to intrude on a private argument. She sensed this was an important moment, a place of no turning back and after a moment she reached out and placed the letter in front of her mother.

'You are perfectly welcome to read it,' said Dorothy stiffly.

'It's between you two,' said Alex. 'Just tell me what's the matter.' She sat down opposite her mother and leaned her elbows on the table, trying to take the sting out of her refusal.

Dorothy snatched at the envelope, stuffing it into her pocket and gave Alex a sharp look. For a moment Alex thought her mother was going to tell her to sit up straight and stop slouching, but instead she sighed heavily and her own shoulders began to slump.

'It's this wretched election,' said Dorothy. 'It seems it is too late to change my address or apply for a postal vote and so the only way I can vote is to go back . . . go to Essex.' She refrained from saying 'back home', Alex noted.

'There've been a few complaints about that,' Alex said carefully. 'A friend of mine says some of her older clients tried to get postal votes but by the time they got the forms, filled them in, got them signed and then back to the office, the deadline was passed. She had one old lady in floods of tears over it. It's a bit of a mess this time.'

'It's an utter disgrace, that's what it is!' snapped Dorothy. 'Think of all the people most likely *not* to vote for the incumbents. Those are the people who need their postal vote and they're the people who won't be able to vote at all.'

Alex raised her eyebrows at this. If she had thought about it at all she had assumed her parents were generally Conservative. The sort of 'blue rinse' Tories who would never dream of voting Labour, considered supporting the Liberals a wasted vote and were generally content to let the status quo rumble on without too much fuss. It was amazing what a few weeks in an open prison could do for an individual's political consciousness. She rather wished something similar would happen to her brothers, Hector and Archie.

'What will you do?' she asked. A part of her was secretly hoping this would help push her parents back together again, though from Dorothy's reaction this seemed a vain hope. Alex loved her mother dearly but she also valued her independence and the freedom having her own home brought her. It had never mattered before, but now, with the arrival of Margie in her life, Dorothy's continuing presence was threatening to cramp her style a little.

Her mother shook her head. 'I don't know,' she said. 'I suppose I can't stay here for ever. No . . .' she held up a hand to forestall Alex's protest, 'you have been so kind, you and

Sue. But I need to talk to your father and as he shows no signs of speaking to me, I will go to him.'

Don't let him push you into it,' said Alex. 'Just because of the election. After all, it doesn't seem to make much difference who we vote for. They're all a bunch of scheming, lying bastards,' she added bitterly.

'Well, I want to at least have some say in *which* scheming, lying bastard represents me in parliament,' said Dorothy.

Alex gazed at her mother in astonishment. Never had she heard her calm, lady-like mother talk like this.

'Oh don't gawp at me like that,' said Dorothy crossly. 'I have opinions, you know. I'm not totally blind to what is going on and how badly it affects so many people. Now, I think we should hurry up and colonise the kitchen before Sue gets home. She said something about taking her turn to make dinner tonight and quite frankly I don't think I'm strong enough for that at the moment.'

Tom bent over the fireplace in Ada's front room, deftly feeding sticks into a small fire that smouldered and sulked in the grate.

'Anything yet?' he called.

There was a scuffling behind him and Ada poked her head through from the kitchen.

'Not as I can see,' she said, eyeing the fire suspiciously. The smoke was starting to roll across the room, making Mouse cough from behind the sofa.

'Shoo!' said Ada flapping the hands at him. 'You 'ent supposed to be in here neither.' The dog lowered its head and sauntered out, the picture of injured innocence.

'So, what you think then?' Ada said as she struggled with the window. The latches were stiff after the long winter and even when she released them the frame squeaked a protest at being forced open.

'Hard to say without poking around,' said Tom, scattering the wood to extinguish the fire. 'How'd you cope in the winter?'

Ada shrugged. 'Don't often use it much now,' she said. 'Was a bit smoky last time but not so bad as is now.'

Tom wiped his hands on his trousers and grinned at her. 'Reckon I'll pop out, have a look an' see if'n there's something come loose on the pot,' he said. 'Otherwise is maybe a bird's nest. Unless you's got some poor dead body up there?' He raised an eyebrow and scooted out of the room before Ada could retaliate, chuckling as he went.

Ada watched him go, wondering at how comfortable she felt in his presence. After so many years of having to rely on herself – because her late husband Frank, let's face it, had been no use whatsoever – she was beginning to enjoy having someone around who seemed willing to share her small sorrows and triumphs. She realised she looked forward to Tom's visits, catching herself peering out of the window at the rare sound of a car or van making its way along the path next to Kings Sedgemoor. Once this would have worried her but now it seemed so natural.

These pleasant thoughts were interrupted as she spotted a figure through the window. Peering through the net curtains, she strained to make out details. He was standing in the shadows of the tree by her gate and it was difficult to make out his face but Ada was convinced it was the same young man who had got into a shouting match with Kevin on his last visit. Now, she wondered, what was he doing, standing in the rain and staring at her house?

'Ada – I was asking you to put on some more of that damp paper,' said Tom coming through the door. 'Oh – what you looking at?' he added, seeing her at the window. He walked up to stand behind her, following her gaze out towards the canal.

'Who's that then?'

'I dunno but he was here a while back, standing and staring. Was Kev as saw him off then.'

'Well, I'll be doin' the same if it's all right with you,' said Tom and headed for the front door. He struggled with the various latches and locks, pulling at the swollen wood before

177

finally wrenching the door open. By the time he set foot on the porch the shadowy figure was gone. Tom stood in the middle of the narrow road, looking both ways but there was no sign of movement. The watcher had vanished, seemingly into thin air.

Tom walked back into the kitchen, thoughtful and a little anxious.

'Say he's been round afore?' he said.

Ada frowned out into the dusk. 'Can't be sure mind but looks like him and 'e was standing in the same place. Just looking. Seemed a bit odd the first time.' She looked at Tom anxiously. 'Don't think is that weirdo do you? That one as runs at the windows?'

Tom was wondering just that but he didn't want to disturb Ada unnecessarily. It could have been someone else – someone looking for Kevin, not realising he'd gone back to the Fair, or even just a casual walker. Maybe it was just someone caught out in the rain, sheltering for a moment before continuing their journey. Somehow he wasn't convinced.

'Would be a brave man as tried running at your house Ada,' he said forcing a smile. 'What with Mickey and Mouse and yer trick with that letter box, reckon any bugger tryin' it on 's likely to be running off singing in a right high voice.'

Despite her lingering anxiety, Ada laughed at the thought before turning her attention back to the recalcitrant fire. It was getting into the fine weather, she decided. They didn't really need it even on wet evenings such as this.

'Maybe might be better to try cleaning out the chimney later in the week?' she suggested, opening the window wider to let the last of the smoke out of the room.

Tom agreed, secretly pleased at her assumption he would be around. If he were honest with himself, he would gladly spend most days at Ada's – and a few nights too, though that was still far away in the realms of wishful thinking. His main concern was ensuring the watcher really was as harmless as they were making him out to be, preferably without alarming her too much. Ada was a formidable woman but her house was isolated, out on a dark and lonely part of the Levels and she had nothing as useful as a telephone to call for help in the event of anything suspicious.

As he drove home he was surprised just how much he felt for her. After the loss of his beloved Bella he had assumed that part of him was gone, buried with his wife, lost with their shared dreams. Yet despite his grief, which was still so sharp he woke some nights to find tears in his eyes, he felt his isolation melt away before Ada's friendship. They had been friends as children and now it seemed as if they had never been apart.

He whistled softly for company as he rattled across the old stone bridge and turned onto the road leading home but all the way he kept looking out for any sign of the mysterious figure. If he spotted him, he thought, he'd stop and have a quiet word. Just the two of them, man to man.

Chapter Thirteen

There was nothing to it really. With Bert's help, Brian and Charlie had the battered metal detector working in a few hours – a few hours where, without realising it, the two lads actually learned something useful. When the lights on the handle lit up and a loud whistling came from the speaker, roughly soldered back into its place on the back of the machine, they could scarcely contain their delight and it was with some difficulty Bert dissuaded them from heading out to hunt for treasure at once.

'Tis late,' he said. 'Look – 'tis raining out and I don't reckon would be a good thing, getting it wet. Is working now but 'ent to say is as good as new. Would be a right shame, getting it broke again. And I don't see you finding another battery in a hurry neither, so better wait 'til you's got a plan. Use it a bit sparingly, I would.'

Reluctantly the unlikely duo let Bert lock the metal detector away in a cupboard for the night and set off, full of grand plans, to seal their new friendship with a few glasses of 'natch'. Bert watched them off the premises, shaking his head as he locked the heavy metal gates shut behind him. A couple of 'natches' and they'd be good for nothing in the morning, he thought. Silly buggers – they never seemed to learn. Just as well they weren't heading out onto the Levels. Cider and the marshes didn't mix, despite the frequency with which the local youth combined them.

To everyone's surprise, both Brian and Charlie were waiting on the doorstep when the first officers arrived the next morning. Despite looking a bit bleary-eyed they were anxious to lay hands on the metal detector and as soon as Lauren located the key to Bert's cupboard they grabbed their prize, heading off under its considerable weight to see what the day might reveal to them.

'Silly sods,' muttered Lauren. 'Look at 'em. Gonna give theyselves a hernia, lugging that great old thing around.'

'Well, it keeps them out of mischief anyway,' said Gordon who had arrived just too late to offer the pair a lift to wherever they were going.

Lauren snorted in disbelief. 'Can't think how,' she said. 'Soon as they spot something they'll be over fences and diggin' up some farmer's field. Will be trespassing and criminal damage at the least they'll be adding to they records.' She climbed down from her stool at the counter and disappeared through the office door, her disapproval obvious in the set of the shoulders.

'Sadly I fear Lauren may be correct,' said Gordon to Sue who was signing in for that morning's court duty.

'I can think of a lot of ways they might be gainfully employed,' said Sue. 'Unfortunately, tramping the Levels with an antique metal detector comes rather a long way down my list. Still, at least they're not hitting each other. That's an improvement.'

'Who's not hitting one another?' asked Alex as she pushed her way through the front door.

'Brian and Charlie,' said Gordon. 'Off across the Levels looking for treasure.'

'Silly sods,' said Alex. 'Any sign of Samuel yet? He's due in for an early call – says he's got a job interview in Taunton later this morning.' She looked around hopefully but there was no-one waiting for her. With a small sigh of resignation, Alex hoisted her bag over one shoulder and headed for her office.

'See you,' said Sue as she grabbed the court pack – a folder containing details of the cases due up on that day along with police notes and reports from the probation service or social services. A quick look through the paperwork was essential as the duty officer could be called on at any point and was expected to have at least a passing acquaintance with the defendant and their circumstances. Sue was relieved to see there were no breaches listed for her. They were supposed to be presented by the breaching officer but this was not always the case, as Alex had discovered in the case of Martin Ford.

In the solitude of her office, Alex unlocked her filing cabinet and unloaded the contents of her bag into the bottom drawer. Resisting the temptation to glance around, she pulled a few loose files over the bottles lying on the bottom and closed the drawer carefully to prevent the glass clinking too loudly. It was a risk, she knew, but she had such a good plan for the final sessions of her alcohol education course and if only she could demonstrate the benefits then Gordon might reconsider his ban. At least, that was the theory. Now she just had to work out how to get a television screen into the centre for an evening.

Absorbed in her planning, she failed to note the passing of time until roused by the phone on her desk.

'I got your 10.30 waiting,' came the disapproving voice of Alison, Alex's designated assistant. 'He's getting a bit agitated but seeing as I've not see Samuel come out yet I won't let him come through.'

Alex blinked at her watch, startled by how quickly the morning had gone. She flipped open her diary and checked the listings. There was Samuel, down for his 9.30am appointment but clearly he'd neither turned up nor bothered to call to let her know he couldn't make it. Damn – a confrontation with that cold, indifferent client was not what she needed now. Everyone was trying to keep a clean sheet – all clients attending, no breaches and – please – no reoffending. Whatever the new senior was like, she was unlikely to get a good first impression from an officer's poor record.

'Right,' said Alex thinking quickly. 'My fault – I'm supposed to see him at the hostel. Check on his progress at the same time, see what Peter Marks makes of him. Who've you got there . . .' She glanced at the list of appointments again. 'Matt? Right, send him down will you?'

Matt was no problem. A hard-working young man who had run foul of the archaic and (in his view) nonsensical law surrounding payment through a gas meter. Short of change one particularly cold evening, he had opened his meter, used a coin from it twice and put in a note to remind himself to make up the difference after the weekend. Unfortunately he forgot and when his landlord emptied the box he reported Matt for theft.

Matt's defence was spirited and contained a lot of common sense. People with other types of meters paid in arrears, he pointed out. They could pay in instalments and run up large bills. No-one charged them with theft. He'd left a note and obviously intended to pay – he just didn't have enough 50p coins. Was he supposed to sit and freeze in the dark all weekend? The answer, it seemed, was yes.

Despite his anger at the verdict, Matt had proved to be a model probationer. He attended regularly, took advantage of the sessions available to him in the day centre and landed a job at the chicken factory where he plucked and gutted dead birds day after day. Alex was full of admiration for his staying power – many workers lasted a few months at most, using the additional income to pull them out of a financial hole. Matt was saving his money in the hope of moving on to college and a better future once he'd earned a decent reference from his employers.

In some ways, she thought as he left the office, the spell on probation had been a good thing for him. He'd had access to help and support, got a bit of funding for his future education and had a chance to talk through his plans with someone who cared. It was exactly what she had expected when she first started the job. If only, she mused, if only there were more Matts and fewer Brians . . .

Arriving at the hostel later that day, she knocked at the office door, peering round to find it empty. Unsure of the layout, she wandered down the main hall to a large open room furnished with half a dozen wooden tables and some battered plastic and metal chairs. There were crumbs on the tables, she noticed. A large metal tea urn stood on a trolley next to the window with a tray of heavy off-white mugs. Some had been used and left next to the unused (she hesitated to label them clean) beakers. No milk or sugar, she noted. Or spoons. Rather odd all round.

'Can I help you?' said a male voice and she swung round to see the warden, Peter Marks, standing in the door of what she assumed was the kitchen. His glasses were steamed up and he looked decidedly hot and bothered. 'Ah, yes. It's Alex isn't it,' he said holding out a rather damp hand. How can we help you?'

Alex shook the proffered hand rather reluctantly, managing a slightly sickly smile. 'I've come to see one of my clients,' she said. 'Samuel Burton. Do you know if he is here?' She felt a flash of annoyance at how stiff and formal she sounded and tried to mitigate the effect by smiling again.

Peter Marks sniffed and rubbed his clammy hands on his shirt.

'He's sick, so he says. Upstairs in his room. We let him stay in today but that's a special concession and I'm not happy about it. It's not as if he even makes an effort. After all, he's been here a month now and not achieved a single thing.'

Apart from managing to rub along in this place without reoffending, thought Alex, but she kept her smile pinned in place and waited. After a few moments Peter cracked.

'Go on up,' he said, waving towards the stairs. 'Second door on the right, down the corridor.'

Alex managed an almost-civil nod and headed upstairs. The smell of feet and cheap aftershave got more noticeable with each step and was strong enough to catch in her throat as she turned down the passage. Lit by a window at the far end, the corridor was dingy and managed to be both cold and stuffy. Truly an exceptional piece of design, she thought.

She tapped on the second door and waited but there was no answer. Knocking a bit louder, she leaned forwards, straining to hear if there was any sound from inside the room. Catching what sounded like a cough, she rapped on the door a third time calling out as she did so.

'Samuel? It's Alex Hastings. I thought I'd just check and see how you are.'

There was another cough from inside which Alex decided to interpret as assent and she opened the door, steeling herself against the expected rush of smells normally encountered in these situations. To her surprise the room was bright, lit by an open window facing the door. The air was relatively fresh and faint sounds of birdsong drifted in, mingling with the sound of an occasional car.

Samuel was lying in bed, propped up on two pillows and he certainly looked ill, with red eyes and flushed face.

She took a couple of steps into the room. 'I was a bit worried when you missed your appointment,' she said, adding 'You're so reliable normally and I know you had an important meeting today. How are you feeling?' Bloody silly question, she thought. From the look of him he was feeling awful.

'Can I get you something? What have they given you for your temperature?'

Samuel managed a short, barking laugh at this before he began to cough again. '*They* haven't given me anything,' he said when he caught his breath. 'I had some aspirin in my things so I took that. I got some water from the bathroom last night. One of the other blokes left a glass behind when he left, fortunately.'

'Hasn't anyone been up to check on you?' asked Alex. She looked more closely at the cabinet next to Samuel's bed. It was neat, tidy and – clear she realised. Surely he should have a cup or plate from breakfast, unless they'd already been moved but judging from the lax way most things were handled in the hostel that seemed rather unlikely.

'I'll get you a cup of tea,' she said and turned away, trying not to slam the door behind her. In no mood to be tactful or conciliatory, she swept down the stairs and up to the tea urn. It was hot to touch and she sorted through the beakers, selecting the least grubby one before taking it into the kitchen and rinsing it under the tap. The water was luke-warm at best but a quick scrub with a cloth served to make the cup acceptable.

The tea, by contrast, was certainly not. When she turned the tap a stream of grey, cloudy liquid ran out. Alex hastily shut off the urn and moved across to the windows to get a better look. If anything, it looked worse in bright light. She sniffed at the contents of the beaker. It smelt a bit like tea so she risked a sip, promptly spitting it back into the cup in disgust. Tea, yes but with milk – sterilised milk from the taste – and a huge amount of sugar already added.

Scrubbing the cup clean again, she put it on the kitchen counter and began rummaging through the cupboards, locating tea bags in one and sugar in another. The milk was presumably kept in the fridge but this, inexplicably, was locked shut with a huge hasp and padlock. Muttering to herself, Alex headed for the office.

'Did you see him?' asked Peter Marks looking up from the book he was reading.

Alex was in no mood for social niceties. 'Has he had any breakfast?' she asked.

The warden shrugged, unconcerned and unheeding of the storm heading his way. 'He's never too bothered with meals here at the best of times,' he said, turning his attention back to the paperback on the desk. 'Hardly ever eats here anyway.'

Alex leaned over and plucked the book from his hands,

186

resisting the temptation to rip it in half down the spine. She had considerable reverence for books, even tawdry pot-boilers like the one now resting in her hands. Closing it, she set the novel gently on the desk before turning round to inspect the rows of keys hung on the wall behind her.

'Which is the key to the lock on the fridge?' she asked. 'And why is it locked anyway?' She was overstepping her boundaries here but she really didn't care. The hostel was supposed to provide safety and security for the most vulnerable offenders as well as a system of monitoring for the most dangerous. From what she had seen over the past few months, Highpoint probation hostel seemed to manage neither.

'There are problems,' said Peter Marks stiffly. 'Problems with certain residents who will simply eat everything they can get their grubby hands on. I found one lad in the fridge, half-way through a block of cheese. A *catering* block mind – a kilo of cheese! We had to throw it away after he'd been gnawing at it and I'm trying to provide decent meals on a very restricted budget as it is. I don't think you really appreciate just how difficult it is.'

'The fridge key?' repeated Alex.

Peter Marks reached past her and grabbed the correct key off a hook, handing it to her with very bad grace. Alex took it, trying not to wrinkle her nose at the whiff of body odour rising from his none too clean shirt.

'What you want from the fridge anyway?' he asked, hovering by the desk as if ready to intervene in defence of his cheese.

'Milk,' said Alex. 'Milk for tea. Samuel should have regular hot drinks even if he doesn't eat anything.'

'Is already milk in the tea,' said Peter. 'Sugar too. All made ready for them in the urn.'

Alex's distaste finally showed on her face.

'What if they don't take sugar?' she asked. 'And surely the milk curdles, heated up in that thing for hours.'

'We use steri' milk for that,' said the warden smugly. 'Don't go off no matter how long is in there.'

Alex pulled a face as she hurried out of the stuffy office. She had encountered sterilised milk as a student and was of the opinion it was disgusting. She'd known feral cats turn their noses up at a saucer of steri'. Somehow it was no surprise to discover the milk in the fridge, used presumably for the staff tea, was fresh.

When she returned with a beaker of tea, the sugar in a saucer (there was no such thing as a sugar bowl that she could see), Samuel was propped up in bed, his top half clad in a spotless white t-shirt and his lower half safely tucked in beneath the covers. He accepted the mug, taking a token sip before blinking at it and taking another.

'Thank you,' he said. 'First decent cup I've had here.'

'Alex proffered the saucer. 'I didn't know if you take sugar,' she said.

Samuel smiled rather grimly. 'Don't, actually. Just empty calories and fit for those needing instant gratification.' He took another drink before setting the beaker down on the cupboard next to his bed.

'Do you want to see a doctor?' Alex asked.

Samuel shook his head. 'It's only a cold,' he said. 'Went for a long walk a couple of days ago and got caught in the rain. My own fault.'

'Do you do a lot of walking?' Alex asked. It was so rare to get more than a couple of syllables out of Samuel, she figured she'd push her luck. Maybe she could learn something to help her understand this enigmatic young man a little better.

Samuel glanced at her and for an instant the bright blue spark flashed in his eyes before he replied. 'Look around. There's not a lot else to do, is there? Don't particularly like the company so I'm happier on my own. As I'm stuck in this place with a bunch of strangers, out suits me best.'

Despite her reservations, Alex felt a pang of sympathy for him. An intensely private person herself, she could imagine how uncomfortable it must be to be thrown into an artificial society such as the hostel – even more so a prison. How on earth had he coped with that, she wondered?

Samuel leaned back in the bed and watched her, studying her face as he searched for any sign of deceit. A lot of people had tried to befriend him, always for their own ends. He was too clever to fall for the usual mock sympathy of a jumped-up social worker. To his surprise, Alex nodded and gave a tiny smile.

'Can't be too comfortable sometimes,' she said.

He waited for her to begin the tedious and predictable talk about working within his situation as she tried to talk him into co-operating with the fools placed in authority around him. Instead she shrugged her shoulders.

'Do you want anything else?' she asked. When he shook his head, Alex glanced at her watch and turned to leave.

'Let me know when you're better so I can reschedule your appointment,' she said. 'I'll clear your absence with the work-shop and have a word with the staff here. You should rest for a few days and stay in bed if possible.'

'Thanks,' he said as she opened the door and stepped out. He didn't know if she had heard but as he settled back down to sleep he couldn't help feeling a tiny glow of warmth deep inside. It had been many years since anyone had treated him with any kindness at all. The fact this small act came from a probation officer left him utterly bemused.

Alex had heard but she gave no sign of it, though the hint of a smile curled the corner of her mouth as she headed down-stairs to have a little chat with Peter Marks.

The problem with going public with an investigation, Dave thought as he shuffled through the pile of notes on his desk, was that the number of false sightings rose almost daily. Now the garden-owning public of Somerset were aware of his existence, the Moth Man was popping up everywhere.

'Reckon he must be flying if'n he's been all these places,' said Sergeant Lynas leaning over Dave's shoulder to peer at the messages.

'So, how do you reckon we should sort out the good stuff from the crazies?'

Dave stared at the heap of paper in front of him and felt his shoulders slump. If he was being honest, he hadn't a clue.

'Maybe try matching them up to what we know about the other three?' he suggested. When Lynas nodded, Dave carried on with a little more confidence. 'I think there are a few important points, markers perhaps, we can use.' He hesitated before adding, 'Of course, it would be best if we could pick out something not in the public eye. Let me check what we kept out of the reports. We did keep some of the details back, didn't we?'

Lynas smiled grimly as he walked towards the incident board at the far side of the room.

'We may not all have the benefit of your education, Detective,' he said. 'Don't mean we haven't picked up a few things along the way. Kept quiet about the stocking over his face so we can chuck out anything where he's wearing a scarf or one of them balaclava things. Same as any with dark hair or ginger. Natural blond – that could be our ace in the hole – if you excuse the expression.' Dave grinned as Lynas continued. 'And we been a bit misleading about the gloves. Didn't say he was wearing any but did let on there was no fingerprints. People reading that, they might assume there were gloves but we never said – or let on what type neither.'

The door to the detectives' room flew open and a flustered-looking young PC stuck his head in.

'Just letting you know,' he said. 'Old-Fashioned's on his way over.'

There was a collective groan from the men and several grabbed their jackets and made for the exit. Dave looked around, puzzled by the sudden exodus. Sergeant Lynas moved smartly away from the incident board and pulled up a chair next to his protégé.

'Just sit still and don't try to be clever,' he hissed as the door slammed open again and the Inspector strode in.

'Sit down, please,' said their senior in a soft voice. The remaining men sank slowly into chairs, exchanging anxious glances with their colleagues.

The Inspector stood by the incident board, studying the

notes, maps and photographs that covered the surface, waiting until there was total silence.

'Look upon this as a motivational visit,' he said finally turning to look at each man in turn. 'Some encouragement in your work. Because you obviously need it.' His voice began to rise as he warmed to his theme and Dave looked on in alarm as his face turned a rather striking shade of puce.

'You have a full complement of officers to help, you have my forensics team working flat out just for you and what have you got to show for all this time and money? NOTHING!'

The whole room of men jumped as he accompanied the last word by striking his fist on the desk.

'People are SCARED out there. They want to know what is being done. I am being pressured from on high and guess what gentlemen? That means I will be pressuring YOU LOT. Find something. Solve this – I don't care how, just DO IT.' He glared around the room, mainly at the top of various heads as each officer stared down at the floor. Finally his eyes met Dave's.

'You – Brown. You're supposed to impress me so get on and do it. You're supposed to be clever – so work something out!'

With that he marched to the door and was gone.

There was a collective sigh as the entire room full of detectives let out their breath. A slow, soft muttering filled the silence as they relaxed again, exchanging rather sheepish grins with one another before turning back to their work with decidedly more focus than previously.

'What did you call him?' Dave asked Lynas.

'Old-Fashioned,' said the sergeant. 'On account of his methods, see? That, my lad, was a good old fashioned bollocking for the team. Works wonders an' all. So – you all spurred on to "work something out" then?'

Dave turned back to the pile of notes and reports heaped on his desk.

'That's about as productive as yelling "score more goals!"

191

at your football team,' he grumbled. Just as he started yet another sort-through he spotted something on the floor. One of the messages had fallen off and was lying, almost out of sight, under the lockable cupboard by his side. With a weary sigh he leaned over and pulled it into the light. Probably yet another sighting of a strange man looking at the windows in a funny way, he thought. He was about to drop it into the mass of useless information before him when he noticed the source. Northumbria Police, he read.

'Sarge – here, I think we might have something,' he called. The excitement in his voice attracted the attention of the officers closest to him and they turned their attention to the young rookie. Dave read through the brief report again and let out a long sigh.

'What?' demanded Lynas. 'Come on, don't play silly buggers. What you got there?' He reached out to take the note but Dave hung on to it and started to read aloud, eyes shining with excitement.

'Reported incidents bear close similarity to a series of attacks last year in and around the Morpeth area. Unknown man sighted in the gardens of large properties in relatively isolated locations. In one incident a man pressed his body against the windows at rear of house. Despite extensive enquiries no suspect was identified. Incidents stopped in September, after approximately six months.'

'Well,' said Sergeant Lynas. 'Good news and bad in that. Get on to them and try to find out the timings, will you? I'll get a decent map and see if there's any clues as to his way of travelling in this.' He hesitated and then said, 'Second thoughts, perhaps we should take this to Old-Fashioned. We want some fairly sensitive information and the higher up the food chain we go the more likely we is to get it.' He noticed Dave's disappointed expression. 'Don't look like that. You get a map and start finding similarities between this lot and ours. Soon as we got more information we'll put it all together and see what it tells us about him.'

'How do we know it's the same man?' asked one of the

detectives. 'Bloody long way away and a year ago, that is. Where's he been since then?'

'I suspect if we can work that out we'll be a lot closer to finding him,' said Lynas. 'This is too clear an M.O. for to be anything other than the same man – or ours is a copy-cat, in which case he came into contact with this joker or was around that area last year and heard all about it. Either way, we know more about him now than we did yesterday.' He stopped at the door and nodded towards Dave. 'Get that map out. I'll be back soonest.'

Dave pulled a clean notepad towards him and began to scribble questions as they rushed into his head. Location could be useful, he thought. Timing too, especially if they were all evenings or on the same day of the week. His current lot were all on a Friday, early evening just as it started to get dark. He stopped for a moment and considered, eyes unfocussed as he chewed the end of his pen. He was oblivious to the men around him, several of whom stared at him, curious rather than hostile towards the newcomer.

Something on the message was niggling at Dave. Should have taken a copy he thought, annoyed with himself at the oversight. Still, there'd not been much time, as Sergeant Lynas had seized the memo and taken it upstairs as soon as he'd read it. What was it about the windows? Only one report said the suspect had rubbed himself against the windows, he was sure. The other times he'd – what – flashed from the garden, maybe. He needed to know which happened first because if the windows came at the end of the series then this could be a sign of escalating behaviour. As the man got more confident he acted out more of his fantasy. The danger was he also needed more reaction, more result, to get the gratification he was seeking. And that meant he might be ready to step up to something even worse.

The house seemed strangely still when Alex got home from work. Sue had left a note saying she was out late doing an evening interview for a report and wouldn't be back for dinner. Alex wandered through the downstairs rooms switching

193

on the lights and closing her curtains tightly. She had waved her mother off at the station the day before and it was a relief to have her home back, yet for the first time in many years she felt lonely in her own space.

Resisting the urge to turn on the radio to fill the silence with empty sound, Alex set about making something to eat. After her visit to the hostel she had spoken to the workshop manager as promised and then spent a difficult half-hour convincing the local job centre not to stop Samuel's money as punishment for missing the job interview.

In a vile mood on her return, she had snapped at Alison, her PA. Alison was not really the forgiving sort and Alex realised on reflection there would be little work forthcoming until she had abased herself totally in that direction. How she longed for a return to her old assistant. Lauren could be tricky and quick to anger, she thought, but she never sulked and a brief exchange of words, preferably accompanied by a cake, would have set the situation right. She missed Lauren's sense of humour, her occasional sharp tongue and her unfailing support. The job seemed so much harder without her some days.

Pushing her half-finished meal aside, Alex sat at the dining table and drummed her fingers on the white cloth. It was a habit her mother hated and despite feeling her absence, a little bit of Alex delighted in the freedom to be annoying in her own home. She rose from the table leaving the remains of her dinner on the table whilst she flicked through the television channels in the fanciful and vain hope a new, fifth broadcaster had miraculously appeared to offer something better than the programming of the existing four channels. She was, of course, disappointed.

Finally, Alex went through to the front room, checked the curtains were still tightly closed and lifted the telephone receiver. She dialled a number from memory and waited, hands only shaking a little, for a reply.

'Hello? Hi.' She paused, uncertain how to proceed. 'I was wondering whether you might – might like to come over and drink that bottle of wine?'

'I can't tonight,' said Margie. 'Got a really busy couple of days coming up and then I'm back to Bristol to wait'n see if I get the job.'

'Of course,' said Alex. A sense of crushing disappointment washed over her and she went hot and cold with embarrassment. 'I'm sorry I bothered . . .'

'I could make it on Friday if the offer's still open,' said Margie. 'Will be lovely to be away from here and wind down a bit with a friend.'

All the breath seemed to rush out of Alex's body.

'Hello? Alex – you still there?'

'Yes,' Alex managed. 'That would be – well, that would be wonderful. Er, don't take this wrong but . . .'

'I will need to stay over if I'm drinking,' said Margie cheerfully. 'Don't worry about it – I'm happy with a couch if needs be.'

'Right,' said Alex. 'Well, see you on Friday then. Oh – you know the address don't you?'

She was grinning like a fool when she replaced the receiver. Then all the doubts came rushing back. Friday would be the first social night since her mother's departure. Was it too early to introduce Margie to her friends, she wondered. And exactly how was she going to do that when she didn't know how Margie saw her. God, life was complicated sometimes.

She returned to the television where, a short time later, Sue found her shouting abuse at a government party political broadcast urging all decent people to back them and ensure the country remained safe for their children.

Chapter Fourteen

Samuel was feeling much better after a couple of days rest and was able to resume his regular routine by the middle of the week. Despite feeling a bit shaky first thing in the morning, he rose early and opened the windows wide, stretching and breathing deeply before rolling his arms and shoulders behind him and above his head. It felt good, loosening the muscles after his enforced idleness and he dressed in a clean t-shirt and track suit, ready for the moment the front door was unlocked.

Slipping into the kitchen, he filled a plastic bottle with water from the tap. It was not ideal but tasted marginally better than the water from the bathroom. Besides, he shuddered to think of the germs crawling over the surfaces in the communal facilities. He was just grateful for the relative space and privacy he currently enjoyed due to the lack of room-mates at the hostel.

Hearing the sound of the locks, he left the kitchen, brushing past Bennie, the deputy warden, with scarcely a nod of acknowledgement. He had not forgotten – or forgiven – her actions last week, ordering him out into the rain without a thought for his health or comfort. Without a backwards glance he began to jog down the pavement, heading for the footpath leading on to the Levels.

Bennie stood at the door, watching as Samuel settled into a rhythm, his stride lengthening as he moved comfortably over the pavement and disappeared round the corner. She was convinced there was something very wrong about Samuel Burton, something more than the familiar resentment at the rules and routine of the probation hostel. Still, she thought, as she went back inside to begin preparing breakfast for the residents, there was nothing she could do until he was caught breaking the rules and at the moment he was behaving himself – just enough to avoid being sent back to court anyway. Or, a much more chilling thought, he was too clever for them all and was already embarked on whatever dark, secret plan he held inside.

She felt a shiver run down her back as she pulled the door closed and set off up the stairs to rouse today's reluctant kitchen assistant from amongst the residents.

Samuel made good time on his run, reaching the airfield easily within his target time. Stopping to drink a little water, he looked around, aware that others also used this space occasionally, but all was still. Listening for the sound of approaching cars, he cut across the runway and made his way to the ruined buildings at the far end. To his consternation, he saw the brush and stones that had concealed the entrance had been disturbed and there were signs of an intruder in the main room. Pulling on a pair of light cotton gloves, he felt around the wall locating his torch still in its hiding place up high on one of the lintels. Switching it on he traced the beam carefully over the floor and walls. Only when he was sure his cache had not been disturbed did he venture over to the pile of debris in the corner.

The smell of pineapple had faded over the past few weeks and he shook out the contents of his tin, examining each item carefully. It was almost time, he thought. Still, the signs of interest in his hiding place worried him. He had not evaded detection for so long by taking risks and he was so close now . . . .

With some reluctance he packed everything carefully in the large tin making sure he left no signs of his presence. Even his footprints, faint and indistinct on the packed mud of the floor, were scuffed and brushed smooth leaving an apparently untouched surface. The torch went in to his pocket and with a final look around Samuel hefted his tin, slightly off-balance from the bulk of his load. All was still outside in the mild morning air and he set off along the edge of the airfield, ducking around the clumps of brambles before sliding through a gap in the fence and settling into a reasonable rhythm across the marshy land.

He had no doubt that that interfering cow Bennie would contact his probation officer and he would be expected in the workshop for the afternoon session. He would have preferred to take his time over the new hiding place and maybe even pop over to the house to have another scout around and check nothing had changed but it was a long haul and he decided it was better to conserve his energy for the weekend.

The Levels are littered with old, abandoned buildings, relics of the agrarian and industrial past and Samuel had explored a large number of them. Steering clear of the more prominent footpaths, he made his way across the empty land to the disused railway line. Here he had noticed the remains of several crumbling buildings, not much more than a patch of scrubland with a scattering of broken brick on the surface. One in particular had a dropped floor and the remains of its door was still lying over the hole. Taking care not to mark the surface, Samuel eased it away from the frame and slipped his precious tin inside. It wasn't ideal but then again it wasn't for long. Soon the contents would be disposed of, untraceable in the thick mud of the great marsh at the centre of the Levels. Samuel always began afresh each time. It was one of the reasons no-one had ever come close to catching him.

He was exhausted by the time he reached the road into town and the sight of the bus rumbling over the pitted road was too much of a temptation. Despite his reservations he flagged it down, climbing aboard, paying the fare and sitting in silence as the green and watery landscape of the Levels flicked past the window. No-one seemed to be paying him any attention and he allowed himself a rare moment of relaxation in the corner of the vehicle. His imagination drifted towards the next few days, the time of anticipation before he was able to fulfil the desire burning inside him.

Not long, he thought. Not long at all.

It was a warm afternoon and Brian and Charlie had spent an exhausting and ultimately fruitless couple of hours crossing the runway, the metal detector becoming a dead weight as they dragged it across the broken concrete and rough scrub of the airfield. After their initial optimism wore off they found the enterprise was rather more like work than anticipated and over the next few days their approach changed from hopefully adventurous to grim determination. As the effects of an evening drowning their disappointment in Robbie's Natural Cider, the most potent and notorious of all local 'natch', caught up with them, their remaining enthusiasm for the project evaporated along with their energy.

Charlie was first to crack, throwing the metal detector one way and his aching body another as he collapsed, a sweaty and bleary-eyed heap beneath the shade of a willow tree.

''Ent nothin' here,' he said. 'Waste of time, this is. Useless girt thing.' He aimed a kick at the detector, scuffing his trainers on the runway but failing to stir the machine into life.

'Watch what you doing,' Brian warned, gathering up his precious possession and pulling it out of the reach of his erstwhile friend. 'Always takes time to find anything decent. If was easy, I reckon would be all gone by now. Probably been picked over already round here anyway. Maybe we'd be better out there.' He waved an arm vaguely in the direction of Glastonbury, a faint smudge on the far horizon. The outline of the Tor wavered in the unseasonal heat and Brian collapsed next to Charlie, nudging him out of the way as he sought some shelter from the sun.

'Don't fancy lugging that old thing all the way to Glasto,' said Charlie sulkily. He was beginning to regret his involvement in the project and was rather wishing he was home with his Gran. His stomach rumbled, a reminder it had been a long time since breakfast and neither of them had given any thought to providing any lunch. More pressing was thirst that dried his mouth and left his throat aching. Robbie's 'natch' was a powerful diuretic and both lads were on the verge of disastrous hangovers.

'Not all the way,' said Brian crossly. 'There's a load of old ruins out there. Factories and forts and whatever. Can't all have been dug over.'

He hauled his aching body upright and slung the metal detector over one shoulder. 'Come on, I got an idea. Is an old dig over past that farm. Found some right nice bottles there once and there was lots of stuff around. You up for another go?'

In truth, Charlie wasn't, but he was not willing to give up just yet. Wearily the two young men trudged across the airfield, slipped through the hedge and headed towards Brian's next target.

Ada rose early, as was her habit, and trotted down the stairs in her cottage to put the kettle on and see to her chickens. Humming softly, she twitched the curtains aside and leapt back in alarm at the face pressed up against her window. Biting back a squeak, she stared for a moment before unbolting the door and, seizing a rolling pin from the draining board, hurling herself at the intruder.

'Get away you nasty, dirty thing,' she shouted, raising the rolling pin and brandishing it at Pongo. The goat looked at her for a moment, tilting his head to one side before turning round and sauntering back towards his paddock. A piece of washing line trailed from his mouth and he munched contentedly on the last of Ada's dusters. Quivering with fury, Ada slapped at his hindquarters, generating a surprisingly mild sound of protest as Pongo ambled back inside his supposedly secure enclosure.

A quick examination of the fence showed the battery for the electric wires had been kicked over, presumably by the goat as retaliation for the mild shock it generated. One of the terminals had become disconnected, leaving the circuit off and the rest of the fence open to Pongo's not inconsiderable strength.

Muttering angrily, Ada struggled to right the posts next to the paddock gate, stopping only to dash inside her kitchen and grab the screaming kettle off the stove. Finally she had the pen relatively secure and was able to go back inside where the dogs had helped themselves to the bread and bacon she'd unwisely left on the table. Surveying the mess in her kitchen, Ada felt her heart sink. Some days, she reckoned, it was better not to get up. Though at least she'd got to the damned goat before he ate her seedlings as well as the washing. And it wasn't as if anything important had been on the line overnight. Mixed blessings, she thought as she settled at the table with a sigh. Story of most everyone's life.

Wary of messing with the battery and either damaging the circuit or possibly electrocuting herself, Ada pottered around the garden keeping a careful eye on Pongo and the dogs. She had considered starting the day turning over the pile of chicken manure but this was round the corner of the house, cunningly hidden between a pile of old milk crates and the remains of an Austin 40. Ada had decided a while ago that the scattered remains of larceny and failed repair projects provided excellent cover for her agricultural endeavours that were hidden away out the back. Most people took one look at the mess in the front and passed by with a righteous sniff. The chicken pile took care of anyone who sniffed too hard. Instead she dug out a new piece of washing line and strung it between the posts and turned her attention to transplanting her salad crops.

She was just considering what she was going to do about the goat overnight when Tom drew up in his battered old van.

'Now then, Ada,' he said cheerfully and then reeled back as Ada vented her fury on him, his fence and his goat.

'Woah,' he managed after several minutes of imaginative and highly personal comments. 'Looks like you fixed it all right and there's no harm done to the garden. Let me check it all over and start that 'lectic fence off again.'

Ada sniffed, wiped her hands on her apron and went inside to put the kettle on, leaving Tom to reset the fence. This time he moved the battery to a box a good distance from the fence and piled some earth around it.

'I'll be putting a top on that,' he observed. 'Don't want the current failing again on account of a bit of rain.'

Ada was mollified but still reluctant to let Tom off quite that easily. 'Don't know as I'd trust it again,' she said pouring out the tea and pushing the remains of a cold pheasant over the table towards him.

Tom helped himself to a chunk of the bird and a couple of cold potatoes. 'Got any pickle?' he asked unperturbed.

Ada rummaged in a cupboard, slamming the door closed as she banged the jar down in front of him.

'Said I wasn't sure how safe he is in there,' she repeated. 'Give me a right scare, leering in through the window like that an' all.'

'Now Ada,' said Tom tucking in to his lunch. 'Was no harm done and won't happen again. I'll go round, check them posts and that battery's well out of reach. This is girt lovely,' he added, spooning pickles onto his potatoes.

'Is just left over veg from last year,' said Ada. 'Secret is lettin' it ferment a bit afore boiling. And a bit of honey, just to take the edge off.'

Tom shook his head in admiration. 'Best I ever had, I swear,' he said helping himself from the jar. 'You ever thought of sellin' them? I know a lot of fellahs as would give good money for summat as good as this. Nothing like a decent heap of pickle with a bite of lunch.'

Ada's response to this idea was lost in a sudden and unexpected knocking at the front door, a sound that caused Tom to rise to his feet and glance uneasily around.

'You expecting company?' he asked.

Ada shook her head, equally perturbed. 'No, I ain't. You don't think is someone from the river board?'

Tom stared at her in surprise. 'Don't reckon so,' he said. 'What would they be wanting with you anyway?'

The knocking was repeated as Ada nodded towards the back garden where Pongo munched his way happily through undergrowth that rightly belonged to someone else.

Tom shook his head. It was much more likely, he thought, the police had decided he'd had enough time free from their attentions and had decided to remind him he was still (and probably always would be) a 'person of interest' to them.

They were standing, frozen by their respective fears in the kitchen, when a face popped round the door.

'I'm sorry to just drop in, Mrs Mallory,' said Charlie Dodds. 'Only I'm gasping for summat to drink. I don't suppose you could spare a glass of water could you?'

Ada glanced at Tom, trying not to laugh aloud with relief. 'You come on in lad,' she said, reaching for a glass.

Charlie slipped into the cool room, his face red and shining from his long trudge across the Levels. He folded himself into a chair with a sigh of relief, bending over to push his battered army surplus bag under the table.

'You been out looking for something your Gran can make for dinner?' Ada asked, hoping to put the lad at ease.

Charlie shook his head as he gulped down the cold water.

'More?' Ada asked and he held out the glass gratefully. 'You sip that now,' she warned. 'Don't want you giving your stomach a cramp, all that cold poured in of a sudden.'

Charlie stopped for breath and set the half-empty glass on the table. 'Thank you Mrs Mallory,' he said shyly. ''Ent nothing to eat,' he added, nodding to the bag. 'Is – well,' he gave Tom a suspicious look. 'Is buried treasure.'

'Is it now,' said Ada. 'And how might you be carrying treasure around with you then?'

"Tis too,' Charlie protested. 'Was down by the bottle pit, over near that old fort. We was usin' Brian's metal detector and there was a whole heap of glass and stuff – look.' He hauled the bag out and dropped it on the table with a loud thump, then began to unpack it in front of them. A variety of coloured glass bottles, most of them dulled by years in the mud of the Levels, lined up across Ada's table. Tom reached out to pick one up, raising his eyebrows to request Charlie's permission first. He rubbed at the surface, spitting on his thumb to clean the deep blue glass.

'This is a lovely specimen,' he said holding the little artefact up to the light. 'Not a lot of these around no more and I know several collectors as pay good money for blue glass. Specially of an age and this is – oh, I think maybe more'n eighty years.'

He met Ada's disbelieving stare with a cool grin. 'Look here,' he said pointing to some embossed lettering on the surface.

'Poison,' read Ada. 'Charming. So – what do that tell us then?'

Tom took the bottle and turned it carefully in the light from the open door. 'Has ribbed sides – see – but nothing else stamped on it. From about 1908 was the law all poison bottles had to say "Not to be taken". This 'ent got that so must be earlier.' He smiled slightly and placed the bottle back on the table.

Despite herself Ada was impressed. 'Well, you learn something every day,' she said admiringly.

Tom shrugged modestly. 'Just pick up stuff, hanging around markets and such. Still, is not often a lad your age knows these is worth something.' He nodded approvingly at Charlie who was staring up in frank astonishment.

'Oh, is not them's the treasure,' he said and fumbled around in the bag once more. 'Is this,' and he dropped a brightly painted metallic object down next to the bottles.

Tom and Ada both leapt back in horror. 'Oh my good God,' said Ada. Tom seized her by the arm and hustled her outside then went back, grabbed Charlie and hauled him through the door.

''Ent safe here neither,' he said looking around the garden. Everywhere there were glass panels – or livestock. 'Where are the dogs?' he asked.

Ada put her hands to her mouth. 'Oh, no. They's in the front room. Oh Tom – oh no . . .'

'Wait here,' said Tom and before she could stop him he slipped back inside the kitchen.

'What's the matter?' Charlie asked. 'What about my treasure then?'

Ada stepped in front of him, blocking his way. With her hands on her hips she presented a formidable obstacle and Charlie, who was basically a sensible young man, hesitated.

'That thing you got in there,' said Ada. 'That's a bomb, you stupid lad.'

A look of horror flitted over Charlie's face.

'But can't be,' he protested. 'Is all bright colours like someone decorated it. Why would anyone do that? And anyway,' he added grimly, ''ent exploded or nothing. Oh heck.' He sat down abruptly as the possibilities if Ada were right hit him. 'Oh bugger. I bin jogging it around and . . .' He went white and rocked slightly.

Despite her anger, Ada knelt down next to him. 'Just sit here,' she said hauling him to his feet and helping him over to a chair looking out over the back fence. 'Maybe lean a bit forwards, put yer head down 'til you feel a bit better.'

Charlie flopped onto the seat, panting for breath as he stared out over the flat, watery landscape.

'Feeling any better?' Ada asked. She glanced over her shoulder anxiously hoping every second to see Tom appear with the dogs.

'I'm right sorry,' said Charlie softly. 'Didn't mean to be no bother to you. I just wanted a drink, was all.' He was close to tears and still looked very pale.

'Just sit there for a bit,' said Ada. 'Don't fret – how was you to know, eh? You stay there mind. Don't want you getting back into no danger.'

Charlie blinked up at her, squinting slightly in the bright sunlight. It seemed impossible, thought Ada, that this menace was lurking in her kitchen, bringing darkness on such a beautiful day.

Her concern for Tom growing with every minute, she hurried back down the path towards the house. She was surrounded by silence, broken only by a brief burst of birdsong from the willows across the stream. It was as if the landscape held its breath, waiting for a resolution. A scratching sound from the front of the cottage and a tiny, almost inaudible bark set Ada's heart racing as she pushed through the new growth surrounding the side gate, pulling at the slightly soggy wood before opening a space large enough to slide through.

She gave a gasp of relief as the front door opened slowly and the two dogs wriggled their way out to safety.

'Tom – oh thank you. Thank you so much . . .' Lost for words for once in her life, Ada flung her arms around him, shedding a few tears of relief as she hugged him tight.

'Now then Ada,' said Tom gently disentangling himself. 'We's not out of the woods yet, so to speak.' He smiled at her, patting her shoulder. 'Don't suppose you got a phone anywhere in there have you?'

Ada shook her head, her attention on the dogs that glided around her legs, tails wagging frantically with excitement.

'I think we need someone to come and get that bloody thing,' said Tom. 'Soonest, too. Could be a dud but could go off any time. Where's that daft lad?'

Ada nodded towards the back garden where Charlie was still sitting obediently on the chair.

'Here, you get yerself and these dogs into my van and I'll go get him,' said Tom handing her the keys. 'I'll drive us into 'Zoyland and let the *polis* know. Get someone to clear it out for us.'

'You lock that old thing?' Ada said taking the keys. 'Out here?'

Tom grinned at her as he shouldered the gate further open.

'You never know,' he said. 'Out here on the Levels, is gypsies and all types around. Can't be taking no chances.'

Friday afternoons were traditionally fairly quiet at the probation offices. Workshop sessions finished around four in the afternoon and not many clients wanted to make the run into town and risk getting caught up in the rush hour traffic as the chicken factory turned out and office and shop workers headed home. Alex looked at her diary and saw she had only one appointment left – Jake Hollis, who was dropping in after work.

When her phone rang she was deep in some planning, setting out the exact details of her clandestine 'drink/drive' evening and her immediate reaction was to shove the notes under a pile of unfinished Part Bs. Stupid, she thought lifting the receiver. Still, it did show how nervous she was about the whole thing.

'Yes?'

'You got time to see Brian?' came Lauren's voice from reception. 'He's all excited and bouncing around out here, going on about making his fortune.' Her voice dropped to a whisper. 'Think he could be on summat – you know. Maybe if you had a word, calmed him down a bit?'

Alex checked her watch and suppressed a sigh. 'Send him down,' she said wearily.

'Cheers,' said Lauren. 'I owe you one.'

Only a few seconds passed before Brian burst through the door, every bit as excited as Lauren had described. Alex held up a hand to stall his excited babble, pointing to the chair in front of her.

Brian dropped into it, a broad grin on his face as he rummaged in the carrier bag clutched in his hand.

'Told you I'd find summat good,' he said. 'Now what do

you think of that?' He pulled out a metal object, the twin to Charlie's and placed it lovingly on the desk.

Alex sprang to her feet, stepping back carefully to avoid touching the surface where the bomb sat, sinister and menacing in its bright painted colours.

'Oh bloody hell,' she said softly. 'Oh shit . . .'

Sliding round the edge of the desk, she held up both hands as Brian lifted his carrier bag and pulled out a second device.

'Put it down very carefully,' said Alex, voice rough with tension. 'Just gently on the floor. Now push the chair back away from the desk – don't touch the bag!'

Brian looked up at her, puzzled and hurt by her reaction. 'But I thought you'd be pleased,' he said. 'Gonna sell um – and the others too.'

Alex took a deep breath and pointed at him sternly.

'Get up very, very slowly and move towards the door,' she said. 'No, don't speak. Imagine that's – oh, a sleeping rattlesnake on the desk. Now, move away from the snake, Brian. That's right – now get out and tell reception to ring the police and report a couple of unexploded bombs in the office.'

Brian's eyes widened in horror and Alex yelled to get his attention.

'Go!' He was out of the door and running before she got past her overflowing bookcase. 'I have *so* got to tidy up a bit,' she muttered, lunging to catch the door before it slammed shut. With a final glance round her room she hurried down the corridor expecting at any moment to hear an explosion behind her.

There was chaos in the reception area as she emerged from the deserted day centre. Lauren had rung upstairs to inform Gordon and a full evacuation was in progress with officers and admin staff scrambling for the door.

'Everyone outside and into the park,' bellowed Gordon. 'Quickly now. Just take what you are carrying – no going back inside.' He pointed to Alison who was dithering by the office door.

'My bag's in there with my new credit card,' she protested.

'Out,' said Gordon firmly. 'Are you all right Alex? Lauren called the police and they're evacuating the rest of the street and getting some bomb disposal chaps in.'

Alex nodded, shaken by events but glad help was on the way.

'Was it a phone call or what?' he asked steering her out of the front door and round the yard to the main gates.

Alex shook her head and smiled grimly.

'It's a Mills bomb,' she said. 'Well, two actually. Brian took that bloody metal detector of his out onto the Levels and unearthed them. Said they were "buried treasure" and unpacked them onto my desk.'

Gordon stared at her, lost for words. 'Right,' he said finally. 'The police will need to know about this as soon as they get here. They want to speak to you anyway and our local Inspector asked if you could be on hand. Stay round the corner from the yard until they get here, mind, just in case.' With that he was gone, cutting across the car park to check everyone was safely out of the offices.

Alex leaned against the gates, shivering as the shock of the last few minutes hit her. For a few minutes she stood, eyes closed against the late afternoon sun that streamed down from the sky, just above the roof line of the old building. The heat seeped into her like warm honey, flowing through her tired body until it rested in her bones. Slowly the tension in her shoulders began to slip away and she felt a sense of calm returning.

Her good mood was cut short by someone stepping between her and the soothing sunlight, casting a shadow across her face. She snapped her eyes open, squinting against the halo surrounding the figure in front of her.

'Oh, Jake. Hello. No, you can't go in,' she said holding out her hand to stop him brushing past her.

'Why not?' asked Jake Hollis stiffly. 'I'm on time for my appointment. What's going on?' He looked around in alarm as several police cars turned the corner at speed, screeching to a halt about twenty yards up the street. In seconds a dozen police officers were knocking on the few occupied houses in the road. Jake eyed this activity nervously, swallowing and stepping back towards the gatepost as the Inspector from Highpoint almost trotted down the road towards them.

'Miss Hastings,' he said, ignoring Jake completely.

Alex managed a rather sickly smile, taking the proffered hand in a slightly moist handshake.

'Now, where did they say the bomb is supposed to be,' continued the Inspector. 'It is probably a hoax but I'm obliged to take anything of this nature seriously, especially considering the run-up to the election and our MP's current job description as Secretary for Northern Ireland.'

He tried a friendly smile, obviously hoping to put Alex at ease but the result was rather too conspiratorial to be reassuring.

Jake, in the meantime, had begun to edge away from them both, seeking to make his escape.

'Excuse me,' said Alex and caught hold of the probationer's sleeve.

'I'm sorry about your appointment,' she said. 'We'll have to reschedule for next week. As you can see, these are rather unusual events.' She gestured towards the people emerging through their front doors, glancing nervously in her direction before being ushered away by the police.

'It's most inconvenient,' said Jake. 'I came in especially after work. I don't see I should have to do it again next week.'

Alex narrowed her eyes and glared at him.

'You will come in when and where I say you will,' she said softly. 'And anyway, you only live down the road in the hostel. You come back past here every night.'

'I had other plans,' said Jake angrily and stalked off, his back rigid as he strove to contain his temper. At the top of the road he stooped to unlock his bicycle, carefully unthreading the chain from some railings before setting off up the street and out of sight.

'What a nice young man,' said the inspector. 'Are they all as charming as that?'

Alex shook her head in frustration. 'He's one of clever ones,' she said. 'Not like Brian who delivered the damn Mills bombs.'

Several officers gathered around her as she described the events of the last hour. 'There was no malice involved,' she repeated several times. 'He didn't do it deliberately. He just didn't realise what he was carrying.'

'Sounds like he was lucky not to blow hisself up,' observed one of the officers.

Alex nodded. 'I think they are old butterfly bombs,' she said. The Inspector raised an eyebrow at this and she hurried on. 'My mother was in London all through the war and she told me about them. Sort of little hand grenades or mines but they were painted bright colours and dropped by parachute so they didn't go off until someone picked them up. Usually a child,' she added angrily.

There was a crackling sound from the nearest car and one of the uniformed men reached in and answered the radio.

'Excuse me, Sir,' he called, his voice strained with the urgency of his message. 'Sorry to interrupt but word is there's another one, out on the Levels near Westonzoyland.'

The Inspector rounded on Alex, fixing her with a stern look.

'We need to speak to Brian,' he said. 'Two incidents of this type make a whole different situation.' He turned away and issued instructions to a couple of constables. 'We must consider him potentially dangerous,' he said. 'Take him to the secure cells and notify the security detail as soon as you find him.' He held up his hand to forestall Alex's protests.

'I'm sorry but there are protocols in place,' he said. 'This should be handled as a potential terrorist situation. The Minister for Northern Ireland is in town at present, canvassing for the election, and he has several high-profile public engagements in the next day or so. This must be handed over to his team at once.'

He turned away, dismissing Alex from his consideration as he issued instructions to the officers around him. Alex waited for a moment before making her way slowly up the street and along the footpath to the park where the rest of the staff from the office was assembled. They would be eager for news, she thought. She hadn't a clue what she was going to tell them.

Chapter Fifteen

It was the worst possible start to an evening Alex had antic-ipated for days. The police had kept them all corralled in the cooling evening air for an hour and a half before finally allowing them to leave. A number of the staff had cars in the yard and there were two issues to be resolved there. Firstly, the police were not letting anyone in for fear the two bombs went off and caused injury or worse. On the other hand, the bomb disposal squad were keen to get all of the remaining civilian vehicles out of range, just in case.

'Not that we anticipate any difficulties,' said the officer in charge standing at the end of the yard and eyeing the vehicles with concern. 'Still, it is very old ordinance and that can be tricky. Don't want to run any unnecessary risks.'

There was some debate about exactly who should go in and move the cars, a discussion rather complicated by Ricky's insistence only he should move his old Austin.

'It's extremely valuable,' he said. 'Tricky to drive too, unless you know what you are doing. I don't want just any-body messing around with it.'

Finally the senior officer had a quiet word with Gordon who took Ricky off to one side. When Ricky returned he was very pale and handed over his keys without a murmur before stalking off to the folly by the main garden. Here he rolled himself another of his trademark tiny cigarettes and sat on his own, smoking and staring out over the park.

'What did you say to him?' asked Sue, eyeing the sulking figure in the background.

'The officer pointed out how unstable these sort of things can be,' said Gordon. 'Even the sound and vibration from a car engine might be enough to set them off. Ricky decided that he would prefer the experts to move his car under the circumstances.' It was a credit to his professionalism that he managed to respond without cracking a smile.

Sue was not so restrained and gave a wicked giggle at the thought of Ricky's precious 'vintage' car being manhandled by a heavy-footed soldier in muddy boots.

'Any idea when we can go?' asked Alex, who was getting more worried with every passing minute. What if Margie turned up early and found the house empty? Would she just go away or would she wait? Alex had planned an elaborate welcome and a special meal but as the minutes ticked away all her hopes began to fade with them. At this rate, she thought glaring at her watch, she'd not have time to cook anything. They'd be eating late into the evening as it was.

'I'm sorry,' said Gordon. 'The police want to talk to you again about what Brian actually said and the bomb squad will need to get more details of exactly what is in the room. I think you'll be here for a while.'

'I only live over there,' said Alex gesturing down the riverbank to the row of terraced houses. 'Can't they just come and get me?'

Gordon shook his head. 'I wish we could all take shelter in your house,' he said. 'I could really do with a cup of tea right now but they were insistent you need to be on hand, at least for a while longer.'

'Can I go?' asked Sue. Alex gave her a hurt look and Sue

added, 'I can wait back at the house and make sure there's someone there to welcome your friend. I could make a start on the dinner if you like.'

Alex suppressed a groan. It was very kind of Sue, who hated cooking almost as much as everyone else hated eating her food, but the thought of the lovely fresh (and expensive) ingredients she had marshalled being subjected to Sue's ministrations was just too depressing.

'I'm sure I won't be long,' she said. 'Could you let her in and maybe give her a drink? Explain what's happened and I'll be back as soon as I can.'

Gordon nodded his agreement and Sue set off across the park.

'Oh, I forgot,' she called. 'What's your friend called?'

'Margie,' Alex replied, ignoring Lauren's sharp look. 'She's from Bristol.' Now why did I say that, she wondered, turning to meet Lauren's gaze. 'What?'

'Nothin,' said Lauren. 'Would that be who we saw out Brean way then?'

Alex shrugged, trying to make light of the whole thing but Lauren was relentless.

'Was Margie at Bristol nick, looked out for Kevin wasn't it. She still here then?'

Despite the temptation to grind her teeth in frustration, Alex kept her face seemingly indifferent.

'Yeah,' she said. 'She's been down here, doing some work at Shepton. I thought it would be nice to make her feel a bit welcome.'

Lauren blinked at her before turning away, disappointed by her friend's lack of reaction.

'Well, seein' as they's got my car out I'll be off home. Maybe see you over the weekend,' she said. She ambled off down the towpath towards the main road where a very uncomfortable looking policeman was struggling to get out of the front seat of her specially modified vehicle. She watched for a moment as the inevitable crowd of gawpers pressed a little too close to the police tape and were ushered back to a safe distance but

215

she was tired after a long week and decided it was unlikely the building was going to blow up, so there was little sense in staying.

Struggling with the seat that the police officer had left pushed right to the end of the runners and down as low as it could possibly go, she settled herself in her car and, executing a nifty three-point turn, set off through town. It would be nice to have a quiet weekend, especially if Dave could get a day off. Not that likely though, with the 'Moth Man' search still going strong. There had been more than enough excitement for one week, she decided. Swinging out to pass a cyclist, she put the car into top gear and roared off down the main road towards home.

No-one was likely to note his absence from the evening meal at the hostel. In fact they would have been surprised if he had actually turned up, so rarely did Samuel deign to eat with his fellow residents. It was perfectly normal for him to disappear in the morning, returning to the hostel just before curfew. As long as he attended his meetings with Alex Hastings and went to the designated sessions at the day centre no-one questioned him, and Peter Marks had given up trying to enrol him on the 'Ladder of Achievement'. It had taken a while but finally everything was in place and Samuel was, to all outward appearances, just doing exactly what he always did.

His afternoon run took him out to the edge of the north moor, a desolate and deserted piece of marshland bisected by the Taunton canal and cut into small, relatively dry areas of peat and bog by man-made ditches and rhynes. There was little in the way of cover but a few trees grew at Northmoor Corner and there were several tumble-down brick shelters nearby, remains of overnight huts for peat cutters but now used by illegal elver fishers during the spring season. Samuel had the location of each one fixed firmly in his mind along with the nearest routes in and out of the area.

Nothing was left to chance and he savoured the moments of calm before the climax of his visit, first rescuing the pineapple tin from its new location. He was pleased to see there were no signs it had been disturbed and the path nearby bore a few tyre tracks from the occasional bicycle but nothing recent. As the sun moved across the sky and the birds began to gather for their early evening flight across the landscape, Samuel settled down in the cover of the trees, savouring the warmth on his skin and the welcome solitude.

His position overlooked the canal and in the distance he could see the tiny village of North Newton. The original cottages were clustered around the crossroads where a few shops supplied the basic demands of the villagers. With the larger towns of Highpoint and Taunton within easy reach, most people shopped outside their immediate area now, picking up their groceries on the way home from work. There was even a special bus, run by a local supermarket, to transport those without cars away from their local shops.

As he watched, a trickle of vehicles began to move down the road from the distant motorway, each finding its way to a house or cottage where the doors opened to disgorge children home from school and eager for the weekend. Samuel settled himself more comfortably in the shadow of the trees, waiting for the next arrivals, the exodus from work. Most people were remarkably predictable, he thought. You just knew they left the office at the same time, got home at the same time, parked in the same place and did the same things over and over, every day.

He knew exactly when she would appear, driving her mid-range hatchback through North Newton before taking the road towards the Grand Estate. Then a left, over the bridge and she was home, pulling up in front of the cottage by the stream. The one with the shiny new windows and the ugly plastic conservatory tacked on to the back. The one they had totally ruined with their lack of taste and crass materialism. Some people needed a lesson, and she was one of them he decided, even before seeing what she had done to the house. She was arrogant, stupid and self-centred, treating everyone around her as an inferior. She had sneered at him the first time they met – and she had scarcely two brain cells to rub together. Samuel realised he was grinding his teeth at the memory and forced himself to relax and enjoy the thought of just how she would pay for that arrogance. Nothing was going to ruin this for him, he decided.

The sun began to sink below the trees and the evening suddenly felt decidedly chilly. Without taking his eyes off the road below, Samuel opened the pineapple tin, sniffing the air as the faint scent wafted past. The sickly sweetness brought back memories of his childhood, pictures he suppressed with a grimace. Canned pineapple – a 'treat' for the poor kids in the class. If he had the freedom to prepare his own meals he would never eat anything out of a can again.

The tin contained his other clothes. Clothes selected to be as unlike anything he would normally wear as possible whilst still being suitably non-descript. He pulled them out and laid them on the grass beside him. Dull coloured clothes, poorly cut and slightly too big for his fit, athletic frame. For his feet he had a pair of old boots, a once fashionable brand with distinctive patterns on the soles. The heels also left an imprint with the shoe size, which was larger than Samuel's fitting. He examined the insides where a lining of old newspapers filled the excess width. Everything was in good condition and ready for him and he stood up, stretched and began to remove his own clothes.

This was the moment when he began to feel the excitement of his actions. All the planning, organising, dreaming, it all came together at this moment. This was where he would begin his remembering as he savoured the event, long after it was over. He stared down the road, hungry for the first glimpse of his chosen companion for the next hour or so but there was no sign of the car yet.

She was never late. He knew that because he had checked, watching one evening after another. She didn't stay late to catch up and was not the type to wait behind and help someone out. When her time was done she was out of the door, into the car and off. He pulled the worn grey shirt over his head, tucking it into the waistband of faded blue jeans. The jeans were a local speciality. Cut from off-blue fabric they were almost (but not quite) the right shape. As a consequence they failed to fit anyone who ever tried them on. The local power station issued them to its workers and around town any ill-fitting trousers became known as 'Hinkleys'. Workers passed them on to friends and relatives and the style was endemic. Everyone had a pair.

Samuel fumbled with the belt, fingers encased in thin cotton gloves to ensure no trace would be left behind when he was finished. The boots were the only striking thing about his appearance. They had once been pink and retained enough colour to attract the eye. Anyone catching sight of him would remember the pink boots – and hopefully very little else.

He tightened the laces, double knotting the bows for security. Patting his pockets, he was reassured he had everything he needed. Key – blindfold – plastic rope, all carefully folded and placed in the right order. He fumbled in the back pocket and located a crepe bandage, useful if she tried to make a noise. At the bottom of the tin was an old-fashioned straight razor, the stainless steel blade folded away in the handle. Samuel reached in and picked it up, opening the blade to check it was still spotless. Quality pays, he thought as he examined the finely honed surface. It glinted in the dying sunlight, bright and clean, without a single blemish.

Satisfied with his preparations, Samuel rolled his own clothes up in a plastic bag and placed them in the tin which he stowed away out of sight in the centre of the undergrowth. His watch was in the pocket of his tracksuit but he could tell the time to within a few minutes from the sun and a strange running count in his head, a metronome that never seemed to stop. He was ready but she was late. She was never late – never. Why was she late today, of all days? The tingling of pleasure was diminishing as he crouched in the shrubbery, replaced by rising frustration. Samuel's eyes shone a bright, hard blue as he stared out over the empty landscape. She was making him angry and that was really not a good thing.

Alex was finally released by the police after six in the evening. Despite her reassurances the bomb disposal officers had swept the building, searching for any more devices. Ignoring her pleas, the police had set up a major incident team and were still scouring the area for Brian. She trudged home through the dusk feeling utterly despondent. Emerging from the tunnel that ran under the road, she was startled to see the lights on in her kitchen. Absorbed in her own problems, she had forgotten Sue had gone on ahead and presumably – hopefully – Margie would be waiting in the house.

Despite the fluttering of nervousness deep in her stomach, Alex felt her mood lift and she found herself hurrying down the path to the back door. Warmth enveloped her as she stepped into the kitchen and the rich smell of roasting chicken filled the air. Margie, looking decidedly stylish in smart black trousers and a flatteringly skinny top was peeling potatoes whilst instructing Sue on the correct way to prepare a salad. To her astonishment, Sue was actually doing what she was told for once.

As Alex stepped through the door, Margie dropped the vegetable knife and reached over to give her a hug.

'I was starting to wonder if you was down in the basement defusing something yourself,' she said with a grin.

Pleased and confused, Alex hesitated, not wanting to look at Sue, but her friend was absorbed in her culinary exercises and just flashed a smile in her direction before returning to the tricky job of extracting the stone from an avocado. Fortunately Margie didn't seem to notice her reticence.

'I hope you don't mind,' she said. 'Sue here let me in and we didn't know how long you was going to be so I thought I'd make a start. Didn't think you'd want to eat too late. Here, have some wine,' and she handed her a glass, brimming with a deep ruby red liquid.

Alex blinked, filled with a sense of astonishment at how – well, how *ordinary* this all felt. How natural, but how right, coming home to her friends, sharing the house with them.

She took a sip from her glass and a powerful rush of sensation flowed across her tongue, warming her through as she swallowed the wine.

'Wow,' she said taking a deep breath before trying another sip.

Margie had returned to the sink and was busy finishing off the potatoes. 'Hope you like it,' she said. 'I think that by the time we get to the end of the week, we deserve something a bit nice. Not that I get all that many weekends, being at Bristol, but I'm really a bit hopeful for Shepton. Would be a good move for me.'

Alex pulled up the high stool she kept under the counter and settled herself on it, leaning her elbows on the worktop and keeping a firm grip on the wine glass. It was, she realised, the first time she'd ever done that. Normally it was Sue propping up the corner, watching and appreciating as hot food materialised before her.

'You really shouldn't be cooking,' she protested feebly. 'I invited you to dinner.'

Margie waved a hand at her casually. 'Is a real pleasure, having a proper kitchen for a change,' she said. 'I'm in the warders' houses in Bristol and quite frankly they is rubbish. I suppose they was built for single men, one time, and they would all eat in the canteen. Now most they have is a bit of a hot plate and a grill. No good for much more than breakfast, that lot. Can't tell you how nice it is, having a real oven.'

She opened the stove door and the smell of roast meat billowed out in a cloud of steam. Alex almost suggested it was time to take the bird out before it overcooked and went dry but closed her mouth without speaking, watching to see what Margie would do.

Deftly juggling the hot pan, she flipped the chicken over onto its back, laid some foil over the steaming bird and covered it in several cloths, sealing in the heat.

'Leave that to rest now for a while,' she said and Alex almost sighed with pleasure. This was a woman who could really cook.

The moment was shattered by an unexpected knocking on the front door. Sue glanced up, raising an eyebrow before sighing theatrically and going to answer it. Left alone for a moment, Margie and Alex smiled at one another rather shyly.

'Are you expecting company?' Margie asked. 'Didn't know how much to do but I can always peel a few more spuds if we need 'em.'

Alex shook her head. '*I'm* not expecting anyone,' she said. 'I'm not sure about Sue but it's probably some last-minute electioneers. They've been a real nuisance this last week. I thought I'd finally got rid of them on Wednesday. Some child campaigning for the incumbent who had a script and was incapable of answering the simplest question turned up and just would not go away. Eventually I told him I'd vote for a bucket of elvers if it kept his lot out of power this time and he went off in a huff.'

Margie began to put the potatoes into a pan of cold water, laughing at the picture Alex painted. 'Perhaps they see you as a challenge now,' she suggested.

There was the sound of voices from the front room and Alex peered through the kitchen trying to see who was at the door.

'Well, come in and I'll ask her,' said Sue from the front room. 'It's not a good time though. She's got company and it's been a rough week for us all. *You* should know that,' she added over her shoulder.

Alex's heart sank as she recognised Lauren's voice and the heavy footsteps suggested she had Dave with her. A glance at Sue's harassed expression confirmed her impression this was not a social visit.

'I'm sorry Alex,' said Sue. 'They're not going to give up. You'll have to talk to Dave.'

Why, thought Alex. Why do I have to talk to him? This is my house and this is my weekend and I don't have to do anything. She suddenly became aware of the startled look on Margie's face. 'Sorry – did I say that out loud?'

'She does that sometimes,' said Sue. 'You'll get used to it.'

'Go on,' said Margie turning her attention to the resting chicken. 'I can get this all ready. You see what they want.'

Alex already knew what they wanted but to refuse again would be horribly rude especially after everything her friends had done to support her over the past few years.

Dave and Lauren were standing awkwardly in the middle of the front room and Alex waved them towards the couch, seating herself on a chair with her back to the window.

'Go on,' she said cutting across Dave's apologies. 'What is it?'

The young detective pulled a thick file from a bag and riffled through it as he spoke. Briefly he outlined the Moth Man case, touching on the lack of any physical evidence, the dearth of witnesses and the new evidence from Northumbria Police. Alex listened in silence, her face increasingly grim.

'So, you're worried he may be escalating?' she said when Dave had finished. 'If this is the same person of course.'

'The samples from Northumbria were a bit basic,' said Dave. 'They match ours broadly though. Another non-secretor and a blond man. Their suspect did go from flashing to rubbing himself against the windows too.'

Alex nodded. 'So, if it is the same person he's already moved from looking to touching.' She caught Lauren's puzzled frown and continued. 'A flasher is seeking the impact on his victim – the shock or horror or fear. It's partly a power thing, I think. But here is a man who needs more. The initial reward isn't enough. He's seeking a physical sensation, otherwise he wouldn't risk rubbing up against the windows. He'd just get closer to see better. Whether he will go any further – I don't know. It is a huge step, and he'd have to risk getting into the house. Of course, if a door were actually open – who knows?'

Dave was making notes as she spoke. 'I wondered about that,' he said. 'Any idea what would make him stop for a while?'

Alex shrugged. 'Could have been a spell in prison or something like that,' she said. 'You've checked that already haven't you?'

Dave nodded.

'So, maybe he moved somewhere else, especially if he came close to being caught. There may be other incidents still not reported, but this is such a strong pattern – what, every four weeks? I don't think it would have gone unnoticed for so long.'

'Could have gone abroad?' suggested Lauren.

'Yes, that's possible. I don't suppose anyone's thought to ask Interpol or someone have they?'

Dave pulled a face. 'We put out a request but it can take months for anything to come back, especially if he was out in the sticks somewhere. To be honest, this would be a very low priority for them.'

'He could also have found a girlfriend,' said Alex. 'Really, you would be amazed what a difference that can make. I sometimes think if we can just keep them out of serious trouble until they're in about their mid-twenties, they'll all settle down and forget all this nonsense. Of course, that's putting all the responsibility on the women,' she added hastily.

'I'm not sure he's the settling down type,' mused Lauren. 'Seems more like the "Who cares, I'm doing what I want even if it's weird" type to me.'

Alex tended to agree with her. It was unlikely this particular lone wolf had succumbed to the love of a good woman. 'Is it exactly four weeks between attacks?' she asked.

Dave looked a little nervous. 'It is, yes. Look, I'm getting into confidential stuff here, details we've kept under wraps. I'm not sure what my sergeant would say if he knew I was talking to you.'

'Well don't blame me,' said Alex. 'I've told you over and again to leave me out of it. I don't know how I can help, not in any real way. All that stuff about being able to identify a character type or tell you what he had for lunch – that's not true you know. All I can do is make the same guesses you do. And you've got all the information, even if you don't know it.'

'Don't none of it work then?' asked Lauren.

Alex shook her head. 'Well, sometimes geographical profiles are useful,' she said. 'It is true a lot of serial offenders stick to their known area. They feel safer and it is easier for them to get away if anything goes wrong.'

Dave looked glum. 'That's one of our big problems,' he said. 'We've got three scenes now, two a long way apart and none of them with any sort of decent road linking 'em. We've no idea how he's travelling either, though he must get to his site a while before the attack. I think someone would notice him if he was totally naked on the bus.'

'You said the scenes are not linked by a direct route? Hang on – I've got a map somewhere round here.' Alex rummaged in an over-full bookshelf, spilling several volumes on the floor before pulling a new edition Ordinance Survey map of the area out from between two volumes of an encyclopaedia.

'Here,' she said, unfolding and laying it on the carpet. 'Show me.'

Dave hesitated for a moment before pointing to the three sites.

'All on the same evening of the week, though they were later each time,' he said.

Alex knelt on the floor and stared at the map for a minute, tracing the main roads with her fingers.

'Right,' she said finally. 'Now we start making some assumptions. Always Friday – why? Perhaps he works and it's the end of the week for him. And perhaps somehow his work links him to these sites. The shift in time is interesting. Does it coincide with dusk?'

Dave looked blankly at her. 'I don't know,' he admitted.

'Check the times in an almanac,' she said. 'If he's waiting for darkness that could mean he's being careful – using it to escape. But if it's dusk, then there's some sort of personal meaning for him. And he will be travelling to his site during sunset at the latest so he's taking more of a risk. You're right about the roads though. The main route runs out towards Monkton but a good way to the west. These others straddle the road out past Durleigh but they're not really connected to Monkton at all.' She frowned at the map.

'Also if he's changing the time it suggests he's got some form of transport. There's not many buses going out to any of these places and certainly not in the evenings. So how is he travelling . . .'

'I'm sure that's the key to it,' said Dave. 'We haven't found any signs of a car or a van and no-one's reported hearing one either.'

'Maybe usin' a tractor?' suggested Lauren. 'Joking, joking. Would make a right racket, I know. Just wondered if'n it would make him – invisible sort of.'

Alex nodded as she pored over the map.

'Actually you're right,' she said. 'Not the tractor, obviously, but about him being invisible. He's choosing these women, studying them and making all his preparations and nobody sees him. Why is that? Someone who's there but not seen. Bus driver – no, too dependent on shift work. Farm worker – wrong season for pickers. Gardener perhaps – freelance or self-employed . . .' Oblivious to Lauren and Dave's presence, Alex ran her hands across the map, muttering and shaking her head as she struggled with the puzzle. Suddenly the phone rang making them all jump.

Alex reached over to the table and lifted the receiver, still staring at the map before her.

'Yes?' she asked. 'Oh. Right, hang on.'

She handed the phone to Lauren. 'It's your brother,' she said and turned back to her own thoughts.

'Who are you,' she mused. 'Or what are you?'

Lauren listened and then glanced at Dave.

'Right, thanks Jonny.' She replaced the receiver and sighed. 'Lovely. Just what we needed. He says your sergeant rang – wants you to call in at once. He didn't want to give Alex's number so I don't think they know you is here.'

Dave reached for the phone, then looked at Alex for permission. She waved at him without taking her eyes off the map. Dave dialled through to the Taunton station and listened for a minute.

'Of course, Sarge. No, I'm in Highpoint but I can get over there right away. Where exactly should I meet you?' He fumbled in his pockets, juggling the telephone whilst searching for a pen. Alex pulled a biro from her back pocket and handed it to him without a word as Dave recited the address.

'Yeah, I've got that,' he said as he scribbled on a scrap of paper on the table. 'What?' He replaced the phone and frowned at Lauren who was mouthing silently at him.

'I know that address,' she said. 'Look.' She knelt down next to Alex, turning the map around until she located the village. 'North Newton – that cottage is out here, see?' She indicated a spot just outside the village. 'That's where Alison lives.'

Alex looked up in surprise.

'What, our Alison? Alison from the office?'

Lauren nodded, squinting up at Dave.

'What's happened?' she demanded. 'No, don't give me all that confidential stuff, neither. Alison's our friend – well, sort of. We don't wish her no harm anyway, so why you getting called out over there at this hour?'

Dave struggled for a moment but the impact of two pairs of eyes glaring at him was too much.

'Her husband rang in,' he said. 'They think they spotted the Moth Man in the garden.' He looked down at Alex and continued. 'This answers one question anyway. He's been on a four-week cycle up to now, same as in Northumbria. This is early. He's escalating.'

'If it is him,' said Alex. 'He's also losing control if he was seen. Go on – we'll take Lauren home. And thanks for leaving me out of this.'

Dave grabbed his car keys, kissed Lauren swiftly and headed for the door. 'Sorry,' he said over his shoulder. 'But Alex – thanks. You've given me a lot of help.' With a quick smile he was gone.

'How do you know where Alison lives?' asked Alex. 'I didn't think you were that friendly.'

'We was all invited over there for her wedding,' said Lauren. 'Just before you arrived it was. She had a right girt fancy party in the garden. Reckon she wanted to show off her house 'cos she was going on about how they was going to put a big conservatory on the back and how close they was to the Grand Estate, almost in the grounds.'

Alex jerked her head up and stared at Lauren.

'What did you say?'

'She was boasting about being on the edge . . .'

'Before that,' Alex interrupted.

'She was telling us about her plans for the cottage. Having a conservatory built and such.'

Alex grinned, a fierce, almost feral smile.

'All of these places, they've got conservatories,' she said. 'The women were all sitting out in a glass house with the lights turned on, lit up like a stage. That's what attracts him. And I think he's a builder – that's how he knows the layout of the properties so well. Lauren, we need to tell Dave as soon as we can. I think he's looking for someone who makes conservatories.'

Chapter Sixteen

He moved down the hill, flitting from tree to tree, then along the dry-bottomed ditch by the side of the road until he reached the hedge surrounding the front garden. All was still and a few birds sang their evening songs, relaxed and drowsy in the warmth of the setting sun. Samuel glanced round the corner of the hedge and spotted the car approaching the house. Finally, he thought. About bloody time. There was usually an hour or so between her return from work and the husband's arrival but that precious window of opportunity was slipping away as he stood, waiting, in the shadow of the garden wall.

He stepped into the long ornamental grasses that lined the west side of the garden, crouching out of sight as Alison turned her car into the driveway, parking on the concrete in front of the garage doors. She looked decidedly out of sorts as she climbed out of the driver's seat, collected her bag from the passenger side and stamped into the house without bothering to lock the car. He smiled, unnoticed in his hiding place. If she had any suspicions she would have been much more careful.

Despite his mounting excitement Samuel forced himself to wait. Better she was relaxed, feeling safe in her precious little home. A few more minutes to let her guard down would be worth the delay. He squinted over his shoulder, looking both ways down the road to check all was clear before making his move. His hands were slick with sweat inside his gloves as he pulled the mask down over his face. As he ran, hunched over to keep out of sight, his legs trembled beneath him.

Rising slowly to look through the window, he felt his mouth go dry and he almost vomited as a fit of giddiness threatened to overbalance him into the fledgling roses. His anger was forgotten now, washed away by the strength of his need for this woman. The blood thundered in his ears and his vision narrowed to a tiny, tight focus as he scanned the room. There she was, standing by an empty fireplace holding a couple of letters and swaying slightly. The sound of a popular radio station reached him, thin and tinny through the glass and the rushing in his head. He slid down out of sight again and began to work his way around to the back door. It was time. He eased the door open and stepped through into the kitchen, rewarded by that first, delicious scream as Alison turned and saw his masked, gloved figure silhouetted against the setting sunlight. Two steps into the room and he had the razor ready in one hand as he lifted a finger to his lips to indicate silence. She stepped backwards, stumbling over the legs of a stool and almost falling in her panic.

This was going to be very easy, he thought. She showed no signs of putting up a fight. She just wanted to get away and that was not going to happen. He took another step towards her and froze at the sound of a car turning into the front yard.

When she was finally allowed back into the office to rescue her bag Alison had taken a couple of minutes to make a call to her husband, Marc. ('Marc, with a "C",' she always said when introducing him). Marc was supposed to be working a bit late that evening, but after hearing Alison's highly coloured version of events decided he really ought to go home.

Alison turned and fled for the front door, screaming in terror as she went. Samuel folded the razor and hastily shoved it back into his pocket, spun round and was out of the door and fleeing across the garden before Alison could open the front door and reach her husband. She flung herself into his arms, weeping hysterically and babbling about moths and Marc wasted valuable seconds trying to calm her.

'Stay here,' he said, pushing her into the car. 'Lock the door. You'll be safe here. I'm going after him.' He set off around the house but Samuel was already through the hedge and racing up the track towards the trees. Marc followed as fast as he could but Samuel was strong, extremely fit and driven by fear of what would happen if he were caught. He plunged through the trees, deliberately heading away from the undergrowth where his precious tin was hidden. He knew if he could lose Marc on the marsh then the enraged husband would return to the house to call the police. Samuel could double back, get his clothes and be off before the law arrived.

Marc was dogged but no match for the younger man and after a few minutes he stopped running, staring after the fleeing figure and trying to fix its appearance in his mind. Later, when the police arrived and he and Alison were giving their statements they could recall very few details. Medium height, they said. Nondescript clothes, rather loose, so it was difficult to give an idea of his build.

'I didn't see his face,' said Alison who had recovered from the worst of her fright and was secretly rather enjoying the attention. 'He had a black mask on and I couldn't see through it. Sort of a ski mask thing.' She was equally unhelpful over how her assailant had been dressed.

'Just ordinary,' she said. 'A floppy shirt and a pair of Hinkleys.' She ducked her head and clenched her hands tightly as she recalled the moment the intruder stepped through her door. 'He had a . . . a knife. Quite thin but very shiny. I saw it in his hand.' Tears filled her eyes and suddenly she was just a very scared young woman sitting in a room she was not sure she would ever call home again.

The sergeant pointed to the attending WPC who walked over and sat beside Alison, speaking softly to comfort her.

'Anything you can remember can help us catch him,' said the WPC. 'It is very difficult but if you can be brave for a little while longer that gives us the best chance to find who this was.'

Alison nodded, sniffed and accepted some tissues from the WPC.

'There was one thing,' she said after blowing her nose loudly. The sergeant leaned forward, looking not unlike an eager retriever hearing a gun. 'Go on,' he said encouragingly.

'His shoes,' said Alison. 'It sounds odd I know but I'm sure they were pink.'

There was an instant's silence before the sergeant cleared his throat.

'Pink, you say – you're quite sure of that now?'

Alison nodded and glared at him. 'I *said* it was a bit unlikely but they were definitely pink. Those posh ankle boots, they were, with the coloured circles in the soles.'

'Right,' said the sergeant nodding to the young constable sitting at the table to make a note of this intriguing piece of information. 'Well, thank you for all your help. I'll just pop next door and see how they're getting on. Maybe you could get some tea?' he added looking at the WPC. She looked back at him, her face expressionless.

'Of course,' she said.

'Two sugars for me,' said the young constable who was scribbling furiously in his notebook.

'You can get your own,' the WPC snapped as she headed for the stove. 'I've got three years seniority on you.' The young man stopped, pencil poised above his notebook and blinked at her as, across the room, Alison managed a tiny smile. After a moment she got up from her chair in the corner and began to help the WPC make tea.

In the front room the sergeant was listening to a run-down of Marc's replies to the same questions he had just put to Alison. The one telling detail was the mention of those pink shoes.

232

'Get that out on the radio,' he said as he hurried out to the car. 'Could be he's easy to spot in them.'

The WPC watched from the kitchen as her colleagues tried to raise a response from their radios.

'Seems we's just out of range,' she said blowing on her tea. 'They'll be in wanting to use your phone in a minute.' They were, but by then it was too late. On the hill, hidden behind the mass of brambles and ferns, Samuel stripped off his outer clothes, changed his pink boots for running shoes and slung the whole lot, gloves, mask and all, in the tin. This slid into an old army pack on his back and, still hidden from view, he was off across the Levels, just one more jogger out training for the summer road races.

Despite his outward calm, he was shaken by the narrow escape and failed to notice the straight-edged razor was missing. It lay in the grass half-way between the narrow road and the sheltering trees until discovered by a searching PC later that evening. The grim find led to an intensive hunt through that area and it wasn't long before someone spotted a set of boot prints, clear and fresh in the slightly muddy ground near the canal.

Dave and the rest of the detectives arrived to take over the investigation and the prints were photographed, cast in plaster and taken away to be analysed along with the razor that Alison identified somewhat shakily.

As the last of the light faded from the sky Dave stood on the hill with Sergeant Lynas looking down on the cottage, now fenced off with crime scene tape.

'Is it just me or do you feel a bit – uncertain about this one?' Dave ventured.

Lynas stared ahead into the darkness for a moment before replying.

'Go on,' he said finally.

Dave swallowed nervously, aware he was in danger of giving away his clandestine meeting with Alex. 'He was dressed,' Dave said. 'It's a week early. And the shoes worry me. We've never found a clear trace before this but now we've got a description, some really distinctive details and a clear footprint.'

'He's losing control,' said Lynas. 'Happens in the end with most of 'em. Needs to do more, needs it more often. Don't look so startled lad. You're not the only one as can read.'

'The razor worries me,' said Dave doggedly. 'That's a huge change and so is going inside the house. Somehow it seems so much more – ruthless.'

'Razor bothers me too,' said the sergeant. 'Probably for different reasons though. Don't like to imagine what might have happened if her husband hadn't come home.'

'But . . .'

'We've got the mask, we've got the gloves, we've got the same day of the week, roughly same time of day an' all. Similar property, woman on her own. Too much in common to be coincidence I reckon. The Inspector agrees with me – this time we got lucky. Our first break in this case and none too soon neither.'

They walked back to the cottage together. Dave hoped Lynas was right but he had a horrible feeling he was not.

The police had arrested Charlie Dodds as well as Brian Morris and the two young men spent a very uncomfortable night in separate cells at Highpoint police station. When it was obvious there was no suggestion of terrorism, the Inspector, who had spent a fairly miserable night himself in the company of the captain of the bomb squad, had a long hard look at alternative charges. As there were two of them he leaned towards conspiracy – any sort of conspiracy would do. He wasn't fussy. Just something to keep them off his patch for a while and to show he meant business. Eventually he calmed down a little, though he was not inclined to let them off with a caution.

'Breach of the peace, at least,' he insisted when the custody sergeant queried their detention. 'And no police bail neither. Keep 'em apart and make sure we have a note of anything the little buggers say that might possibly be used in evidence against them. They're at least sitting there over the weekend.'

With that, he marched out of the station, got in his car and headed home to his house, one of the new-build 'executive' buildings Kevin had viewed scornfully on his ride across the Levels. It was after midnight when he got home to find the remains of his evening meal dried out on a plate in the oven. It was not quite the evening he had been anticipating.

In her house beside the River Parrett, Alex found her evening was heading into areas she had hoped to avoid for a few weeks, until she and Margie had a chance to get to know one another a bit better. She had imagined a few quiet meals and perhaps another drive out somewhere rural and undisturbed. Maybe a stroll across the hills or a walk through the Saturday market at Taunton. All of this was accompanied by warm, golden sunshine and a dearth of curious friends who lacked the tact to withdraw and give the two of them some space.

With Dave's departure they became four at dinner. It was scarcely possible to bundle Lauren into a car and ship her off home and even Alex realised such an action was unlikely to endear her to Margie so Lauren settled down to the meal with the three of them. Alex declined any more wine, aware that she would have to drive Lauren home later that night and she watched rather sadly as Margie's special bottle was shared around the table. Lauren sipped appreciatively rolling a little around her mouth before swallowing theatrically.

'That's right lovely, that!' she declared.

Despite all the disruption, Margie seemed to be enjoying herself and the group chatted happily, comparing work experiences and telling stories about themselves until Margie suddenly looked at Alex.

'So, I couldn't help hearing some of that before. Tell me if'n is confidential but why was the police asking you about all this?'

Alex tried to seize the escape clause offered by supposed confidentiality but Lauren was too quick for her.

'Is this nutter running around gardens and up against the windows,' she said cheerfully. 'Getting a bit much and, to be honest, most of the police don't have much idea who it is or why he's doin' it. Dave needs to do something good these next few weeks, seeing as he's only acting detective, so he come over to see if Alex can help. Does anyone else want that?' She swooped on the last roast potato, added a dollop of gravy and began to eat happily, oblivious to the mixture of confusion and resentment she had generated.

'I got most of that,' said Margie slowly. 'Just wondered why he was asking you, Alex. Not that I'm saying you don't know your stuff, mind, but – well, seems he was talking like you was an expert.'

Alex took a deep breath, glaring at Lauren who had almost finished her potato and looked as if she was about to say something more.

'I did a bit of psychology at university,' she admitted reluctantly, trying to ignore Sue's raised eyebrows. 'It seemed interesting at the time and – well, I studied some of the traits and patterns of criminal behaviour. When I switched to philosophy that got mixed in with my final thesis on ethics and society. How psychotic behaviour is not necessarily psychotic if the society in which it occurs is *also* psychotic. Honestly, it sounds a lot more interesting than it is.'

'So all this time I've been sharing a house with a mind-reading psychologist?' said Sue.

Alex slammed down her glass of orange juice and pushed her chair back only to be restrained by Margie.

'Think she's teasing you,' Margie murmured.

Alex sat down again, a tight smile on her face. 'Sorry,' she said. 'I'm a bit jumpy this evening. It's been a bit more exciting than usual, what with Alison's stalker and bloody Brian and his treasure.'

Margie smiled, an easy, relaxed smile as she reached over to collect the plates.

'I can imagine what is like,' she said. 'Up at Bristol we get students from the university coming in sometimes. Most times they is useless. Got no clue about talking to our lads and they get wound up by them a treat. Sometimes, though, there's one as seemed to have a gift. Get the inmates talking, even get them thinking. One student, last year it was, she came and told us there was trouble coming on the wing. One of the men, he was gathering a lot of attention from the others. He was having an 'undue influence' – that's how she put it. He'd not said nothing to her, and 'tis all confidential in them sessions anyway, but that was what she made out, watching them.

'Couple of the blokes on the wing, they laughed about it but she was right an' one of 'em got hurt real bad when it all kicked off. Luckily some of the warders was more open and looking out for trouble so was prepared. You'd 'a' thought they'd be grateful, seeing as it could 'a' been a whole lot worse, but they all closed ranks on her. Went muttering around as if she'd set it up or something stupid. My senior, he says psychology 'ent natural. I heard him talking in the rest room one day and he called it a "dark art". Seems people all over is just scared of what they don't understand.'

Alex listened to Margie's story, nodding at intervals.

'There's the other side to it,' she said. 'When you get it right then people start on about mind reading and nonsense like that. But a lot of the time it's just educated guess-work or at best the most likely outcome. So then you get it wrong and you're a fraud. If you're lucky then no-one gets hurt but sometimes it can be a total disaster.'

'That why you don't want to help Dave?' asked Lauren.

'I do want to help Dave,' snapped Alex. 'I just don't think I will be helping him by pretending I know anything about this Moth Man. I know a bit about that sort of offender – but so do you, Sue. And Margie, you've spent longer in the company of dangerous offenders than any of us.'

The tension around the table was broken by the ringing of a telephone bell and Alex scrambled to her feet to answer it. Whilst she was in the front room, Margie and Sue cleared the plates and prepared the pudding.

'It's only shop-bought,' said Sue as she pulled an apple pie from the warm oven.

'Sorry to say it but that's preferable to you trying to make one,' said Lauren wickedly.

Sue sniffed and sat down, pulling the custard jug out of reach.

'Apologise,' she said sternly.

Lauren groaned, stretching as far as she could but the jug eluded her.

She was spared the humiliation of replying when Alex called her through to the front room. 'It's Dave,' said Alex handing over the phone before returning to the table.

'Everything okay?' Sue asked helping herself to pie.

Alex nodded rather absently.

'I think so. Alison's husband . . .'

'Marc-with-a-C,' said Sue.

Alex grinned at her. 'Yeah, Marc-with-a-C came back and the man ran off. Dave sounded a bit shaken by it all though. This time the man broke in to the house.' Her face became serious as she contemplated Alison's ordeal. There had been some differences of opinions between them in the past but, as Lauren said, she didn't wish any harm on the woman.

Lauren came trotting back through looking relieved.

'Alison's fine, Dave says. He won't be back for a while though so if I could take you up on that lift . . .?'

Alex nodded wearily. 'Of course. No problem.'

When Sue and Lauren were engaged in the kitchen, clearing away and washing up Margie leaned over the table and took Alex's hand.

'You are a good person to have around in a crisis I reckon. And a right good friend.' She nodded towards the kitchen to emphasise her point.

Alex squeezed her hand in reply and managed a smile.

'Is a shame about the wine,' Margie continued thoughtfully. 'Probably just as well I got another bottle.'

Alex's smile was much more genuine this time.

'Were you hoping to get me drunk?' she said softly.

Margie's eyes sparkled in the light of the lamps.

'Can't blame a girl for trying,' she said.

Alex took a deep breath and stepped out into the unknown for the first time in many years.

'I think you might be assuming I need all that much persuading,' she said.

There was an instant's silence as their eyes met but Sue hurried back into the room, seized the last of the serving plates, threw them an absent-minded smile and was gone again.

Alex swallowed nervously, aware that they were still holding hands. Margie disentangled her fingers gently, stroking Alex's thumb with her own before sitting back slightly and picking up her half-empty wine glass.

'I'll go and give them a hand,' she said taking a sip. 'See if we can hurry them along a bit.' She raised the glass in a mock toast as she disappeared through the door, leaving Alex alone at the table, her heart beating frantically. She imagined could feel Margie's touch on her hand, warm and soft and gentle around her fingers. She was still sitting there, her eyes closed, when Lauren returned clutching her coat.

'Thanks for this,' said Lauren. 'And dinner too. I like your friend,' she added as she clambered into Alex's dilapidated Citroën and giggled a little as the suspension filled, lifting the car as Alex turned the key. 'Why you still running this old thing?'

Alex was lost for an answer, taken aback by the abrupt change of subject. She had been dreading Lauren meeting Margie, imagining all sorts of probing questions and intrusive speculation. Perversely, she was almost disappointed.

As Alex sped out along the main road towards Nether Stowey, Samuel was picking his way carefully and stealthily back along the tow path by the canal. The tin containing his clothes and the pink boots was buried safely in the old mine workings and in his running gear he was unlikely to raise much interest. The paths back had been deserted apart from one encounter with an old van near Huntworth Bridge. The vehicle sped up behind him too quickly for him to hide in the undergrowth but Samuel was not too concerned. He was jogging with his head down, his face partly hidden by the hood of his track suit and with the poor light it was unlikely he would be recognised, even if there were ever any call to identify him.

He was much more concerned over the loss of his razor. Checking and re-packing the tin before hiding it once more, he had discovered its absence. A flash of cold fury ran through him as he rummaged in the pockets of his Hinkleys, to no avail. The blade was gone and he could only hope it was dropped somewhere in thick foliage, away from prying eyes and eager policemen. He had been very careful, always handling it whilst wearing the cotton gloves so he had no worries about fingerprints but the fact he had not noticed it was gone troubled him deeply. The whole evening had been a disaster and Samuel was not used to failure. He didn't like it and he wasn't going to risk coming that close to being caught again.

Samuel had taken considerable care to disguise his nocturnal activities. His record – his criminal record – was a patchwork of minor offences, many of them 'taken into consideration'. When younger, he had been more reckless and on several occasions found himself in the wrong place at the wrong time – or, 'in suspicious circumstances' as the police had put it. Pleading guilty to a whole raft of minor offences had allowed him to escape with relative impunity, though it had landed him with a record and, for the moment, the attention of the probation service.

Whilst he would have preferred to escape detection entirely, Samuel considered his reputation as a petty criminal useful on occasions. Having already been identified as a minor nuisance, an opportunist and not too smart thief, he was unlikely to enter anyone's thoughts when they were hunting for a serial sex offender.

He had little respect for most members of the criminal justice service. In his opinion they were slow, predictable and often lazy. The fact he had been rewarded with a lighter sentence for lying and accepting all those little offences just to get them off the unsolved list illustrated just what the authorities' priorities were. He was considerably cleverer than the average policeman and he knew it. Still, he reflected as he jogged through the front door to the hostel a few minutes before curfew, he needed to be wary of Alex.

Her unexpected kindness had made a big impact on him, awakening a long-buried sense of obligation. Used to viewing most women as either stupid and therefore to be despised or desirable and therefore prey, Samuel now had a woman in his third category. Alex was a thinker, someone who did what she believed in. Alex just might be his intellectual equal and as such she deserved his respect.

Chapter Seventeen

Alex woke on the Monday feeling happier and more content than she had for years. Drawing back the bedroom curtains she looked out at a bright morning and smiled. In the kitchen she found herself humming, softly at first but then a bit louder to get above the noise of the kettle.

'Good God, woman, are you mad?' snapped Sue from the doorway.

'It's a lovely day,' said Alex, gesturing to the door leading to their tiny garden. 'You can hear the birds singing . . .'

'Then they're bloody mad too,' Sue said. She picked up a beaker, added a teabag and emptied all of Alex's hot water on top of it before sweeping out into the quiet of the dining room. Alex refilled the kettle, made herself some coffee and followed her, sitting down opposite at the table.

'About the weekend . . .' She began sipping her drink and keeping her attention fixed on a plate of slightly burnt toast in front of her.

'Mmm,' said Sue, reaching over and helping herself to breakfast. 'This is burnt.'

'Don't eat it then,' said Alex crossly.

'It was fun,' said Sue chewing contentedly. 'Apart from the Alison part, obviously. We should do it more often.'

'I'm hoping we can,' said Alex. 'Especially if Margie gets the job in Shepton Mallet. Um . . .' She was uncomfortably aware of her face turning red.

'You should,' Sue continued, oblivious to her friend's discomfort. 'Do you good. I was getting worried you were turning into a work-obsessed hermit.' She looked up from her empty plate and pulled a face.

'Oh come on, how old are you? You're blushing like a schoolgirl.'

'No I'm not,' said Alex, glowing even more. 'It's just – well, it's hard sometimes . . . you never know what people might think or how they might react. It's . . . difficult sometimes.'

Sue snorted impatiently.

'Well, I've know from almost the first moment we met,' she said dismissively. 'And I suspect so does everyone else. It's not a big deal you know. Just adds to your charm and mystique.'

There were tears in Alex's eyes as she stared at Sue. 'It is getting to be a big deal,' she said softly. 'This Clause 28 thing could be very nasty if they get it through parliament. There's a lot of ugly stuff going on around here. Just ask Lauren about some of the things Jonny has to put up with.'

'Well, they have to get back in first,' said Sue. 'The way it's looking, we should finally get a change this time round. You wait – this time next week it will all be over.'

'I hope so,' said Alex. 'I'm just sick of it all. I know people who've left the country they're so scared.'

'Seems a bit extreme,' said Sue. 'Anyway, fortunately the probation service has an anti-discrimination policy so you've nothing to worry about.'

Alex envied Sue her confidence. Some days, listening to the casual abuse swirling around the day centre, she doubted she could stand another week without leaping on to a chair and yelling the truth at the room. She wondered just what sort of a riot that would provoke.

On her arrival at work there was a message from the police station at Highpoint.

'Is the Inspector,' said Lauren. 'He kept them two lads in all weekend and they's off to court later today. Think he might want a word.'

Something was nagging at the back of Alex's mind as she took the call. Something Brian said just before he emptied the butterfly bombs onto her desk. Frowning, she tried to recall the sequence of events. He's said he'd found some kind of treasure, boasted he was going to sell it and then . . . .

'Oh bugger,' she muttered into the receiver.

'I beg your pardon?' came the outraged tones of the Highpoint Inspector.

'Sorry, sorry.' Alex hurried on before she lost her train of thought.

'I've only just remembered. When Brian came to see me on Friday he said there were "others". He was going to sell the two bombs he'd found and then "the others". Only he didn't know they were bombs. It was purely innocent on his part.'

'I'm not sure I agree with you entirely on that estimation,' said the Inspector. 'His actions were reckless and resulted in enormous inconvenience, not to mention expense, for the emergency services. He was almost certainly trespassing when he obtained these devices and that means he and his companion are guilty of theft.'

'Did you hear what I said?' asked Alex impatiently. 'Brian claimed there were more of these damn things. He's found them out on the Levels, digging in an old bottle pit. If he found them then someone else is likely to stumble over them and we might not be so lucky next time.'

There was a moment's silence at the other end of the phone.

'Well, in that case young Brian Morris had better cough up the location and pretty smartish too,' said the Inspector.

'Let me talk to him,' said Alex. 'I'm sure we can come to some arrangement.' Without waiting for a reply, she put the phone down and turned to Lauren who was leaning on the counter and eying her curiously.

'I've got to go down to the police station,' she said. 'If they get to him first then Brian is just dumb enough to tell them where the wretched bottle dump is. If I can speak to him then perhaps we can negotiate a caution or something. Oh don't look at me like that,' she added crossly. 'It's my job to help him – and poor dumb Charlie too. It's not like they've really done anything wrong but the police seem determined to charge them with something for the inconvenience.'

Lauren sighed and slid off her high stool.

'Alison's not in, big surprise, so I'll check the diary, see what I can do about your appointments. Go on, push off 'n' save Brian and Charlie. Lord knows, someone's got to.'

Alex grabbed her car keys from the counter, whirled round and crashed straight into Ricky who was heading for the desk, a scowl on his face.

'Hey, watch it,' he said, fending Alex off with one hand and brushing imaginary dirt off his court suit with the other.

'Sorry,' Alex called over her shoulder. At the door she stopped and looked at him over her shoulder. 'How's the court duty going?' she asked waspishly. 'And I do hope your car was okay after last Friday.' She was gone before Ricky could retaliate, almost tripping over her feet as she hurried across the car park. Ricky glared at her from the counter before turning and catching Lauren grinning at him from the office door. Snatching the court pack from the tray just behind the counter he pushed his way through the door to the stairs, heading for his office. Lauren could not be certain but she thought she heard him mutter something as he turned away. It sounded horribly like 'Little freak'.

On her arrival at Highpoint police station Alex was escorted to an interview room where Brian was sitting at a table. Actually slumped over a table would be more accurate, Alex thought, as she opened the door and walked across the room. Brian lifted his head slightly, gave a grunt of recognition and closed his eyes once more. He looked decidedly the worse for his two nights in the police cells and it was obvious from the smell of him that he had not availed himself of the washing facilities, assuming they had been on offer, which Alex rather doubted.

Ignoring the odour of sweat and misery that surrounded him, Alex sat down opposite Brian.

'Good morning,' she said.

Brian stirred, groaning softly. ''Ent so good from where I'm sitting,' he said.

'Would you like something – a cup of tea?' suggested Alex.

Brian lifted his head and nodded. 'Wouldn't mind,' he said.

Alex got up and went to the door, tapping to indicate she needed it unlocked. It was opened suspiciously fast and the young constable standing outside nodded and hurried off to the canteen without a quibble. Well, thought Alex, they're very eager to hear what he has to say.

Brian had levered himself up into a sitting position and was now leaning on his elbows, blinking at her hopefully.

'You come to get me out?' he asked.

Alex held up one hand and said softly, 'I want you to listen carefully, Brian. Don't talk just yet, okay?'

The young man shrugged, rubbing his eyes and scrubbing at his face. He was obviously exhausted and Alex wondered how long he had left sitting been in the interview room. Much brighter souls than Brian had started talking, just to get away from the bright light or on the promise of a place to lie down.

'We'll wait until your tea comes,' she added. A few seconds later there was the sound of a key turning and the same young constable entered the room bearing a large mug. He put it down in front of Brian and left without a word, turning the lock noisily behind him.

Brian grabbed at the beaker and took a great gulp, letting out a gasp as the hot liquid hit the back of his mouth.

'Gently,' said Alex. 'You'll burn yourself.'

Brian nodded, his eyes watering a little as, with some reluctance, he put the tea down on the table.

'Now, when you came to see me on Friday you said something about there being some more of the butterfly bombs. "The others", you said.'

Brian opened his mouth to reply but Alex silenced him with a gesture.

'Just listen for a moment. Obviously it would be a great relief to everyone if we could find these. They could be quite dangerous, especially if some children came across them. I'm sure the police would be very grateful if you would help them locate and remove the rest of the cache. I would expect them to look very favourably on this sort of action. In fact, I would be surprised if they pursued the case against you any further, in light of such co-operation. I expect Charlie will be helpful in finding them too. Perhaps with both of you working on it we could locate them quickly, before anyone gets hurt.'

Brian gave a slow smile as he caught on to Alex's plan.

'Reckon,' he said taking another, more cautious, sip of his tea. 'I was working the detector most times so was Charlie knew exactly where we was.'

The door to the interview room opened with a loud bang and the Inspector strode in, his face a picture of fury.

'You should damn well show us where they are and take what's coming to you,' he said before stopping abruptly, aware he was losing control of his temper in front of a civilian. 'Take him back to the cells,' he called and the attentive constable hurried in and seized Brian's arm.

'Hey, watch my tea,' Brian protested as he was helped, none too gently, out of the door.

The Inspector glared at Alex. 'I do not appreciate this sort of interference in police business,' he snapped.

Alex took a deep breath. She was aware her actions were bordering on unprofessional and it was important she had a decent working relationship with the local constabulary but she was not going to allow Brian – or Charlie – to be railroaded into custody when all they were guilty of was stupidity – and a little bit of trespassing.

'I can understand that,' she said. 'I don't mean to interfere but I thought Brian would be more likely to talk to someone he knows. I've been working with him, and Charlie too, for a while now and I believe they trust me. I know how important it is to find the bottle tip and the other bombs. They're decent enough lads and both of them are trying to turn their lives around, especially Brian. Let's give them a break and I promise I'll do all I can to make it work out.'

The Inspector stood for a moment, looking at her as if weighing up his options, though actually he had very few of those left.

'All the credit for the find goes to you and the police, of course,' Alex added. 'You've done all the real work.' She waited to see how this little fabrication went down.

'That is not my main concern,' said the Inspector. 'I do not see why they should just walk away from this scot-free.'

'Oh, I would expect a caution at least,' said Alex. 'And believe me, they won't be boasting about this round town when I've finished with them.'

'I seem to have little choice,' said the Inspector grudgingly. 'I want that bloody metal detector though. I'm not leaving it in the hands of a couple of delinquents like them.'

Alex's heart sank, knowing Brian would refuse, but she managed a tight smile.

'Of course,' she said.

''Ent got it,' said Brian. ''Ent got it so you can't have it.'

'Look, that's the deal. You are very, very lucky and we need to get out there and find the rest of the stuff before there's an accident. Because if there is, the police will have something they can really put you away for. So come on, I need the metal detector.'

'Told you. Ent got it. My Dad, he was drunk when I got home and took it off us. Said he was gonna throw 'er in the canal, seeing as I bring the police round to his house.'

He would not be shifted on his story and after some careful questioning the arresting officers confirmed they had caught up with Brian at his family's house on the Levels and his father had indeed been at home.

'Abusive he was too,' said one. 'Drunk and shouting, threatened all sorts of things and just shoved the lad out the door.'

They also confirmed Brian had not been carrying anything when he was delivered into their arms and a subsequent search had not revealed the item concealed about his person. Brian's father was known for his temper as well as his unpredictability and there was a marked reluctance amongst the officers to make more enquiries as to the fate of Brian's metal detector.

Charlie was even less helpful. 'Dunno,' he mumbled, shrugging his shoulders. 'Didn't see it after Brian left. Went home and stopped at the Mallory place – you know 'bout that. Don't know nothing.'

Alex was not entirely convinced but it seemed to her more important to find and defuse any further butterfly bombs. She could easily deal with Brian the next time he was caught wading across the Levels on an illegal search and eventually the Inspector came round to her point of view.

Given the poor radio reception on much of the Levels, the police waited until a detachment of the bomb squad could join them at the station. Then, with Brian and Charlie in the back of a van, they set off in convoy into the marsh land to find and hopefully neutralise the remaining ordinance. Alex had done all she could and so she returned, somewhat reluctantly, to the office.

There was also some unexpected fall-out from Brian and Charlie's little adventure for the Mallory household. The police had arrived with commendable speed and removed Charlie's 'treasure' to a place where it could be disposed of safely. However, they also did a quick search through the house, just in case there were any more suspect items. Whilst they did not find any more bombs they did find Ada's unlicensed shotgun, several knives of illegal length and type and an unmetered electricity supply. On their departure they removed the weapons and the next morning an engineer arrived to disconnect the power supply.

Ada stood in the kitchen, watching in silence as the man took away her only source of power, tears of fury in her eyes.

'We will be in contact with you over this,' said the young man as he locked his van prior to departure. 'This sort of theft is dangerous and we will prosecute. There will also be a substantial bill to pay.'

Ada sat in her dim, cold kitchen and began to cry softly. Her husband, the late (and largely unlamented) Frank had 'arranged' the power hook-up some years ago. She had not known the details and had deliberately not asked. Now it seemed she might find herself in danger of imprisonment herself for there was no money to pay even a regular bill, let alone a hefty fine.

When Tom arrived after lunch he found her still hunched over in her chair, the marks of dried tears on her face.

'I could kill that stupid little hooligan,' he said. 'Bringing trouble to your door. Is not right.'

Using the range in the kitchen he brewed some tea and sat with Ada whilst she drank it.

'Don't do no good, threatening the lad,' Ada said sadly. 'Was me at fault anyway. I knew there was something dodgy about the power, seeing as I've never had a bill. Couldn't have afforded it though and if'n I'd tried to get it put in proper they'd have found that one anyway so I'd 'a still been done for it. Seems once you start, is very hard to stop.'

Tom nodded thoughtfully. 'You're not wrong there,' he said. 'Maybe we should go talk to someone. Was not you put the 'leccy in, after all. Could maybe plead was already done when you got here.'

'Don't be daft,' said Ada. 'What about me not ever getting no bills?'

Tom stared into space for a moment. 'Perhaps is their fault,' he said. 'They don't ask for it, well you can't pay. And you've had a lot going on for a while, what with losing Frank and the problems with Kevin. Is easy to lose track of time.'

''Ent like I uses it much anyway,' grumbled Ada. 'Always stuck with my range for cooking and I got an old back boiler so there's warm water most days too. I does like the lights, mind. And Kev brung us a television, though there's not much on worth watching most times. They's still goin' to want a heap of money, though, and to be honest, Tom, I don't have it. Kevin sends some regular now and that keeps me going along with that pension after Frank died. Is not much, though, and all I got in the world is this house and a bit put by in the tin up there.' She nodded to the mantelpiece where an old tea caddy stood, one corner poking out from behind the clock.

Tom rose and crossed the room, reaching out to lift it down. As he did so a letter in a brown envelope fluttered to the floor. He stooped to retrieve it and stopped just as he was tucking it back out of sight.

'Forgive me being nosy,' he said staring at the address printed on the flap. 'You never opened this. Could be important.'

'Ada flapped a hand at him angrily. 'Nothing good never comes in them brown envelopes,' she said. 'Don't know why it didn't go on the fire along with the rest. Must have been distracted.'

She reached for the letter, intent on disposing of it in the stove but Tom stepped back out of reach.

'Seriously, Ada, I do think you should take a look at this 'un.'

'Well, why don't you open it if you's so keen,' she snapped. 'Give me my tin so as I can do a count up.'

Tom stood staring at the letter for a minute whilst Ada emptied the contents of the tin onto the kitchen table and began sorting and counting the coins, making an angry rattle and clatter as she did so. Finally he tore open the envelope and pulled out an official-looking missive. He squinted at the closely typed paragraphs, tilting the paper in an effort to get more light. Ada, who had been studiously ignoring him, stopped her sorting and looked up at him.

'Want to borrow my glasses?' she asked.

Tom scowled, blinked at the letter once more and held out his free hand. 'Don't know where mine is,' he conceded. 'Bella was always on at me to be wearing 'um but never could get on with the damn things.'

'Is because they makes me feel I's getting old,' mumbled Ada turning back to the table.

Tom grunted in agreement, adjusting the spectacles up and down his nose to get the focus right before returning to the letter in his hand. He read it through once, then a second time and stood for a moment, staring thoughtfully through the back door until Ada's patience snapped.

'Come on then, what is it got you all tied up?' she demanded, all pretence swept away by a rush of curiosity.

'You had any more like this?' Tom asked.

'Don't know what this one's like,' said Ada. 'So I can't rightly say.'

Seizing the piece of paper from Tom's hand, she held it up, struggling to read until Tom handed back the glasses.

'Don't understand this,' said Ada finally. 'What's this on about? I 'ent made no claim to no-one.'

'Says it was made on your behalf,' said Tom. 'By a Mr Mallory. Kevin perhaps? He say anything about that?'

Ada shook her head, utterly bewildered. ''S'pose it might be,' she said. 'Don't know as how there's any more Mallorys out there. None I know of as would be interested in summat like this anyway. Well, so what's it actually mean?'

Tom took the letter and glasses again and skimmed through the text.

'Seems to say they considered your claim for compensation and – well, they's sending you a payment. For Frank, on account of him bein' killed by Derek Johns. Oh bugger – Ada, you burned any more of these letters recently?'

Ada opened her mouth to deny it, then stopped and a worried look came over her face.

'Had a bit of a clear-out, about a week ago,' she conceded. 'Must 'a missed this one but a load of old stuff got just thrown out.'

'When you say "thrown out", do you mean in the bin or in the stove?' Tom asked.

Ada frowned, struggling to remember. 'Was the day that strange lad was staring at us across the road,' she said. 'I 'ent sure but I think it was the bin, 'cos we was having trouble with the stove round that time. Yes, I is sure was the bin.'

Tom was out of the back door in a second and Ada heard the sound of her rubbish being turned out as he began searching for any more letters. Ada piled the coins up in neat rows before following him outside.

'You's worse than an old fox,' she said. 'Look at the mess you's making.'

'Hell with the mess,' said Tom, his voice echoing as he dipped into the dustbin once more. 'Could be hundreds of pounds in here and you just chucked it away!'

'You think so?' said Ada, shocked at the thought. 'Why would anyone give me all that money on account of Frank?'

Tom stopped his rummaging and gave her a hard look over his shoulder.

'Well, he was released for helping 'em catch Newt and Biff,' he said. 'Looks bad, letting their grass get killed and not even offering something by way of compensation.'

Ada shook her head. 'Seems Frank was a better provider dead than he ever was afore. I don't know, don't seem right somehow.'

'Well, is going to be theoretical if we don't find the rest of them letters,' said Tom grimly. He dug down through the layers of paper and occasional food cans, moving with more caution as he encountered a sharp tin lid.

'Ah, *suwin*,' he said, jerking his hand out and started to put the cut finger in his mouth.

'No you don't,' said Ada, stopping him just in time. 'Come in and I'll clean that off.'

Tom sighed loudly. 'Don't think there's anything in that bin,' he said sadly. 'Don't know what we do now if is gone.'

'Well, I had nothing but the money in the tin a half-hour ago so it's not like I lost anything,' said Ada as she led him inside and pointed to a kitchen chair. 'You sit there and I'll get something to disinfect that. Looks like a nasty cut, off the edge of something.'

Tom sat quietly as Ada cleaned his cut hand and dressed it, bandaging the torn edges neatly together. They sat quietly at the table sipping hot, sweet tea and Tom felt a rush of deep affection for this woman. So hard on the outside yet so kind once you got past the prickly shell she wore. One day soon, he thought, he would get up the courage to tell her just how much she meant to him.

Charlie Dodds was reduced to tears by the tongue-lashing he was treated to by the Inspector on their return from the bottle pit but Brian Morris was made of sterner stuff. He stood in front of the officer's desk, hands behind his back and waited until it was finished, nodded his head to indicate he understood he had received a formal caution, and ambled out into the waning sunlight. Because, of course, the metal detector had not gone into the canal at all. In fact Brian, who knew his father only too well, hadn't even taken it home.

After checking he was not being followed by Charlie – or an overzealous policeman – he set off for the bus station where the free supermarket bus waited. Despite the fact he was obviously not a shopper, the driver waved him aboard and Brian collapsed into the worn seats, breathing in the smells of fresh bread, dairy goods and muddy boots that permeated the vehicle. No-one sat next to him, probably because he smelt worse than the bus after his long weekend in police custody.

Alighting at the junction of the road near Westonzoyland, he continued on his way, whistling softly and tunelessly as he walked along the path by Ada Mallory's house. He stopped for a moment, recalling Kevin's unexpected kindness the last time he'd been home but the sight of Tom Monarch heaving the rubbish bin through the gate on to the roadside made him reconsider and he trotted off down the track, Tom's eyes following him out of sight. Resigned to an evening in the company of his family, Brian turned onto a narrow footpath and set off, the spring gone from his step as he contemplated the likely beating he could expect from his father.

His steps slowed until he was barely moving, weighing up his options. They were pretty well non-existent for in the absence of any ready cash he could not even get himself something to eat. He had worn out his welcome at the houses of most of his friends and the only one within reasonable walking distance was Charlie Dodds' place. Given recent events it was unlikely Charlie's grandmother would give him much of a welcome. It was not particularly cold but he was hungry and only had a thin jacket. His shoes, too, were not particularly warm and the damp of the path was seeping through the worn soles. Not for the first time he considered doing something stupid – and public – to get himself sent to the hostel.

Tom almost ran him down as he swung the van around the corner, braking just in time.

'Girt fool boy!' he shouted out of the window. 'What you doing, standing there in the middle of the road?'

Brian shuffled out of the way, barely glancing in his direction. Tom put the van back in gear and started to inch past but something made him hesitate. Perhaps the droop of the lad's shoulders or the way he seemed close to just collapsing by the side of the road.

'You okay?' Tom asked.

Brian mumbled something and took another step, pressing himself against the stone wall leading to the bridge.

'Hey, hang on a minute,' said Tom. He set the handbrake and jumped out of the vehicle, striding over to the miserable figure. Brian shivered, flinching away from this large, threatening stranger. Tom stopped a few feet away, lowering his voice as if talking to a frightened animal.

'Is okay, I 'ent going to hurt yer. Just a bit startled to see you there, is all. Where you heading? I could give you a lift, seeing as is getting' dark now.' He peered through the gloom, trying to make out the lad's face but Brian hunched over, back turned towards him.

Tom sighed and stepped back towards his van.

'Come on lad, seems the least I can do seeing as I almost ran you down.'

'Brian looked over his shoulder.

'Don't matter,' he said miserably. "Ent got nowhere to go anyhow.'

'Well, you can't stay out here,' said Tom. 'Is going to rain later. Where's your home?'

"Ent welcome there,' Brian mumbled. 'Not with my Dad home. Thought I'd head for the airfield maybe.'

Tom folded his arms, shaking his head slowly. There was something about this young man that reminded him of Kevin, Ada's son. The same fragile confidence, easily damaged; the same impractical approach to life's problems. Kevin had been very lucky in that his mother had sheltered him, protecting him from the consequences of his occasional bad choices until he found a place where he could grow and flourish, at the travelling Fair. There were a lot of Kevins in the world and most of them went bad – or disappeared, unremarked and un-mourned.

Cursing himself for a soft old fool, Tom had one last try.

'Come on, I'll take you to mine and you can sleep on the couch,' he said. 'Get some supper in you and you'll feel better.' It occurred to him this might be seen as a rather dubious proposition on the lad's part. It also occurred to him that, although he had very little worth stealing he was opening his home to a total stranger. He would have been greatly encouraged had he known neither possibility occurred to Brian.

Chapter Eighteen

Ada was surprised the first time Tom arrived at her gate with Brian Morris in tow. Brian cut a slightly hang-dog figure, though was much improved by a wash, some breakfast and the loan of a clean shirt. Tom nudged the lad through the gate past the dogs who were sniffing and giving suspicious growls.

'Go on then,' said Tom.

Brian looked down at the ground, scuffing his feet in the dirt.

'Sorry,' he mumbled.

'Sorry for what?' asked Ada. 'What's all this then, Tom?'

Brian sneaked a look at Ada before returning his gaze to the area around his feet.

'Sorry 'bout all the trouble with Charlie and stuff,' he managed. 'Was me as found them bomb things in the bottle tip. Didn't mean no harm, Mrs Mallory.'

Ada stood looking at him for a moment, arms folded across her chest. Then she shook her head and sighed. He was so like her Kevin in many ways and he had some manners at least.

'No real harm done,' she said. 'Apology accepted. Now, come in and we'll have some tea.'

Brian flashed a smile at her and his whole face suddenly seemed illuminated. Then he turned his head, sniffed and stepped off the dirt path, away from the open kitchen door.

'Is that an Anglo-Nubian you got?' he called excitedly, ignoring the dogs who hurried after him and threatened to snap at his heels.

'Well, what do you know,' said Tom softly. He followed Brian across to the enclosure where Pongo was trying to get his great head over the wire without getting a shock from the current.

'Mind now!' Tom called. 'Is electric that fence. Give you a bit of a buzz.'

Brian stopped just short of the wire and lifted his arm, holding his hand out so the goat could sniff at him. After a moment Brian reached forward and stroked Pongo gently on the nose.

'Is a beauty,' he said, turning to look at Tom with shining eyes.

'Don't you two be coming into my kitchen if you touch his head,' called Ada. 'You wash off under the tap first.'

Brian grinned at Tom.

'Stud goat?' he asked.

Tom found himself grinning back. 'Reckon. Though he's here on loan, doing a bit of land clearing. All Bob's young 'uns is his get, so Bob's bought in a new stud. They fight something awful so Pongo had to go, poor old fella.'

Brian nodded understandingly.

''Ent he a bit lonely, out here on his own?' he asked. The goat was nudging at his shoulder and Brian obligingly resumed petting around the animal's chin and ears.

'You seem to know an inordinate amount about 'em,' said Tom.

Brian shrugged. 'Was goats on the farm down at the Borstal I was at,' he said. 'Most kids, they won't go near 'um but I liked 'um better'n the pigs. Got more brains than chickens and even horses. Enjoyed looking after the goats, I did. There was Alpines too but these is the best, I reckon. Give nicer milk too.'

'You two want this tea or not?' Ada called from the kitchen.

'Come on, lad, don't do to get her riled,' said Tom and together they rinsed off and heading into the house.

After the tea Brian headed back out to Pongo again, the dogs following him.

'Seems a decent enough lad. Just needs a bit of a helping hand,' commented Tom.

Ada gave him a hard stare.

'You's planning something,' she said. 'Don't you give me that innocent look neither. I know you, Tom Monarch and you is up to something.'

Tom laughed, raising his hands in protest.

'I'm as surprised as you,' he mused. 'Never thought to see a lad like him so struck with goats. Still, he's got nowhere to go, nothing to do and he's a sniff away from getting into real trouble. Next time he's for the big prison and that's going to finish him off. I was thinking, maybe he could stay with me for a bit and we could see if that probation officer could find him a place in the farm college. She done right by Kevin.'

'What do you care 'bout some little hooligan boy from town?' Ada asked. 'You's taking a big risk, letting him stay at yours.'

Tom struggled to find the words to express himself. In truth, he wasn't sure exactly why he felt the need to offer Brian a hand but, just as he couldn't pick up a stray dog off the road and then abandon it again, he felt a responsibility for the boy. Tom had never had a child of his own and he was cut off from the rest of his family by the consequences of his marriage outside the tribe. In spite of his recent past and his numerous dubious business practices, Tom was a good man and he wanted to make a difference to someone.

'Just seems like the right thing to do,' he said with a shrug.

Brian turned up with Tom each morning that week and after a couple of days the dogs stopped following him around, contenting themselves with lying in the shade, snapping at early season flies and watching as he worked around the little smallholding. Pongo had done sterling work on the rough scrubland to the left of Ada's garden and Tom was eager to repeat the process on the other side.

'Make all the difference, having an extra pair of hands,' he said as they sat around the kitchen table eating the lunch Ada had prepared for them all. 'If'n you can help with the digging we can maybe get the fence moved over and not have to get a second lot. Ada can keep an eye on Pongo while we does the building.' Tom smiled at Brian over his cup of tea.

'I can't come tomorrow,' said Brian. 'I got to go an' do something. I'm sorry,' he said to Ada. 'Just – is something I need to do.'

Ada frowned at Tom before reaching out to touch Brian's hand reassuringly.

'You don't need to be saying sorry all the time,' she said firmly. 'Is nice having you here but you don't owe us nothing. You got your own life to lead. Don't need to be hanging around all the time with us old 'uns.'

Brian turned bright red and almost spilled his tea in his confusion.

''Ent that,' he said. 'I really enjoys this. Feels as if I'm doing something, for a change. Is only, I got to finish off something afore I start anything new.'

'Hope it 'ent nothing a bit dubious,' commented Tom. 'Wouldn't want to be harbouring no fugitive, would we.'

'What did you say that for?' asked Ada crossly when Brian was back in the garden and out of earshot.

'Well, what's he got to finish off? All he ever done for years is get into trouble,' Tom grumbled. 'Still, I can take you into town tomorrow. Cast our votes and see if there's anything worth having in the market. What you say?'

'I don't reckon I'm casting no vote,' said Ada firmly. 'Pack of thieves and liars, the lot of 'em. Don't listen to us and don't

260

pay no mind soon as they's voted back in. You ever see one of 'em down here in the winter storms? Bet they's not even own a decent pair of wellies.'

'If you's on the list then you should vote,' said Tom firmly. 'Only way we can register any opinion and is more important then ever this time. You want this lot to think they done a decent job? I for one want to tell 'em they's not.'

He rose and went to Ada's clock where the post was starting to mount up again. Flipping through the litter of paper, he pulled out a white card and held it up.

'See, you got a voter's number, right here. You come with me tomorrow into town.' He began to shove the rest of the envelopes back out of sight when the return address on one caught his eye.

'Ada,' he said softly and held it out to her. 'When did this 'un arrive?'

Ada took it from him, turning it over a couple of times in her large, rough hands.

'Don't recall,' she said finally. Maybe couple of days ago.'

They stood for a moment, both staring at the envelope before Tom sighed.

'Better open it?'

In silence Ada tore the top off the brown envelope, pulled out the letter and read it, before taking a couple of steps backwards.

'Steady now,' said Tom, seizing her arm and helping her into a chair.

Ada held out the letter, her face frozen in disbelief as Tom read its contents.

'Well,' he said finally. 'Seems you is now a rich woman. Even if they decided your Frank was guilty of – let me see now – "contributory negligence", that's still a good chunk of money. You got a bank account?'

Ada shook her head.

'What would I be doing with one of them?' she asked scornfully.

Tom flipped the letter over and waved the slip at the back towards her.

'Need one now,' he said. 'Got to pay this into a bank account or something like it. Can't expect the corner shop to cash this like they does yer widow's pension.' He squinted at the cheque, counting the figures again to make sure he'd got it right.

'Reckon most of the shops in Westonzoyland don't see six thousand pounds from one year's end to the next.'

Alex rose early on Thursday and hurried off to the polling station to cast her vote. The papers were full of speculation, last-minute opinion polls and quotes from the notable and the knowledgeable and according to some of them it was a forgone conclusion. According to others it was too close to call. So, she thought, as she marked the ballot paper and posted it in the metal box, no-one really knew.

She was early in to work that morning too, carrying an unusually large bag over her shoulder. She waved towards Lauren and Pauline who were standing by the reception counter but did not stop to chat.

'What's up with her then?' Lauren wondered as she watched her friend manoeuvre the heavy bag through the doors and hurry on towards her office.

Pauline shrugged. 'Who knows. I expect she's trying to get all her preparation ready for the session this evening.'

Lauren nodded, remembering it was the penultimate class in Alex's Alcohol Education group. So far it seemed to have been a success, with only one of the participants falling foul of the law since attending and a drop in the number of tipsy clients propping up the desk in the day centre. Lauren knew Alex had some unorthodox ideas and Gordon had vetoed several of her more imaginative plans, but even so, the whole scheme had been well received and it seemed likely the magistrates would adopt it as a viable alternative to sentencing for the numerous alcohol-related incidents they faced every day.

In the privacy of her office, Alex unpacked a portable television, a small tape recorder, two joysticks and a black

262

plastic boxed keyboard bearing the logo 'Commodore 64+'. The last items were her Christmas present to herself, a moment of total indulgence she had rarely regretted. Telling herself it was important to keep up with modern technology, she had started to use it as a word processor, only to find she needed a separate printer as neither of the machines at work would read the floppy disks she used. With a show of reluctance she put her educational aspirations to one side and dived joyously into the new and exciting world of video gaming.

Most of the games involved hunting for treasure, exploring strange buildings or (her personal favourite) helping a small red ant avoid death at the claws of large purple scorpions. Several, however, did have an educational element to them. She had spent several happy evenings running a cartoon builder around some scaffolding whilst attempting increasingly complex mental arithmetic and was pleased to discover her grasp of the seven times table was greatly improved.

Her focus today was on the racing game. The object was to drive a motorcycle at high speed around a racing circuit, preferably faster than both a real-life opponent and those controlled by the computer. Alex and Sue had once sat up late into the night steering and crashing their riders until they agreed they were far too intoxicated to drive. It had been a salutary experience and Alex hoped the young men who insisted they drove better after a drink or two would learn something from the game.

There was, however, one drawback to her scheme. She needed them to experience what the difference between 'sober' and 'a bit tipsy' made to their ability to manoeuvre the little bikes, and that meant she had to defy Gordon. In the bottom of her filing cabinet was a case of beer and half a dozen water glasses. Each was marked to show how much beer comprised a unit (a surprisingly small amount). She also had a police-issue reusable breathalyzer to test the lads after each 'crash'.

All she needed was an empty office building so she could run the session without interruption and she had chosen the evening with care. On election night everyone would be eager to get home, to watch the shape of the next five years unfold through the miracle of television. Alex was prepared to contain her desire to see some politicians humiliated if it allowed her to run the class undisturbed.

When the offices emptied, she moved her computer game and flip chart into the main room of the day centre, stowing the illicit beer and glasses in a box behind the corner table. As the class arrived she encouraged them to relax, chat and play a few games of pool, a welcome change from the serious approach she had maintained in the previous sessions. When she was sure they were all nicely loosened up she ran through a few of the key points from the earlier classes and was pleased to see they had all remembered at least some of the information.

Most of them knew what a unit of alcohol was and could list the main side-effects of excessive drinking. They could cheerfully discuss liver damage and the possible damage to the brain, the impact of dehydration and the total lack of effective cures for a hangover. What was concerning her was their difficulty in linking all this to themselves and to real life. Most of them still maintained they could 'manage' an inordinate amount of alcohol and still function normally. For at least half of them this meant they thought they could drive quite safely after five or six pints. The evening she had planned was designed to disabuse them of this notion.

The first round of 'racing' went fast as the class took to the game with juvenile enthusiasm. Even the sole middle-aged man in a suit, a drunk driver sentenced to the class by an enthusiastic magistrate, entered into the spirit of the competition. Before long there was a leader board marked up on the flip chart and everyone was clamouring for a second go. Alex let them all try a second run and, as they finished, handed each of them a single unit of beer by way of a 'reward'. Several of the brighter lads eyed her suspiciously but the lure of a free drink was too much of a temptation and they all swigged their way through their glasses before embarking on a third set of races.

The next lot of scores were not as good as the first two and when everyone had finished Alex handed round the reusable breathalyzer. Everyone was under the drink-drive limit but another drink pushed them over it, though no-one admitted to feeling any effect whatsoever. It was surprising how much difference the last two drinks made – surprising for them anyway. Half the players crashed their bikes and no-one finished even close to their original times.

It was a rather sobering experience for all concerned, Alex thought as she packed up the computer, threw the bottles in a plastic bag for discrete disposal in the outside bins and rinsed out the glasses. Locking up behind her, she failed to notice one window was still lit on the upper floor. Heading off home through the empty car park, she forgot that Ricky, still slightly traumatised by the events of last week, had taken to parking his car in the old bike shed, out of sight (and hopefully range) of the main building. Hurrying through the back gate into a now deserted park, she didn't feel Ricky's angry eyes fixed on her retreating form.

As soon as she was out of sight, Ricky hurried down the stairs, cancelled the alarm and began a search of the day centre. He had been disturbed by the sounds from Alex's class and stormed down the stairs to protest the interruption. At the door he had stopped, watching through the glass as a group of young men jostled and laughed, drinking beer and playing some stupid computer game. No wonder she seemed so popular with the clients, he thought. This was a disgrace – thoroughly unprofessional and probably verging on fraud. He wondered what Gordon would make of it but stopped as he remembered Gordon's days as acting senior were about to come to an end.

Ricky knew the new senior from his days at college and he knew exactly what she would make of the situation. All he needed was some evidence to back up his complaint. After ten minutes searching he found it in the form of a dirty beer glass that had rolled out of sight under the table. Coupled with the used breathalyzer tubes and Alex's scorecard for the computer game which he found torn off and shoved into her bin he had more than enough. Satisfied by his evening's work, he reset the alarm and headed off to catch the early election results. Ricky could wait for his revenge. In a few weeks someone with the right sort of attitude was going to take over and Alex and her little cabal were in for a nasty surprise.

Thursday morning was fine and bright and Brian rose early, preparing tea and toast for Tom before they left the house.

'Sure you don't want a lift some place?' Tom asked.

Brian shook his head and waved as he set off across the marsh, hopping over the narrow rhynes and dodging the boggy places until he reached Langmead Drove, the ancient track cutting across the lowland towards the airfield. He knew it was foolish but he really had to try one last time with the metal detector. There was something good out there, he knew. Something waiting for him that would transform his life. Such was the lure of easy money and Brian could still not ignore its call.

The metal detector was stowed in an abandoned rabbit warren and was none the worse for lying several days unprotected in the ground. Brian brushed off the dirt, switched it on and was pleased to see the battery was holding up just fine. It was unlikely he'd be able to get another and so he intended to get the most use he could from the aging machine. When it finally died on him, well then he'd look for something a bit steadier as a living.

The airfield was too exposed to curious gazes and anyway it had been picked clean long ago, but Brian had seen several other places where the ground looked as if it had been disturbed recently and so he slung the metal detector over his shoulder and marched off across the Levels, heading towards Currey's Bridge where the River Parrett flowed, thick and viscous in the distance.

It was hard work, walking and swinging the heavy machine in front of him and several times Brian considered chucking the thing over a hedge and heading off towards Ada's cottage. She was going out, though, he recalled. No chance of a cup of tea there, so he persisted, moving slowly and carefully along the narrow track. He was just across the bridge when he got his first hit and he switched off the machine, dropping to his knees to scrabble at the loose earth before stopping abruptly. He had been very lucky last time, he recalled. Might be a good idea to go a bit gently on this one.

He rummaged around in the hedge, scratching his hand on the thorns before pulling a medium sized branch free to use as a shovel and slowly he loosened the dirt, turning it aside to see what was underneath. There was a soft clanging sound and he froze, memories of the deadly little butterflies still sharp in his mind. Very, very gently he moved the earth away to reveal a large metal tin. Not long in the ground, from the look of it. No signs of rust on the lid or down the sides, he noted as he prised it loose from the damp soil. The tin was surprisingly heavy and he sat down, placing it between his knees to steady it before levering off the lid.

As it popped open there was a faint burst of fruit from inside. Brian sniffed, trying to place the smell. Pineapple, he thought. He had always liked pineapple though rarely had it, except the tinned sort that turned up occasionally at school for pudding. Tilting the tin towards the light, he poked his hand inside, wary of the sharp edges. His hand met cloth, a rough, heavy fabric, tightly wound up and pushed down the sides. Groping around some more he managed to extricate a shoe, then its companion. Brian pushed the tin to one side and examined his find. Decent leather boots, he noted, with good, strong laces. They looked about the right size too. Thrusting his foot inside one, his toes met resistance from the newspaper linings. It was the work of seconds to yank this out, discarding the faded sheets in the ditch behind him. A bit of pulling and wriggling and the boots fitted perfectly.

Brian couldn't believe his luck. His old shoes were cracked and falling apart, the soles worn away from years of wear. These, he thought as he stood to admire his feet, these were expensive boots. He'd never have been able to afford a pair of these even if they were a bit worn and scuffed in places. He decided to ask Ada if she had any polish, though he wasn't sure what colour. Was there a special polish or should he darken them down with black?

He turned his attention to the rest of the contents but even he was not desperate enough to covet the Hinkleys. After a moment's hesitation he rolled up the work shirt and shoved it in his jacket pocket, abandoning the rest of the find by the track. Today, he thought as he sauntered along towards the River, today was a good day.

Friday, in contrast, was not a good day. Alex sat up long into the night watching in disbelief as the election results trickled in. Although only about a third of the constituencies had been announced by the time she gave up and crawled into bed, it was obvious which way the country had voted. When she dragged herself out again the next morning it was apparent the government had been re-elected by a landslide. All her hopes that the changes in the way offenders were treated were dashed. It was all set to continue and, worse for her personally, it looked as though the controversial 'Section 28' was now to be enacted.

'You look like total shit,' said Sue, peering at her over a cup of tea.

'So would you if you'd seen and heard some of the gloating last night,' Alex grumbled.

Sue shrugged her shoulders.

'There's nothing we could do to change it,' she said. 'Too many greedy people don't give a damn about the rest of the country. Why should they give up their nice share offers because a few criminals need a helping hand. No-one cares anymore.'

'Except for us,' said Alex stubbornly.

'Yes,' said Sue. 'Except for us. And look where that's got us. I don't know about you but I was better off as a student than I am now. I don't know how you manage the mortgage

on this house. We just get more clients, less say in their pro-
grammes and everything goes up except our salary. You
know.' She fixed Alex with a stern glare over the top of her
beaker. 'I've half a mind to go back to teaching for a bit. At
least we got to take our holidays.'

'I didn't know you were a teacher,' said Alex. She was quite
startled by this bit of news, not least because the thought of
Sue being responsible for thirty young, impressionable minds
was rather disturbing.

'Oh, it was at my college in Exeter,' said Sue. 'I had the
hooligan element, of course. Actually it was quite enjoyable a
lot of the time. I came into probation thinking I'd be able to
make a difference to some of those in real trouble, not just the
YTS drop-outs. Fat chance, the way things are going now.'

In the probation offices there was an air of subdued gloom,
not improved by Ricky's appearance at the tea room door, a
wide grin on his face.

'Anyone sit up to see the election last night?' he asked.
'Fantastic!' With that he was gone, taking the stairs two at a
time and whistling as he went.

'Well,' muttered Lauren. 'Glad someone's happy.' She was
still mulling over Ricky's remark on Monday. With some
reluctance she had mentioned it to Pauline but her line manager had advised against saying anything to anyone else.

'You're not sure that's what he said?' When Lauren shook
her head Pauline continued, 'Even if he did – and I'm not saying that's a fact – he can just deny it and it would make things
much worse. Look, if he is behaving like that and you can
prove it, come to me. It is not acceptable and I won't have my
staff treated to abuse. But until then I can't really do much.'

Lauren knew Pauline was right. She was also sure Ricky
knew it and was extremely unlikely to ever say or do anything
so unpleasant in front of a witness. Gathering her belongings,
she made her way down the stairs and set to work on the
pile of notes Ricky had left on her desk. She was just getting sorted when her phone rang and Ricky demanded her

presence upstairs. Replacing the receiver with a sigh, Lauren slid off her high chair and headed for the stairs.

Ricky was on the top floor, right at the farthest end of the building and she was out of breath by the time she reached his office. Ricky didn't bother to get up as she shoved the heavy door open, glancing at her as she walked across the room to stand in front of his desk. Ricky took a few seconds to finish reading the letter in his hand before looking up.

'Oh, I'm sorry, I forgot to ask you to bring your diary. Run and get it could you?'

He turned his attention back to the files in front of him as Lauren turned and struggled her way through the door, along the corridor and down the stairs. Three flights of steps took their toll on her fragile lungs and she stopped to rest for a moment before heading off again, clambering upwards with grim determination.

When she pushed open the office door for a second time Ricky made a show of glancing at the clock before holding out his hand for the book. Lauren handed it over in silence, grateful she did not have to speak, as her breath was coming in short gasps.

Ricky flipped through the diary pages, grunted and handed it back.

'Thanks,' he said and looked down at his desk.

Lauren's hands were shaking in fury at this abrupt dismissal but she turned and walked out without a word, clutching the diary to her chest. She took the stairs rather more carefully on the way down as her legs felt as if they were made from rubber. She had scarcely got back to her desk when the phone went again. This time he was asking for one of the 'dead' files to be brought up. Quickly please as he needed some information from it before he headed off to court.

Wearily Lauren located the buff folder and set off up the stairs once more. By the time she reached the top she was feeling a bit sick and there were flickering black dots in front of her eyes. She took a deep, if slightly uneven, breath and hurried towards Ricky's office. Again he stayed at his desk, holding out his hand in silence and making her stand in front of him like a schoolgirl summoned for misbehaviour.

'Fine, that's all,' he said and Lauren headed back downstairs again, her feet dragging on the worn carpet as she tried not to stumble. The stairs seemed steeper with every flight and as she turned the corner at the bottom her legs gave way completely. She grabbed frantically at the handrail but it was already out of her reach and she tumbled the last half dozen steps, hitting the door at the bottom with a dull thud.

Pauline was first on the scene, closely followed by Eddie and Alex, who were just inside the day centre. Gently lifting Lauren in his arms, Eddie carried her small frame into the office where he laid her on the rest room couch.

'Lift her head a bit,' said Pauline, who was hovering anxiously. 'She has trouble breathing – she told me once she can't lie down flat at night.'

Obediently, Eddie lifted Lauren's head and put a small cushion under her neck before placing his fingers on her wrist to check for a pulse.

'She's still breathing but her heartbeat is all over the place,' he said. 'I think you'd better phone for an ambulance.'

Chapter Nineteen

Dave Brown took the call from probation sitting at his desk in the Taunton detectives' room. After thanking Pauline, he spun out of his chair and headed for the Inspector's office.

'You just go,' said his senior officer. 'We're just waiting here for results and stuff from the lab. Nothing likely to happen for another week or two, going on the past couple of months. You take the time you need.'

Dave was not totally convinced by this argument but he was too worried about Lauren to argue and anyway the last thing he wanted was to sit around in the detectives' room waiting for something to happen. Nodding his thanks he grabbed his bag and coat and headed out of the door.

Lauren had been taken to the hospital in Highpoint, a Victorian monstrosity decorated with numerous fake Greek architectural features and several redundant porticos. Dave had often marvelled at its ugliness in passing but today he bounded up the steps without a second glance at the mock Corinthian columns. Hurrying past the glassed-in reception desk, he trotted down long, featureless corridors painted a series of depressing greens. The floor was slippery underfoot and several times a nurse frowned at him as he hurried by, but Dave was blind to anything but the desperate need to reach Lauren.

At the door to the intensive care ward he stopped, taking a moment to steady his breathing and smooth his hair down a bit. A nurse barred his way as he tried to step past the door.

'I'm sorry, only close relatives are allowed,' she said. She didn't look very sorry but she was certainly extremely determined. For a moment Dave considered pulling out his warrant card but he had a feeling that would probably make her even less willing to let him in. Over the far side of the room he caught a glimpse of Jonny hunched over a bed, his posture radiating his anguish.

'I'm her fiancée,' Dave whispered. 'Please, I've come over from Taunton. I only heard a little while ago.'

'Wait here,' said the nurse and turned towards the single occupied bed. There was some hurried whispering and Jonny looked up, staring right into Dave's eyes, holding his gaze for a heartbeat before nodding. Dave was halfway across the room before the nurse had beckoned him in.

Lauren lay propped upon her back in the centre of a mass of wires and tubes. She looked tiny and so fragile, surrounded by the forest of medical equipment. Her face was a sickly yellow colour and she was so still he wondered for a moment if he was too late. Then he noticed a screen on the left showing a green line that peaked regularly as it ran across the monitor and he let out his breath with a sigh.

'She's stable now,' said the nurse softly. 'You may sit with her but not wake her up. Any sign she is disturbed you go out, both of you.' With that she marched back to her post by the door, leaving Dave and Jonny to stare at one another.

'Any idea what happened?' Dave whispered.

Jonny shook his head. 'No. I'm going to see Alex and Pauline at probation later. I didn't want to leave her alone in case she woke up. Here, you sit in this chair. I'm dying for a piss.'

Dave settled next to Lauren, taking her right hand in both of his. For a little while he just sat, feeling the gentle pulse beneath his fingers and gazing at her face. Finally he leaned forwards and touched her cheek very lightly. There was no response from Lauren and as the nurse shot a warning scowl in his direction Dave settled into the chair.

People came and went through the day, trickling in to stand beside the bed and look helplessly at Lauren's tiny figure but Dave did not stir. It was quite late in the evening when Alex arrived, her face grim as she sat on the opposite side of the bed.

'Do *you* know what happened?' Dave asked.

Alex shook her head. 'No,' she said. 'Not really, though I have my suspicions. I think Lauren's being bullied at work and I'm sure I know who's responsible but I can't prove anything. I should have been looking out for her but I've been so wrapped up in my own problems, I just didn't see what was going on.' Alex blinked back tears, unable to meet Dave's eyes.

'You can't blame yourself,' said Dave sadly. 'Lauren always seems so . . . so strong and bloody minded, to be honest. She's not the easiest person to help.' He gave a rather lop-sided grin, then his eyes slid past her to focus on the door.

A porter stepped into the unit, whispered something to the duty nurse, a slightly more sympathetic woman than the last. She nodded in the direction of Lauren's bed and returned her attention to the papers in front of her. The porter's shoes squeaked on the polished floor as he made his way over to where Alex and Dave waited.

'Sorry,' said the porter. Alex wondered if he were apologising for the shoes or the interruption. 'Sorry,' he repeated. 'Detective Constable Brown?'

Dave nodded. 'There's a phone call for you. They insisted it was urgent otherwise I'd not have disturbed you.'

Dave rose to his feel, stretching the stiffness out of his back and shoulders.

'Don't worry,' said Alex in response to his unasked question. 'I'll stay here until you get back. We're not leaving her alone.'

274

Dave nodded his thanks, gave Lauren's hand a tiny squeeze and followed the porter out of the door.

Alex leaned back in the hard hospital chair and sighed softly. It had been a long and very depressing day, culminating in the rescheduled appointment with Jake Hollis. He had been even more abrupt and unforthcoming than usual and she had been tempted to send him on his way early so she could get to the hospital but decided she wasn't going to give him that satisfaction. As a result, they spent a bad-tempered and unproductive hour in the empty offices before Alex finally put them both out of their misery at half past six.

She had stopped off at her house to grab a sandwich and let Sue know where she was going before heading for the hospital. Now she felt the weight of the last few weeks on her shoulders and when Dave failed to reappear she resigned herself to a long, lonely vigil. As night fell the nurse turned on the lamp at her desk, the light casting long, thin shadows across the small ward. Lauren lay without moving in the bed, only the flickering tracks of the monitor screens to show she was still alive. Half-way down the night, the nurse brought her a cup of tea when she checked on the patient. Finally Alex surrendered to her exhaustion and slept.

'This is not good,' said Sergeant Lynas as he opened the door to the car and Dave hopped in the passenger seat. Lynas glanced over his shoulder swiftly before making an illegal turn in the street and heading off at top speed.

'Where we going?' asked Dave trying to put his anxiety over Lauren to one side.

'Just south of Pethy,' said Lynas using the local slang for the village of North Petherton. 'Same as the others – well, same as most of 'em anyway. Lonely house, woman sitting alone all lit up, naked man landing on the windows. You know.'

'Bit different from last week then,' said Dave staring at the scenery as it whizzed past the windows of the car.

'Could be he had more time to prepare, take off his clothes and stuff' said Lynas but his voice lacked conviction.

275

'Old-Fashioned thinks it's so close to the last one on account of him being interrupted last week so we's to treat them all as one series of offences.'

They drove in silence, both unconvinced by Old-Fashioned's reasoning but neither with the authority to challenge it. On arrival at the cottage they found the crime-scene officers already hard at work and this time there was more good luck.

'A tyre print,' said the officer who met their car. 'Finally we have something on how he's travelling.'

Dave and Lynas glanced at one another but kept quiet. The officer led them to the back of the garden where several people were photographing and measuring a muddy patch. Sure enough, running through the centre was a tyre print. Narrow but with a thick tread, it was too small to be a motor vehicle and the track was too confined for a car.

'Moped?' suggested Dave.

Lynas considered for a moment before shaking his head. 'Would be heard,' he said. 'Anyway, they leave a smell behind from that bloody horrible fuel mix. And them treads is very marked for a moped but it 'ent all that deep so there's not the weight you'd get.'

They stood in silence, watching as the photographers finished and the mould man stepped in to cast the tread as evidence.

'Bike,' said Dave suddenly. 'Those – what do you call 'em – like trick bikes with the big springs. The sort the kids use all over the hills.'

Lynas blinked as a torch shone towards them before refocusing on the ground. 'I think you'm maybe right,' he said. 'There was bike tracks all round Eleanor Bradshaw's place out by Enmore too. Check for a match against BMX tyres first,' he told the plaster tech before turning back to Dave. 'Well done – we might just have something to go on, finally.'

The two detectives turned towards the windows and Dave hesitated, recalling something Alex had said last week. In the excitement and tension of the attack on Alison it had slipped his mind completely.

'Sarge,' he said softly. 'That's a new conservatory, right?'

It was so new there were still a couple of stickers from the glass makers on the windows.

'All of the women, they were all sitting in conservatories. New conservatories, put up in the last six months or so. Maybe we should check, see if the same firm built them all.'

Lynas looked at the young detective admiringly. 'Now that's what I call good thinking,' he said. 'You see if anyone else inside can tell us anything useful about that whilst I'm doing the preliminary interview with our victim. And then I want you to get back to the station and follow up on this. Contact the other women and find out if they had the same builder.'

As Dave turned away he added, 'Take the car – I'll get a lift with the tech boys. And go back to Highpoint for this one. You might need to look in at the hospital.'

Alex woke, stiff and cold in the chair beside Lauren's bed and for an instant couldn't recall where she was. Then her eyes focussed on the still form and it all came rushing back. A dark shape emerged from the shadows by the door and resolved itself into Jonny, his face tight with worry and fatigue.

'Thanks for staying,' he said softly as he slumped into the other chair. 'Where's lover-boy gone?'

'He got an emergency call from Taunton,' said Alex. 'I said I'd stay but I must have fallen asleep.' She wiped her chin surreptitiously in case she had dribbled. 'What time is it?'

Jonny squinted at his watch. 'Gone midnight,' he said. 'I've been over to see Mum. She's worried sick and it was all I could do, stopping her from rushing over. Nothing she can do, of course, but I promised to go back, let her know if there's any change.'

Alex shook her head. 'Well, I've been asleep but I think she's about the same,' she said sadly. 'Do they know what caused her to collapse like that?'

Jonny scowled and suddenly his beautiful, open face became a mask of fury.

'Was something close to a heart attack,' he said. 'She struggles with her breathing sometimes, 'specially under stress. Seems she was running up and down them stairs at work, got her breathing all tangled up and she just collapsed. Seeing as she was still half a dozen steps up she done some damage, landing heavy like she did.' He gave Alex an angry look over Lauren's sleeping form. 'Don't suppose you know *why* she was doing that?'

Alex shook her head. 'I think we need to ask Lauren,' she said. She was saved from further questions by the appearance of Sue at the door to the little ward.

'Only two at a time,' said the nurse, rising from her chair and holding up her hand. 'In fact, you really shouldn't be here at all at this hour. We can make an exception for family members but I'm afraid the pair of you must go now. You can come back in the morning.'

'Can they stay a few more minutes while I find a phone and let my Mum know how she is? Don't want her waking up and finding she's alone in a strange place,' asked Jonny.

The nurse sniffed and started to speak. 'I really don't think she's . . .' She stopped abruptly. 'Very well, five minutes. There's a phone box just down the hall.'

Sue walked over to the bed and stood at the end. There were tears in her eyes, tears of anger.

'This is that little bastard Ricky's doing,' she hissed. 'Pauline said he had her running up and down the stairs just after he got in. Gordon hauled the little shit into the office this afternoon, along with Pauline. Do you know what he said?'

'You're getting a bit loud,' Alex murmured. 'Volume control . . .'

'He said, "It's not my fault if she can't do the job. She shouldn't be here if she's not up to it",' hissed Sue.

Alex went cold with fury. 'Whatever you do, don't let Jonny hear that,' she said. 'Not yet anyway. He's desperately upset and I dread to think what he's do . . .' She broke off as Jonny came back into the room.

'What?' he said, looking from one to the other.

'Nothing,' said Alex hastily. 'I think I need to go Jonny. Can we bring you anything? Have you eaten?'

Jonny shook his head. 'I'm fine,' he said. 'You go and thank you so much for staying with her. I'll call if there's any news.'

Sue reached out and hugged him, much to his surprise.

'Phone if you need anything,' she said. 'We're just over the river.'

By the time they reached the door Jonny was sitting next to his sister, holding her right hand, oblivious to anything but Lauren.

The ringing of the telephone woke Alex the next morning and her first thought was something had happened at the hospital. Hurling herself down the stairs, she reached the door to the front room just as the sound stopped.

'Bugger, bugger, bugger,' she muttered. Then she heard Sue's voice and peered in as her friend replaced the receiver.

'What?' Alex demanded. 'Is it Lauren? What's happened?'

Sue's eyes were wide with shock as she stepped back into the dining room.

'Sit down Alex. That was Dave.' She held up her hand to forestall Alex's cry. 'It's not Lauren, don't worry. Dave was ringing to let you know they've arrested someone for the Moth Man attacks. It's Brian Morris.'

Brian had taken a bit of a ribbing from Tom when he appeared at the cottage on Thursday night in his lovely new boots.

'Where the hell you get them then?' Tom asked, trying not to laugh.

'Found 'em,' said Brian. 'Right smart, 'ent they.'

'Excepting the colour,' said Tom.

'What you think Ada?' he asked the next morning when they arrived to work on the new goat enclosure.

Ada looked at Brian and shook her head.

'What's wrong with 'em?' Brian demanded. 'Need a bit of a clean but I reckon they'll come up smashing.'

'Where you going to get polish to match round here?' asked Ada.

'Thought I'd maybe use some black on 'em, make 'em a bit darker,' said Brian.

Tom and Ada exchanged glances and then Tom rose from the table.

'Reckon I'll be checking on them nets for covering the salad,' he said and strolled out into the sunshine, leaving Ada glaring at his back.

'Right, well now Brian. Let me see – what colour's this then,' she asked pulling the tea-cosy off the teapot.

Brian looked at her suspiciously but said, 'Green of course. I 'ent blind.'

'Hmm. So, them boots of your'n, they's green too?'

'Sort of grey-green, yes,' said Brian peering down at his feet.

'Sit down for a minute,' said Ada. 'I got a couple of bits of news for you, neither particularly good. First off, I think you is probably colour blind, at least a bit. That tea-cosy, that's red, not green.'

Brian blinked at her but didn't say a word.

'Second off, them boots of your'n, they ain't green, nor grey-green, nor green-grey. They's pink.'

Brian gaped at her in horror, then down at the offending boots.

'What'm I supposed to do then?' he said. 'I only got these. Chucked the others away, they was so far gone. I can't be seen out in no *pink shoes*.'

Ada struggled to keep a straight face. What was it about the colour pink, she wondered. It couldn't be aesthetic. After all, Brian couldn't even see the colour.

'Don't know if putting black on them's a good idea,' she said. 'Maybe if we could find some red . . .'

'I'm off into Street early tomorrow,' came Tom's voice from the door. 'Could take you with us an' we could probably pick up some there. Only place I knows of with more shoe shops than pubs, is Street.'

'That's sorted then. Now, you here to chat or look after Pongo and help with the fence?' said Ada briskly.

The rest of the day passed quickly and it was with a sigh of relief that Tom and Brian clambered into the van at the end of it.

'Just time to pick up something for tea,' said Tom as he started the engine.

Brian looked down at the grubby floor, trying not to visualise the real colour of his boots. He was really looking forward to getting some red polish and putting a bit of a shine on them.

The next morning they set off early. Brian sat in the van, bouncing on the seat across the rough ground. Occasionally he would slip his hand into his pocket to feel the crackle of a five pound note on his fingertips. Ada had pressed the money into his hand as he was leaving the cottage last night, cutting short his protest.

'You been a great help here. Couldn't have managed without you, to be honest. Don't expect you to keep working for nothing and anyway, I bet red shoe polish is a sight more expensive than a tin of brown. Now be off – and don't you mention this to Tom neither.'

For once he was not thinking of all the 'natch' he could get for a fiver. He was wondering if there'd be much left from the red polish and if he could maybe get some flowers or something for Ada. The casual care he received from her and Tom, the sense of being valued, was slowly chipping away at the false bravado he wore around his emotions. Brian was actually starting to think of a life beyond the next day. Maybe, with a bit of support, there might be a future for him that was not numbered in probation orders, lost days of drunkenness or 'short, sharp shocks'.

After parting company with Tom he walked down the middle of the road, hands in his pockets. The bright shop fronts were looking a bit faded and there were a lot of racks selling bargain shoes lining the pavements. Brian was not the most experienced of shoppers but even he could tell there was a desperate air about the town. Too many red stickers, too many shop staff, too few customers, especially for a Saturday. He knew the place was in real trouble when, instead of the shop staff scowling at him when he stepped over the threshold, he was greeted politely by an assistant who, as soon as he produced the five pound note from his pocket, called him 'Sir'.

After some discussion and a close examination of his pink boots he left with a jar of red colour-restoring polish, a new pair of laces and enough change to get a decent bunch of flowers for Ada. As he walked towards the florist Brian felt proud and happy, a young man with money he had earned in his pockets and a sense of what he might do with his life. As he smiled, the gap knocked in his front teeth was a reminder of some of his less sensible actions but nothing could take away the rush of happiness he experienced.

Nothing, until a sharp-eyed constable, not much older than Brian, spotted him striding down the road. The policeman's eyes were drawn to Brian's feet and the pink boots, now the focus of a county-wide alert. Grabbing the radio fixed to his pocket, he called in the sighting and set off after his quarry.

The florist was startled when a police van screeched to a halt outside her shop and three officers rushed in to seize the young man who had just purchased a rather large bouquet of flowers. As they grabbed him from behind, Brian struggled, trying to put his flowers back on the safety of the counter whilst protesting his innocence of any wrongdoing. In the ensuing melee Ada's bouquet was dropped on the floor where it was trampled by three pairs of police boots. Brian was dragged, shouting and swearing into the back of the van, leaving the bemused florist to lift the crushed flowers and count Brian's carefully husbanded change into the till.

In the back of the van, Brian was flat on the floor, a police size eleven boot on his back.

''Ent done nothing!' Brian gasped, almost crying in fury. 'What you doin'?'

'Shut up you little pervert,' snarled the officer in the front. 'You wait 'til they get hold of you in Taunton. They'll get the truth out of you, no mistake.'

'Why we takin' him all the way to Taunton?' asked the officer in the back.

'Special instructions,' said the the officer in the front. 'Seems he's to be questioned by the *detectives*.'

In the Taunton station there was an air of subdued excitement when the call came through about the arrest. Sergeant Lynas and Dave Brown had done a lot of the work on the case and they were determined not to be pushed aside by more senior men, most of whom were eager for the glory a successful conclusion would bring. Dave was particularly anxious for he was coming to the end of his probationary period as acting detective and was not sure all his work in the background would be enough to get him confirmed in post.

Lynas hurried off to speak to the Inspector as soon as they heard the news and put the case for their involvement as forcefully as he could.

'We've worked this for weeks,' he said. 'We know more details than anyone, we been to all the scenes. Come on, Sir. If anyone can catch him out, is us.'

The Inspector recognised the truth of this. Lynas was one of his best men and he had developed a lot of respect for Dave but he was aware of how important the first interview would be. After careful consideration he went for a compromise. The actual interview would be conducted by senior officers but Dave and Lynas would observe from behind one-way glass. It was not ideal from anyone's point of view but he hoped to get the best result by involving both groups in the process.

Dave was torn between anger at being shut out of the Moth Man case and the rising anxiety over Lauren. His phone call to the hospital had elicited only a bland, generic reassurance and the promise to contact him should there be 'any significant change'. Dave was dizzy with fatigue, worn out by the stress of Lauren's accident and heartily sick of the whole business of chasing this elusive offender around the county. It was probably just as well he wasn't going to be in the room, he thought. At the moment he wanted nothing more than to knock the little bastard's teeth down his throat.

When he took his place in the observation room he leaned forwards, peered at the dishevelled figure of Brian Morris seated facing them and turned to his sergeant.

'That's not him.'

Lynas peered through the glass, slightly cloudy with the reflective coating on one side and shook his head.

'Why's that then?'

'Look at him!' said Dave. 'He's far too skinny and small to outrun anyone like the bloke near Newton. He's not blond, he's sort of mousey and as people never cease to remind me, our chap is a *natural* blond. And I know this guy. He's a total loser and a pain in the arse but I can't see him as a sexual predator. And he can't even ride a bike properly. I know *that* because his probation officer made me teach him about three months ago. He's rubbish at it, to be honest. No way could he manage the rides across the hills and out to some of the scenes.'

The Inspector had slipped into the room unobserved and cleared his throat as Dave finished. The two officers jumped to their feet, Dave blinking at his commanding officer nervously.

'You make a good case,' said the Inspector waving his hand to tell them to sit again. 'However, he was wearing the boots worn by the intruder at North Newton. They are being checked now but they are the right size, the sole is distinctive and there are a number of matching abrasions. He also had some red shoe polish in his possession, presumably to disguise the colour. And despite your opinion of his skill in that area, we know he owns a bike of the right type and can ride it.'

Dave knew what he had to do now was keep quiet and listen to his superiors. 'The hair, Sir,' he said. Inside his head he was shouting, 'Shut up, shut up, *shut up!*'

The Inspector stared at him. 'And?'

Dave swallowed nervously. He could feel Sergeant Lynas shifting carefully from one foot to another beside him. 'The hair on the glass,' he said. 'It was blond. Brian Morris has brown hair. There's no way those hairs came from him. Sir.'

His commanding officer studied Dave for an instant, then turned his eyes upwards, gazing at the grey ceiling as if searching for exactly the right words.

'Very well, Acting Detective Brown,' he said finally. 'By your own admission you are acquainted with the suspect. In fact you have established some sort of rapport with him. I would suggest therefore you may take your place in the room and practise that good old fashioned skill known as "good cop, bad cop". You will be the good cop, of course. I want to know where he was last week, where he was last night and why he was buying coloured polish to disguise those boots.'

Brian stared at Dave when he entered the room, then turned his head away.

'Hi Brian,' said Dave, pulling out a chair and sitting opposite the lad.

'Bugger off,' said Brian. ''En't done nothing and en't talking 'til I get my solicitor. I already been stitched up once by you lot an' is not lettin' it happen again.' He leaned back in his chair, folding his arms with a glare.

'That's not very friendly,' said Dave. 'You'd better watch your tongue when my colleague gets here.' He realised he had no idea who his 'colleague' was going to be – or even when they were going to arrive – but he ploughed on hopefully. 'Just want to sort this out so you can be on your way. I'*m* not convinced you had anything to do with these attacks, to be honest, but you were wearing the exact shoes used in last Friday's incident. That's pretty compelling evidence, you must admit.'

To his surprise Brian gave a short, humourless laugh.

'Last Friday?' he said. 'Well, shows what you lot know, don't it. Got me a *alibi* for Friday. An' a right good'un an all. Now, what about my solicitor?'

There was something wrong here. Brian was not the strongest of characters and he regularly folded when interrogated but this time he showed no signs of any concern.

'You don't have a solicitor,' said Dave. 'You've never been able to afford a solicitor Brian. Why do you suddenly want one now?'

'Duty bloke'll do,' came the reply. 'Just want someone here as my witness. Now that's all I's sayin' 'til he gets here.'

Dave got up and left the room, leaving Brian to stare defiantly at the one-way mirror in the room.

'Get him the duty solicitor,' said the Inspector shortly. 'I want to know how he got those shoes and just exactly what this bloody alibi is. And I want to know now.'

When Dave returned to the interview room he was accompanied by the duty solicitor, a thin and nervous associate from one of Highpoint's three firms, and Sergeant Lynas who was preparing himself to play 'bad cop' should it prove necessary. The seniors, it seemed, had decided to let the junior officers take the blame for this should it prove to be a disaster.

'I would like to consult my client,' began the solicitor rather nervously but Brian shook his head.

'Just want you here,' he said. 'And that on.' He pointed to the tape recorder on the table.

Dave and Lynas exchanged glances before the sergeant started the recording by identifying the people in the room. Something was wrong and this interview was not going as planned. Acutely aware of the witnesses just the other side of the glass, Dave waited for Lynas to make the first move but as the silence stretched out painfully he realised he was going to have to say something.

'So, tell us where you were last Friday evening,' he said.

'I'm instructing my client not to answer that question,' the solicitor said.

Brian brushed his intervention aside, leaned forward and grinned, his chipped front tooth giving him a feral look.

'Was banged up in Highpoint on account of them little bomb things I found,' he said gleefully.

At the mention of bombs the solicitor turned very pale. This was more than he had bargained for and he looked as if he wished the floor would open and swallow him up. Dave understood exactly how he felt and from the sudden stillness of Sergeant Lynas beside him, he knew they were about to be made into fools in the eyes of his superiors. His desire to strangle Brian returned in all its fury, though for a different reason.

'So how did you come by the boots?' he asked, desperate to salvage something from the situation.

'Found 'em,' said Brian with a shrug.

'What do you mean, "Found them"' asked Lynas. 'What, they were just lying around in the road and you picked them up? Someone gave them to you? Elves left them on your doorstep?'

Brian glared at him. 'Found 'em in a tin,' he said. 'Out by Currie Bridge, they was. Buried under a hedge.'

'So if they were buried as you claim, how did *you* manage to stumble across them?' Lynas demanded.

'Was using my detector,' Brian said. 'Got a good loud signal so I dug around, found this tin and there was clothes and stuff in it. No name 'nor nothing so I kept they boots 'cos they's right smart and mine was full of holes. Shirt too – chucked the Hinkleys mind.'

Dave jumped in, his heart pounding with excitement. 'What about the tin,' he said. 'Where's the tin, Brian?'

'Threw 'um back,' said Brian. 'Along with the old paper and stuff.'

'What "old paper"?' pressed Dave, barely able to contain his impatience.

'I really think I need to talk to my client,' the solicitor squeaked.

'Was a load of old newspaper in my boots,' said Brian. 'Sort of packed around the sides but I couldn't get my feet in so I pulled it all out and they fit perfect. When do I get 'em back then?'

Alex arrived at Highpoint police station to protest Brian's arrest at the same time as the phone call came through demanding verification of his arrest and detention. Receiving short shrift at the desk, she made her weary way across the river and plodded into the hospital where Jonny sat, red-eyed and exhausted by Lauren's side. Alex sent him off to get some breakfast and took his place, holding the small, cool hand in hers.

There were still no other patients in the intensive care unit and so she talked softly to her friend, knowing she wasn't going to disturb anyone. Secure in her isolation, she found herself opening up, telling Lauren little stories from her childhood and events from her past. It felt good to share more of herself after so many years of silence although she was fairly sure Lauren couldn't hear her. Even if she could, it was unlikely she would ever remember anything when – if – she woke.

There was a footstep behind her and Alex glanced up to see Sue at the door beckoning to her. Reluctantly Alex followed her into the corridor.

'Another phone call,' said Sue. 'This time from Taunton. They're going to release Brian – obviously – but he's got no shoes. They're keeping his as evidence apparently. Have we got anything in the store at the day centre?'

Alex sighed and dug her keys out from her pocket. 'Here – do you mind . . .'

'Oh, who needs a weekend anyway,' said Sue. 'You'd better take my house key so you can get back in. I'll drive him home or wherever he's dossing at the moment and maybe then we can lock the door, put on the stereo and get happily drunk for the rest of the day.'

As she returned to Lauren, Alex had to admit she was sorely tempted. In fact, she wished she could share the proposed boozy weekend with Margie too. Her head full of pleasant imaginings, she sat down and slipped back into her reminiscing. Without realising it, she moved into some of the areas normally kept guarded and hidden. In fact, she was so absorbed in the soft telling she didn't notice Lauren's breathing had changed along with her heartbeat until the nurse hurried over from the desk by the door, shoved her aside roughly and dragged the curtains around the bed.

Chapter Twenty

Lynas arrived at Highpoint police station to find Dave had been called into the hospital and with sinking heart he drove over the bridge, abandoning his car in a space marked 'Senior Registrar' before running up the stairs two at a time. At the door to the intensive care ward he stopped, taking a deep breath before opening it.

'Really, this is too much,' said the duty nurse crossly. 'This is a hospital not a social club. Who are you and what are you doing here?'

Lynas fished in his pocket, flashed his warrant card and kept walking without a word, leaving the nurse trailing in his wake.

'You must not agitate the patient. She needs as much rest as possible and this level of excitement is not good for her.'

As the implication of her words struck home, Lynas turned back, grabbed one of her hands and squeezed it tightly.

'Thank you!' he said, a big grin over his face.

Behind the curtain Dave sat on one side of the bed with Jonny on the other, standing behind an older woman who was sitting by Lauren and holding her hand. Alex stood off to one side, a dopey smile on her face as she watched Lauren who was now propped up in the bed with several fewer tubes and wires issuing from her small body.

Jonny glanced over, acknowledging Lynas with a nod before turning his attention back to his sister. Dave raised his eyebrows questioningly at his sergeant. Lauren whispered something and Dave leaned over to catch what she was trying to say.

'Go on, I'm fine. Got people here so you get off to work.'

Dave bent over and kissed the top of her head before sliding out of the curtained area.

'Good to see her doing better,' said Lynas leading Dave off the ward with a nod of thanks to the nurse at the desk.

Dave let out a long, deep sigh. 'I can't believe how close we were to losing her,' he said. 'She'll be in hospital for a few more days at least and then she'll need complete rest at home for a while.'

Lynas, who had encountered Lauren on several occasions, hid a smile.

'Good luck with that, then,' he said.

On their return to the car there was a note attached to the windshield, fluttering in the light breeze. Lynas ripped it off, tore it into several pieces and tossed the keys to the vehicle at Dave.

'Just be a moment,' he said. At the reception window Lynas pushed the remains of the note over to a rather startled porter who was sitting at the bench having a cup of tea.

'Official police business,' said Lynas. 'Clue to that is written on the side of my vehicle – says POLICE, right? So I don't expect to be hearing any more about this.' Whistling cheerfully he headed back to the car. Things were going their way at last.

Sue had found several serviceable pairs of size 11 shoes in the emergency clothes cupboard and drove with them over to

Taunton. Brian was waiting in reception and received these offerings with a distinct lack of enthusiasm.

'Was lovely, my new boots,' he grumbled, trying on a pair of sneakers. 'Now I got this tin of red polish – what'm I gonna do with that then? Waste of two quid, that was if'n they's not givin' 'em back.'

A quick enquiry at the desk ascertained they were certainly not giving them back. The boots were evidence to a serious crime and, in the desk sergeant's opinion, Brian was damn lucky they weren't charging him with something.

'Well, what about my flowers then?' Brian asked.

It took several more minutes to work out the basis of this complaint but Sue finally decided it was not worth taking this one up with the desk sergeant.

'Tell you what, Brian,' she said, 'we'll pop into a florist on the way over and get some flowers. I'll sort it out here later.'

The sergeant sniffed and turned his back at this but Sue went over to the window, forcing him to look up from his paperwork.

'Is Brian free to go?' she asked and he nodded reluctantly.

'We may need to speak to him later,' he said. 'He must inform us immediately if he ceases to reside at . . .' Here he scrabbled at the forms on his desk. 'At Caravan Cottage, Sutton Mallet.'

Sue looked over at Brian, surprised by this. She was under the impression he was still residing, somewhat uneasily, with his family.

Brian nodded he understood and rose to his feet, heading out into the bright light of the morning. Sue followed, wondering how Ada fitted into all of this. She felt a little guilty about not visiting for so long but life and work had been so hectic it had just not been possible.

Once Brian had a new bunch of flowers they set off towards the low, watery plain of the Somerset Levels. Brian looked around Sue's car approvingly.

'Nice motor, this,' he said. 'Not like that weird thing Alex drives. Never could get used to all that rising and falling.'

Privately Sue agreed with him over the eccentricities of Alex's aging Citroën but she was not about to criticise her friend behind their back.

'That is a classic car in the making,' she said. 'You just wait. In twenty years people will still be talking about it.'

Brian was not really interested enough to get into a squabble so he just nodded and returned to staring out of the windows.

'So, what's this with you and Ada?' Sue asked as she navigated the turn from the main road onto the Levels proper. The car jolted and bumped along for a few yards before the track smoothed out and the wheels hissed softly as they gripped the gravel and mud of the surface.

'Was Tom took us in,' said Brian. 'Said I should apologise on account of Charlie and them bombs 'cos they's causing all kinds of problems what with the electricity and all. Then I started helping around a bit, 'specially with Pongo. He's girt lovely is Pongo.'

Sue took a deep breath, let it out again and decided not to bother. Really, she should have known better than to expect any sort of sense from a lad like Brian Morris. When she opened the car door and stepped out beside Ada's cottage, Sue sniffed the air, wrinkling her nose.

'What is that smell?' she demanded.

Brian managed to disentangle himself from the seat belt and emerged, still clutching his flowers protectively.

'What smell? Oh – is Pongo,' he said hurrying up the path and disappearing through the side gate. Sue locked the car doors and followed him, a trifle reluctantly as the smell got stronger with every step. Stepping through the gate she found herself facing the source of the aroma. Pongo, she decided, was very well named. He was also huge and the strange horizontal pupils in his large brown eyes gave him a slightly devilish look. Pongo ambled up to the fence, pushing through the as-yet uneaten undergrowth and chewing reflectively. Sue beat a hasty retreat towards the kitchen door just as Ada looked out.

'Well, come on in then' she said, holding the door. Inside it was warm from the old range where a battered kettle hissed and bubbled ready for tea. Half of the room was in bright sunlight streaming through the door, the rest was dark, lit only by the soft glow of an old paraffin storm lantern. Sue took a seat at the table and watched as Brian moved around the kitchen taking out cups and saucers, pouring milk into a jug and setting the table for tea. He seemed perfectly at home and Ada was obviously equally comfortable with him. Well, thought Sue, you never know what you're going to find out on the Levels.

'Have you had a power cut?' she asked as she peered around the dimly lit end of the room.

'Told yer,' said Brian. 'Is the trouble with that electricity.'

'Hush now!' Ada said. 'Is nothing to worry her with.' She handed a cup of tea down the table followed by some rather delicious-looking gingerbread.

'Wow, thanks,' said Sue. She took a large bite and the cake was as good as it promised to be. 'This is really excellent. Did you make it?'

Ada smiled at her. 'Is some advantages to using the old range,' she said. 'Always makes right decent baking even if is a bit slower.'

Sue nodded, her mouth still full of cake. 'Even so Ada, Brian said something about there being a problem. Maybe I can help.'

Ada scowled at Brian but she was worn out with worrying and even the knowledge she had all that money put by now didn't seem to offer much reassurance. She'd been poor most of her life and that didn't scare her but the threat of going to court, even possibly ending up in prison – that did. She trusted Sue almost as much as she trusted Tom and after a moment she set down her cup, went to the mantelpiece and unfolded a letter from the electricity board.

'Here,' she said placing it in front of Sue. 'Came just yesterday. To be honest, I don't have no clue about what to do.'

Alex left the hospital and made her way home just before lunchtime. Lauren had her family around her including a bewildering number of cousins and aunts and the duty nurse was reduced to ringing around the empty hospital in the vain hope of locating someone with sufficient authority to enforce the 'only two visitors at a time' rule. Eventually it was Lauren herself who imposed some order by declaring she was very tired, she was delighted to see them all but she really would appreciate some privacy while she ate her lunch.

Alex joined the exodus, rather shaky now from hunger, stress and lack of sleep and arrived back at her empty house with the beginnings of a very nasty headache taking up residence in her skull. Forcing herself to eat a rather dry sandwich, she took her tea out into the garden hoping the quiet would help.

She was startled to see old Mr Pond from next door scuttling out of sight behind the fence and walked over to the edge of her garden, curious to see what had prompted his odd behaviour. Glancing over into next door's, she was just in time to see the back door slam. At the join of the two houses she noticed the raspberries were just starting to fruit and stopped to examine the canes. Most of the berries were still small, green and hard but a few were already turning red. One or two looked as if they were ripe and she picked these, savouring their tart sweetness on her tongue. Feeling the fatigue flooding through her body, she abandoned her garden to the birds, picked up the cup and went back inside, dragging her way upstairs to the crumpled but so-welcoming bed.

It seemed only a few minutes but a glance at her watch showed she had been asleep for almost two hours when a hammering on the front door roused her. Groaning softly and silently cursing herself, she got up and peered out of the window. Her heart sank as she recognised the car parked across the street and she tottered downstairs and wrenched the door open with a decidedly bad grace.

'What?' she demanded as Dave Brown stepped inside, clutching his case file. 'Not Lauren? She was fine when I left.'

Dave looked guiltily around and shook his head.

'She's fine. And thank you again for all you've done. I feel really bad, imposing on you like this but . . .' He set the file down on the table and started pulling out papers and forms.

Alex knew when she was beaten. She might as well get on with whatever he had in mind and get back to sleep as soon as possible.

'This is what we've got,' said Dave as he explained about Brian Morris, the metal detector and the pineapple tin.

'I knew the little shit hadn't lost the damn thing,' said Alex.

'Just as well for us he hadn't,' said Dave. I doubt we would have uncovered it, however hard we looked. As it is, we've got a lot more information but I'm worried we may be running out of time. There was only a week between the last two attacks and if he's escalating he may strike again at any time.'

Alex picked up a copy of the local map, studying it closely. 'These are the sites of the incidents, right?'

Dave nodded, leaning over her shoulder to point. 'This one first, then here, here, across here to Alison's place and then last night, er . . .' He searched for a moment before locating the bridleway out of North Petherton, 'There you are.'

'No,' said Alex shaking her head. 'This one,' she pointed to North Newton. 'This one is wrong.'

Dave sat opposite her, staring at her earnestly.

'Are you absolutely sure?' he asked.

Alex nodded firmly. 'Oh yes. Look, all the others are to the west or south west of Highpoint. All accessible by footpaths or bridleways too. This one is the wrong side of the motorway. Are there any other differences?'

Dave took a deep breath, aware he was not authorised to say any more. 'Right, the bloke was dressed, he escaped on foot somehow – at least from the immediate vicinity, he went into the house – first time that's happened. And he had a weapon.'

Alex nodded. 'Well, the theory of geographical profiling tells us someone like this will most likely stick to an area he's familiar with. Somewhere he's comfortable and he's been before. Now, your idea of a bike is good because there's no sign of a car or motorbike but these places are a long way apart for someone on foot. Normally we'd draw a rough circle round the sites, like this,' she indicated with a finger. 'He's most likely inside that area. But this one,' she stabbed at North Newton again. 'This is stuck out way beyond.'

Dave peered excitedly at the map.

'So, he could live at . . .' he searched the centre of Alex's circle. 'There's nothing there. Kings Cliff Wood, a couple of quarries and.. Oh. I don't think he's there.' He pointed at the only residential building in the target area. 'Crows Nest Farm. There's a small enterprise estate next to the old farmhouse and not much else. No,' he held up his hand. 'I'm *not* going to check out the farmhouse. You know who lives there? My senior Inspector, "Old-Fashioned". And before you ask, he doesn't have a son and he's not a natural blond. Not any more, anyway.'

'Maybe our Moth Man works there then,' said Alex, peering intently at the map. 'This enterprise estate thingy – what sort of businesses are there?'

'You're still thinking about the conservatories aren't you,' said Dave as he scribbled some notes. 'One of the victims, let me see, Miss Taylor out at Goathurst, she said he looked a bit sunburned. As if he'd only just started working outdoors. That was . . .' He flipped through his notebook, trying to find the dates. 'March 20th. Friday evening, but quite early on. He's been getting a bit later each time . . .'

'Dusk,' said Alex who was tracing the roads and tracks between the sites. 'He comes out at dusk, drawn to the lights. And the four week thing – it's full moon. No,' she said looking up at Dave. 'I don't mean he's necessarily feeling the magical aura or some such stuff but Friday seems to be his chosen evening and if he's out riding these tracks after dark the moon will give him a bit more light. Even so, it would be pretty dangerous . . .'

'You're not a biker, are you?' Dave asked with a grin.

Alex pulled a face and shook her head.

297

'That's part of the fun apparently; the danger, the thrill of it all. Most of them seem to be adrenalin junkies . . . Is that why he's doing it?'

Alex glanced up from the map and shrugged.

'I don't know – it could be. Then again, he may be using that sort of bike because it's the only one he's got . . . oh.'

'Oh?' said Dave. 'Oh what? Oh, the theory's fallen apart or Oh I've just had a breakthrough?'

'Just "Oh", at the moment,' said Alex, a thin squirming thread of anxiety twisting in her stomach. Probably just co-incidence, she thought. So many young men had those bloody BMX bikes now, it could be any one of them.

Dave was sifting through the contents of his file and pulled out the notes on the pineapple tin. As he did so a thin piece of A4 fluttered to the floor. Bending to retrieve it, he stiffened and let out a sigh.

'Ah, this came in a couple of days ago. Why didn't anyone tell me? Damn it . . .'

Alex interrupted him, 'You've been a bit preoccupied,' she said. 'Whatever it is, unless it's a name – in which case the others would have been after him by now – it can't be that urgent.'

'It's from Interpol,' said Dave excitedly. 'I contacted them back in April. Almost forgot about it, to be honest, but look – have you got a calendar or a diary or something?'

Alex pulled open the drawer under the table and extricated a diary, plonking it in front of them. Opening it at the calendar page, Dave began to scan from the telex in his hand to the diary. Alex offered him a pencil.

'Go ahead,' she said. 'I don't mind and we can destroy the evidence of our collusion later.'

Dave scribbled on the message, ringing dates on the calendar and counting back as he went. He didn't have to say anything when he'd finished. The pattern was set out clearly in front of them. The previous year showed five similar incidents, all on the Friday of the full moon, then a gap of five months before they resumed with Miss Singleton in Goathurst.

'Okay,' said Alex finally. 'Where was he before we were blessed by his presence?'

'Holland,' said Dave. 'Place called Bergen, north of Amsterdam.'

Alex felt the thread in her middle tighten into a knot. 'Five month gap,' she said trying to keep her voice calm. 'So it could be there are some the police missed, either in Holland or back in the UK.'

'Might have been in prison,' said Dave absently. 'Though, then, he could be one of yours by now.' He grinned at her mischievously before returning to the telex message.

'Yeah,' said Alex softly. 'Could be one of mine.' A thought floated across her mind and she grabbed at it, grateful for the distraction. 'You said there was something in the boots when Brian found them?'

'Yes, old newspapers he said, packed around the sides. Perhaps to help them keep their shape?'

'Or what if they were a bit too big and so the paper held them on firmly,' said Alex. 'That would be a good piece of misdirection – the boots are your main piece of evidence, the one thing that stands out about his appearance, but they're the wrong size. If he planned on dumping them sometime it would be hard to use them against him, if the paper lining was gone.'

Dave nodded, 'The same idea occurred to me. We had a poke around but there's a lot of rubbish in the hedges and it's hard to tell which bits of paper came from the damn boots.'

'I suspect someone capable of planning all this is too careful to use anything that ties him to an incriminating location,' said Alex.

Dave paused and added, 'This last one though, he wasn't as well prepared or something went wrong and he couldn't get away as cleanly as before. I think he's unravelling a bit.'

'Maybe something made him change his plans,' said Alex and the thread inside tightened another notch. 'I'm sorry Dave, I'm really tired and I need to go and lie down. Call me later and let me know how it's going.'

Dave looked disappointed but gathered up the papers, stuffing them into the file before standing up and stretching.

'You really have been a great help,' he said as he stepped out of the front door. 'And I cannot thank you enough for everything you've done for Lauren.'

'She's my friend,' said Alex softly, closing the door. As soon as Dave was gone, Alex scrabbled around for her office keys, her heart sinking as she realised she'd given them to Sue. She dare not try to borrow a set from anyone – there would be too many questions asked and as yet she had no definitive answer. Musing on her next move, she checked through her briefcase where several files rested, waiting for their updates. She had been so busy she had not been able to do much more than rudimentary notes and had shoved the top few into her bag, just in case she found time to do some catching up. She breathed a sigh of relief when she read the name on the third folder. Perhaps she could lay to rest that horrible, burning thread of suspicion after all.

Settling by the telephone, Alex began to add more scribbles to the notes left on the calendar. After about ten minutes she put down her pen and gazed at the results. It was not conclusive but it did make a substantial if superficial case. According to her records, Jake Hollis had the means and opportunity to commit all of the attacks, including those abroad. He had been in the north east for a while before disappearing and there was a handy ferry from Newcastle to Amsterdam. If he had been running from the police it was a good escape route.

The attacks in Bergen stopped when he was in prison prior to his deportation from Holland – for theft, she noted. Nothing to suggest he might be a sex offender though. That put a bit of a dent in her case – a lack of obvious motive. Still, Alex was sure she had something and after a final check she lifted the telephone receiver and dialled the detectives' room at Taunton. After a brief conversation she hung up and crawled over to the couch where she lay, exhausted, drowsing in the sunshine as it poured through the window.

He spent the first part of Saturday at the jet wash, cleaning his bike. As the mud washed away down the central drain he felt some of the tension in his back and shoulders go with it. By the time he had finished there was nothing left to tie him to the track behind the house in North Petherton and, just to make sure he had covered all the options, he wheeled the wet machine behind the cover of the washing screens where he removed the rear tyre. Replacing it with a new one of a different make, he slung the old, distinctive tyre into the garage's skip before throwing his leg over the bike and setting off down the road, bunny-hopping on and off the pavement as he went.

It was a fine day and he decided to take a ride across the countryside. Perhaps he should go out to Kingston St Mary, to look over the track by West Deane Way. He would have been there last night if his plans hadn't been disrupted and now he was regretting the hasty actions that had almost been his undoing. It would have been better to wait and proceed as planned than rush – and now one of his chosen ones was wasted. He should have saved her for next time. She deserved so much more, he thought with a twinge of anger.

The ride was exhilarating and his good mood was soon restored as he pushed his body as hard as he could. The sun was warm on his back and arms, now a golden brown from the work outside and the time spent riding across the hills. The only things still niggling at him were the endless, stupid restrictions placed on him by his court order. He was a grown man, he'd done his time for the petty offences with which he had been charged. It was a ridiculous state of affairs, expecting him to live with a bunch of knuckle-dragging morons in a grubby, smelly hostel.

Ahead of him there was a ridge, a good jumping point with a spectacularly fast and dangerous downhill section. Taking aim at the centre of the crest, he pumped on the pedals with all his might, relishing in the surge of power as it propelled the bike up the hill and over the top, hanging in the air as he flew between two little girls who were pushing their bikes just below the top of the hill. The BMX descended fast and he only just managed to pull to one side, landing awkwardly and ripping his knee open as the bike slid away from under him.

'You stupid little shit!' shouted a man who was running up the hill towards him. 'You could have killed someone.' Behind him the two little girls burst into tears, more scared than hurt but obviously distressed by the near miss. Ignoring them, he clambered to his feet, grimacing with pain as he limped over to the bike, now lying on its side, one wheel still spinning.

'Did you hear me,' yelled the man who was fast approaching. 'Where do you think you're going? It's idiots like you . . .'

He stopped abruptly as there was a hand around his throat.

'Fuck off and leave me alone. And take them with you,' he gestured towards the crying children. 'Get them out of my sight before I really hurt you.'

The man landed in the dust of the track, choking and struggling for breath as his assailant remounted and set off down the hill at a furious pace his whole leg burning and throbbing. The sun seemed to have gone from his day and after a couple of miles he gave up, turning round and heading back to Highpoint by way of the minor roads.

Unknown to the bike rider his actions had been captured on camera. A local man, who was out with his two dogs, had stopped just below the summit and snapped his canine companions using a shiny new Polaroid camera. When the picture emerged from the front he watched eagerly, only to see the attack by the enraged BMX rider framed nicely in the background. Muttering in disgust, he was about to stuff the picture into his pocket when the victim hurried over, anxious to obtain evidence for his ordeal.

The police at Highpoint took one look at the photograph and identified the culprit immediately.

'Do you want to make a formal complaint?' asked Sergeant Willis with poorly disguised eagerness. Only his professionalism stopped him adding, 'Please do – go on.'

The father looked over at his distraught children and nodded.

'Would I have to stay here if you do?' he asked. 'I'm just visiting from Dorset, see.'

Willis hastened to reassure him. They might need to call him when it went to trial but this would only be for a day. It would be a public service, he said, as well as some justice for the family. After a few minutes' hesitation it was agreed and the sergeant handed him over to one of the constables to take a statement.

Once the family was safely on the way home Sergeant Willis put a call through to Taunton. At the weekend there was no senior officer in Highpoint and any large operations needed a higher level of authorisation than he could give. To his dismay he was connected to the head of the Special Action Group, known locally as the 'Saggers', the heavy-duty end of law enforcement in the county.

'I'm not sure we need that sort of response,' he said. The Saggers were known for their rather over-enthusiastic actions and had a habit of turning up at unsociable hours dressed in full riot gear. Wherever possible, Willis, a decent, old-fashioned policeman, liked to talk his suspects into the car rather than hurling them in head-first.

'I think this is exactly the sort of operation we are supposed to handle,' came the reply. 'This is obviously a violent and dangerous criminal who behaves with a reckless disregard for the safety of others. We'll be in touch later. I'll pass you over to my co-ordinator to check all the details.'

Sergeant Willis seethed at the arrogance of the man but there was nothing he could do. Glumly he supplied the address and phone contact for the probation hostel and replaced the phone, wondering if they would even see the culprit before he was usurped by Taunton and added to their success rate.

Samuel was resting upstairs in his now empty four-bed room when there came a tremendous banging from the downstairs hallway. Footsteps pounded up the stairs and he sprang to his feet as the door was flung open and three huge figures crowded into the room. Clad in dark blue overalls with black boots and black leather gloves, each carried a short, heavy truncheon. Their heads were protected by blue and black motorcycle-type helmets and each wore a tinted visor down over their faces. For a moment the figures stared at him whilst Samuel fought the urge to run, to escape somehow, even if it meant a fall from the window. Then the lead figure raised one leather-clad finger up in front of his visor, warning him to keep silent, before turning away, gesturing the others to follow.

Samuel let out a long, juddering breath as he sank down on his bed, his heart hammering in his chest. A cold sweat burst out over his body as he listened to the heavy footsteps beating up the corridor before there was the sound of another door being flung open. This time it seemed they had the correct room as a barked order was followed by cries of alarm. Samuel rose from the bed, treading lightly as he crossed the room and peered round the edge of his door.

Flanked on both sides by the blue-clad police, Jake Hollis was hustled down the stairs and out into the waiting van. Despite the fact he was obviously in pain from a nasty injury to his knee, the officers ignored his protests, dragging him across the floor when he stumbled and almost fell in the hall. There was the hollow, metallic sound of a door being slammed shut and locked and then the roar of the engine as the van took off down the road at high speed.

Samuel closed his door softly, his hands trembling. He was no longer afraid, just shaken by the violence of the arrest. Slowly his heart rate returned to normal and he lay down again, pondering on this strange event. He had been sure they had somehow uncovered his secret, perhaps through the pineapple tin. It would be a very, very lucky copper who stumbled over that but, even so, he decided he had better dispose of it and its contents, just to be on the safe side.

Should he go now, he wondered? He could take advantage of the distraction offered by Jake Hollis's arrest. No, let attention swing away from the hostel. Just do the same as he did every weekend, he decided. No-one expected him to eat there any more and he could be out on Monday morning whilst all the day trippers and yokels were back at work. He would dress in his running clothes, get to the tin, destroy anything incriminating and be back without raising any questions about his whereabouts. Whatever Hollis had done, he had also unwittingly done him a big favour.

Sue returned to Highpoint leaving Brian with Ada and Pongo, and passed the hostel just as the SAG van cut across the traffic and roared off down the road, blue light flashing and siren blasting. Alarmed at this ominous sight, she turned into the tiny car park at the front and scurried into the office where Bennie was trying to raise the warden, with no success.

'Bastard,' she hissed between her teeth. 'He's supposed to be on call but there's no answer from either of the numbers he left. First time I've ever needed him . . .'

Sue made some suitably supportive noises followed by a strong cup of tea and Bennie was only too happy to share her understanding of Jake's arrest.

'I think they are looking at assault,' she said. 'Possibly threatening behaviour or ABH too. He seems to have left bruises on the man. It's the kids I'm sorry for. They were really scared apparently and Jake almost crashed that bloody bike down on them. He could have killed them.'

Sue rather doubted that but she wasn't going to interrupt whilst Bennie might still have some useful information to impart. Besides, Sue had formed an intense dislike of Jake over the past few months having seen how difficult, arrogant and rude he was to everyone at the probation offices. She really didn't care much about defending him to the hostel, especially as it was looking very unlikely he would be returning anytime in the near future.

When she finally got back to the house Alex was dozing uneasily on the couch, a notepad and the local map on the floor next to her.

'Planning a walk?' Sue asked cheerily.

Alex struggled to sit up, her eyes sticky and her head swimming with fatigue. 'Oh, hi. Is Brian okay?' she asked.

Sue sighed, nodding as she headed towards the kitchen.

'He's fine. I've got some early salad here from Ada. Shall I put it in the fridge?'

'What? Oh, yeah. So what was all that about?' Alex asked.

Sue waved the question away impatiently and hurried back into the room, plonking herself down on the end of the sofa to relate her news from the hostel.

Alex listened, her eyes growing wider with each detail.

'Oh no – there's going to be hell over this,' she said. 'Still, at least we know he's safe in custody. That's only part of the story mind.'

'What?' Sue demanded.

Alex picked up the map and stared at it thoughtfully before going through the notes she and Dave had made earlier.

'The one thing I realised was – look here. All the sites are within a mile of the workshop on the Crows Nest estate but the last one, this one in Pethy.' She indicated with her finger. 'This is also the exact same distance from us at Highpoint.'

'You think he's been going from work,' said Sue walking her fingers across the map.

Alex nodded, 'I do. There's something else.'

'This is getting rather intriguing.' said Sue.

'I don't think that was the original victim last time,' said Alex. 'The whole thing was muddled, less organised, as if done in a hurry. I think this was someone he'd marked down for later but something forced him into a last minute change of plan. Like an unexpected appointment in Highpoint, for example. The week before was Brian and his butterfly bombs and we had to reschedule all our final clients for the day, remember?'

Sue nodded. 'Still, that could also be anyone from the afternoon and it is all a bit circumstantial.'

Alex smiled grimly, holding up her hand for attention.

'Oh, there's a lot more.' Swiftly she went through the previous attacks, including those in Holland, and the five month hiatus.

'Perhaps it was too cold for that sort of thing?' Sue suggested. 'Maybe he almost got his thingy stuck to an icy window?'

Alex laughed at the thought, 'I guess that would be some sort of justice,' she said. 'No, I think he might have been in prison for something else, in which case . . .'

'He's probably one of ours,' said Sue softly.

'Yep. So here's my theory,' said Alex. 'Jake Hollis was shipped back from Rotterdam after he served two and a half months for petty theft, was caught trying to break into sheds at Harwich and then turned up here in the hostel a few months before all this started. He's been working at the unit that designs and builds conservatoires and just before the first attack he was promoted to the fitting team for part of his week. That's how he finds his victims and finds his hiding places. And he's got a BMX bike from the workshop project and Dave's fairly sure that's how the Moth Man has been getting around undetected,' she added gloomily. 'I expect there'll be a bit of a stink over that.'

'But Jake Hollis isn't blond,' said Sue. 'He's got sort of – reddish brown hair.'

'I rang the hostel,' said Alex. 'They said he was demoted and put back in a four-bed room for a couple of weeks because he ruined a whole batch of their towels using some sort of hair dye.'

'So he's a *natural* blond,' said Sue trying not to giggle.

'Yes,' said Alex and suddenly she was overcome by a fit of laughter too. 'God, let's have a drink, raise a glass to Lauren's recovery and toast the capture of Jake Hollis, Moth Man and natural blond.'

Chapter Twenty-One

Alex's first call on Monday morning was a trip across the Levels to see Iris. Newt was due to be released in about ten weeks and the prison authorities had finally decided he was no longer a flight risk. This meant he was back on the outside work party and enjoying the early summer sunshine after fifteen months locked up inside Dartmoor.

''Bout time an' all,' said Iris as she glided around her spotless kitchen making tea and putting out the best china for her visitor.

Alex sipped a little nervously from the fragile cup. Her history with fine china was not good and whilst she appreciated the gesture she would have preferred something a little more robust.

'I've spoken to his tutor at the prison,' she said setting the cup down with exaggerated care. 'He says Newt has a real talent for figures and he's almost mastered the computer already.'

Iris frowned at her.

'Computer? What's that then? I was hoping he'd be doing something useful for when he's out not messing around with silly games and stuff.'

Alex was by no means an expert but she was beginning to grasp the potential these new computers offered and she spent an interesting, if slightly frustrating, half-hour trying to explain it all to Iris. Ever practical, Newt's mother seized on the main flaw in any business plan Newt and Alex might come up with.

'So how much is these PC things then?' she asked.

Alex sighed, 'Well, they're not cheap . . .' she began.

'How much?' Iris demanded.

'About five, maybe six hundred pounds,' said Alex.

Iris snorted in disgust. 'So where is we going to get that sort of money?' she demanded. 'Could live a long time on that, never mind spending it on this – whatever it is – on the hope it'll be some use some time in the future. I reckon maybe I'll see if'n I can find something on one of the farms, seeing as Billy's been out in the work parties again. Something steady with a bit of security.'

Alex mused on this as she drove back across the soft, empty landscape of the Levels. It was a large sum of money to gamble with but she was convinced Newt was more likely to stick at something he found challenging rather than a routine job he could do without much thought. Part of his problem was that he was clever – smart, quick and imaginative. He wouldn't last a month cutting peat or weeding gardens. This was supposed to be the time of the enterprise culture – well, she was going to see whether anyone might be willing to take a chance on Billy 'Newt' Johns.

Humming to herself, she swung the car off the tarmac road and onto the bumpy track leading to Ada's cottage. It was only a short diversion and would save her some time later, she reasoned. Pulling up outside, she noted the neat flower bed and clear areas ready for planting, a marked contrast to the frontage she had encountered on her first visits to the Mallory home. With Kevin's departure and her husband's untimely death, Ada had taken control of her surroundings, getting rid of the old motor vehicles so beloved of some young men. The whole place was starting to look quite smart, she thought.

The sight of Brian, stripped to the waist and wrestling with a fence-post only a few inches shorter than he was, brought her up with a start. Brian looked over as the gate clanked and gave her a cheerful grin.

'Morning,' he called, dropping the pole into one of several holes dug in a line next to the scrub bordering Ada's garden. Then, as the breeze changed direction slightly, she got her first whiff of Pongo.

'Whoah, Ada!' she gasped as she stumbled into the kitchen. 'I'm hoping that's your famous goat and not Brian.'

'I heard that!' Brian's voice floated through the door as Alex closed it against the smell.

Ada grinned wickedly and indicated a place at the back of the table. Alex, familiar with the etiquette after more than two years in the job, waited for yet another cup of tea and whatever cake or biscuit might be forthcoming. Once they were both settled Ada leaned forward and said, 'I was hoping we could do somethin' for that lad.' She indicated towards the garden where Brian was happily toting goat nuts for Pongo, chattering away to the animal as he did so. 'Seems is the only thing he's any good at, but he's a real talent for it, I reckon. Seems a shame he has to get hisself put in prison to be able to work with un.'

Alex put her cup down on the table and looked at Ada.

'You think he might be worth a place somewhere?' she asked. 'Only, we have to be very sure. Most of the colleges don't have all that many empty rooms and they're naturally reluctant to waste one on someone who's going to disrupt everyone else, act up and then leave. We need to keep their goodwill if we are going to help *any* of our clients and I have to say Brian does not have a very good record.'

Ada was wearing her stubborn look. 'I don't care 'bout what he done before. I only know what I sees and he's been out there, grafting away and never a murmur from him. Is what he's meant to do, I reckon and if you don't help him, well who will, eh?'

Alex knew when she was beaten. There was something indomitable about Ada, especially when she was fighting for someone else. She often failed to stand up for herself, but there was no-one Alex would rather have by her side in a fight.

With a sigh Alex signalled her surrender. 'I'll do what I can,' she said. 'Promise, okay? Now, I really came over to see if I could help you.'

Gingerly she broached the subject of the illegal electricity supply. Sue had spent some time explaining the details of Ada's dilemma and together they had worked out what they hoped might be a winning strategy.

'It wasn't you that rigged the electricity cable, it was Frank,' said Alex.

Ada nodded, her eyes dark with anxiety as she looked at her across the table.

'Well, they will probably argue you benefitted from it and should have known something was wrong when there were no bills.'

Ada sighed. She had indeed known something was not quite right but Frank wasn't around to ask and she was only too grateful for the comfort the electric light brought her in the long, dark nights.

'What have you got that you actually use?' Alex asked pulling out a notebook.

Ada frowned and looked around the room.

'Well, is mainly the lights,' she said. 'Don't have much else. Had an old radio but it packed up last year and Kevin got us one of them transistor things. Runs on batteries, though is not the lovely sound I got from the old one. Apart from that, only that old television out there.'

Alex refrained from asking if Ada had a licence for *that*. Sometimes it is better not to ask the question, especially if you were already fairly sure of the answer. She scribbled a few notes and looked around the kitchen.

'What about cooking?' she asked. 'How do you manage that?'

Ada turned and gestured towards the iron range that dominated the back wall.

'Always used that,' she said. 'I don't think I'd know what to do with all this new stuff.'

Alex suppressed a grin at the thought of an electric cooker as 'new stuff'. She considered asking if Ada had a kettle or a toaster but realised this was likely to bring a whole heap of scorn down on her head.

'Now, how long have you been connected?' she asked.

Ada thought for a moment, tapping the table in front of her and muttering softly.

'Was just after he got out for that stupid poaching charge,' she said finally. 'Couple of days later he was back on remand over the cheques.'

Alex felt a flash of sympathy for this proud and patient woman who marked her life by the crimes of her family. She resolved to do everything in her power to spare her the ultimate humiliation of a court appearance.

'Actually I don't think you can owe them much anyway,' she said. 'I expect the connection charge will come to more than the power used and it's only for a fairly short time. Are you sure it was less than a couple of years ago?'

Ada nodded firmly.

'Still got the old lamps I used most of my life,' she said. 'How d'you think I is managing now? Mind you, is surprising how dim they is, once you's used to the 'lectric.'

Alex finished her notes and glanced at her watch. She was due back at the day centre and it was past noon, so with a sigh she rose to her feet.

'One thing you must promise, Ada,' she said. 'You have to open the letters from the electricity company. If we can get the supply put back on, you must pay the bills. Agreed?'

Ada scowled at the thought, glancing at the ever-expanding thicket of despised brown envelopes behind her clock.

'I suppose,' she said reluctantly. 'Oh, I was wondering – any chance of gettin' my shotgun back soon?'

On her way back across the Levels, Alex let her mind run over Ada's dilemma. She was fairly sure she could get the electricity company to come to an agreement, especially if they realised any court case could cost them more in the end than they were ever going to recover. Publicity surrounding the prosecution of a widow whose dead husband had been responsible for the illegal instillation could also be very damaging to a company already under fire for its hefty profits and recent price hikes. Alex hoped this would outweigh the urge to make an example of Ada, for the sort of illegal hook-up she had been using was not uncommon in the more remote rural areas and the company was determined to do everything they could to eradicate it.

The shotgun was entirely different and Alex had spent an extra ten minutes explaining to Ada she was very, very lucky that the police had decided not to press charges and were instead going to confiscate the weapon. Dave Brown had a quiet word with his sergeant who had spoken to someone else and they had unearthed the original licence for the gun, now long expired. Sue had testified unofficially to the officer concerned over Ada's refusal to read official mail and stated her firm belief Ada probably hadn't realised it needed renewing after five years.

In fact Sue had gone a bit further than that, pointing out in her sweetest, most reasonable way that the police had a responsibility to follow up any non-renewal and, if necessary, remove the gun and they had, unfortunately, failed to do this. It hadn't made her any friends in the Highpoint station but this, coupled with the fact Ada had kept the gun safe, unloaded and separate from the ammunition, had been enough to persuade them it was better to drop the matter.

Alex had a quiet grin as she manoeuvred her temperamental Citroën around a particularly large pothole. She had seen Sue in full 'sweet reason' mode and it was a frightening sight. Rounding a sharp bend, she was startled by a glimpse of a familiar figure disappearing into the shadows under the Currie Bridge. Unable to stop on the dangerous corner, she carried on down the road towards Highpoint, her attention now focussed on what Samuel Burton might be doing, skulking around in the undergrowth.

Samuel had left the hostel as soon as the front door was unlocked, waiting only until the temporary warden disappeared back into the office before hurrying off down the footpath that ran behind the building and on to the track beside the river. He had a small folding spade in his backpack along with several pairs of latex gloves, a disposable lighter and some lighter fuel. It was a nuisance but he had decided, on reflection, it would be better to dispose of the contents of his tin rather than risk it being found by the police.

He knew there was a problem as soon as he crested the bridge. The ground had been disturbed and he forced himself to keep jogging, passing the site of his buried tin without a glance. On the other side he kept going until he had turned a slight bend in the track and would be hidden from view. Here he waited, crouching in the tall grasses and peering through the rough hedge until satisfied no-one was watching the site. The ground was dry where it had been turned over and left in the warm sun and it was fairly obvious from the dip in the earth that his tin had been removed – by person or persons unknown.

Heart pounding, he scrabbled around the edge of the area, though he knew it was pointless. The tin was gone, along with the clothes and his striking pink boots. He was not worried about losing the clothes, just the circumstances surrounding their loss. He must have been careless, he thought as he scanned the hedge for any sign of the tin or its contents. It was inconceivable anyone could have unearthed the tin by chance so he must have left some tracks – or maybe been seen. The latter idea sent shudders down his spine. Still, if he'd been seen then the 'Saggers' would have come for him, he decided. Running through his actions, he was reassured there would be nothing to connect him to the cache. No fingerprints, no sign of who he was or where he might have acquired the clothes.

There was a moment's hesitation as he remembered the newspaper lining those pink boots. It was local – the *Highpoint Herald*, an evening paper read by half the town so no clues there, but if someone was clever enough they just might work out that the man they sought had feet a size or so smaller than the boot print.

He was suddenly aware of the sound of a car engine approaching. Instinctively he dived across the road and slipped into the shadow of the bridge, listening for any indication the driver had seen him. The car kept moving, heading off towards Highpoint without slowing and he gave a soft sigh of relief. Whatever had happened to his stash, he decided as he brushed himself down and wiped his hands on the grass, it was gone and there was no point hanging around by the bridge, possibly attracting attention. He packed his spade and the latex gloves back into the rucksack on top of the lighter fuel and set off towards Highpoint. Bloody probation workshop session this afternoon, he thought. Oh, could his life get much worse? Still, there was always next time. Soon, he decided. It had to be soon. There were others out there waiting for his visits and now the coppers had Jake Hollis they wouldn't be expecting anything else. He smiled slowly as he began his long jog back towards the town, his eyes gleaming a bright, hard blue.

It was very quiet at the probation office in Highpoint. Alex had contrived to miss the weekly meeting, primarily as she really did not want to be in the same room as Ricky Peddlar. It seemed very strange, pushing the front door open and not seeing Lauren's head bob up over the counter to greet her. She felt a twinge of apprehension as she considered what life might be like if Lauren did not, or could not, return to work.

Scarcely had she reached her desk in the tiny ex-storage area than served as an office than the phone rang and Gordon was requesting her presence upstairs. Alex suppressed a groan. She liked and respected Gordon enormously but she was desperately tired after the stresses of the weekend and the paperwork that demanded her attention from her desk seemed to be growing every day.

Clambering up the stairs to the first floor, she was aware for the first time how steep they were. None of them had realised just how difficult Lauren must have found the climb, day after day. No one except Ricky, of course. By the time she reached Gordon's room at the end of the long, sunny corridor, she was grinding her teeth in anger again.

'I'm sorry you missed the meeting this morning,' said Gordon, peering at Alex over his glasses. Alex resisted the urge to twist her fingers and shift in her chair. Gordon, for all his mildness and approachability still carried the unmistakable air of a head teacher. The sort you tried very, very hard to please at school. She started to mumble something but Gordon held up a hand, waving her excuse away.

'I wanted to speak to everyone about Friday's unfortunate incident,' he continued, ignoring Alex's look of outrage. 'I understand there was some bad feeling afterwards and can quite appreciate why that might be. However,' he continued, raising his voice slightly. 'However, this is a team and we will work as a team. I hope you will accept my word when I tell you I have already taken steps to ensure this never happens again and I have emphasised that this type of behaviour is never acceptable, in work or outside.'

He stared at Alex, forcing her to meet his gaze, waiting in silence until she nodded her understanding.

'Good,' said Gordon, leaning back slightly in his chair. 'Now, our new senior, ah, let me see.' He rummaged amongst the papers in the tray on the end of his desk. 'Yes, here we are, Rosalind Marchent. She will, I understand, be arriving on July the first, although I think she may pop in to have a look around before then. She has an assistant, um . . . Yes, here we are – a Mrs Debbie Jones. I don't know if Mrs Jones is a probation officer or not but that was all arranged at headquarters so that will be the situation after this month.'

Back in her subterranean office, Alex wasn't quite sure what to make of all that. She'd never heard of a senior bringing their own assistant along to a new office but then the service was changing so fast it was hard to keep up sometimes.

She remembered Ricky's delight when he heard of Rosalind Marchent's appointment. It seemed they already knew one another and he approved of her methods. That, Alex concluded gloomily, could not be good.

The rest of her day passed in a whirl as she met with clients, worked on the ever-growing number of forms required to keep track of every minute of her day and snatched a few minutes to put the finishing touches to her final alcohol education session. After the success of the drink-driving evening she was feeling very good about the whole course and hoped to end on a high note, dispelling the final myth, so firmly held, that the new low alcohol and alcohol-free beers tasted, in the words of one young man, 'like rat's piss'. Of course, this held almost as much danger as last week's session but once more the centre was likely to be deserted and this time she was technically serving mainly soft drinks.

A quick call to the hospital gave some good news. Lauren was responding well – so well in fact that they were getting rather anxious to get rid of her. Leaving a message for the reluctant patient, Alex returned to the logistical nightmare that was her workload as she tried to juggle regular clients and running the day centre whilst still fitting in an occasional appearance in court. Not to mention the odd sleep, she thought.

One disadvantage of the final sessions was that she had to buy the drinks herself and it seemed every month her budget shrank a little more. Only last week she had disgraced herself in the local supermarket by squeaking with excitement and giving a little jig at the sight of a jar of half-price mayonnaise. The memory brought a flush to her face and she bent over her notes, determinedly forcing her mind back to the problem of finding anyone marginally competent to run the new sessions the court were so keen she should offer.

The two workers she had were good, especially now she'd done away with the original workshop guy, but they lacked the training for a lot of the courses and this left Alex leading almost half of the provision herself. It was an impossible task and she felt a rush of gratitude when her phone rang. Her pleasure didn't last long however as the voice of the manager from the Quantock Conservatory Company boomed angrily down the line at her. It took all Alex's tact and patience to dissuade the man from making an official complaint over Jake Hollis – his absence, his arrest, the damage this would do to their company . . . When he finally rung off Alex was left in no doubt that was one placement the service had lost for good.

Dave prepared himself for his final interview with some trepidation. He knew he had done the best job he could and felt he had made a real contribution to the 'Moth Man' case. Sergeant Lynas had been encouraging and Dave was fairly sure he'd not alienated anyone in the close-knit detective squad but, even so, there was no telling whether he had made the grade or not. No-one had mentioned his progress or offered much in the way of advice, apart from Lynas, of course, and he had no idea what to expect as he walked along the corridor and knocked on the door to 'Old-Fashioned's' office.

'Come,' barked his senior and Dave pushed open the door, trying to look as confident and smart as he could when actually his legs were threatening to collapse and his mouth was so dry he was sure he could only croak if asked anything.

'Brown,' said Old-Fashioned from behind his desk. 'Good. Attention please.'

Dave forced his body to stand upright and still, eyes in front as he awaited his fate. Much as he wanted to make detective for himself, he wanted it even more for Lauren and the thought of taking news of his failure back to her was almost more than he could bear.

Old-Fashioned started by running through Dave's qualifications, commending him on his record at Hendon and then moved on to the time at Highpoint.

'Some issues here,' he rumbled. 'Still, often see it in a promising young man. If you can stick it for the two years it shows discipline, self-control. Ambitious are you?'

Dave was still trying to decide whether his 'issues' at Highpoint were a good or a bad thing and the question took him by surprise.

'Yes . . . Yes, Sir,' he stammered.

'Good. Well, it shows in your work. You've certainly put the hours in and your sergeant thinks highly of you. Not a bad spell here for your first probationary period . . .'

Dave's heart sank at the word 'first'. First generally meant there was a second following behind. He didn't want another chance in two years time, he wanted it now. With body rigid and an expressionless face he waited to hear his fate.

'Overall, an exemplary three months,' continued the Inspector. 'Apart, of course, from your unfortunate inclination to involve civilians in police matters.'

Dave blinked at his words. Whatever he had been expecting it wasn't that.

'Confidentiality is vital in our work, as I am sure you know. A case could be severely jeopardised by outside influence or the suggestion that evidence has been shared with an outsider.' Old-Fashioned stopped and stared at Dave before continuing. 'I am, of course, referring to your sharing of case files with Miss Hastings.'

Dave felt himself turn bright red. He had no idea how his senior had found out but he couldn't dispute the facts. He was tempted to open his mouth in an attempt to justify his actions. She was an officer of the court, he could argue. She had knowledge and skills the force needed and the police were turning to civilian experts with increasing frequency. Then he remembered the words of his training sergeant at the academy and kept silent.

There was a slight pause as if Old-Fashioned was waiting, expecting him to speak. Then the Inspector gathered up the papers in front of him, slid them into a folder and rose to hand it over the desk.

'Well, it has been an interesting experience for us all. My best wishes on your next posting.'

Numb, Dave took the folder. 'Thank you, sir,' he said and

walked out of the office. He didn't think he could face the detectives' room. They would know the outcome the moment they saw his face and besides, he had to work out how he was going to tell Lauren.

Half-way down the corridor, Lynas stepped out the detectives' room and held out his hand.

'I'm going to miss you, lad,' he said. 'You've done well here. Maybe you'll give a thought to coming back next time round?'

Dave stared at him bleakly.

'I don't know if there'll be a next time,' he said softly. 'Not sure I can hack another two years in uniform.'

'What the holy hell are you on about?' asked Lynas. 'Is only three months you'll be away and half the time is plain clothes anyway. Who you been talking to? They been pulling your leg for sure.'

Dave gaped at him in astonishment.

'Three months?' He opened the file he was carrying and peered at the top sheet of paper. 'I'm going to Hendon,' he said.

'Course you are. Only place they do detective training,' said Lynas with a grin. 'Come on – your mates want to stand you a drink so I hope you got enough on you for a taxi home. Don't want to be spoiling today with a pull for drunk driving, do you.'

It was very quiet in Tom's kitchen that Monday evening. Brian sat in front of the tiny black and white television but nothing caught his interest and finally he turned the set off and ambled over to join Tom at the table.

'Would really appreciate it, if'n you could give us a lift into Highpoint Wednesday afternoon,' he said.

Tom glanced at him over the top of his newspaper.

'Oh yeah? What's that for then?' he asked.

'Got an interview with Alex Hastings, my probation officer. About trying for that farming college out Cannington way. Was Ada had a word and she said maybe I could get a place, learning about looking after animals and such.' Brian's eyes were shining at the prospect and he was transformed from the scruffy, skinny waif Tom had rescued on the road into a confident and enthusiastic young man.

'Might be a test or something,' said Tom. He hated to sound negative but it would be worse, he reasoned, for Brian to think it was all settled, only to be let down once more.

Brian shrugged at this.

'Most likely,' he agreed. 'Still, they has classes at that day centre an' if'n we can, I'm goin' to go and work there so's I has a good chance at it.'

Tom raised his eyebrows at this. He had never heard Brian express the slightest interest in any kind of study before. There was a pause as Brian contemplated his future before he caught Tom unawares with a sudden change of subject.

'I know is not really my business but is there trouble with you an' Ada? Only,' he hurried on. 'Well, you 'ent stopped off for a few days. Just drove us there an' been away again. Seems a right shame, seeing as she do seem so fond of you – an' there 'ent so many people she has as friends, neither.'

Tom's immediate reaction was to tell Brian to mind his own business but he hesitated. It was obvious Brian had great affection for Ada and, if he were honest, the lad was right. Folding his newspaper carefully and placing it on the table before him, Tom leaned on his elbows and tried to explain what was wrong.

'Now, 'afore I talk about this, I want your word this is between us, as men, right?'

Brian nodded, startled by this. He was not used to being taken seriously and was suddenly relieved his words had not offended.

Tom hesitated, trying to choose the right way to say what he was feeling and Brian waited, silent and attentive across the table.

'You say Ada's maybe fond of me – well, I can tell you I'm just as fond of her. Always have been a bit sweet on Ada, if I speak the truth, even when we was just little 'uns, running round the fields and lanes. Don't get me wrong – I loved my Bella, was true to her 'til death, just like we promised, and I didn't think I could stand it when she went. But now I see Ada and I feel like I might have a bit more life left still. We's both had a few hard knocks, both had a lot of tough times, only I was with someone as cared, someone as made everything better for us both. Ada never had that – don't know what she was thinking, marrying Frank.' He glanced up and saw Brian's frown.

'Don't you look like that, neither. Maybe we ain't supposed to speak ill of the dead but there was precious little good about that man. Even now he's gone, is still causing her grief over stuff he done.'

'If you feeling that, why's you not telling her then?' asked Brian.

Tom sighed, 'I was all set. Figured it was enough time past for us both an' we was getting on fine. Then there was that letter. You know, all that money the government sent her on account of Frank bein' killed by that nutter Derek Johns. Couldn't say nothing then, could I?'

'What you mean?' asked Brian.

Tom shook his head sadly. 'I know what folk says about us *Rom* but I 'ent the sort as would prey on a woman once she's got money. So, well, seems as how I left it too long. Should have told her how I felt afore this. 'Tis too late now.'

'What about what Ada wants?' Brian asked. 'All right you being so high and mighty and such but what about how she feels? You asked her?'

Tom was startled by his vehemence. It was easy to view Brian as a thoughtless lad but in truth he was growing up and sometimes – just occasionally mind – he was right about something. And this, he thought, this was one of those times.

'Course, if you care more about what folks think than you does about Ada, well she's probably better off without you,' said Brian.

Tom sat, open-mouthed in astonishment for a moment, then threw his head back and laughed.

'You'm right,' he said. 'You is so right. Go on, get us a couple of beers from the fridge an' we'll drink to Ada – and wish me luck.'

Alex's last stop at the end of a long day was the hospital where Lauren was residing in a side room off the main ward.

'Don't know why I can't go home,' Lauren grumbled. 'Got all my stuff there and would be a lot more comfortable. I'm supposed to rest but is like lying on a plank of wood, this bed. And is so high I can't get out on my own. Have to call someone to help. Can be right embarrassing.'

Alex sympathised with her friend. A desperately private person herself, she viewed the routine indignities of a stay in hospital with something close to horror.

'Still,' said Lauren reaching for the box of biscuits Alex had fetched along. 'Be out soon and I just had some real good news from Dave.' Munching happily on ginger snaps, Lauren told her of Dave's success.

'Course, he's got to go away for the extra training but is only three months and he says he'll be able to come back some weekends.'

Alex added her congratulations but she was so tired that her head was starting to spin and she wasn't really paying attention as Lauren chattered on about the case that had made Dave's trial as detective such a success. Then something made her sit up and listen more closely.

'Would be perfect except he's still fretting over that tin they unearthed by Currie Bridge . . .'

'Sorry, what was that about Currie Bridge?' she asked leaning forward in her eagerness.

Lauren gave a sigh to express how difficult her life was, surrounded by people who didn't even listen properly. Then, with exaggerated patience she explained about the tin, its missing contents and the origin of Brian's pink boots.

Alex listened in silence as inside her head several pieces of a puzzle fell into place. All her early questions about Samuel

Burton resurfaced as she considered one explanation for his obsessive behaviour, his inconsistent and flatly contradictory criminal record and his presence by Currie Bridge that morning. She thought of those strange, flat eyes with their bright blue sparks of anger and remembered the flash of revulsion she had experienced on their first meeting.

She had been convinced the attack on Alison was the work of a second man but lacked any real evidence to back up her argument. Now she was sure she knew who was responsible – but still had no way to prove it.

Leaving the biscuits with Lauren and promising to look in the next day, she made her way home, struggling with just what she should do with her knowledge. However she looked at it, she had nothing concrete, nothing that would stand up in court. Jake Hollis was still vehemently denying anything to do with the attack on Alison but even without it, there was enough against him to send him away for two years, especially when the CPS added his breach of the hostel conditions. Samuel Burton, on the other hand, was going to get away with it.

Back home in her little house wedged between the river and the main road, she sat for a while, sipping a cup of tea and turning the events of the past few months over in her mind. Then she rose from her armchair and checked the curtains in the front room were properly closed and the window was locked. Out there, less than a mile away, was a highly intelligent sexual predator. He knew who she was and he almost certainly knew where she lived and every week she would have to sit down in front of him and discuss his progress, knowing all the time that he was simply waiting until he could move on, remake himself and emerge as someone new, with the same old desires.

She felt a shiver run down her spine and resisted the urge to go to the window again, just in case. The sound of the phone snapped her out of her cycle of fear and she answered it, not caring if it were her family with a new crisis or someone from work or her most boring friend. Until Sue got home from her evening visits she just wanted to talk to someone.

'Alex?' came a familiar voice. 'Alex, got some good news, I hope. They finally made their minds up and offered me that post at Shepton. Starts beginning of August. Alex?'

Alex felt the tension drain out of her body and a slow grin spread across her face.

'Margie – that's wonderful. Congratulations – I know how much you wanted it.'

'Yeah, so I'll be down your way all the time,' said Margie. 'If you's free this weekend we could meet up and you can give me some tips on where's best to live . . .'

Alex replaced the receiver and went out to the kitchen where the evening meal was bubbling away in a pot. She had started to feel her ties with Highpoint were loosening as the work changed more towards punishment, the demands of management grew larger and louder every month and her friends suffered mishaps or worse but now . . .

Now she knew she would stay and do her absolute best for all the broken lives placed in her care. Now Samuel faded into the background and lost the power to frighten her. Now she had something to hang on to.